VIOLENT TRIUMPHS

USA TODAY BESTSELLING AUTHOR

JESSICA HAWKINS

I've become a queen to the forsaken, a leader to thieves, and the wife of a man who instills fear in all who cross his path. He was the husband I didn't want. Now, I can't fathom life without my king.

I should've been ready for anything. Like the caterpillar that feeds on poison during metamorphosis, I was raised in the dangerous world of cartel crime. But nothing could've prepared me for Cristiano de la Rosa, his brother's poison, or the Calavera cartel.

This is still a story about a love strong enough to topple households, unite enemies, and divide brothers. Resilient enough to bring down those who would try to destroy it . . . and selfless enough to make the ultimate sacrifice. But I was warned, and so were you. Death's day always comes.

This time, it will find what was once a caterpillar is now a butterfly—and hell hath no fury like the White Monarch.

1

NATALIA

I *suspect you might even like the feeling of surrender.*

Cristiano's distant words echoed through the darkness falling over my mind. He hadn't meant submitting to death, but the hands around my neck demanded that.

The back of my skull throbbed where it'd been slammed against the tile floor. One moment, I'd been trying to tell Cristiano something important over the phone. The next, dragged through our bedroom and pinned on my back by an immovable weight.

Now, pinpricks of white light pierced the black. Stars in the night sky, promising peace. It wouldn't be difficult to walk toward them. The dark had always been a fierce presence within me. Unknown. Ever-inviting.

Surrender would be simple. My body and my training had failed me—I hadn't even fought back. Or maybe nothing up to this point had been real. Maybe this had all been a dream, and I was being torn from sleep.

As my windpipe closed under the grip around it, my screams relented. The shrill house alarm faded into a peaceful buzz. My fear ebbed, an ocean of tranquility rising in its place.

Heaven.

Mamá waited with open arms.

Go to her. Be with her again. Submit.

I wasn't waking up; I was dying. Cristiano was the last person I expected to see at the gates of Heaven, but there he was, waiting in his suit and tie. Thank God. Wherever I was going, Cristiano was there, and he wouldn't let anything hurt me.

He and my mother would be the light, the serenity, the prize for giving in to death.

All I had to do now was succumb. Go to him . . .

Cristiano.

"Cristiano is dead." A scratchy male voice took hold of me the way strong hands locked around my throat. "You have nothing to fight for," he said. "Go to sleep."

The word scraped through the dregs of my consciousness. *Dead.*

That was why Cristiano waited for me at the gates to eternity.

But he could not die. He was *untouchable.*

What was a world without Cristiano de la Rosa? Grief flooded me, but just as quickly, it ebbed. And in its place, fury swelled. Someone had *killed* Cristiano.

The voice above me thought I had nothing to fight for, but it'd just given me a reason.

Nobody—*nobody*—would get away with murdering my husband.

Fight, Natalia. Surrender is not an option.

Reality flickered. Carotid arteries. No oxygen. I forced myself out of the encroaching darkness. Clawed at the tightening fingers around my neck. I arched my back until I was looking upside-down in the bedroom mirror propped against one wall. My first night here, we'd stood in front of it—Cristiano wrapping his arms around me from behind, demanding my submission. I hadn't given in then. And over time, I'd grown stronger. Mentally, emotionally—and physically. Under Cristiano's guidance.

I wanted those moments with him back. For him to survive so I could look him in the eye and tell him I'd resisted, and I'd won.

Because he'd taught me how. He'd taught me strength.

With a clicking noise, I struggled to turn my head and see where it was coming from, but my vision blurred. Moonlight glinted off metal. A knife? *Fuck.* I began to thrash under him.

"*Shh*," he said. "This won't hurt."

I had no defenses against a knife. No weapon. Nothing on me but flimsy satin pajamas and plenty of exposed skin. But my breath . . . it was coming back.

Change your mindset, Cristiano had told me. *You're in control . . . you* can *take down an attacker . . . you* can *fight for your life and escape.*

That was all I had to do. Escape. Run. I wasn't at the level I needed to be to win, but I had the will to survive on my side—and the fact that he'd removed a hand from my neck to pick up the blade. I only needed to incapacitate him long enough to outrun him and get to the panic room.

My first self-defense lesson on the lawn had taught me more than hand-to-hand combat. There was the art of diversion. The magic of distraction.

Have you ever been to Disneyland? I'd asked Cristiano as his bar of a forearm had locked around my neck from behind.

The sound of Cristiano's answering laughter heartened me.

Words scraped from my throat. "Cristiano . . . isn't . . . dead."

The attacker's face bent toward mine, giving me my first close-up glimpse of him in the dark. Crooked nose, foul breath, beady eyes. "What?"

"He's not dead. I can"—I let my voice falter—"take you to h-him."

He leaned closer. "¿*Qué*?"

I rammed my forehead into his mouth, and blood burst from his lip. "¡*Cabrona*!" he cursed.

The butt of my palm slammed into his trachea. Plastic clattered to the ground. I only had enough strength to shock him, but it was all I needed. He loosened his other hand around my neck, and I punched him in the same spot, harder this time.

Alarm crossed his face with his guttural shout. The fact that he could shout at all meant I hadn't crushed his windpipe. I fisted my left hand and made good use of the extravagant diamond Cristiano had saddled me with. I jammed my wedding ring into the man's throat over and over until he'd released me completely to grab his own neck. Blood trickled onto me as he wheezed so hard, my own chest went tight.

With a bare foot, I kicked him in the crotch, crawled out from under him, and jumped up. I'd taken only two steps when his hand grabbed my ankle, and I fell forward. My head cracked the mirror. It teetered, and I rolled away a split second before it toppled to the ground.

The short fight had winded me, but he hadn't gone down yet. Movement from the corner of my eye spurred me to get back up. I grabbed the biggest shard of broken glass within reach and got myself to stand. The moment I was on my feet, the man seized me from behind. He pinned my elbows to my sides with one arm, grabbing at the glass with his other hand. I held onto it until blood dripped down my fingers, but he wrestled it from me and put it to my throat.

"Nobody . . . told me . . . you'd fight back," he panted, struggling to speak. If his mouth hadn't been in my ear, I wouldn't have heard him over the blaring alarm. "Your husband teach you that?"

"Fuck you."

"It's a nice surprise. Very *exciting*. But I'll cut your throat if I really have to." His front flush against my back, he lifted my chin with the glass as his tone turned from amused to foreboding. "Your husband stole from us. This is the price. For every woman Cristiano took, we'll kill two inside these walls."

I'd been in this position before, at the mercy of a menacing man and his whims. And I'd been just as scared.

But Cristiano had taught me a valuable lesson that day he'd simulated jumping me on the lawn.

I was not to be underestimated. I'd survived my time in the Badlands by doing my best to protect myself from every angle—mentally, physically, emotionally. Cristiano had pushed me as far as he could without injury. But now, I had to be willing to get hurt.

I yanked on my attacker's wrist with all my body weight. The glass sliced the length of my throat as I rotated until the man's arm was twisted at an unnatural angle. I wrenched it as far back as I could and kneed him in the nose. He stumbled backward through the archways to the balcony as blood gushed from his face.

Run? Or stay and fight? I had to decide—

"*Maldita perra.*" He charged at me with the shard of glass. "You fucking bitch."

Too late. I'd broken the first rule Cristiano had ever taught me.

Don't hesitate.

I covered my face and ducked a second before a gunshot exploded through the room. I lowered my arms as his body jerked and staggered onto the balcony. He coughed, reaching for me, blood gurgling from his mouth.

I wouldn't hesitate twice.

I sprinted at him and shoved him as hard as I could. He flipped backward over the wall and tumbled down the rocky cliff. His guttural yells echoed through the mountainside until he hit a crag with a *thud* and landed on the strip of shore below.

Silence descended. Even the alarms became white noise. I'd killed a man. I hadn't thought about it. Just rushed him . . . pushed him . . . murdered him.

I clutched my neck. Something warm and sticky filled my palm. I pulled my hand away—blood. He would've killed me without a second thought. I didn't owe him one, but I peered over the edge anyway. There was just enough moonlight to make out his shadowed figure, arms and legs splayed like a broken action figure. A dark shadow seeped over the sand. "Oh my God."

"He's dead." I whirled to find Jaz's petite frame in the doorway, her gun aimed at me. She raised her voice over the sirens and added, "It's a long way down."

A beat passed as we stared at each other. "Thank you," I said.

She lowered the pistol. "They cut the electricity and killed the generators," she said. "We have to take the stairs to the panic room."

"They?"

"There are more men in the house."

I glanced back over the wall. High tide. The frothy ocean licked at the distorted body on the shore. "He said they're here for us," I told her. "The women. As payback."

"Are you with me?" Jaz asked.

A breeze passed over my half-naked body. "I should—"

"There's no time," she said, turning. "Come on."

She hurried through the room, and I followed as we sprinted down to the second floor. "Wait!" I said at the mouth of the staircase and turned back.

"What are you doing?"

"We have to get Pilar." Keeping my back to the wall, I made my way down the dark hallway to her bedroom, where I hissed her name.

After a second, Pilar slid out from under the bed, her face streaked with tears. "Natalia. *Ay, Dios mío.*"

"Come," I said, squatting to help her up. "Hurry. Are you hurt?"

"N-no." She shook as she got to her feet. Jaz guarded the door, poking her head into the hall before beckoning us over.

Pilar gasped. "You're covered in blood."

"I'm fine."

"Who's doing this?" she asked. "What do they want?"

"Come *on*," Jaz whisper-ordered.

I took Pilar's hand and let Jaz lead us through the dark, trusting her intimate knowledge of the house. When we reached the ground floor, she ushered Pilar and me ahead of her. "Run. I'll watch our backs."

We crossed the main room and slowed as we approached the kitchen, the quickest route to the cellar and panic room. Jaz raised her gun and entered first, her eyes narrowed sharply as she surveyed the room.

"It's clear," she said, nodding at a door that led to the garage. "Through there. You know the way?"

"*Sí*," I answered. "What about you?"

"Right behind you."

I grabbed Pilar's arm and sprinted forward. My bare feet slapped the tile, and we were within reach of the handle when Pilar tripped and pulled me down with her. My head just missed the corner of a table, but my cheekbone smacked the ground. Pain shot through my face, but I quickly forgot it when Pilar screamed.

I looked back and slapped a hand over my mouth. We'd fallen over Rocío, a woman who'd worked alongside Fisker in the kitchen. Blood splattered the ground and cabinets, darkening the floor around her.

"*Shh.*" Jaz yanked Pilar to her feet and, when she didn't quiet, silenced her with a slap across the face. Jaz squatted. Held her fingers to Rocío's neck. Glanced up. "She's dead."

My throat closed. "She—she was going to the panic room, too."

"Maybe." Jaz made the sign of the cross, picked up a gun next to Rocío's body, and nodded toward the refrigerator. "But she went down fighting."

I followed her gaze to what looked like a man's body slumped in one corner. "Is that one of them?"

"He's not one of *us*. Other cartels don't realize that we *always* fight back. Every one of us. We win, or we die trying." Jaz handed Pilar the gun. "But everyone in this house fights."

"I don't know what to do with this," Pilar said, holding out the Glock like it was a ticking time bomb.

"If anyone comes at you, pull the trigger," Jaz said, closing Pilar's hand around it. "You need to watch Natalia's back. She's probably the one they want. And she's going to get you both to the panic room."

"What about you?" I asked.

Jaz's eyes dropped to Rocío. "I told you," she said, swallowing. "I fight."

"No, Jaz." I pulled her arm to get her to face me. "You

don't understand. Those men are here for us. They're looking for any woman, and they will kill you."

"I have a job to do. Just like Rocío did."

I still didn't know exactly how Jaz had ended up in the Badlands, but I could piece some of it together. My first morning here, she'd revealed that she'd used sex to survive at some point in her past. Cristiano had said earlier tonight that Jaz hadn't known much kindness. Considering the Badlands had partly been built as a safe haven and rehabilitation center for victims of the pleasure trade, forced labor, and more, Jaz most likely fell into one of those categories. "Maybe they won't kill you," I said. "What if they *take* you instead?"

She froze, fear clearly working through her. "I—I can't hide down there while . . . while the others defend us."

"You're not hiding. You're protecting us." I wanted to yell to get through to her, but I struggled to speak as it was, my throat aching. I gripped her arms and shook her until alarm crossed her face. "We need you. If you don't come with us, then I'm staying here with you."

"No, please," Pilar begged through a sob, her wide eyes fixed on Rocío. "You can't leave me alone."

Jaz shook her head. "If you die, and Cristiano survives —he'll kill me himself."

"So where do you think he'd want his most tenacious fighter?"

"With you." Jaz's jaw firmed. "Fine—let's go."

We all tumbled through the door, into the garage, and down the staircase to the cellar. At the door to the panic room, I was shaking too hard to get my thumb on the fingerprint scanner, so Jaz took over. Within seconds, it lit up green, and the lock clicked open.

I let Pilar and Jaz go in first. After the near complete darkness of the house, the safe room's overhead lights seared my eyes and turned everyone a dull shade of gray. I pushed the door shut, and the slam echoed in the otherwise complete silence. Even Pilar had stopped crying. Locked in the vault, I pressed my forehead against the cool steel door.

Cristiano.

Even from a distance, he'd saved me. If it weren't for my self-defense lessons, I wouldn't be standing here. But where was *he*?

I need you to save yourself and come home to me, he'd told me once.

I *was* home. I'd saved myself.

Had he?

My breath stuttered.

"Cristiano is dead. You have nothing to fight for. Go to sleep."

Taunting words as I'd been held down. No air. Barely enough hope to save myself. My throat constricted as ghost hands wrapped around it.

I made two fists, fighting back sobs that rose fast and overwhelming in my chest. Cristiano hadn't sounded right on the phone earlier. He'd called my name as if in slow motion, from a distance. And there'd been a man in the background. What had he said?

My temples pounded as the back of my throat ached from holding in tears. We'd been talking . . . my heart rate quickening with an unfamiliar and scary kind of excitement.

Come back.

That was the important thing I'd been trying to find a way to tell him without betraying the person I'd been when I'd arrived here.

If I'd known those were his final moments, I would've just *said it*.

Come home.

I turned and leaned back against the door. One of the walls opposite me had been slid open to reveal shelving, like the inside of a large locker. Jaz passed Pilar a blanket and water, even as she held her gun close in her other hand. In a corner, a TV monitor flickered with security footage of the house. Not that there was much to see when it was deathly still and silent.

I opened my mouth to tell Jaz what had happened. Maybe I could connect the upstairs attack with what I'd heard on the phone with Cristiano. But Jaz's words from earlier came back to me.

If he doesn't make it back, you *won't make it out.*

She'd warned me nobody in the Badlands would forgive Cristiano risking his life on my behalf. If Cristiano was in danger, *I* was in danger. Jaz had made herself clear not even hours ago.

It would be my fault if he didn't make it home.

The cost of his life would be mine.

Pilar was suddenly in front of me, trying to get me to move away from the door. "You don't look well."

"She hit her head," Jaz said, shifting brown, almond-shaped eyes to me. "Do you feel . . . *¿cómo se dice?* How do you say in English? Sick to the stomach?"

"Nauseous." Pilar twisted her dark hair on top of her head, secured it in a knot, and took my elbow. "You should lie down."

"She should do anything *but* lie down," Jaz said.

"Where's everyone else?" I asked Jaz. Pilar tugged on my arm, but I stayed put. The pounding in my head could wait. "Where's Alejandro?"

Jaz shook her head. "Fighting or dead."

"You saw him?"

"No, but I know. Some cartel thinks it can come in and slaughter us, but nobody who enters will make it out alive.

We can defend ourselves, and we will. They can't know that every person in this home will fight to the death for what we've built."

The Badlands wasn't Cristiano's town. It belonged to all of them. And apparently, I wasn't the only one Cristiano had equipped to defend herself—and this place—in the event of his absence.

Pilar returned to the locker, searching the shelves. When the door beeped behind me, I moved, and Alejandro ushered in two women from the staff who ran into Jaz's open arms.

I grabbed Alejandro's elbow. "Have you heard from Cristiano?"

"I've been looking for you." His eyes roamed my face as Jaz and the women talked over each other in Spanish. "What happened?"

"Have you heard from him?" I repeated loudly, and the bunker went silent.

Cristiano is dead.

This is the price.

Alejandro glanced at the ground. "I have to get back up there. Stay here until I come for you."

"Max?" Jaz asked from across the room. "Daniel?"

Hearing the names of the two men who'd gone with Cristiano on his mission, Alejandro turned his face away. Grease smeared his cheek. "Nothing."

My heart missed a beat as panic rose in me. "*Nothing?*" I asked.

"Nobody's answering my calls."

"Maybe they're not able to," Pilar said. "They could've put their phones down or gone to sleep—"

"They were attacked, too." Alejandro sighed, clearly torn about whether to stay or go back up, and maybe even how much he should say. "And in an emergency like this—

danger out in the field, an intruder or attack within the walls—we always check in within ten minutes. No matter what," Alejandro said. "It's a rule."

The air around me constricted. My vision narrowed on a bloody smear on Alejandro's green, long-sleeved shirt. I could still hear Cristiano's deep, *alive* voice over the phone. His hard-earned laugh. His controlled, unnerving command for me to get down to the cellar when the sirens had sounded. There'd been no alarm on his end. Only my name. And the voice in the background.

"A gift from Belmonte-Ruiz, cabrón. You've fucked with us for the last time."

"Belmonte-Ruiz," I whispered. Mexico's most pervasive human trafficking ring. They wanted Cristiano dead, and with good reason. He'd stolen from them. Evaded their attempts to stop him. Taken pride in hurting them, and in the fact that he was still standing.

It was only a matter of time before it would catch up with him, though. And yet, even knowing it put his home, his people, his wife, and himself in danger—he'd persisted. He wouldn't be deterred from helping those who couldn't help themselves.

I wanted to be mad at him for it, but it only showed the kind of man he was. A man I had doubted and maligned every chance I'd gotten. Some good in this garden of evil. And I hadn't gotten the chance to tell him before they . . .

I choked back a sob. "They tried to kill him."

"They might've succeeded," Alejandro said.

A wave of nausea hit me. I touched the blood-caked gash on my throat. All at once, everything throbbed. My neck. My hand. My forehead where I'd smacked it against the glass, my cheek from hitting the floor.

"Check her head," Alejandro said to Jaz. "She looks too pale."

"I'm fine." I had to be. I needed answers, not more problems. I grabbed Alejandro's rumpled shirt. "You have to find Cristiano. His phone could be broken," I said. "They could've lost signal. Or been forced to leave their things behind. He can't be . . . he needs us."

"I've deployed a team to find them," Alejandro said, a failed attempt to sound reassuring. "According to GPS, Cristiano and Daniel haven't moved. I think that's good. But Max . . . his phone is offline."

I frowned. "Why?"

"Hell if I know, but he'd answer if he could."

"What happens if you don't hear from them within ten minutes of an emergency?" Pilar asked.

"It's never happened," Jaz answered.

"*Never?*" I looked to Alejandro for confirmation. "In all the years you've known Cristiano, there was never *once* a miscommunication, an accident, a—"

"Never." He checked his watch. "We always find a way to make contact, even if we have to find a phone somehow. It's been over half an hour." Alejo sniffed and grabbed the door handle. "I have to get—"

"That doesn't mean anything," Pilar said, her voice rising as she glared at Alejandro. "Phones fail all the time. And you need to work on your bedside manner."

"I'm just trying to prepare Natalia." Despite his brusque tone, worry etched the lines around Alejo's eyes. "Even putting aside the ten-minute rule, if Cristiano was alive, he never would've let this long pass without checking on Natalia."

Oh, God. My limbs weakened, and I grabbed Pilar's arm. Alejo was right. Cristiano's silence spoke louder than anything. He and I had a turbulent history, a marriage that better resembled a battlefield, and we'd been sparring for weeks—but my gut knew. He would've done anything in his power to make sure I was safe.

And even though I'd wished him out my life more times than I could count, I wanted safety for him, too. I wanted him back.

The world began to swim. I slid down a wall and dropped my head between my knees.

If I'd had any doubts, they vanished before my eyes.

Something he'd said at the costume gala came back to me . . .

It had been Cristiano's dying wish to hear me scream.

And the heavens had granted him that.

2

NATALIA

My world shook, and I startled awake. Jaz hunched over me, backlit by the humming white lights that seemed as bright as the sun. "What month is it?" Jaz asked.

"What?" I sat up slowly. I didn't remember lying on the ground or curling up with a blanket.

"Do you know your age?"

"I . . . twenty. Why—"

"Good enough." Jaz stood abruptly and moved back to her side of the room. She sat in a corner, pulled her legs to her chest, and held her gun on the tops of her knees.

I pressed the butt of my palm to my throbbing head to find it bandaged. My hand had been wrapped, too, from the shard of glass. "What happened?"

She kept her eyes on the door. "You passed out."

My vision doubled. Blankets and pillows had been arranged around the room. More women had appeared. Everyone slept except for Jaz.

"How long was I out?" The question came out as a scratchy whisper, my traumatized throat protesting.

"I don't know. A couple hours?" She heaved a sigh. "Alejandro says upstairs is clear, but they're handling the bodies."

"Bodies? Plural? Is there news about . . ." I couldn't bring myself to say his name. *Cristiano*. Even thinking it made my heart sink.

"All the women who survived are in this room." She shifted. "Nothing from Cristiano."

I fought back another wave of nausea. *Nothing* was the worst possible scenario. All signs pointed to his death. I had to believe he was alive, though. That he, like I, had fought back as hard as possible. For all the faith he'd placed in me over my lifetime, I owed him the same.

"No one checked in—not Max, Daniel, or Cristiano. They're dead." Her small, pointed nose twitched. "What are you going to do about it?"

"What?"

"They killed your husband. Not just any man—the leader of a powerful crime syndicate. Our savior. Our protector."

I lifted my head. She expected me to take on Belmonte-Ruiz? *No.* She expected me to cower and fall, or to run away. Maybe that would be wise. If Cristiano de la Rosa couldn't beat them, neither could I. Then again, I'd just taken down an attacker who'd had every advantage against me.

But I couldn't think of something so daunting now. I rubbed my elbows, the newest, but not only, aching spots. "Did you bandage me up?" I asked Jaz, noticing the open first-aid kit by her side.

"I woke you up to make sure you don't have a concussion," she answered. "I don't think you do."

"How do you know?"

"I've done this lots of times for Cristiano and the guys.

You'll probably be fine." Jaz pulled her knees more tightly to her chest. "Which is too bad. It would've saved me some trouble. I told you the price of Cristiano's life."

Mine.

Pilar sat up from her makeshift bed in the corner, rubbing her eyes. "What does that mean?"

"Your fate is linked to his." Jaz looked to Pilar. "Yours too."

"Cristiano put himself in danger for me," I told Pilar. "According to Jaz, it's my fault if he dies."

Pilar raised her unsteady hands to her mouth. "And they'll kill *us*?"

I had always tried to protect Pilar, but if Cristiano had taught me anything, it was that no weapon could match the truth. The more she knew, the better chance she'd have of making it out of here alive. "They'll try."

I held Jaz's gaze. She didn't scare me. Her threats only came from concern—I knew, because we were both afraid of the same thing.

Losing Cristiano.

And she wanted what I did—his survival.

The question was why I cared? I'd fought Cristiano at every turn. Stripped down, with no indignation to hide behind, only my basic, unadulterated, inexplicable hope remained.

That he'd live.

That he'd come back to me.

That I'd get the chance to tell him I wasn't the same girl who'd arrived here. And that I didn't see him as the same man.

Time passed differently in the vault. I had no concept of how much of it had gone by when Alejandro finally reappeared.

I jumped to my feet, steadying myself on the wall when I got woozy. "Well?" I asked.

"A chopper is inbound. It's not one of ours, but we've made contact." Alejandro looked from Jaz and the women waking up on the floor to me. "Cristiano is on it."

I covered my mouth and released an unexpected sob. "He's alive?"

"*No sé.*" Unsure, Alejandro shook his head. "But we've got great doctors on hand to receive him."

I'd get to lay eyes on him. Touch him. Tell him I wanted him to stay. That *I* no longer wanted to leave. "I should be there when he lands," I said, pushing through a sore throat.

Alejandro hesitated. "Respectfully . . . you'd probably be in the way. We have it under control. Might be best if you stay down here."

"Might be best if I *don't*," I shot back.

Alejandro arched an eyebrow. Up until now, I hadn't given him—or anyone—reason to believe I'd want Cristiano to return alive. But despite my best efforts, my feelings for Cristiano had been building. I hadn't wanted to admit it, but now, I had no choice. I had nothing left to hide behind. My soul ached to my core at the thought of losing him, of never hearing his deep, solid voice again, of things left unsaid.

"You said yourself Cristiano will want to know that I'm safe," I said. "Maybe having me there will—will give him hope."

Alejandro nodded behind him. "Come on, then."

Outside the metal box, my chest loosened. I could breathe again. I was taking action. We made our way briskly upstairs to the garage.

Alejandro drew his gun as we entered the house through a back door. "Stay by my side."

Though some of the lights had come back on, my skin crawled with the eerie stillness, as if the house had been deserted for months. Alejandro stayed close to me, his posture stick-straight.

"I thought you said the coast was clear," I whispered.

He didn't respond. According to Cristiano, a hundred percent confidence in anything was a death wish.

We entered a wing of the house I'd rarely had a chance to explore on our way to an elevator I'd only heard mentioned in passing.

Once we were inside, I asked, "Where does this go?"

"To the helipad on the roof."

We exited the elevator and stepped onto an open, brightly lit landing pad. It wasn't even the roof—the top floor of the house was well below us. It was just the endless, black night on the top of a mountain. I had looked up into the same sky earlier and reveled in the array of stars. Now, they were in hiding, drowned out by floodlights.

We walked toward a raised concrete circle outlined in white paint with an "H" in the center. A team of men in jeans and t-shirts waited, hands in their pockets, furrows in their brows.

"Who are they?" I asked.

"The trauma team. Other medical professionals are downstairs tending to the staff." Alejo pointed to the only woman. "She's leading the charge and has worked on Cristiano before."

I bit my thumbnail, looking them over. I'd only ever known sterile hospitals, white lab coats, stethoscopes, high-tech machines. Even when Papá or my grandfather had needed medical attention, the doctors looked professional. And they never would've accepted a female physician at the helm, as senseless as that was.

"Are you sure about this?" I asked. "I could call my

father. He'll know where to find the country's most capable people."

"Doctor Sosa is highly regarded. Cristiano trusts her." Alejandro clasped his hands behind his back with an inhalation, searching the sky. "If he's alive when he lands, he'll be in good hands."

With a whir in the distance, we each whipped our gazes behind us. A blinking dot in the skyline came into view. I laced my fingers over my breastbone as it neared.

I just wanted to see his chest rise and fall, his lips and hands warm and pink with life, his long lashes flutter as he opened dark, ruthless eyes that would soften at the sight of me.

Was that so much to ask?

Please, I prayed.

I held my hair down as the helicopter hovered in front of us. As soon as the landing skids touched down, the team was moving, opening the door, reaching in, helping out a woman in a short, slinky red dress with legs for days . . .

The unexpected sight of a siren with curled, auburn hair and fire-engine red lips left my mouth hanging open. Freshly applied makeup made it seem as if she'd come straight from a dinner party.

"Who is that?" I asked.

Alejandro followed my line of sight. "If I had to guess . . . could be Natasha."

Natasha?

The name set off warning bells. Cristiano had mentioned a Natasha before, but he'd made her sound fleeting, like a one-night stand.

A gurney appeared, transferred quickly from the chopper to the pavement. My heart dropped to my feet seeing the lifeless body strapped to it. Cristiano had never been so still. I didn't remember running toward him, but suddenly he was within arm's reach. Gloved hands restrained me. Men yelled at me to get back. Cristiano's ripped-open dress shirt revealed blood-soaked bandages around a once elegant, now shredded, *always* powerful torso.

Cristiano's body bounced gracelessly on the gurney as they rushed him off the helipad.

Beneath an oxygen mask, his pallor alarmed me. "Is he a-alive?" I heard myself ask.

"You have to step back, *señora*," one of the men said.

Alejandro held the elevator doors for them. I started to board as well, but claws on my elbow tugged me back. "They told you to stay clear."

As the doors closed, I turned to face the sharp, female voice and acrylic nails that had kept me from Cristiano. Had she not been wearing heels tall enough to turn her into a tree in an obscenely short dress, we would've come face to face.

"Who are you?" I asked.

She released my arm. "*I* am the reason Cristiano is alive."

He's alive. Was she sure? How did she know? It didn't matter. It was the only answer I'd gotten so far, and I'd take it. I made the sign of the cross and silently thanked Our Lady of Guadalupe.

"You," the woman said over my head to Alejandro. "Are you head of security?"

"At the moment." He hit a button to call the elevator back up. "I'm Alejandro."

"Ah, yes. You spoke to my pilot." She held out a hand. "Natasha Sokolov-Flores. An old friend of Cristiano's."

They shook, and Alejandro tilted his head in my direction. "This is Natalia, Cristiano's wife. She's as much the head of household as I am while Cristiano's incapacitated."

I appreciated the vote of confidence, especially after Jaz's earlier opinions.

Natasha returned her eyes to me. Or to my rings, more specifically. "Is that wise?" she asked. "Cristiano made it seem like this was a marriage of convenience. I'm certain he would not like his business managed by a girl he can barely trust."

"And I'm certain he wouldn't like you speaking to me that way," I said.

I was as surprised as she looked at my response. *Mindset*, Cristiano would remind me. Natasha had the wrong one about me. So did I. Cristiano would expect me to step up in a situation like this.

"Mrs. de la Rosa has many advisors," Alejandro assured her.

Natasha's eyes flitted over me then back to him. "I'm sure you want to know what happened. Is there somewhere we can talk?"

She and Cristiano had been . . . together? Tonight? He hadn't mentioned that on the phone—but why would he? In any case, I couldn't let that bother me now. Cristiano's condition was far more important. "We can talk here," I said. "Now."

The elevator dinged, and we boarded. "Maybe it's better you let us handle the business side of things," Natasha said to me. "It isn't pretty."

I'd own the ivory tower, and I'd rule from it. Cristiano had told me that once our vows had been exchanged. If I didn't believe I could take over in his absence, nobody would. "I need to be included in any discussion."

She looked to Alejandro as if for permission. "Cristiano trusts her," he said. "With all due respect, you're the stranger here, Natasha."

The elevator stopped at the house, and the doors parted to the top floor. "Call me Tasha. Cristiano does," she said, walking out.

I tried to keep up with Alejandro as he strode down the hall to my bedroom—until he stopped abruptly at the doorway and turned back to me with a frown.

"What is it?" I asked.

"You can't let her or anyone intimidate you." He glanced at the ground. "If Cristiano doesn't make it . . . you're in charge. All this is yours. And I don't mean that figuratively—he was adamant that your marriage be legal."

To torture me, I would've once thought. Now, I wondered if Cristiano's reasons ran deeper than that. A need to connect with me on some level when I'd wanted nothing to do with him. An attempt to protect me, even, if something should happen to him.

"You have my loyalty, Natalia," Alejandro said, reading my mind. "Cristiano would've wanted that."

I swallowed, glancing through the doorway. The broken mirror was gone. I assumed the body on the beach had disappeared as well. Alejandro and his team moved fast.

My gaze moved to Cristiano as he was transferred from the gurney to the bed. "We shouldn't speak of him like he's gone. Not yet."

The team of doctors worked so swiftly, I could hardly keep the four of them straight, much less get closer than a meter from his bed. In no time at all, Cristiano had been hooked up to a heart monitor that'd appeared out of nowhere, irrigated, prodded, and injected. White patches dotted his torso as IVs branched from his chest, arms, and hands.

His dark, disheveled hair had fallen over his clammy forehead, and I resisted the urge to push the strands out of his eyes. "What happened?" I asked anyone who might respond. "Was he shot?"

Tasha turned to me with her slender arms crossed. "Stabbed."

This close, I could see Cristiano's blood had stained her red dress. She'd helped saved his life while I'd been accused of putting it at risk.

If I had the energy, I'd hate her for having information about my husband that I wanted. And for a pointed chin that gave her a markedly heart-shaped face, her sultry, Eastern European features, and a smooth indistinct accent that made her sound exotic.

Alejandro beckoned us toward the fireplace and away from the doctors. "Tell us what happened," he said to Tasha.

"Cristiano pissed off the wrong people with his little operation," she said.

She knew the truth of what went on here in the Badlands, then. She and Cristiano were close—but how close? Enough to have discussed my marriage, but not enough for her to know it wasn't a complete sham.

"Cristiano's operation is anything but little," I said.

She lifted a manicured eyebrow. "You're aware of it?"

"My husband's business? Yes." Across the room, masked doctors convened near Cristiano's head. I spun my diamond around my finger and added, "We're already aware Belmonte-Ruiz is behind this."

"They hit us here, too," Alejandro explained. "You said he's alive because of you?"

"Cristiano's attacker is dead," she said. "I didn't have time to double-check, but my father's men have confirmed it, and they're taking care of the body now."

"I have men en route to look for Max and Daniel." Alejandro glanced at his phone screen. I'd lost count of how many times he'd checked it. "Did you see them at all?"

"Only at the event," she said. "One of them guarded the door while Cristiano and I spoke privately on the balcony." She licked her bottom lip, keeping her eyes on Alejo. "Cristiano left before I did. When I came out, I saw a valet attendant standing over him with a knife. Cristiano had been stabbed several times. The valet was about to finish him off."

"And?" I asked. "Then what?"

Tasha took her time unsnapping her slim, snakeskin clutch. She pulled out a tiny handgun that just fit in her palm. "Elena. Named after my late grandmother. Neither lady has ever let me down."

"You *shot* him?" I asked.

She tossed her chestnut-colored curls over one shoulder. "Wouldn't you, darling?"

My cheeks warmed. Cristiano wouldn't even let me carry a gun. Where was the White Monarch now? Still in his office at *La Madrina*? I had the next best thing. My silver, gold, and pearl wedding ring, modeled after the elegant 9mm, had acted as a weapon hours ago.

"We were talking when it happened," I said. I'd heard his smile through the phone when he'd realized I was calling out of concern. To ask him to abandon such a risky mission. After weeks of resistance on my part, how horrible it must've been for him to think he finally had me on the hook—that the only danger was the usual minefield our conversations presented—only to be met with . . . a *knife*.

"Did you see his phone, Tasha? It's offline," Alejandro said. "Was he holding it?"

"Cristiano was barely conscious, slurring his words, unable to do much more than lie on the ground," she said.

"Slurring?" Alejandro asked. "If he was drugged, it would explain why he didn't fight back, and why he didn't alert us to trouble." Alejandro unlocked his phone and began typing. "See if your men can locate and destroy his cell."

I tried to keep up without getting emotional. On the ground? *Drugged?* Cristiano loomed over everything, and not just physically. At the thought of him unable to defend himself, a lump formed in my throat. "How'd you get him here?" I asked to shift my focus.

"My bodyguards," Tasha said. "I didn't know what else was coming, so we got him into my car. Maksim didn't pick up, and I didn't have anyone else's number, so I called my father. He sent a helicopter for us. We did our best to stem the bleeding."

"He could've died on the way," I said. "He should've gone to a hospital."

Tasha snorted. "Don't be naïve. They'd have sewn him up and turned him over to the authorities."

"Do you think I care as long as he'd lived?" I asked, heat rising up my neck. "It wouldn't matter anyway if he was detained—Cristiano de la Rosa can get himself out of any situation."

"Assuming he survives," she said, taking a compact from her clutch, "he may not be able to much longer."

Alejo paused and looked up from his phone. "What do you mean?"

"If Belmonte-Ruiz is on to Calavera's games, others

will be soon, too." She checked her lipstick in the handheld mirror and ran a finger along one corner of her mouth. "Rumor is, Cristiano has stopped supplying arms to those who do business with BR."

"And any syndicate heavily involved with human trafficking of any sort," Alejandro said with a nod. "It's not a rumor."

She glanced sidelong at him and snapped her compact shut. "That's a big enough number to ruffle some feathers."

"It is," Alejandro agreed. "Especially if the truth about the Badlands gets out. But it's what we all decided as a team."

I bit my lip, struggling to keep up, but still following. The truth about the Badlands . . .

Gruesome rumors surrounded the Calavera cartel, a reputation Cristiano and his men had cultivated in order to insulate themselves. Calavera was a top dealer in weaponry worldwide, and that made them nearly untouchable. But would it be enough to protect them if word spread that the Badlands actually acted as a rehabilitation hub for those the other cartels had sold into slavery?

The leaders of this underground world I'd grown up in could justify and support nearly anything. But the disruption of the way things were, theft that dearly cost Cristiano's rivals, and the unraveling of decades' worth of industry . . .

That was business nobody around here would support.

But it wasn't anything I could worry about now. Cristiano's life was on the line.

And I didn't want to think of what could happen to all of this without him.

3

NATALIA

The balcony doors had been shut, and the curtains drawn, but through the sheer white fabric, the night sky lightened to royal blue as dawn began to break.

Doctor Sosa stepped away from Cristiano's bed to make notes on a clipboard. It was the first time she'd separated from the trauma team, and I didn't waste my opportunity to try to get answers. "Doctor Sosa? I'm Natalia," I said as I approached her, and added, "de la Rosa. Cristiano's wife. Is he—will he live?"

She stuck the clipboard under her arm. As she pulled her surgical mask's straps from behind her ears, pieces of her light brown hair fell around her face. Judging by her haphazard bun and the puffiness around her eyes, she'd been asleep when she'd gotten the call. "*Sí.*"

Air rushed out of my chest. I hadn't expected a simple "yes" for an answer. I opened my mouth but couldn't find the words. "He—really?"

"Cristiano was stabbed three times," she said. "Two

deep but clean lacerations in his abdomen, and one that just missed his heart."

I covered my mouth. Hearing his brush with death put so bluntly, my chin wobbled.

A hand on my shoulder alerted me to Alejandro. "'Just missed' is a good thing, Natalia," he said.

"Cristiano is very lucky," Doctor Sosa agreed. "Well, either that or the attacker was extremely skilled."

"I . . . what?" I asked. "I'm sorry, it's been a long night. It sounded like you said he was *skilled*."

"I heard the same," Alejandro said. "What does that mean?"

"He didn't hit any vital organs," she explained, pointing to her own abdomen. "With three tries, it's almost as if he was trying *not* to kill him."

"That makes no sense," Alejandro said. "But it sounds like good news?"

She nodded. "He's lost blood, but he's smart—or foolish—in that he banks some before each major trip outside the Badlands. There are matches within the town who are donating, too." She reviewed her clipboard and sighed. "Someone less stubborn likely would've gone into hypovolemic shock by now, but fortunately, we're prepared to do a transfusion. I have to observe the wounds for a bit, then once I'm sure there's no infection, we'll sew him up."

"So he's going to be okay?" I asked slowly.

"It's never wise to make guarantees in this kind of situation, but the outlook is good. There's some tissue and muscle damage, plus the sutures, so I'll need him to stay in bed for a couple weeks or so."

"He won't like that," Alejandro said. "He's been confined to bed in the past—we all have for one reason or another, and I know him. He's too impatient. You remember the last time he was shot."

I frowned. "The *last* time? How many times . . .?"

"He was back in the field soon after," Doctor Sosa answered. "Just remind him that if he makes this worse, it could result in surgery. Or an infection. Keep his wounds clean, make sure he takes his antibiotics, and keep him off his feet for as long as you can. He should be on the road to normal soon."

Normal.

Did I want that?

My body answered for me. I didn't even know how to handle the relief flooding me. I hadn't prepared myself for good news. My limbs fatigued as exhaustion set in, but I held myself together. "Thank God," I said. "No—thank *you*, Doctor."

"Of course, but my work isn't done yet."

"Far from it," Alejandro agreed, looking me over. "Would you take a look at Natalia next?"

"I feel fine," I said to the doctor. "Cristiano needs you more."

"My colleagues can handle him for the moment. Come. Sit," she said, guiding me by the elbow toward the couch in front of the fireplace. "I see you have some battle wounds of your own. Headache?"

"A little, yes."

"That's to be expected. But your speech sounds fine, which is good. Let's take a look." She sat me down, unwrapped my bandages, and inspected the cuts. "They look worse than they are," she observed. "Surface wounds, though the neck and this one on your cheek are likely to leave a scar."

I glanced at Alejandro. "At least I'll have proof I defended myself when Cristiano wakes up."

He smiled. "He'll be in need of some good news."

After Doctor Sosa stitched me up, I curled up on the

couch, watching them do the same to Cristiano.

Fingers sifted through my hair. I basked in the comforting touch. *Cristiano*. He was here. He was . . .

Injured.

I opened my eyes. Pilar perched on the edge of the sofa in Cristiano's bedroom where I'd fallen asleep in front of the fireplace.

"How do you feel?" she asked, tucking me in with a throw blanket.

"Is Cristiano awake?" I asked, sitting up.

"Not yet."

I glanced over at him. The room had emptied out. Only the heart rate monitor's steady *beep* indicated any life.

Pilar glanced at the bedroom's closed door and whispered, "We could go, you know."

I rubbed the remnants of my headache from my left temple. "What?"

"I . . . about what Jaz said in the panic room . . ." She moved her loose ponytail over one shoulder and curled the ends around her hand. "I know Cristiano is supposed to recover, but anything could happen. You and I could be in serious trouble if he doesn't. Or even if he does. We could run. Now. Before he wakes up."

Had Pilar been paying attention at all? "*Nobody* runs from Cristiano," I said. "Especially me. If that were an option, I would've tried weeks ago."

"It's probably the last thing you want to think about right now, but this may be our only chance. He's unconscious. Two of his best men are missing. And the others are distracted looking for them." She gripped one edge of my blanket. "We can go to your father and Barto. Barto will help us, I know he will."

"Cristiano is as strong as he looks." I shook my head, looking her in the eye. "When he wakes up, and I'm not here, he'll come after me."

With her shirt sleeve, she wiped sweat from her temple. "You could . . . you could *kill* him." She winced and rushed out, "We could find a way—poison, overdose, smothering him in his sleep—and escape before they know it was us."

I bit the inside of my cheek. I understood where Pilar was coming from. In the last twenty-four hours, she'd been kidnapped by Alejandro, ferried to a place rumored to exploit women—run by a man she'd feared ever since childhood, when she'd witnessed him beat up her cousin—and endured an attack that could've easily ended her life.

Since Cristiano's return to town, the man she'd known as *El Polvo* had chased her off the dancefloor at *La Madrina*, made her watch us marry against my will, then ordered her brought here.

But she'd heard the worst of him from me. Pilar had been one of the people I'd turned to after my mother's death.

Cristiano had done unforgivable things. What did it say about me that I had no desire to run? That I wanted to be the first person he saw when he opened his eyes? That I didn't even want to *try* to hide my feelings for him from Pilar—or from Cristiano, from myself? Not anymore.

I didn't *want* to consider what it said about me—because I'd made the mistake of blindly trusting a man before. For Diego, I would've done anything—for him, I *had*. Was this any different? I didn't know.

But the idea of losing Cristiano had shown me I wasn't ready to say good-bye. Despite all we'd been through, he and I were only beginning to learn who the other person was. My attacker's declaration that my husband was dead had spurred me to fight for my own life—so that I could avenge his. I'd sworn Cristiano my loyalty, and whether I'd known it at the time or not, I'd meant it.

Cristiano had done unforgivable things, yes—but he'd done admirable ones as well. He'd put himself at risk to get me closure. Except for my questions surrounding my mother's death, he'd always told me the truth, no matter how brutal. He'd taught me strength in many ways.

And though she didn't know it, he'd helped Pilar from the shadows as well.

"Cristiano didn't just bring you here to make me happy. He did it to protect you from Manu." I took her hand and squeezed it. "Did you know your cousin was the one who molested your half-sister?"

She gasped. "Nessa? Yes, I knew—but that's not supposed to leave my family. How did *you* know?"

"Cristiano told me. That's why he roughed him up so badly years ago. Not just for stealing, but so he wouldn't—*couldn't*—hurt Nessa again."

Pilar opened and closed her mouth a couple times. "I . . . I didn't know. Are you sure?"

"He told me earlier tonight." Earlier tonight, when things had been so different. When I'd been so close to figuring out my rollercoaster of a relationship with Cristiano. "He's not who you think he is. There's a very big heart in there, though he tries to hide it. Stay with me." I gave her an encouraging smile. "Spend time with him. You'll see."

"If you say it's true, I believe you." She bit her thumbnail. "But . . . please don't tell him I suggested we try to kill him."

I pulled her in for a hug. "Will you find out from Alejandro if there's any new information?"

"Of course." She stood and fixed her hair as she left the room.

I got up from the couch and folded the blanket over the side. Grateful for my first moment alone with Cristiano, I crossed the room, lowered myself onto his side of the bed, and fit my palm against his warm one. We'd held hands once before, when we'd been staked out in a car, watching Sandra fight for her life.

Some of the last words he'd said to me rang through my mind.

"Sleep well. I will, knowing you're one of the protected."

I'd said nothing back. He slept almost too peacefully now, but there was life in his hands—and blood under his fingernails.

Anxiety tightened my chest at the sight of his wounds. Cristiano had always seemed invincible to me. Even when he'd fled our house to escape my father's wrath, he'd done it unscathed.

The truth was, without Cristiano walking this earth, I wouldn't feel as safe. And I didn't mean *just* in the cartel world.

He was a protector—*my* protector.

I'd thought he was the enemy—but maybe he never had been.

Feelings hadn't been blooming inside me—they'd been planted long ago, taking root without my knowledge.

I couldn't pretend that in my darkest hour, I hadn't fought harder so I could get back to him. Had it been the same for him? Was that how he was still standing?

Because he should've been dead. Alejandro suspected he'd been drugged—I'd forgotten to ask the doctor about it. That would mean the attack hadn't been spontaneous. Belmonte-Ruiz had had Cristiano at their mercy and hadn't even done any serious damage. It made no sense.

"You can't sleep there," I heard from behind me.

I looked over my shoulder. Jaz stood in the doorway with an armful of towels, a green plastic bowl, and a sponge. "He needs to be cleaned up," I said.

She entered the room. "That's why I'm here."

My husband receiving a sponge bath from another woman? That wasn't going to happen. I rose from the edge of his bed. *Our* bed. "I'll do it."

She set the items on his nightstand and unfolded a towel from the top of the pile. "I've been tending to *señor* de la Rosa for years.'"

"That was before," I said.

"Before what?" she asked but kept her eyes on the task in front of her. She knew the answer.

"Before me," I said.

Alejandro had been right earlier—gone were the days of conceding to others. Cristiano needed me to step up now and act as his wife. To care for him as one, and to make decisions in his best interest.

"You care about Cristiano," I noted.

She paused and dropped the towel to her side. "And you've made it clear you don't."

"Things change," I said. "People change."

Jaz shook her head. "People don't change. Circumstances do. I don't trust you alone with him."

"And I didn't trust you, either," I said. "You eavesdropped on my call with him last night, then threatened my life, not for the first time. But you also helped get me and Pilar to safety."

She shrugged and took the bowl and sponge to the bathroom. "I did that for Cristiano," she said over the sound of running water.

"Then we do have something in common," I said. "Our loyalty to him."

She poked her head into the room. "You call feeding outsiders information *loyalty*?"

The cell phone Diego had given me. Jaz had likely helped Cristiano find it. "I never shared information outside these walls," I promised. "It was a mistake to accept the phone. I paid the price. Cristiano has forgiven me."

She turned off the faucet and returned to his bedside with a bowl of soapy water. "He's blind when it comes to you."

Her words echoed the distrust she'd made clear to me the night before. But then there was also that *other* thing she'd said. The one I hadn't remembered until this moment.

"Even if he doesn't know it yet, he loves you . . ."

Last night, I hadn't known how to feel about that, but now? Was it possible I felt the same about him and hadn't known it, either?

I went quiet with the startling thought. Then pushed it away, considering Jaz tilted her head as if she could read my mind.

"Nobody can deny you've been good to him," I said. "But you have to make room for me, because if it's one or the other, you know who Cristiano will choose."

Jaz crossed her arms. "You're sure about that?"

I couldn't fathom Cristiano having to pick between the two of us, but he'd worked hard to get me here—and even harder to ensure I couldn't just walk away. I pulled my shoulders back as I nodded. "I am."

"Jaz." Alejandro leaned in the doorway. How long he'd been listening, I wasn't sure. "This is Natalia's job now."

Jaz sighed. "I hope you prove me wrong," she said to me and walked away.

Alejandro winked, then shut the door to give me privacy.

I picked up the sponge.

And I prepared myself to tend to the devil. To fix the monster who'd destroy all other monsters. To bring my husband back to life.

4

CRISTIANO

I'd opened my eyes once and seen my dark angel above me, silhouetted by sunlight streaming through the balcony's arched doorways. She wasn't here now. Maybe it'd been a dream, but she was one I hoped to have over and over. And yet, I'd almost died without having her even once.

I ached for her gentle touch, the curled ends of her midnight-black hair brushing my skin as her oval eyes soothed me, even when they were filled with defiance. "Natalia."

"Welcome back to the living." It was Alejandro who stepped up to the bed, crashing through my fantasy with a grin on his face. "You're a little slower to recover in your old age. I had my money on you waking up this morning."

Reality hit with brutal force. I shot into a sitting position, pain searing through my chest and down my side. "Where's Natalia?" The words scraped from my dry-as-fuck throat as the machines around my bed beeped faster, louder. "What happened to her?"

"Don't move." Alejandro laid a hand on my shoulder

to try to ease me back down. "Your wife is here, *don* Cristiano. She's sleeping." He nodded backward to where her sock-clad feet stuck out over one arm of the sofa. "She hasn't left your side."

Even my relief was exhausting, hitting like a tidal wave and forcing me back against the bed. "Is she okay?"

"She's fine, but she hasn't slept much in the last thirty-six hours." His voice deepened. "I can wake her, but first, I should debrief you."

"Let her rest," I said, despite my demanding need to look into her eyes and hear her tell me she was all right. "What happened?"

"Belmonte-Ruiz. They've claimed responsibility for your attack and for the one here. They targeted every woman in the house."

My wife's blood-curdling screams echoed through our bedroom. A room where, until recently, I'd never felt anything but safe. Anger roiled through my chest like a Mack truck. "Natalia. Someone put his hands on her?"

"She fought back. She survived. Not everyone was so lucky. I'll fill you in later."

I closed my eyes to steel myself against a pain far worse than some stab wounds. Some of my people had paid the price for what had started as a personal vendetta. It'd grown into much more over the years, and Calavera had the support of everyone in the Badlands—but I'd let them down. "I'm sorry," I said.

"We'll arrange a service for them," Alejo said. "Once you're recovered, that is."

With Natalia's safety established, and my immediate concerns eased, hazy details from the attack at the hotel came into focus. My wounds announced themselves, tight and throbbing. Tension in the bridge of my nose made my head feel on the verge of exploding.

I'd experienced worse, but this particular strike had me on edge. I wasn't sure how many times the attendant had stabbed me, but even once was too many. I hadn't been able to stop it. The assault had seemed to go on forever, delivering me slowly to death's doorstep. What had kept Max and Daniel away?

"Why aren't I dead?" I asked.

"Because your attacker is."

"Max got him?"

Alejandro hesitated. "No."

"Daniel?" I asked. "I think I heard a gunshot, but I was out of it."

Alejandro glanced at the ground, taking too long to respond.

"What?" I asked.

He raised his eyes. "Daniel's dead. Found around the side of the hotel. His body's in transit so we can give him a proper burial with the others."

Fuck. My throat constricted. It'd been some time since one of my immediate team had taken a bullet for me. Things had happened so fast, and at the same time, they hadn't. This had been an organized attack. My final moments with Daniel played through my head—him teasing me for being overly protective of Natalia. The insinuation that I was paranoid. And yet, he'd always done exactly as I'd asked, up to his final moments. "And Maksim?"

Alejandro inhaled, his chest expanding. I tried to brace myself for the same news, but there was no preparing for that. Daniel had been a good and loyal man, but Max was more than a comrade. He was as good of a friend as I'd ever find. We'd been together since the start and had defeated many who'd like to have seen us both dead.

Finally, Alejandro exhaled. "They have him."

It took a moment for his words to register. And when they did, the heart rate monitor beside me went haywire. "What?" I asked. "What are you talking about?"

"Belmonte-Ruiz captured Max. The good news is, he's still alive, which means they need him. I've seen proof of life."

Blood rushed in my ears as I sat up. "Then what the fuck are we sitting here for? We have to go after him."

Alejandro's brows furrowed. "We will. But first, we need a plan. And in order to make one, we've got to figure out why they tried—or didn't try, according to Sosa—to kill you and not Max. If he's bait, then they must've known—"

Despite the way my torso protested, I swung my legs over the side of the bed, nearly knocking over the monitor. "If you think I'm going to sit here while Max is in trouble"—I yanked an IV from my inner elbow—"then you don't know jack shit about me, Alejandro—I'd do the same for you."

"*Ay. Tranquilo.* You need rest—"

"Don't tell me to relax."

Alejandro shoved me. Already out of breath, I went down easy, and the resulting pain was enough to remind me I could still make things worse. "I wouldn't ask that of you, and neither would Max," Alejo said. "You're useless to us dead, and that's what you'll be if you go after him at anything less than a hundred percent."

"You underestimate me," I said, failing to control the volume of my voice. My face burned at the thought that Max had been gone for over a day, and we'd done nothing.

"You're a danger to yourself, but also to those who go with you," Alejandro reminded me. "We'll get him. But not today."

"We *don't* leave men behind—"

The air in the room shifted. I looked past Alejandro, and my anger immediately fell away as my gaze landed on Natalia.

Long, dark hair in disarray, breathless and pink-cheeked in a white satin robe, she stared at me as if she'd seen a ghost. "You're—you're awake."

"You're alive."

Natalia drew toward the bed. Did she also feel the magnetic pulse beating between us? She scanned me head to toe. "And you're bleeding." She looked to Alejo. "Why is he bleeding?"

"He's trying to leave the bed," Alejandro said—the fucking snitch.

A dark, red rivulet ran down my forearm. I didn't even feel it. I wanted Natalia in my arms as soon as possible. "Leave us," I told Alejandro. "Stabilize everyone within these walls who can fight. We're going after Max."

"With all due respect, sir—"

"You're too polite, Alejandro. The answer is *no*," Natalia said. Her voice faltered but not with doubt—her vocal cords sounded strained. Her posture lengthened as any sign of distress left her. "You're not stepping foot outside this bedroom until you're fully healed."

I slow-blinked at her. "You're telling me no?"

"She just did, and she's right." Alejandro lifted his chin, no doubt smug that he had backup. "We're not ready. We'd only be leaving ourselves open to another attack here and putting more men at risk. Max knows that—so does Belmonte-Ruiz."

All at once, exhaustion hit—along with the urge to promise Natalia I'd never leave her side again as long as she wanted me there. "Call a meeting," I said. Still woozy from whatever medication had been administered, I could admit I wasn't in the best state of mind to make decisions. But I would be soon. "We'll finish this discussion then."

Alejandro exited the room, leaving me with my shame. My partner was in trouble because of me, and I was doing nothing. And yet, Natalia was here. She was safe.

"Come here," I said, and softened my command with, "*mi amor.*"

"How do you feel?" she asked as she approached slowly. "What can I get you?"

The warble in her voice resounded in my chest. I couldn't go to her. I was still hooked up to more than one machine, and even if I hadn't been, my body didn't move nearly as fast as I needed it to. My weakness was on display.

"Just you." Everything smarted when I reached for her. "Please. Come."

"Lie back, and I will."

Willing to concede to anything in that moment for her touch, I rested against the mound of pillows behind me. "You're losing your voice."

She ignored me and opened the drawer of my night-stand to take out a cloth. "Let me just call the nurse Doctor Sosa arranged for us—"

I stopped her. "Please, Natalia. You are my medicine. Only you can heal me."

Her lip curled as her eyes went foggy. I couldn't tell if she was smiling, grimacing, or trying not to burst into tears. She sat on the edge of the bed, scooting closer until the heat of her body warmed me. The contempt, resentment, and anger that sometimes marred her face when she looked at me had vanished. So I *hadn't* imagined the intimacy of our last phone call, then. The girl who'd once pointed a gun in my face seemed relieved to see me alive.

"Here." She held out a glass of water from the nightstand. "Drink this."

Damn it, Natalia. She was just trying to take care of me, but I needed answers more than fluids or nurses. I gulped down the water as quickly as I could while she disappeared into the bathroom.

When she returned, I gave her back the glass, and she pressed the now dampened cloth to my inner arm where the IV had ripped. The wound was the equivalent of a scratch, but I couldn't bring myself to stop her.

"I'm sorry I was asleep when you woke up," she said, wiping the area clean.

I'd seen glimpses of her over me, her hand in mine as I'd drifted in and out of consciousness, her normally violet eyes gray.

My freshly stitched wounds protested as I lifted my arm to touch her cheek, but it was worth the pain when she turned her face into my palm. "I know you've been here," I said. "What happened? Tell me everything."

"One of the valet attendants attacked you. How much do you remember?"

"I don't mean me." I took the cloth from her, discarding it on the floor. It hurt like *fuck* to lift my arm, but I took her chin and turned her head to examine the nasty looking cuts on her forehead and cheek. She had her own stitches. When I spotted a long, scary gash running from under her chin down her neck, my free hand curled into a fist. "Who did this to you? What happened here?"

"Tasha shot him, by the way." She ran her thumb over the red mark on my arm. "The Belmonte-Ruiz member who attacked you. She came on the helicopter, and she's here now."

Tasha. So that's why I was still alive. "She's at the house?" I asked.

Natalia nodded solemnly and added, "She . . . she saved your life."

"That's the least of my concerns." Tasha was a good friend, and I owed her, but I didn't care to think of that now. "You were screaming on the phone, Natalia."

"I was scared," she rasped. "For you, and for myself."

My eyes drifted once again along the slash. Bruises darkened her slender neck. I urged her chin up. "What are these marks? The cuts? Your voice—it . . someone . . . were you strangled?"

"I fought back," she said, smiling softly. "And I won. That's what matters."

Pride swelled in my chest. My girl. She'd done well, but a victory was hardly enough to placate me. "Don't protect me, Natalia."

As I tried to sit forward again, she kept me in place with a bandaged hand on my shoulder.

"What happened there?"

"Please. Lie back—"

"Stop telling me to lie back. Give me every detail, or I'll go find someone who will."

She glanced at the heart rate monitor. "I don't want you to get upset."

I caught her wrist and brought her palm to my bare chest so she could feel my pulse. "The physical pain is nothing. I've felt worse," I said. "But every second that ticks by without knowing what happened to you, the ache grows. My anger grows, and my heart—"

"Okay," she said, her voice soothing despite the way her eyes darted over the screen as it picked up my increased heart rate. She scooted closer, keeping her warm hand over my heart. "All right. I'll tell you. Belmonte-Ruiz had a mission. For all the women you took from them, they wanted to repay the favor."

"They targeted you."

"All of us. We fought back," she said quickly. "Not everyone survived, but Jaz, me, Pilar—we're all safe."

That wasn't good enough. One life lost, one scrape, even—it was too much. I shut my eyes. "I swore to you that you were safe here. That I'd be here to protect you. All of you." Jaw clenched, I looked away. "I failed you."

She got even closer. "You *were* here, Cristiano. A man entered the room while I was on the phone with you. He put his hands around my neck and squeezed until I saw stars."

I would tear him limb from limb. I would rain fury on his family, his brothers, anyone he cared about. A hazy film shuttered my vision as I shook with an impending explosion. All I could see was another man in my bedroom.

Threatening my wife.

Touching her.

Hurting her.

Visions crashed across my mind like waves against sharp-edged rocks. "I'll kill the motherfucker."

"I already did," she said, her eyes locked on mine.

What? My temper simmered as the words registered. "You . . ."

She nodded slowly, a proud smile forming on her face. "I told you. I fought back, and I won. You *were* here. You taught me." Her expression turned serious again. "I panicked, though. I wasn't in the right mindset, and I couldn't fight him off, and I started to give up. I did everything wrong at first. But he didn't expect me to defend myself, and that was his mistake. I don't think any of them expected that of us."

"He underestimated you," I said. "But you didn't underestimate yourself."

"You gave us . . . you gave *me* the tools to defend myself, and I did."

"How?"

"Jaz helped." She curled her fist against my chest. "I'll tell you all the details later, and you can tell me how to do it better next time."

I shook my head, half-awed, half-wishing I'd seen it with my own eyes. "You did everything you were supposed to. You survived."

"Rule number one—don't die." She took my wrist, dipped her head so I wouldn't have to reach much, and brought my fingers to her stitches. "They're a badge of honor. You warned me I might get hurt, so I was ready for it. You have scars. Now I'll have them, too. And they'll remind me that sometimes . . . things might seem scary and impossible. But that doesn't mean they are."

Was she talking about more than her attack? Everything about me and my life had frightened her when she'd arrived. I hoped this was her telling me that I'd prepared her well, taught her to defend herself, and now she was ready to open herself up to the possibility of scary and impossible things—like *us*.

"The scars are a part of you," I said, "and they represent the second chance you gave yourself." I ran a thumb over her bruised, cut cheek. There was a glaring question I couldn't ignore, though, and I worried the answer could set me off in a way I wouldn't be able to come back from, but I had to know.

"Natalia. Did he touch you . . .? Did he . . . did . . ." I urged myself on. She was my wife. We shared a bed. I'd threatened the universe that no man should come near her. If he'd tried anything with her, it would change everything. How I approached her, touched her, even spoke to her. It would break my heart in two and send me to the depths of a hell I didn't want to even acknowledge, but I had to take care of her before I could worry about myself. "I have to know if he raped you, or even if he tried."

She drew back, shock clear on her face. It was blunt, but it was the only way I could ask. I had to know the fact of it—immediately.

"No. No, no, no." She squeezed my hand with both of hers. "They weren't here for that. They just wanted us dead."

My heart rate steadied as resolution settled over me. "I will find a way to make this right. His brothers, his family, will pay—and I will blow up the Belmonte-Ruiz cartel. What I did before, trying to hinder their business, was nothing. Now I'll come for them."

"But first, you'll rest," she said, drawing the sheet to my chest. She picked up the fallen IV, sliding the metal stand closer to the bedside. "And you won't hurt anyone innocent on my behalf. Take comfort in the fact that no man who entered these walls with ill intentions survived."

"That gives me little comfort. They're just the tail of the snake." I sniffed, though admittedly, I was happy to hear it. "Not even one made it out?"

"Not even one. Hold still." She lifted the edge of a bandage on my torso, examining the wound. "Some came close to escaping, but your men blasted their helicopter out of the sky. You've equipped your staff—your people—well. They're composed in the face of danger, like you. Most of them are alive because of it."

It was hardly the time for praise, but I could see she was trying to comfort me. Her interest in my feelings was new—and very welcome. "They came in through the roof then," I said.

"Alejandro thinks they hacked the security system via the cell phone I snuck in. See, when Diego gave it to me at my dad's house, he wanted me to get info he could pass on to Belmonte-Ruiz." She took a breath, her cheeks pink as her theories spilled out. "They'd then be able to access the cameras around the house to get a lay of the land. They would've needed that to down the system long enough to breach the walls via helicopter, enter through the roof, override the backup generators and security—"

"I get it." I didn't need to hear more.

They'd flooded my home. Hurt my staff. Entered my bedroom. Threatened Natalia's life.

They'd put something in my drink. Cornered Max. Shot Daniel.

Distantly, I heard Natalia call my name. "They'll pay for this."

She forced my fist open, slipping her delicate hand in my bruised and roughened one. "Cristiano, please, calm down. You're in no state to get upset."

"They know I won't sit back and do nothing," I said.

"Which is why you have to," she said. "Nobody knows what's happening yet. It could be a trap, or some kind of diversion, or . . ."

I didn't hear the rest. Just her touch brought my heart rate down to a manageable level.

Natalia sighed as if she carried the weight of the world on her shoulders. "Don't you want to know how *you* are?"

I could tell without hearing from the doctors that my injuries were relatively mild. I'd been stitched up, and no doubt they'd try to keep me in bed for some ridiculous amount of time. I knew from experience, though, that the pain could be worse, and since I was already restless, that I'd be on my feet in no time.

It made no sense, though. I should've been dead. Nobody had ever gotten me on my knees and at their mercy for long enough to stick me—what, three or four times? They'd completely immobilized me. I could've watched him draw a gun and put it to my temple—and done nothing about it.

"Some of the doctors think you were lucky," Natalia said softly. "But I know you make your own luck. The valet didn't hit any vital organs, and he missed your heart completely."

I brought her hand to my mouth, watching her face, asking silent permission as I pressed a kiss to her knuckles, her palm. "That's because I'm no normal man, as I've told you. My organs are impenetrable."

"And your heart?" she asked. "Is it impenetrable, too?"

"No, but it wasn't where he thought it would be," I said. "Because it was here. With you."

"Cristiano," she said on a breath. She pushed some of my hair off my forehead, and it took everything I had not to close my eyes and give in to the feeling of her fingers on my skin. I'd already had her out of my sight too long, though. I wanted to get my fill of her. "The doctor didn't say you hit your head. Are you feeling okay?" she asked. "Has this near-death experience made you . . . romantic?"

"Only reinforced what I already knew—time is precious. I won't waste it anymore by holding back."

"You, hold back?" she asked and ventured a small smile. "Since when?"

I wished she'd crumble once and for all, fall into my arms, and seek safety in me, but still . . . *she* held back. Something had changed—I could feel her giving in, but she wasn't completely there yet.

She moved close enough that we could speak in whispers. "You scared everyone," she said.

"You?"

"Yes. Me. Are you going to tell me why you went?" she

asked. "What you were looking for? What was so important that you'd risk your life for it?"

"You'd know the answer if only you'd let yourself see it."

She bit her lip as her eyes roamed over my bandaged body, her raven-colored hair falling around her face.

"You, Natalia," I continued. "I went for *you*. I was looking for *you*. I'd risk my life for *you*."

Her gaze shot up, and she grabbed my cheeks so suddenly, I flinched. She forced me to look her in the eye. "No."

I frowned. "No what?"

"No more searching for closure or proof or whatever it was that took you away. I don't need it, Cristiano de la Rosa. Don't you *ever* go looking for closure for me again."

"But it's not just for you. It's for me, too." I placed my crude, unworthy hands over her soft, injured ones, engulfing them. "There will always be a hint of doubt in your mind about my involvement in Bianca's death, and I won't live that way."

She drew back slightly, surprise playing out on her face. Her brows drew together as she looked sideways, away from me. What was it? Did indecision war inside her? Anything to do with her mother, she wanted answers. But that meant letting me continue down that path.

"Do you know something?" she asked.

"Only suspicions I'm trying to verify."

She inhaled deeply through her nose. If she asked me to go back, I would—just as soon as I had a plan in place to retrieve Max and retaliate against Belmonte-Ruiz.

"Don't go," she said finally. "I want you to stay here. Stay home. Don't go looking for answers, and don't go after Belmonte-Ruiz."

I must've misheard her. She would put my wellbeing

above learning more about Bianca's murder? Above revenge? In that moment, all my wounds were healed. The loyalty and the trust of my wife was the salve, the anesthetic, the cure for a lifetime of rejection and loss.

It was, finally, the first indication that she could find a way to love me.

The other night, this was all I'd wanted to hear from her—stay.

But she and I both knew it couldn't be.

I had always been and would always be in this life. In the line of fire. At risk. No guarantee of tomorrow. I wasn't letting anything go, and now that Belmonte-Ruiz had struck against us, I would have to retaliate tenfold. Natalia might not like it, and her concern was almost enough to make me think twice, but I couldn't let Daniel and the others die for nothing. And I couldn't leave Max behind— even if, deep down, I knew what his fate would be.

"Enough business talk." I ran my hand up her forearm and squeezed her biceps. I wanted her to come even closer, but we'd made a lot of progress already tonight, and I didn't want to push my luck. "Did you sleep by my side last night?"

Slowly, she shook her head. "You needed space."

"You swore you'd be in my bed." My tone dropped. "It's the rule, *mi amor*."

"Extenuating circumstances."

"If I'd woken up and you weren't there, I'd have sent everyone out looking for you."

"They wouldn't have had to look far. They would've found me on the couch. Still close—in case you needed anything."

"I *need*, Natalia. I need you like I haven't needed anything in a long time. Maybe ever." I drew her closer by her arm until our faces were centimeters apart. "I won't force you to fill that need, but you should know it runs deep in me."

If one thing had kept me from falling into death's grip, it was the promise of her sweet mouth taking my cock again. I dreamed of it, of the last night we'd spent in the same bed, of the way she'd willingly gotten to her knees, and then of our kiss. Those memories had kept me alive.

And the fact that I owed her the same.

If I thought I could reciprocate with all the vigor I intended, I would've splayed her out in front of me now.

It would be the first thing I did once I was back on my feet—devour that pussy like the piece of candy it was.

Warmth crept up my neck as my hunger for her stirred deep inside me. Fuck trying not to scare her. I'd never let that stop me before. "If I told you to climb on top of me now, what would you say?"

Her lips parted for a breath. "It would probably kill you. The doctor said if you rip your sutures, she'll have to perform surgery."

"Nobody knows the medicine I need. Get on. Put me inside you; it will heal me. And if it doesn't, it will give me something to live for."

The rosy flush of her cheeks pleased me. I looked forward to seeing how she'd demur or lash back when she was so clearly trying to be nice to my injured self.

But then she glanced over her shoulder. Leaned into me. Brushed her mouth along the outer shell of my ear. "Okay."

I nearly choked. "O-*kay*?" I asked, not bothering to keep the surprise from my voice.

She nodded, running soft fingertips along my hairline, then against my scalp.

My eyes fell shut in pure bliss. My beautiful queen

would finally give what I had practically begged for. What I'd trade my kingdom for just then.

My heart thumped, its *ba-bump* speeding with the machine's *beep-beep*.

God, don't let me die from satisfaction before I even truly taste it.

"I only ask one thing," Natalia whispered in my ear.

I opened my eyes to look into her sparkling ones. "Anything."

"If I climb onto your lap and finally take you inside me . . ."

I salivated, my hand on her arm tightening as need coursed through me. "Yes?"

"Do you promise to lie still so you don't worsen your wounds?"

My hope crushed like a vehicle flattened to a pancake by a compactor. I could've cried if I didn't have the urge to laugh. My temptress knew exactly how I'd answer. God was not merciful.

"*Lie still?*" I asked. "I vowed to prove that your virginity was still intact by utterly destroying it. How can I do that if I don't move?"

"*Ah.* Shame." She wet her lips, blinking lazily at me. Did she want it that bad, too? Or was she teasing me? "You may be willing to risk your life for one night of sex, but I'm not." She kissed my cheek—her touch gentle as my body answered with desire's violent pull. "It won't be tonight. Or tomorrow night. But it *will* be," she said. "Heal, Cristiano—so you can make good on that promise."

Fuck me. She was ready, then? Her admission was the sweetest consolation. She was going to give herself to me. I weighed the idea of delivering on my promise now and dying in the process against having to wait even longer, knowing it would *finally* happen, and living to enjoy it.

If I thought I could ruin her tonight without ending up on an operating table, I might've tried. I'd have to be content knowing there was light now where there had only been darkness before.

But if it meant opening my wife's eyes to what we could be, I couldn't help thinking I should've gotten myself nearly killed sooner.

5

NATALIA

I n our dimly lit master bathroom, Cristiano stood directly under a soft, warm bulb that shone on him like he was a statue in a museum. From the doorway, I admired him in the mirror. He brushed his teeth wearing only low-slung, black sweatpants that showed off the muscles rippling all the way down to a defined "V" . . . and beyond. His sculpted definition spanned so far south, I wondered if his *size* could be the result of some special kind of workout.

I crossed my arms over my nightgown to hide my nipples as they stood at attention. "You should be in bed."

Gauzy bandages glowed white against his abdomen. His smooth, bronzed skin had been marred and scarred— and not just by this attack. "Doc says I've been healing up nice the past few days," he said.

He put his every effort into hiding a grimace as he bent at the hip to spit into the sink, but I knew better.

"Really?" I asked. "Because I spoke to her this morning, and she wants you off your feet for at *least* another week."

He snorted. "A *week*? No, *mami*. I'll go crazy if I'm bedridden more than a few days. And it's been a few days."

It wasn't the first time we'd been over this. I tried to be understanding of the fact that he'd had a traumatic experience, but I'd had one as well. Cristiano wanted to be back in action. And I . . . I didn't ever want to suffer through the crippling fear of thinking I'd lost him again.

"You can't recover in days," I said. "You—"

"I've done it before. It's far more dangerous for me to be off my feet, Natalia. It leaves us vulnerable." He ran his toothbrush under the faucet. "The best way I know how to heal is to get back to work."

"I forbid it," I said. "I forbid you from leaving our bed."

Cristiano paused, then glanced up at the ceiling. "*Ay, Dios mío*, I've waited a long time to hear you say that. I'm happy to stay in bed for weeks if you join me."

He'd certainly retained his dirty mind and insatiable hunger to take me to bed. "If you have to go into surgery, you'll be off your feet for much longer."

"It would be worth it for a night with you."

Jaz entered with ointment, pill bottles, and the items for his sponge bath. "You're supposed to be in bed, *señor*."

I didn't bother hiding my *told-you-so* smirk.

He slow-blinked at the items in Jaz's hands and shook his head. "I already told you both—I'm perfectly capable of showering."

"*La doctora* said you're not supposed to be moving around yet," she said, setting everything on the counter. "Natalia needs to clean the wounds and change the bandages. I showed her how. It'll take two minutes—just stand there."

"Jaz, in five seconds, I'm going to hop in the shower,"

he said, undoing the tie of his sweats. "So in three seconds, I'm pulling down my pants."

"You're too unstable. You could fall."

Jaz was right—he could slip and hit his head. He could barely raise his arms without pain, though he tried to hide it. He needed help, but he'd never admit it. "I'll join you," I said.

His eyes glimmered as they met mine in the reflection. "Join me? You mean . . . in the *shower?*" The teasing in his voice almost made me rescind my offer.

"I owe you," I said. Last month, I'd been the one injured in my bathroom as he'd removed glass from my feet. "For helping me after the warehouse fire."

Any hint of jesting vanished from his face. "I'm the reason you were hurt in the first place."

"I haven't forgotten." But he'd come for me. He'd scaled the side of a building about to blow just to help me. Diego, on the other hand, had left me to fend for myself as he'd tried—and failed—to salvage the Maldonados' drugs.

I stepped toward Cristiano, hoping my cheeks wouldn't redden. Flirting with my husband a few nights ago had been a glimmer of fun in a dark time, and we could certainly use some fun. "You cleaned and bandaged my wounds," I said. "Let me do the same."

"Thank you, Jaz," Cristiano said. "You're dismissed."

With a twitch of her lips, she nodded once and left the bathroom. At least this time, she didn't argue. Or else she saw what I was also coming to terms with—things had shifted between Cristiano and me.

I didn't recognize this forward behavior in myself, but I'd seen it before. From the man in front of me looking pleased by my demand to take care of him.

I was staking my claim.

He'd told me many times before—I was his.

And for the first time, a small voice in my head answered back.

He was mine.

Cristiano watched in the reflection as I approached him from behind. "Lift your arms a little if you can," I said.

He raised them slowly to give me access to the bandages around his middle.

"Does it hurt?" I asked, as I focused on peeling off the gauze.

"Will you kiss it better?"

Relentless. I hid my smile. "No."

"Then no, it doesn't."

I frowned at the clean, red gashes, no longer than a toothpick, but wide enough that they needed thick, dark sutures to close them. After peeling the dressing from his chest, I discarded everything in the trash. I crossed the bathroom to flip on the shower, and when I turned back, he was there, standing in front of me. "Can't shower in these," he said.

My eyes dropped to his pants. "Do you need help?"

"Yes." He cleared the rasp from his voice. "It hurts to bend anywhere."

I had no doubt it *did* hurt, but since he rarely shared when he was in pain, I recognized his ulterior motives. Tonight, though, I'd let him get away with it.

My fingers grazed his skin as I worked the sweats over his muscular ass. I released a breath, grateful to see he wasn't hard. Doctor Sosa had explicitly warned Cristiano about straining himself, but if he got sex on his mind, I wasn't sure he'd heed her warnings.

But the sight of him exposed and in need of my help stirred my desire.

The designation of *husband* had taken on many meanings over the past several weeks. Tormentor. Protector. Teacher. I nearly shivered knowing how it would change again soon. *Lover.* The thought of sex with him had always excited me, even when it scared and shamed me. But as the days passed and Cristiano began to heal, my anticipation to finally submit to his advances grew more urgent.

It couldn't be tonight. He was still far from healed.

But for all the times he'd enjoyed making me squirm, I could finally return the favor.

I held his gaze as I drew my nightgown over my head and dropped it with his pants. His eyes jumped to my breasts. My nipples were still two pebbled points, showing off for him.

I stepped into the shower first and held out my hand to help him.

As he moved under the stream of water, I soaped up a sponge and touched it to his back.

"No wounds back there," he said over his shoulder. "You don't have to be so gentle."

I glided the sponge across the broad expanse, reaching to get his shoulders. I followed a long scar from the right one as it crossed his spine. Other marks on his sides, arms, and back told the story of a violent life.

"This isn't your first brush with a knife," I guessed and ran my thumb over some raised, pink skin under one shoulder blade. "Is this from a bullet?"

"I told you—I've been knocked off my feet before."

I'd read a piece in the newspaper years ago about the infamous, anonymous leader of the Calavera cartel. It'd claimed he'd taken more bullets than drugs in his life. I moved around to Cristiano's front, fascinated by each clue to his past. "What happened?"

"Many things," he said. "I'll tell you one day if you like, but the long scar on my back is the only one with any significance. It started it all—my father's belt."

I froze, raising just my eyes to his. I wished hearing that surprised me more, but it was no secret his father had been abusive. Diego had talked about it now and then, but he'd played it down. Was that because he'd been mostly spared? Had his older brother borne the brunt of it to protect him? Weeks ago, I would've never come to that conclusion, but I was beginning to know Cristiano as that kind of man. One who'd shoulder as much as he could to protect others.

"I hate your father," I said. "And I'm sorry he did that."

"I've come to terms with it, and I've worked through my issues with him," Cristiano said. With effort, he raised a hand and leaned against the tile. "I was rarely surprised by how far he'd go. Diego, on the other hand—I never saw his betrayal coming."

Diego and Cristiano were each other's only remaining immediate family, so back then, of course they'd been close. I could see things more clearly from Cristiano's perspective now, though. Diego had turned on his brother, accusing Cristiano of a brutal crime that could've gotten him killed.

I eyed another bullet wound above his left pec. "You've been through so much I don't even know about."

"It made me who I am," he said. "The rest of these scars, they're barely worth talking about, Natalia, so don't worry about them. The same will be true of my new wounds once they heal. We move forward stronger. ¿*Entiendes*?"

"I understand." I moved on to washing his wounds,

ensuring they were thoroughly clean—and trying not to fixate on the fact that we were physically very close, and stark naked, and for once, I wasn't scared, anxious, or nervous.

As I silently soaped him, his cock twitched. Once, that would've scared me. Now, it reminded me of our last night together before all of this. Upstairs at his nightclub, *La Madrina*, as I'd advised him to go after what he sought, unaware of the trouble it would bring. And then, as I'd gotten to my knees to comfort him . . .

I turned away as a flush worked its way up my chest and exchanged the sponge for his shampoo. Any movement was an effort for him, but there was no way he'd be able to get his arms above his head. I'd need a damn step stool to even reach his hair, though.

I squirted some shampoo into my palm, went to the opposite end of the shower, and climbed up onto the bench to stand over him. When he just stared at me, I said, "*¿Entonces?* Well?" I raised an eyebrow. "Come here."

I could've sworn he chuckled as he walked toward me. I sank my hands into his hair. There seemed to be even more of it when it was wet—abundantly silky and inky in my hands.

He closed his eyes and dropped his forehead to my stomach as I lathered. He scraped the sensitive spot between my breasts with his stubble, and I bit my lip to keep a moan inside. That would only encourage him, and his control had proven slippery. We had to be good, so I had to be the strong one.

He slid his hands up the outsides of my thighs and rested them on my hips, his fingers splaying over my ass cheeks. "Natalia," he murmured. "*Te extraño.*"

I miss you. I was right here, and yet I understood. Between everyone fussing over him the past three days, and

Tasha and Alejandro monopolizing his time, plus every-thing I'd been doing to keep the household running, we hadn't been truly alone since he'd woken up. His drugs knocked him out at night, and I slept on the couch to give him space.

My heart beat in my stomach. Maybe I wasn't only worried about *Cristiano's* control. Stripped bare, with his massive hands on me, and my resistance to him no longer holding me back . . . desire pulled in my depths in a way it hadn't since before he'd left. I'd fought him for so long. I didn't need to anymore. I didn't want to.

When Cristiano had woken up, it had hit me as we'd come face to face—up until that moment, I'd been *terrified* he wouldn't survive. That I'd lost him. That I'd be left on this earth to defend myself against Diego, Belmonte-Ruiz, and even my father. The relief I'd felt had been palpable but equally scary in a different way.

It didn't mean he wasn't still the man who'd forced me into this marriage. Who'd stood over my mother's dead body, and who'd left me, a grieving child, in a dark tunnel for hours. But he'd also once protected my family and had made sure my every need had been met since my arrival here in the Badlands.

On our last call, I'd wanted to ask him to stay but hadn't been able to find the words.

And I'd almost lost him. Time was precious, as he'd said, and it shouldn't be wasted.

Instead of trying to tell him all that, I put my arms around his neck and hugged him to me.

He pressed his lips to my skin, working his mouth up my chest before tilting up his head. "*Por favor,*" he said slowly. "Please—don't deny me anymore."

I could bend and kiss him for the first time since the night he'd left *La Madrina*. And this time, I could admit that

I was willing. I wanted that. I wanted him to heal. To have what he needed. That meant I cared. But I had cared for Diego, too. I'd overlooked warning signs and had believed anything he'd said or done. After my horrible judgment, could I trust myself? Could I trust Cristiano?

Suds dripped from his hair into his face, so I reluctantly peeled his arms from around my middle. "You need to rinse."

"You don't know what I need, Natalia."

I sighed as I got down from the bench and led him under the stream of water. He took my face in his hands, staring into my eyes. When I moved closer, his erection pressed against my stomach. I wanted to give in. To soothe him.

Maybe he was right to believe that I was the one thing that could heal him.

"Remember the last time you saw me, before all this?" I asked.

"I was stabbed, not hit over the head." He brushed his thumb over the corner of my mouth. "My memory's as sharp as ever. It was the night I caught you with the cell phone and punished you at the club. Are you still angry with me?"

I shook my head. "That's not the last time you saw me."

"You're right," he said. "You were asleep as I packed a bag."

"I'm not talking about that." I took him in my hand. "I mean when I looked up at you from my knees."

"*Christ*, Natalia." He inhaled a breath, his fingers digging into my cheeks and inspiring a thrill that ended right between my legs. "Be careful talking like that."

Last time, we'd been in the dark. Now, I could see everything. He was nearly as thick as my wrist, even more veiny than his brawny forearm, and his pink velvety skin stretched as he grew against my palm.

His eyes turned anguished as I stroked him, and I'd never had such an urge to chase someone else's demons away.

"We can't kiss—you know where that will lead," I said. "But will this help? You have to promise to stand very still and not strain yourself."

"I could never stay still with your hands on me." Water dripped down the bridge of his nose. He caught my wrist, and I released him as he laced his hand with mine at our sides. "That's not what I need anyway."

"What then?"

He tilted my chin back with his other hand, lowering his face to mine. "Have your feelings changed now that you've almost lost me?"

"Yes." I held his gaze. "But you can't expect our relationship to transform overnight."

"I don't. But if there's anything you want to say, say it now."

As determination entered his voice, a warning alarm sounded in my head. "Why?" I asked, my shoulders tensing.

"I have to go, Natalia." He pressed his lips together. "I can't let Max stay with Belmonte-Ruiz any longer."

Goddamn it. Frustration flared in me, and I stepped back to cross my arms. Cristiano had almost been *killed* a few days ago. What would it take to get him to pull back? "I know you can't let them get away with this—it's the nature of this world. But *you* can't go. Make a plan, and send Alejandro and your men after Max."

"I'm the one who put Max in danger." Lines deepened in his forehead with a frown. "I can't send others to do *my*

job. I'm done playing games with those *cabrónes* and understand me—I'm going to blow the motherfuckers up."

He couldn't do this. Not now. I was finally letting
myself see Cristiano for all he was, and he was going to put
himself back in the line of fire. Wasn't this all he'd asked of
me the past few weeks—to open myself to the idea of us?
To stop fighting him? And now that I was ready, he was
going to go back out there when he wasn't even at half
capacity and get himself killed? "You're not ready."

"You have to trust me to know what I am and am not
capable of."

"You're a fool."

He paused, blinking at me.

Now that I had his attention, I didn't hold back. "You
think you're a superhero, but you're not. You're mortal.
You can die."

"I never said I couldn't."

"You're acting like it. Physically, you're not even close
to healed. If you leave now, you'll come home in a body
bag."

"Do you really believe that?" He straightened, bearing
down on me. "Or are you provoking me in hopes I'll prove
just how capable my body is?"

"You're not ready mentally, either. You've barely given
yourself a chance to recover from an attack on your life.
You're acting irrationally, from emotion—"

"You don't know me at all if you believe that."

"You don't know *yourself*." I rose to my full height,
holding his gaze as it darkened. "You're a man, and you
can fall, Cristiano. You have people here depending on
you."

"You don't think I know that?" He clenched his jaw
and turned his face from me. "It's all I ever think about. All

the lives that're endangered when *I'm* in danger. That's why I have to go."

"That's why you *can't* go after Max. In your state, you're more vulnerable than usual, and that puts those around you at risk. Don't be stupid, Cristiano."

He stepped into me. "Brave little girl. You think you can call *me* names?"

"You can try to intimidate me to keep my mouth shut, but when your life is on the line, I won't."

"Why?" he asked.

"You almost *died*."

"I've come closer than that."

I wanted to yell at him to get it into his thick skull that he could be more helpful to Max here than in the field, but that wouldn't get us anywhere. I took a breath and tried to reason with him. He flinched as I placed my palm over his chest wound. "*Escúchame*, Cristiano. Listen to me. You're not weak to rely on your men in a time of need. Can't you see it makes you stronger to know when to stand back and let more capable people help?"

He made a fist. It hurt him that an enemy had succeeded in debilitating him and would keep him from doing everything he could for his comrade.

His hand flexed. Covered mine on his pec. "Every one of your touches comforts me. Heals me. But as you soothe me, the opposite is being done to Max. He's a prisoner, not a guest."

I shut my eyes against the idea, but the image only became clearer in the dark. If Max was still alive, there was no doubt he was being tortured. I tried to fight the vision of him tied up in a dark room, bloody and swollen. "I understand," I said. "I want Max to come home, too. But we need more information. Maybe they took him to bait you."

"Can't bait a dead man."

"Maybe you weren't supposed to die."

After a beat, his eyebrows cinched. "What?"

"I've had a lot of time to think about all of this," I said. "'If you're going to aim, kill.' You taught me that. So why take Max? Why go to the trouble of attacking your home if they'd planned to kill you at the hotel?"

Recognition dawned as Cristiano picked up my line of thinking. "Any message would be pointless if I was dead," he said, his expression easing. "They wanted me to live. And you, too."

"Me?" I shook my head. "My attacker almost choked me to death. He almost slit my throat—"

"Almost," Cristiano said. "He might've had orders to get you out alive. He had a syringe on him."

"*What?*" A hazy memory returned of the man holding up what I'd thought was a blade. "A tranquilizer?"

"You would've been their first target. Why not just shoot you?" He swallowed. "My *worst* fear, as I thought I was dying, was that they'd take you, Natalia."

I refrained from shuddering. This new information changed that night entirely. There'd been more at risk than my life. I could've been in Max's position now, in the grips of a rival cartel with an axe to grind.

I *did* want Max out. Desperately. But Cristiano's life meant more to me, so I spoke to him in a way I knew would get through to him. "Are you going to take me with you to retrieve Max?"

The corners of his mouth drooped. "Why would I?"

"Because you'd be leaving the Badlands unprotected again if you go. You'd be leaving *me* vulnerable. If they want me, they may try again."

Torment marred his features, but it didn't deter me. I

needed him to understand what he could lose if he acted recklessly.

"They might be waiting for you to walk—no, *run*—into a trap," I said. "And if they have you, then they have me, too."

He brought my palm to his chest. "I . . . I can't let him sit there and rot, Natalia. And if I can't help him, I've failed him."

I threw my arms around his neck, our wet, naked bodies flush. "*Hay un tiempo señalado para todo,*" I whispered, quoting from the bible. "*Un tiempo de matar, y un tiempo de sanar.*"

There's a time for everything. A time to kill, and a time to heal.

"You didn't make these decisions alone. Max knew what he was getting into," I said. "He can handle it. He would never expect you to save his life at the expense of everyone else's. He's strong."

He shuddered. "What do I do?"

I had one of the most ruthless, foreboding crime lords in my arms, asking for my help. It wasn't the first time. My advice to him in the upstairs bedroom of his nightclub had been wrong. If I hadn't told him to go, maybe he would've stayed and neither of us would've faced death.

Then again, we wouldn't be here now.

He'd returned to me. Not just physically, but emotionally. He came back to me for help.

In the possible event of his death, I'd known I'd have to step up. Why should that change since he'd lived? More than ever, I could be the woman he thought I was. The queen he'd chosen for his bride.

I smoothed my cheek against his bristly chin, while all six-foot-five inches of him stood powerful—and naked. Emboldened by the juxtaposition of his masculinity and vulnerability, I drew back and said, "You make a plan. You assemble a team. But you don't rush. Max is tough and stubborn. He will hold on until your men can get to him."

Cristiano rested his forehead against mine. "We," he said. "We will make a plan. We will assemble a team. *We* will get him out."

I was in it now. I had been for a while. With a few words, Cristiano told me I was no longer here against my will. And I accepted that.

I let Cristiano in. I stepped into the role he'd been pushing me toward. I stood by his side in the ivory tower.

We were Calavera royalty.

6

NATALIA

News of Cristiano's latest brush with death had spread through the Badlands, and in the following week, it became a full-time job receiving well wishes in the forms of home-cooked meals and handmade goods such as pottery, candles, and tequila. It was a celebration of his good fortune rather than what could've been, and I was grateful for the distraction.

But as I came in from the town square one evening, I was reminded that I still had other, more personal matters to deal with. I peeled off gloves dirty with soil from planting trees and left them in the entryway as I followed voices to the dining area.

The last two voices I wanted to hear—Tasha and Cristiano.

Regardless of where in the house Tasha was, she was becoming a more unwelcome presence each day, but more maddening was Cristiano's aversion to rest.

I strode in and found them chatting at the far end of the long table, where nobody ever sat. "Do you have wings now?" I asked, satisfied with how my voice carried and my sandals slapped the tile.

Cristiano stopped mid-sentence to turn his gaze on me. "*¿De qué estás hablando?*"

He wanted to know what I was talking about? *Pfft.* I slapped a cordial smile on my face. "I know you didn't walk downstairs since the doctor explicitly ordered you not to. And the elevator's out of service while it undergoes security upgrades. So did you fly? Or is there a slide from the top floor I'm not aware of?"

"I've been in bed for two fucking weeks," he said.

"It's been eleven days—don't exaggerate."

"Doctor Sosa was just upstairs with us," Tasha said, "and she told us it was fine."

Us? I turned my glare on Cristiano. I shouldn't need to forbid him from being alone in our bedroom with a woman who wasn't Jaz or Doctor Sosa, but apparently I did. And to make matters worse, not only had he used the stairs, but he'd gotten dressed—and he looked infuriatingly handsome in a pressed, white dress shirt and slacks. It was the first time he'd been out of loungewear since he'd been delivered home to me bloody and half-dead. Did he think he was going somewhere?

"Lighten up, Natalia," Tasha added. "Cristiano heals at a superhuman rate."

"No, he doesn't." I walked to stand by his chair. "Because he's *not* superhuman. He's a man, and he was stabbed three times."

"I'm still struggling to understand why you care." Her narrowed eyes stayed trained on me. "What did you call your marriage, Cristiano? An alliance between you and Costa? Nothing more."

I *hated* the idea of Tasha thinking this was all for show. She'd been intimate with Cristiano. She knew what he liked, and—considering they'd been spending time together without me—how to get his ear. Not to mention she was a beautiful woman who likely knew her way around a man as experienced as my husband—where I was still a girl in many ways, especially when it came to sex.

I turned to face Cristiano. "The doctor was here? What'd she say?"

His eyes twinkled. "That I'm cleared for *almost* everything."

A flush made its way up my chest. "I'll have to hear that from her mouth."

"You would've if you'd been by his side," Tasha said behind me. "Where were you?"

Gardening suddenly sounded unimpressive, but spending time in the Badlands was much more than that. Without Max, Cristiano, or even Alejandro to talk to, the residents had issues to be resolved, and I heard some of them while helping out around the chapel.

I turned to Tasha. "Handling business. Teresa was showing me some things." I held up my left hand before adding, "She's the goldsmith who made my wedding rings."

Tasha checked her manicure. How it was still perfectly intact after the last couple weeks was beyond me. "*Ten cuidado*, Cristiano. You should be careful," she said. "When a mafioso falls, there are always vultures lying in wait."

Cristiano pushed back from the table, rose, and placed his hands on my shoulders. "Are you suggesting I've fallen?" he asked.

Tasha wet her lips. "You will if you don't take control of this situation. Word is spreading."

She'd indicated something similar before, when she'd first arrived. Before I could ask her to clarify, Alejandro opened the door to the kitchen, holding it for Jaz to pass through.

"How many places should I set for dinner, *señor?*" Jaz asked.

"Set it for five," I answered. "Pilar will be joining us as well. Will you get her, Alejandro?"

"Of course," he said, nearly jogging off in the direction of the library where Pilar had been spending most of her time.

As Jaz distributed silverware and napkins and filled glasses with red wine, Cristiano moved to the head of the table, walking almost as if he was back to normal. That didn't mean he wasn't still in pain, though.

I linked my elbow with his and lowered my voice. "How are you feeling?"

"Better than ever," he said without looking at me.

"Tasha said word is spreading. Does that mean people beyond Belmonte-Ruiz are beginning to learn the truth about the Badlands?"

"We're not discussing this now."

"But—"

"I said *no.*"

Tasha and Jaz quieted, looking at us.

"It's not a topic for dinner." Cristiano grabbed one of the elaborate candelabras from the center of the table and thrust it toward Jaz. "Get rid of this. Nobody can see each other with these *malditas cosas* in the way."

My mouth fell open as he cursed something as stupid as candlesticks. Even though he and I had argued since his return, it was the first time he'd snapped at me. I wasn't even entirely sure what the topic *was*, but it was obviously a sore one.

Pilar's laugh floated in before she did with Alejandro.

He'd clearly said something to amuse her, but when her eyes landed on Cristiano, her demeanor shrank.

Cristiano hadn't left our room much since he'd been confined there, which meant . . . this was the first time Pilar had seen him—at least while he was conscious—since our wedding. She wrung her hands in front of her, her nerves palpable, even from across the room. "Wh-where should I sit?"

"Anywhere but in Natalia's seat," Cristiano said, standing behind his chair at the head.

Pilar's eyes darted around. Since we rarely ate at the table, she had no way of knowing whose seat was whose. "Here," I said, holding out a hand for her. I led her to the chair next to mine. "Alejandro, you sit opposite her."

Cristiano pulled out my chair but spoke to Pilar. "I take it you'll be staying with us a while."

Pilar glanced at Alejandro as she tucked a napkin on her lap. "I . . ."

"The fiancé won't be bothering Pilar again," Alejandro replied for her.

"Good," Cristiano said, gesturing for me to sit.

I stayed where I was, feeling suddenly out of the loop. "What are you talking about?"

"Whose fiancé?" Tasha chimed in.

"*Siéntate.*" Cristiano ordered me to sit, waiting as beads of sweat formed on his upper lip. Knowing he wouldn't relax until *I* did, I obeyed. He helped scoot me under the table and asked, "What kind of food do you like, Pilar?"

I gave her an encouraging smile.

"Traditional," she said.

"Traditional what?" Cristiano asked, taking his seat at the head. "Traditional Vietnamese? Do you like pho? Indian? Chicken curry?"

"You know what she means," I told Cristiano. What was his problem? Whatever nerve I'd hit earlier, it was obviously still tender. "Most people count their blessings after a near-death experience—you just come out even grumpier."

Pilar shifted her horrified stare to me. In her world, women didn't go around calling dangerous kingpins *grumpy*.

Cristiano paused in the middle of unfurling his napkin into his lap and looked at me. "You haven't seen grumpy yet, *mamacita*."

"She has a point," Alejandro said from across the table. "Maybe it's because you stopped the painkillers."

"When?" I demanded.

Cristiano sat back in his seat, massaging the bridge of his nose with a hefty sigh. "Days ago."

"What's wrong?" I asked. "Is it a headache?"

"It's becoming one, yes," he said.

Pilar giggled, then sucked in a breath when Cristiano looked at her, as if laughter might get her into trouble. She was still scared of him. I didn't blame her—he'd kidnapped both of us—but he wasn't going to hurt her.

Cristiano wasn't going to hurt *me*.

It hit me for the first time—I'd known all along that he wouldn't.

Cristiano would *never* hurt me.

Not back then, as a child, when he'd chilled me to the core with the White Monarch under my chin. Not when he'd had me alone and stripped down in my bathroom at Papá's house, or when I'd been at his mercy in the church. Not when I'd stood before him as his new bride, claimed as his property.

My gut had told me so, but as the full realization passed over me, I peered at him. Perhaps all along, Cristiano had simply been pursuing me at any cost. That didn't make what he'd done okay, but it didn't make him the monster I'd thought he was, either.

As I studied Cristiano, his eyes traveled from Pilar's shoulders, which were practically at her ears, to her hands laced tightly on the table. She wore a long-sleeved dress, but I knew Cristiano was seeing the faded bruises beneath it.

He dropped his hand from his face and gave her a comforting smile. It was clearly forced, but he was making an effort. "I'm sorry I was short with you just now. And I'm sorry about Manu."

She looked down. "It's—I'm fine."

Cristiano had just spent the last several weeks trying to convince me he wasn't a threat—now he'd have to start all over with her.

But then, she lifted her head with a hint of a mischievous smile. "I'm better than Manu at least."

Cristiano released a genuine laugh. "Yesterday went well then?"

"Yesterday?" I asked. "And what's wrong with Manu? If somebody doesn't tell me what happened . . ." I threatened.

Tasha puckered her crimson lips. "Who the hell is Manu?"

"Pilar's ex who got physical with her for the last time," Cristiano explained, then turned to me. "I promised Pilar that she wouldn't be a prisoner here. Yesterday, Alejandro took her home."

I gaped at my friend. How had I missed that? With my time split between caring for Cristiano and handling Badlands business, I hadn't seen much of Pilar lately. She'd only planned to spend a weekend here, for God's sake, and it'd completely slipped my mind to check in with her.

"You went home yesterday?" I asked her.

"*Sí*, and she *chose* to come back," Cristiano said, not bothering to hide his smirk. "Imagine that."

I rolled my eyes. "Let her speak for herself."

He responded with a scolding arch of his eyebrow.

From the short, quick shake of Pilar's head, she didn't *want* to speak, but I urged her on. "You want to stay?"

She nodded slowly, her eyes darting from Alejandro to Cristiano. "On the condition that I can leave anytime I want. I just couldn't see any other way out of my engagement to Manu. I had to tell my parents, though, and pick up some things from home, so Alejandro came with me."

I reached for her hand across the table. "I'm sorry I haven't been here for you."

"You've got plenty to deal with," she said. "I'm settling in now—don't worry about me."

Jaz and the chef came through the kitchen door to deliver salads adorned with peach slices, feta, pecans, and dried cranberries.

Tasha forked a small bite into her mouth and moaned. "*Divine.* Where do you get such perfect peaches?"

Cristiano grinned. "Right here in the Badlands."

"Doesn't Fisker make the best meals?" I asked, smiling at him and then Pilar. She knew food best of all, and I hoped a comfortable subject would help ease the tension in her shoulders. "My husband may not have much going for him, but his food is straight from the ground, and he employs a world-class chef."

Cristiano narrowed his eyes on me. I lifted a corner of my mouth enough to convey I was teasing. He opened his hand on the table to me. It was the perfect chance to show Pilar that I was comfortable around him, so she could be, too.

When I placed my hand in his, he brought it to his lips

briefly, then lowered it under the table. "Surely your *husband* has something else going for him," he said.

The sudden masculine power underneath my palm sent memories of our shower together flashing across my mind and a tremor of excitement through my body. Part of it was the anticipation of knowing Cristiano was counting the days until he was healed enough to have me.

"Forgive me for staring at my wife. I so love when she calls me *husband* without sneering." Cristiano moved our hands to my upper leg and leaned over to whisper in my ear. "You want me to stay in bed so I'll heal faster. But remember that the faster I heal, the sooner that tender spot between your legs is mine to devastate."

I released a shaky breath. What once had been a threat was now a delicious promise. Tenderness wouldn't do. Not our first time. And he knew it, biding his time until then, teasing me with his words.

Cristiano didn't wait for my response. As his fingers slipped up my inner thigh, he turned to Alejandro, who was buttering a slice of bread. "How did Manu react?"

Alejo set down his knife. "As you'd expect." He took a bite, chewing as he added, "But I handled it."

"He tried to stand up to Alejandro, but instead, he got knocked on his ass," Pilar said. "It was fun to watch."

I laughed at her uncharacteristically wicked grin, glad to see she was loosening up. After all, who better to take down her greatest threat than the most threatening men she knew? "Alejandro's a good fighter," I said.

"Is he?" Cristiano asked as he slid his hand down my thigh and squeezed my knee in the exact spot that tickled.

I gasped, grabbing his wrist and trying not to laugh. "But Cristiano is better," I added quickly, and his hold on me released.

"Ah, thank you for saying so, *mi amor*." Cristiano

winked and turned back to Alejandro. "I assume you did more than knock him down."

Alejo dipped his head marginally. "Not in front of the lady."

"And your parents?" Cristiano asked Pilar.

She nodded. "I said just what Alejandro wanted me to."

My focus faltered with Cristiano's hand still resting on my leg. My mind had begun to register that when it came to sex, Cristiano would always wait for some kind of cue to proceed. With the promise of his fingers so close, my stomach somersaulted.

"What?" I asked, sounding as dazed as I felt. "What did Alejo tell you to say?"

"Alejandro gave me instructions," Pilar offered.

"They came from Cristiano," Alejo said.

Tasha looked back and forth, as if watching a tennis match, and not a very exciting one. Every now and then, she sighed at her plate.

"I told Manu and my parents I wasn't going through with the marriage," Pilar said, "and that I was coming here to work. For Cristiano. Against my will."

Against her will. The lie was for the best. Being here with me was better than the future with Manu she'd been unable to avoid on her own. And it perpetuated the myths surrounding Cristiano and the Badlands. I understood why Cristiano wanted that—but how did he feel that so many people thought he was the same kind of evil he fought against?

Was he able to employ logic to remove his emotion from the situation?

Or did it cut deeply, and he'd gotten good at hiding it?

"I confirmed your marriage was a sham," Pilar continued, glancing from me to Cristiano and back, "and that

Cristiano had only done it to forge the alliance with Costa, but that both Natalia and I were unharmed."

Two servers entered and placed steak and baked potatoes in front of us.

"Thank you—for letting me stay," Pilar added, and I could see her trying to be gracious to a man she'd feared for so long. "But my family never let me do anything. Just work in their shop and try to find a husband. I'd like to pull my weight, maybe help around the house, or—"

"We can get you your own place if you like," Cristiano said. "Help you start a business—whatever you want."

"What *do* you want?" I asked her.

She sat back. "*No sé.* I . . . I'm not sure."

That didn't surprise me. I doubted neither her parents nor Manu had ever asked. "You can start over here."

"Can I change my name?" she rushed out.

The four of us just looked at her. It was both a small and enormous request.

One dinner, and Pilar was coming out of her shell. Perhaps she'd believed what I'd been trying to tell her about Cristiano. Or maybe it was Alejandro's presence that comforted her. I was pretty sure they'd been spending some time together—another reason, I suspected, I hadn't seen much of her.

"Well . . . of course," Cristiano answered. "Countless people within these walls have changed their identities."

"Esmeralda," Alejandro said, suddenly laser-focused on cutting his steak. "It's, ah, a good name."

"Yes." I picked up his line of thinking. "For her emerald eyes."

Pilar smiled to herself. "Esmeralda. It's pretty."

"It suits you," I said.

"This is *very* touching," Tasha said, "*pero, por Dios*, is it boring. I don't understand why none of you are discussing what really matters." Her teeth scraped her fork as she took a bite, chewed, and swallowed within seconds. "Almost two weeks have passed, and Max is still missing. You haven't struck back, and it makes you look weak."

"Don't mistake strategy for weakness," I said.

"You've run out of time for strategy. It's time for action," she said, looking from me to Cristiano. "A true crime lord would never let this happen."

"Tasha . . ." Cristiano warned.

"Nobody even knows where Max is," I said. "It's better to strike quietly, when they least expect it, once we're certain of his location."

"That could take months. In fact, you may never know his exact location. And every day that passes, people talk." Tasha dabbed the corners of her mouth with a napkin. "You look even weaker for the fact that the truth is coming out."

Cristiano looked at his plate and didn't deny it.

"Go on," I invited.

"Calavera's ruthless reputation has been enhanced by the mystery shrouding them. But with these attacks, and Cristiano's refusal to arm certain cartels, it's becoming popular gossip that Calavera is working for the wrong side."

"Because he isn't trafficking anyone—he's helping them," I said.

"Right," Tasha said. "How do you think that makes him look? Like a traitor. And not just to Belmonte-Ruiz."

I'd heard it twice from Tasha now. Even Alejandro had seemed to think it was possible. But Cristiano had yet to bring it up to me. "Is this true?" I asked him.

He looked up at me. "Give me a moment with my wife."

Alejandro stood first, picking up his plate. "We'll move to the kitchen."

Pilar followed suit, but Tasha took her time pushing her half-eaten dinner away and rising from her seat. "Ignoring the problem won't make it go away," she said. "And it will get Max killed."

I followed Tasha with my eyes until she'd made her way through the room and disappeared up the staircase.

"Tell me what's going on," I said.

Cristiano sat back in his seat and crossed his arms. I got the sense he hadn't dismissed the others so we could talk candidly. "Don't question me in front of others."

"I didn't."

"Did I not make myself clear earlier?" he asked. "I told you the topic was closed during dinner."

Ah. Well. If he didn't want to discuss business, then I didn't mind changing the subject at all. And since he kept insisting he was better, then there was no reason to keep letting him off the hook. I raised my chin. "Then tell me this. Why is Tasha still here? Who is she to you?"

7

NATALIA

Cristiano ate his last bite of steak the way he had all the others—chewing fast and hard before washing it down with a gulp of wine. Injured or not, he held true to his claims that he ate as if someone might take his plate away before he was finished. "*Chin-chin.*" He raised his wineglass. "*Brindis, a mi bella esposa.*"

"Toasting 'your beautiful wife' won't get you out of answering my question," I said. "Why is Tasha still here? And what does it mean that people are learning the truth about your business?"

"Her family has an extensive network here and in Eastern Europe." Sucking his teeth, he set down his glass. "She knows this world well and is good for information, so she's been helping me find things on Belmonte-Ruiz. But ask me to send her away, and I will."

"Send her away."

He paused and tilted his head, clearly unprepared for that answer. "Why?"

How could he even ask? Did he not see the way she

looked at him? At me? "She's pressuring you to make rash decisions."

"Nobody pressures me to do anything," he said. "And I'm nothing if not thorough."

"Remember, you were going to charge in guns blazing after Max was taken without even considering it could be a trap. I talked you down. You think you're immune—that you can do no wrong and survive anything."

"This again. I understand your point of view—I have heard it. I have heard Alejandro's." His silverware clattered to his plate. "I've made a decision, and you will stand behind it. Alejandro and his team will leave tomorrow."

"Why? Because Tasha bruised your ego?"

He curled his hand into a fist on the table. "How do you think it looks to have you question me? Argue with me? I told you I didn't want to discuss any of this at the dinner table, yet you and Tasha push me."

"Then let's instead discuss how you told her our marriage means *nothing*—that's none of her business."

"Haven't you discussed our arrangement with Pilar?"

"That's different."

"How?"

"I was confiding in Pilar, not trying to sleep with her."

"Ah." He gripped the arms of his chair and crossed an ankle over one knee, looking amused. "Is that why you think I told Tasha you mean nothing to me?"

"Why else? You were out of town. It would've been the perfect excuse." I shifted in my seat, discomfited over the idea of Cristiano at the political event with another woman on his arm. Especially statuesque, cunning Tasha, a guest in our home. "An arranged, celibate marriage means you wouldn't *technically* be cheating."

"You think Tasha cares if I cheat on my wife? If I

wanted to fuck her, I would. Don't I have every right to? My own wife won't even sleep in my bed."

My face warmed at his bluntness. "I've removed any temptation—for your own good."

"We're hardly alone. And when we are, you're always moving around. There are constantly people in my room, and at night, you go to the couch." One eyebrow rose. "Perhaps if you treated me like your husband instead of a pariah, she'd get the message."

"I don't treat you that way." I frowned. "I've been a good wife to you. On one point, I won't back down—your recovery is my priority. I won't allow you to risk your health for Max, or so you can get laid." The hint of a smile on his face only spurred me on. "If that makes me the villain while Tasha treats you like a superhero, then fine. But I want you alive and strong."

He ran one hand down his chin, his eyes unnervingly fixed on me. "Get laid?" He chuckled. "You don't have to sit on my cock to make me feel wanted around here. All I ask is to have you at my dinner table and in my bed."

I inhaled through my nose. It hadn't been my intention to spurn him, only to make things less difficult. As it was, the heat of his stare could conjure all the promises he'd made over the past few weeks—to erase Diego. To show me what it was to have my virginity taken. To wreck me. "I don't . . . I don't trust myself to sleep by your side."

He ran the tip of his tongue over his bottom row of teeth, then wet his lower lip. It glistened in the warm light of the overhead chandelier, full, sexy and tempting. "And why not?"

This went beyond sex, but I hadn't given him much on the emotional front, either. Both topics were scary. I sighed. "When you called me from the political event, I was about to ask you to come home," I said. "I was worried."

"I know," he said. "Had you asked, I would've come running. I'm here now."

"But so is she. I wouldn't have been so daring over the phone if I'd known you were with a woman you've been intimate with. So answer me—did you sleep with her that night, or any time during our marriage?"

"You're jealous." He didn't bother to hide his grin. "My God, it's even more spectacular to witness than I could've ever hoped."

He was enjoying this too much. With a sigh, I started to get up from my seat.

"Tasha's an old friend I met early on in the second part of my life—after I left Costa," he said. "She comes from a very powerful *familia Rusa-Méxicana*."

"I have old friends, too," I said, sitting back down. "If that's your excuse to fool around, I should get the same pass."

He snort-laughed. "Any man who tries with you can't value his own head too much."

When he stood, I looked up at him. "Does that mean I get to decapitate *Natasha*?"

He froze as one corner of his mouth twitched. "During our short marriage, you've accused me of sleeping with Sandra, Jaz, and now Tasha. While I sit here celibate and desperate for release—and no, not the kind of release you've already given me." I moved against the back of my seat as he stepped forward until his feet met the legs of my chair. "Although, I do dream of the moment you'll swallow my cock again."

My cheeks flamed. Well, Cristiano was certainly back to his old self. The vulgar but hot picture he painted made me squirm—and reminded me of what he'd told me about Tasha before all this. "*She* did that for you, too."

"But not like you. Nobody will ever do it for me like

you. I don't want to get my dick sucked or handled or anything of the sort." He dragged out my chair, with me in it, and stood over me. "I want. To fuck. My wife."

I was finally ready for it. He wasn't, but by the look in his eyes, I wasn't sure I could stay him any longer. If he was willing to put himself in surgery to have me, he would. I'd tasted the power of unraveling him before, and it was just as sweet now. He only wanted me. At any cost.

"But . . . I can't," Cristiano said finally. "Not how I plan. I don't know what kind of sex Doctor Sosa has, but she'd probably *never* clear me if she had any idea what I've got in store for you."

Oh, God. I didn't know what to feel—relief? Disappointment? I wanted him. Having *all* of him, without reservation or an injury to slow him down, scared me. But there'd be no other way with him.

Gripping the edge, he sat back on the table. "You want to know about the women in my life? I'll tell you, and then we're going to drop this bullshit about whether I'd keep a mistress when I have perfection at my fingertips. Understood?"

I chewed the inside of my cheek. Cristiano was a god, and he called *me* perfection? He declared his loyalty to me when I'd fought him tooth and nail up until recently? I agreed more out of curiosity than anything. "Understood."

"Jaz was half-dead when we found her. It has been a long and arduous road to rehabilitate her. It will be a while still before she lets a man touch her, and I'm one of the only people in the world she trusts. Eduardo and Alejo, too. So, no, she's not, and never was, a mistress." He drummed his fingers along the table's wood edge. "She can be scrappy, but when it comes to learning more technical hand-to-hand combat, there are still too many triggers.

Sandra, on the other hand, took to it very well. She wants to fight back."

I curled my hands in my lap. I shouldn't have brought Jaz and Sandra into this, but apparently, something about Cristiano with another woman changed the chemistry of my brain—and it had even in the beginning of our marriage. "I'm sorry," I said.

"Sandra—I already told you her aunt sold her into prostitution—she doesn't sleep well, so some nights, we stay up late strategizing how she'll attack the ones who bought her years ago. She's hoping to take down all of them on her own—and then her own family for the way they betrayed her." He cocked his head. "That's why you found her in my office so late at *La Madrina*. We were breaking down her strengths and weaknesses in the fight earlier that night."

I had the infuriating urge to apologize again. It was a strange feeling for me, believing every word Cristiano said. But instinctively, I knew—he wouldn't lie about this. The subject was too raw, and the evidence of his efforts to help was all around me.

He'd only ever shown such undeniable honesty with his kiss and his touch, when we'd each been stripped of anything but primal urges. I had never doubted our chemistry, but I *had* his words. I didn't now.

"None of that changes the fact that you've been intimate with Tasha, and now she's under this roof." I never would've deigned to tell Cristiano how to live before, and even now, I faltered. It was my place, but it would take time to grow into this role. Time, and practice. "I don't care if she saved your life," I said. "It's disrespectful for her to stay."

His eyes scanned my face. "I told her our marriage was simply an arrangement between two families for the same reasons I told Senator Sanchez you're a spoiled brat who doesn't compare to the kind of women I can get."

My face heated. "Then why didn't you steal one of *them*?"

"You know why. Because I wanted *you*." The buzz that came with hearing that never wore off. With Cristiano's knuckles whitening against the table, and his lids lowering, I had to restrain from arching toward him. "Because even though marrying Natasha would've been a better business move," he continued, "it never crossed my mind to marry *anyone* until Diego laid you at my feet. I knew you were bait, and I bit the hook anyway."

Cristiano—hooked. I'd done something no other woman in the world had been able to, and I was sure many had tried. "Why me?" I whispered.

He undid the button at his collar with one hand. "No one else has been able to give me what I want."

"More power?" My eyes dropped to the pulse at the base of his neck, the veins running along the back of his muscular hand. "No," I said, answering my own question. "That's not what you're looking for. There's no lack of powerful families with eligible daughters around here."

"You're not a spoiled brat. Nor did I make our arrangement solely for business reasons. I said those things, and I keep you at arm's length in public, for your protection, Natalia."

He slid one foot forward. His nearness, and his protectiveness, only made me want to be closer to him. I moved my sandal to graze the inner edge of his dress shoe. Making a fist in his lap, he ran the sole up my ankle. I couldn't help my shudder. How could such an innocuous touch send a thrill up the inside of my leg?

"I don't have many attachments." His tone remained firm, but softened at the edges. "My cartel is one, but its people can fend for themselves. As you did when you were forced to. It's why I go overboard with the safety measures. When someone suspects my weaknesses, they attempt to exploit them."

I hadn't forgotten Jaz's words to me—that Cristiano loved me, even if he didn't know it. *Did* he love me? And did he know it now? He'd been ordered to care for my family and me in the past—maybe all this was because he'd never stopped. "*I'm* a weakness of yours."

"Diego knew it before I did."

My heart skipped painfully. Diego had used me; that wasn't news. But Cristiano could easily do the same. I was here because of deals they'd made behind my back—how could I trust Cristiano after all that he'd done, after years of hating him? But the bigger problem was how I could trust myself. I touched my neck. "The last thing I want is to care about someone again—and have him betray me."

"Then hear me." He leaned forward. "I've been trying to tell you this for a while. You are more than a conquest to me. More than an exchange of power. You're Bianca and Costa's daughter." Grabbing the arms of my chair, he dragged it forward until our faces were centimeters apart. "You're the girl I was hired to protect, and would have, if I hadn't been framed for Bianca's murder and forced away. You're my wife." His breath teased my lips, and I resisted from closing the short distance between our mouths. "And if seeing me on my deathbed wasn't reason enough to convince you of that, then I'll have to get creative."

I didn't need more convincing. But his declarations and determination were too good not to indulge. I met his eyes. "Creative how?"

He ran the backs of his knuckles along the length of my throat. With that one touch, my mouth went bone dry, but I got very wet somewhere else—the tender spot Cristiano grew more and more impatient to claim.

"I believe I owe you a debt, Mrs. de la Rosa—and you're about to collect." He took my chin in a gentle touch that contradicted the hardness in his gaze. "You've sworn to be at my dinner table every night." Rising to his full, intimidating height, he looked down on me. "Now I want you *on* it."

8

NATALIA

It was time to collect on a debt Cristiano owed me.

Words I'd never expected to think . . . and especially not in this context.

Dinner was over before it'd begun, and Cristiano stood above me, looking hungrier by the second. "Do I need to repeat myself?" he asked. "I said get on the table so I can make your cunt my next meal."

Butterflies exploded in my stomach. I barely managed to contain my gasp at his vulgarity, but I *couldn't* control the gush of warmth between my legs. "But your wounds—"

"My mouth still works."

I rose from my chair. "The doctor said—"

"Your husband is hungry." With a knuckle under my chin, he raised my face. "I've waited long enough to see how you taste, and you've waited patiently for me to pay my debt. You don't have to tell me you want it—only if you don't." He stepped aside and nodded at the long, sturdy table that seated at least twenty people. "You have until my face is between your legs to object."

Desire coiled in me. At one time, keeping him at arm's

length had been the right move, but the best part of resisting him up until now had been giving in. "I can't object once you've started?"

"You can"—he picked me up by my waist and plopped me on the table—"but you won't."

"Maybe I should shower first."

"I'll take you any way, including ripe. *Especially* ripe."

What? My mouth fell open. "That doesn't bother you?"

He took my ankle to untie the straps of my leather sandals. "Nah," he said, removing each shoe. "Some other time, I'll make up for it by scrubbing you clean with peppermint soap. Just breathing on your pussy will make it scream."

"Cristiano—"

"Don't pretend you're scandalized." He slid my ass to the edge of the table. "Now, put your feet up and bare yourself to me."

I stared at him for a moment. I *wasn't* pretending. I'd truly never been in the presence of someone like him. The most Diego had ever demanded of me was a kiss. And what had I thought back then? That Diego and I would unleash our passion when the time was right?

It didn't work that way. Heat had been smoldering between Cristiano and me since the start, and each time we struck against each other like flint, we came dangerously close to setting fire to everything around us.

I lay back and lifted my heels to the table. As if he hadn't just affectionately removed my shoes, he tore a hole clean through the crotch of my leggings.

"What—"

"I'll buy you new ones." He kept his eyes on my face as he slid a finger under the fabric of my thong, his knuckle grazing me. Goose bumps exploded over my skin. He snapped the sliver against my clit, and I gasped at the sting.

"That's for arguing," he said, "but don't worry—I'm about to make it better."

I bit my bottom lip, not bothering to hide my excitement. "What if someone sees?"

"They won't, I promise you that." He pulled up a chair like he was sitting down to a meal, then spread my legs and pushed his face between them. With the thong between his teeth, he let it snap against me again.

"As much as I enjoy making you squirm," he said, picking up a steak knife, "the underwear has to go."

I inhaled sharply. "What are you doing?"

With the serrated edge, he sliced through the thin strip of fabric. "Unwrapping your candy pussy like I promised so I can lick and suck until I find what I want—your sweet core."

His black eyes bored into mine, beckoning me to the dark side. This was the submission he'd promised I'd enjoy, if only I'd listen to my body and give in. Warmth seeped over me, pulling me under.

Cristiano grew serious. "I understand why your guard is still up, but starting now, it comes down. I want you to think long and hard about the past several weeks, Natalia. To wake up by my side and know without a doubt that I mean it when I say I want you and only you here as my wife. That I've promised to care for you. That I'm trying to protect you and others from things no person should ever witness, much less experience. And in case none of that is a good enough reason for you to accept me once and for all as your husband, then tomorrow morning, you will remember how I ate your pussy so good, you can't imagine a future without sitting on my face whenever you feel like it."

He sank his mouth onto me like I was a juicy steak, obliterating any shock I might've felt over his declarations.

Having only ever experienced Diego's gentle tonguing, I wasn't ready for Cristiano's onslaught, the way he gripped my hips and pulled me onto his face so hard I wondered how he could breathe.

Nothing could prepare me for his animal growl vibrating through me.

Or how he thrust his tongue inside me and shredded the last of my willpower to resist him.

My feet jumped to his shoulders. He sucked on my clit. A whimper escaped my open mouth. Pleasure so severe it bordered on painful ripped through me, but it was due to more than a skilled combination of tongue and teeth. It was his voraciousness to devour me that made my spine arch to the point of snapping and my moans echo through the hall.

Consumed, I closed my thighs around his ears, but he pried them right back apart, holding them open. "Don't close your legs again," he said, licking his lips. "I need my hands."

He spread me wider. With the unexpectedness of a long finger inside me, I sucked in a breath. He added another, easing both in as if testing me. He withdrew them, stuck them in his mouth, and grinned wolfishly. "Wanna taste?"

"No," I nearly choked out, horrified at the suggestion.

"More for me."

The faster his fingers slipped in and out, the wetter I got. I hadn't known I could even drip this way. His tongue sucked and explored my clit like it was his new favorite toy, lavishing attention on it until my insides flurried and contracted around his fingers.

"I understand why your guard is still up, but starting now, it comes down."

With my surrender, bliss radiated from my core to the tips of my fingers and toes, scorching anything in its path.

He removed his fingers, took a bruising grip on my hips, and burrowed his face between my legs. His tongue invaded like he was mining for gold. His voraciousness brought on my climax, simultaneously spurring it on and easing the raw, agonizing pleasure with groans that vibrated along the waves of my orgasm.

By the end, I was pulling his hair as my thighs quaked. He kissed me gently, his tongue tender on my quivering pussy as he helped me back down to Earth.

He uncurled my hands from his hair and stepped away, taking me in. A satisfied rumble from his chest made me feel as if I'd pleased him.

Even in my haze, I wondered how he seemed as content as I was.

I was almost too shy to look him in the eye. He'd transformed from man to beast, and me?

I'd loved it so much, I'd come as hard as humanly possible.

With a mouth like his, I'd be a fool not to chain myself to him.

If there'd been any question about whether I could learn to follow the devil . . .

I had my answer.

In our bedroom, I unbuttoned Cristiano's shirt from my body as he watched from the bed, naked from the waist up. He stuck his arm behind his head. "If you take even one step toward the couch, I will carry you back to this bed—and you wouldn't want to risk me opening my wounds, would you?"

I smirked. Suddenly his condition was a concern of his?

But the truth was, I didn't *want* to sleep apart—I hadn't for a while. I'd chosen the sofa the last week and a half to give him space. Let his body heal. Remove temptation.

And, if I was honest, this part was still new to me in many ways—not just because I'd had only one lover, one time. Cristiano had been right to call me out for having my guard up, but it was more about wading into unfamiliar territory than resistance. About moving past the shame of having fought so hard against him only to give in practically overnight.

"I didn't see you take your antibiotics," I said, holding the dress shirt closed over my naked body.

We'd already undressed his wounds, and now they breathed. I'd gotten used to the sight of them, but my anger still simmered over what they represented. "So give them to me, Nurse Natalia," he said.

I went to the closet to change into a nightgown, discarding his shirt and my destroyed pants in a pile. In the bathroom, I washed my hands for thirty seconds like the doctor had told me to, soaked a gauze pad, and carried his pills, fresh bandages, and antibiotic ointment back to the bed.

"The first night I brought you here," he said as I climbed onto the bed next to him, "I thought you'd instantly see how well we fit together once I got you in my arms. I'd already known from the moment I'd seen you at the costume party that there was an attraction between us. I assumed you'd fight it, resist it, but that once we were alone, you wouldn't have to fear it anymore." His gaze, nearly as potent as his touch, drifted from the hem of my short, slinky slip down my bare legs. "As my wife, you'd have the freedom to give in."

"You didn't know me as well as you claimed."

He shook his head. "I don't consider myself a naïve man, but when it came to you, I suppose I was."

He'd never intended to force me. His only mistake had been overestimating his male prowess and underestimating my will to hate him. It made more sense that he'd stormed out of my father's house after bandaging up my wounds from the warehouse fire. I'd made it clear that morning that I believed he had it in him to rape me. Or how he'd grilled me about whether Diego had been forceful with me by the fountain the night of the costume party.

I sat back on my heels. Ghosting my fingertips around one wound, I asked, "Does it hurt?"

"Much less than it did a moment ago."

"What was it like?" I asked as I gently touched the wet gauze to his torso. "Were you scared?"

He watched me. "Terrified."

My eyes jumped to his, surprised by his admission.

"Not for myself," he added. "For you."

"Do you regret any of it?"

He paused, digesting the question. "I can't, Natalia. I never want to put you in danger, but so many lives have been bettered because of everything leading up to the attacks."

I was glad to hear he'd do it all again. If I hadn't survived, at least my death would've been in the name of something good. "Why?" I asked. "Why is helping these women so important to you?"

"Do I need a reason?"

I smiled sadly as I patted his skin dry. "In this world, yes. Nothing is free. Nobody acts with good intentions."

After a few silent beats, he reached up and cupped my cheek in his large, warm hand. "You do, don't you?" His thumb touched the corner of my mouth. "What do you think Bianca would've wanted for you?"

How often did anyone bring up my mother to me? Rarely, if ever—as if the topic of her death was off-limits, when really, I relished the chance to talk about her. "I don't know what she'd want for me," I said, "but it wouldn't be to stay in such a dangerous life."

"She was raising a strong woman who wouldn't allow fear or shame to rule her. Bianca would've approved as long as you were honest and unwavering in your choices." He dropped his hand to my thigh and squeezed gently— not playfully this time, or even sexually. Just comforting. "If you truly want out of this life, then go, Natalia. But you'd be running away because wanting it scares you . . . and I think your mother would've made you question that. Confront it. If you want a place by my side, the way she stood by your father, then take it. Own it. Don't feel ashamed that the cartel runs in your blood."

Cartel life was maim, murder, and supplying evil with the means to tempt the good. "It *is* shameful," I said, unscrewing the top of the pill bottle to shake his antibiotics into my palm. "Innocent people pay the price for what we do."

"Was your mother innocent?" he asked. "Was mine? No. But they made no apology for it."

I wished I could believe in my mother's innocence the way I had as a child, but there was no such thing as a bystander in this business. But if my mother had helped Papá make decisions, or even stood by without protest— did that make her as ruthless as him? My father had killed, and so had she. I leaned over to trade the pill bottle for a glass of water on his nightstand. "The women in this world aren't to be underestimated," I said, handing him his meds.

"They're good caretakers, too." He tossed back the antibiotics with a quick sip and set down the glass. "I look forward to the day you finally realize what Diego is, and I pray all your mercy will have been used up by then."

"I already know, Cristiano. He's a coward and a manipulator." Something that resembled pain passed over Cristiano's face—but I hadn't hurt him. His relief had. Perhaps because he wanted so badly to trust that I'd finally come to that conclusion after all his efforts to get me there.

Since Cristiano's return, he'd never wavered in his hatred for his brother. "Diego told me once that you two could never trust each other again," I said. "And he was right."

"He blames Costa and me for our family's demise. And if Diego can't understand why our father had to die, then I worry what else he can justify."

"He must've aided in the Belmonte-Ruiz attacks," I said. Up until very recently, I wouldn't have thought Diego capable of putting me in harm's way, but I'd had no idea what I was dealing with. He'd already admitted his involvement with Belmonte-Ruiz, but if he'd fed them information, then he'd known I was a target as well as Cristiano.

"It's . . . it's my fault," I said. "I brought the phone into the house."

"True." Cristiano rubbed his jaw. "But if that hadn't worked, they would've found another way. Trust me."

"Then I'm also to blame that the truth about your business is leaking."

"No, *mi amor*. It was only a matter of time," he said quietly. "It's why I've formed many powerful partnerships over the years, amassed as much money as possible, and insulated my people. And if I were truly worried, I'd shut down my operation."

"You're not going to?" I popped the cap off the ointment and dabbed some on each of his wounds. "Where are the girls you rescued the night I was with you?"

"In a safehouse a few blocks from here. Trained staff helps them work through the stages of recovery. After, we set them up here, or somewhere else if they choose."

He had an answer for everything. "So, what happens now, Cristiano?"

"I don't know, but we're not going to stop. Does that scare you?"

I chewed on my bottom lip. Both Diego and my father had said at different times that I'd be safest with Cristiano. Even California would leave me exposed if someone really wanted to get to me. Cristiano wasn't trying to hide that I was in danger, and I appreciated that. More, I didn't have to wonder if I'd risk my safety so Cristiano could help more women, men, and children. "No," I said. "I'm not scared."

"I thought by presenting our marriage as no more than a contract, people would be likely to leave you alone. They didn't."

"Maybe you should try the opposite approach," I said.

A corner of his mouth lifted. "Not a bad idea. I said the Badlands were treacherous as well, yet they came for us anyway. So perhaps now I'll make it clear that you belong to me in every sense of the word. And there's no question that the rumors about what I do to those who fuck with my things are true."

The scary way his voice dropped sent a bolt of excitement through me. Cristiano had warned me plenty of times that he was very protective, but it'd never felt truer than in that moment.

I unwrapped a fresh bandage and set my hands in my lap, studying him. "Are you going to tell me why?"

He didn't ask for clarification. He knew what I meant. He'd evaded the question once tonight, but I wasn't going to keep quiet like I had when I'd arrived. His hesitation meant there were reasons behind why he did what he did, and I wanted them. I wanted to know more. To know him.

He scratched under his nose. "I've always had, uh, a physical advantage over most others," he said. "I've used it. And I hope anyone I've killed has deserved it."

"But . . ." I played with the corner of the paper packet. "You deal in weapons, Cristiano. You arm the bad guys and give them an advantage over everyone."

"I'll never be the good guy. I'm sensible. Our country, our people, rely on the production and movement of contraband. Take that away, and we'll fall. That's just how it is."

"In this case, sex is contraband."

"If we fall because I disrupt the sex trade, then we deserve to."

I was equally warmed and horrified by the pride that spread through me. His conviction moved me as I tended to the physical evidence of what had resulted from him advocating for good. Equally scary was how wrong I'd been about him.

"But if it gives you any comfort," he said, "I never armed Belmonte-Ruiz. And I've stopped selling to anyone who does business with them."

"Tasha and Alejandro told me. That's another reason they're coming after you?"

"*Sí.*" He held out his hand for the last bandage. "*A ver.* Give me that."

"I still need to wrap your chest."

He gestured for me to hand the packet over. When I did, he set it aside and took my forearm, tugging me down to the bed. I let him guide me into the crook of his neck. "When we drove into the Badlands the first time," he said, "what'd you think you'd see?"

I shut my eyes like I had that day, transporting myself

back to that moment. "The worst," I admitted. "Rundown buildings, beggars, prisoners, prostitutes. I think I half-expected a guillotine. I could've sworn I saw people huddled into the cargo space of a semi."

"Those who'd chosen to leave the Badlands and make their homes elsewhere." He ran a hand up my arm. "I won't ask what you thought of me."

"I thought you were a monster."

With a deep breath, he shifted under me. Whether from physical pain or something else, I wasn't sure. "I am, Natalia. No question there."

I tilted my head to see his face better as I half-whispered, "You're scarier than any monster."

"You remember."

"You said that to me one night after a nightmare, when my mother was still alive. You promised you'd keep the monsters away. But if you're the *good* guy, what does that make everyone else?"

"Not figments of our imaginations, unfortunately. They're bad. So I have to be worse. I've made peace with it, but that doesn't mean I can't also stand for something."

I scooted over on the bed, getting even closer to him. He'd talked of owning my wants and needs. I *wanted* to know him better. I *needed* to know why—why I sat beside him now, why he felt compelled to help, how he'd gotten to this place.

"Is there really no reason you do all this?" I asked.

"Nobody should need a reason to help those people," he said and paused.

"But you have one," I guessed. I slipped my hand into his. He tensed under me but then relaxed. Offering him comfort was new for us.

Or maybe I was the one who needed it.

Getting to know the innerworkings of Cristiano's mind,

heart, and soul wasn't a task for the faint-hearted. Wondering what I'd find scared me—but not enough to pull back. Not physically, and not from whatever new emotional territory we were wading into.

"Tell me what happened," I said.

9

NATALIA

With each inhalation, Cristiano's massive chest expanded underneath my cheek, but his arm remained firmly around me. Silence permeated our bedroom. Secured in the crook of his arm, it would've been easy to change the subject back to something safer. Why rock the boat with questions about his past, now that we'd set sail on smoother waters?

But he'd always encouraged me to ask questions, to look closer, to live this life with wide-open eyes—and he hadn't shielded me from the ugly sides of it. So, the longer he remained quiet, the more anxious I became. If Cristiano struggled over opening up about his past, I suspected that meant it was deeply painful for him. Could I be the comfort he needed? Had I made him feel safe?

Was that even possible when I'd only just begun to concern myself with his safety and comfort?

Maybe that was his hesitation. To open up about what haunted him, he'd have to take a leap of faith.

After a while had passed, he shifted. I placed my hand

on his chest and raised my eyes to his. He nodded toward the bedroom door. "Growing up, our household had staff, like yours. Like mine does now."

"It's not unusual."

"My dad had groomed me my whole life to help with, and eventually take over, his business. Diego, too, but he was much younger. I was significantly more involved. My father had a warehouse near the border of Juárez and El Paso. He had to hide it from your father and the other families around here. There, my parents trained and housed mules, prostitutes, and slaves. I visited several times before their deaths, and I saw the innerworkings of the sex trade."

"How old were you?"

"Thirteen when it started." He closed his fingers around my hand on his chest, veins protruding from his forearm. "I watched him quietly build that business. Anytime I tried to speak up, he'd beat me. After a growth spurt, I tried to physically interfere with a deal. The next day was the first time he brought Diego to the warehouse. He was only eight."

Cristiano's punishment had been Diego's introduction to the darker side of that life. His father must've known how that would affect Cristiano. I flipped my palm over to squeeze his hand. "I'm sorry."

His dark eyes drifted up to the ceiling. "He tried to get me to see people as commodities. No different than weapons or drugs to be moved across borders for a profit. Same with my mom. They didn't see faces, just dollar signs. And control. Maybe I would've, too, if not for . . . for Angelina."

Just hearing a woman's name, especially since Cristiano struggled to get it out, put my nerves on edge. She had to be the reason. "Who's Angelina?"

He slid his hand up my back, pulling me closer by my shoulders. "It's weird to say her name aloud after this long. She was the daughter of the head of our household staff. I had no time for girls, but she worked around the house a lot and was the kind of beautiful everyone noticed. I had a harmless crush—at least, it was harmless until my father noticed it."

His hand became clammy in mine—or maybe I was the one sweating. I didn't want to ask, afraid I already knew the answer, but I had to. "What happened to her?"

"The last time I stood up to my dad, he didn't beat me, and he didn't involve Diego."

"He beat her?" I guessed.

"I wish he had." The haunted look in his eyes turned the pit in my stomach into a sinking rock of pure dread. "I wish he'd just fucking killed her."

The back of my neck bristled. To hear Cristiano, champion of innocent women, admit *that* of all things . . . it said everything. "How come?"

"He sold her to a Ukrainian man for a couple hundred dollars. I was in the room. My father had me restrained as the man beat her, raped her, then took her. And then my father gave me the money."

I covered my mouth with both hands as bile rose in my throat. I'd heard his parents were malicious from my father, Diego, Cristiano, and others—it was common knowledge, really. But it'd mostly been in the context of their business and plans to overthrow my family.

This, though?

It was a whole new level of evil. Just hearing the horrific words brought tears to my eyes. "I had no idea. I . . ." My chin trembled. "I'm so sorry, Cristiano. Diego never said anything."

"He was young. I used to talk about it with him, so he

knows—but he only witnessed the tip of the iceberg in person."

Cristiano pinched the inside corners of his eyes and breathed through whatever was working its way through him.

I brought his palm to my heart. "You don't have to be strong," I said. "You're strong for everyone, all the time, but you don't have to be that way with me."

"I was forced to be," he said. "Our father wanted to make damn sure I understood that there was *no* room for attachments in this world."

"What did you do?" I asked.

"I knew my father wouldn't stop at that. Diego was getting older, and he'd start seeing more. I wanted to protect him from our parents, but also . . . I couldn't live in a world where I knew that was happening. I had to get us out or stop them—and there was no getting out."

I clenched my jaw to stem another wave of tears that heated the backs of my eyes. It broke my heart, after all the strife between the brothers, to hear that Cristiano had once wanted to shield Diego so badly, he'd put himself in harm's way. And that Diego didn't know it, or even the extent of his father's business . . .

"As you know," Cristiano continued, "your father, mine, and some of the other cartels in the area had formed a pact against human trafficking. So my parents would have to take them out in order to expand their business."

"That's why you chose my father to ask for help."

"At that point, I was barely fifteen and had no resources. I used the money from Angelina's buyer to get a gun and transportation to your house. I'd known Costa to be fair, and your grandfather to be ruthless—the right combination for what I needed." Resolve entered his voice as his shoulders drew back. "I figured as soon as they heard what my parents were doing, and that they were planning to overthrow the other cartels to get away with it, they'd be my best shot at stopping them. And I was right—you know the rest."

My heart raced. If there was no more to the story, then it didn't have a happy ending. "But what happened to Angelina?"

He finally lowered his anguish-filled eyes to mine and shook his head.

"You don't know?" I asked.

"I never found her. I've tried. I started in Ukraine and Russia. That's where I met Tasha's grandfather, whose family had built a strong network in both México and Russia over many generations. But even with their help, it'd been eight years since she'd been taken. It was like looking for a needle in a haystack. But it led me to other men and women that society had cast aside and left to fend for themselves. From Eastern Europe, we went on to see more of the world." He took a breath and resolution firmed his jaw. "I'm certain Angelina's dead by now. I hope she is. Some nights I lie awake thinking of everything she endured—all because of me."

"Oh, no. No, no, no." I got up on an elbow and took his chin to force him to look at me—something I'd learned from him. "It was *not* your fault, Cristiano."

"I've done a lot of work to overcome my past with my parents. They have no control over me anymore. But Angelina . . . I cared about her, and that ruined her life." He took my wrist, running my palm along his stubble before he kissed the inside of my hand. "You can see how that has affected me. Why I keep you a secret from the rest of the world."

"Because you . . . care about me."

He frowned. "I've always cared about you, Natalia. Always." He tucked some of my hair behind my ear as I looked down at him. "In a twisted away, every time I've scared you, hurt you, pushed you away—it was to ultimately protect you."

I had the overwhelming urge to lean in and kiss him. To kiss *Cristiano*—willingly. To chase away the sadness in his eyes. But then, they grew distant.

"But there's no guarantee I *can*," he said. "That's why you need to learn to fight for yourself. I couldn't protect Angelina, and I failed your mother—I can't fail you."

"Both situations were outside your control." The last eleven years, he'd been accused of the crimes of his father. Acknowledging that meant admitting I'd been wrong about everything—including my mother's murder. "You really didn't kill her, did you?" I asked through a rasp in my throat.

"No."

I opened my mouth to form some kind of response, but what could I possibly say? I couldn't give him back the years he'd lost. The life he'd known. The family stolen from him. And I'd played a part in it.

"You never had enough evidence—or reason—to believe otherwise," he said, reading my mind.

Moving forward, knowing all I did now, I could help him rebuild. I sat up, swallowing over and over. "We're going to fix you up," I said quietly. Carefully, I taped the last bandage over the gash nearest his heart. "We're going to fix this."

"I don't need fixing, Natalia. With you on my side, I'm a force to be reckoned with."

I shook my head and pressed the tape down, sealing the bandage. "Sit up."

He pushed off the mattress and into a sitting position. I picked up a roll of elastic wrap and moved forward until we were face to face. He stretched his arms as I reached both of mine around his middle to bind him.

As his breath warmed my cheek, I raised my eyes to his full bottom lip and then higher. I wasn't sure what I expected to find in his eyes—sadness, regret, pain. But he seemed perfectly content just to watch me work.

"Do you still look for her?" I asked.

His Adam's apple bobbed. "It's been almost twenty years, Natalia. Maybe I could've saved her back then if I'd had the resources I do now." He spoke quietly, inches from my face. "I'm using what I learned back then to help others. But no, I don't look for her anymore."

I snapped the clips on the bandage tape closed, securing it as my soul wept. That door would never be closed. He'd always wonder what had happened. His parents would forever have that hold on him from their graves. "Are you afraid to love anyone again?"

His expression fell as if I'd sucker punched him. After a moment, he lowered his arms, took my biceps in a firm but gentle grip, and looked me in the eye. "I didn't love her—it was a boyhood crush, but that doesn't lessen the devastation of what happened to her." He paused as if choosing his words carefully. "If it'd been you, I would damn well still be looking."

Was he trying to tell me something? Was it possible that in the last several weeks of darkness, love had bloomed?

"It wouldn't have been me," I said. "Your parents would've murdered my entire family . . . if you hadn't stopped them."

"Then I've done at least one thing right in my life."

"And . . . what about now?" I asked through the lump forming in my throat.

"If someone took you now? They'd better kill me in the process, because I'd never stop until I found you. There'd be nothing left of this earth. And then, I'd keep going in the afterlife."

"Where would you look first?" I asked. "Heaven or Hell?"

"Heaven," he said immediately. "If you stay here by my side, though, that will change. There's only the underworld for people like us. But down here, we don't burn. We rule."

Physically, it would take almost nothing to lean in and kiss him, but it would cost me in other ways. I'd consent to my downfall. To descend with him. To bleed for him as he'd promised I would.

He cupped the back of my head and pressed his lips to my forehead. "I'm not scared to fall in love," he said against my skin. "If anything, I'm scared not to. Your parents set high standards for what a true partnership looks like, but I don't back down from a challenge."

All bandaged up, but not yet healed, he lay back against the pillow and let his eyelids fall shut.

It wasn't the first time Cristiano had referenced my parents' marriage and their love for each other. It was the *everything* he'd been seeking. It had to be. That would answer many of the questions that had surrounded him from the start.

I let my eyes drift over my strong, menacing, yet achingly vulnerable husband. He was right. With me by his side, we'd be a force to be reckoned with.

We?

Weeks ago, it might've surprised me that I'd want that, but I didn't think it would've ever truly shocked me. It was why I'd fought all of this so hard.

It felt entirely and alarmingly natural to stay, put on my crown, and descend deeper into the darkness with Cristiano.

But that didn't mean I had any idea what I'd find once everything went black.

10

NATALIA

F lat on my back on the front lawn, I struggled to breathe under Cristiano's considerable weight and brawn. He pinned my wrists over my head in the grass, and with speed a man of his size shouldn't possess, he maneuvered his hips between my legs, wedged his thighs beneath mine, and spread them.

"You're helpless against me, Mrs. de la Rosa," he said with an infuriatingly smug smirk.

I bucked my hips as hard as I could, knowing it would do no good.

"Third time this morning—and *I'm* injured. Have the last several weeks of training been for nothing?"

Between my shorts and his joggers, only thin fabric separated us. "I fought off a real attacker. It's just *you* who's too strong for me."

"What have I told you? A limited mindset will always be your greatest liability." He bent until his face hovered over mine, and his eyes dropped to my mouth. "Once you defeat me, then you'll know you can take on anyone."

I licked my lips to see if I could keep his gaze there. "Cristiano?"

"Hmm?"

The thing about lightweight workout gear designed to fit like a second skin was that it didn't leave much to the imagination. Cristiano had too much happening down south to hide anything. Even when he wasn't hard, I could feel him between my legs, but now, something stirred. "I think you're the one with the wrong . . . mindset."

"Yeah?" he asked.

I shifted my hips, teasing him with a warm home for the thick, ridged monster rising between us. Reminding him that with the baggy openings of my running shorts, he could unfasten, tug, shift, and be inside me in seconds.

His grip loosened as he inhaled. "*Yeah*," I said.

Flattening my foot against his thigh and using the advice he constantly repeated to me, I put my weight behind my shoulder, pushed off his leg, and rolled out from under him.

"*Oof.*" He flopped onto his back, clutching his abdomen.

I jumped up to straddle him, careful not to sit near his wounds. "Sorry, but I win," I said, smiling down at him. "Did I hurt you?"

"Nothing a few new stitches won't fix."

As I leaned forward, my ponytail hung over my shoulder, the ends brushing his chest. "You left yourself open."

"I did." He seized my biceps, yanking me down until our bodies were flush—and I was back under his control. "But, no, you didn't win. The fight is never over."

His heart pounded against my breasts—or maybe it was mine. Either way, our breath mingled, and our eyes searched each other's faces. In the weeks since we'd kissed, the electricity between us hadn't dimmed. Just the opposite

—it'd become even more charged. At one time it'd been exactly what I'd been worried would happen—that a kiss would be powerful enough to make me forget why I hated him.

But I'd already forgotten. Or maybe he'd given me enough reasons to change my *mindset*.

Not for the first time since he'd opened up to me about his past, I didn't just *want* to kiss him. I craved it.

The need in his eyes had been growing even stronger since he'd begun to fully heal, and it betrayed his power-lessness. I could've asked for anything in that moment. Or, I could be the one to initiate, sliding up the hard length of his shaft, controlling my tempo, his orgasm, and mine . . .

I'd been sleeping by his side as I had the first weeks I'd arrived—only now, he'd pull me into his embrace each night, mouth in my hair, my hips nestled into his, our bodies learning how to share a bed. How to have restraint.

He'd woken up this morning ready to spar. And if he could wrestle me to the ground, then I knew what was next. It'd been coming a long time. He'd been waiting even longer. His unwilling bride would ask for it, and he would answer tenfold. With the ache growing stronger between my legs each day, maybe I'd even beg. He'd warned me I would.

"I see you're fully recovered, sir," Alejandro called cheerfully from somewhere far too near.

I shot into a sitting position so quickly, I almost tumbled back into the grass.

Alejo sauntered toward us, not bothering to hide his grin.

Cristiano fixed my shorts and patted my hips to get me to climb off him. "What are you doing back? You're supposed to be in the south."

After our meal with Alejandro, Pilar, and Tasha—

which had turned into dinner for one when Cristiano had decided to *eat out* instead—Alejandro had assembled a team and taken them on an attempt to recover Max . . . against my advice. They'd loaded Tasha in a car to return her to wherever she'd come from, and according to Cristiano, they hadn't had much to report since.

In this case, I worried no news wasn't good news. But by the spring in Alejandro's step, it looked as if I was wrong.

"Did you locate Max?" I asked as I stood, brushing grass off my legs.

"Afraid not. Believe me, Cristiano will be the first to know when we do."

When Cristiano moved me in front of him, I didn't have to ask why—the reason pressed into my backside. "You have that look," Cristiano said.

"Which one?" Alejandro asked.

Like a cat who'd caught the canary. I noticed it, too. "You know something," I said.

"I know two things. First, Max's trail went cold again, but we're extremely close to securing a rat within Belmonte-Ruiz."

"Someone's willing to help?" I asked.

"Willing? No. But he agreed when I presented him with an alternative that didn't end well for his family in the States. Now, we put on the pressure until he caves, then wait for the right time to pounce."

"Then why aren't you closing the deal?" Cristiano asked.

"I don't need to be there for that." He widened his stance and crossed his fists under his arms. "I wanted to deliver this next part in person—we were successful in a *different* mission." He winked, and, in a very odd turn of events, he hooted. Like an *owl*.

Cristiano's hands tightened on my shoulders. "*¿El Búho?*"

"*Sí, patrón.* When we took Tasha back to the city, we got more information from her family. Since we've been waiting around a lot while trying to track down Max, we decided to put that intel to good use."

"Fuck," Cristiano said, but there was no anger behind his curse. If anything, he sounded pleased. "You know where the Valverdes are, don't you?"

"The Valverdes?" I asked, the *apellido* a faint echo in the back of my mind. "Why do I know that name?"

Alejandro nodded, and if he'd looked smug earlier, now he looked downright prideful. "They're closer than you think, boss."

"Not in the south?"

"Not anymore."

Cristiano stiffened behind me. "Don't fuck with me, Alejandro."

I glanced back, twisting to look up at Cristiano. "Are they what you left to find?"

"*Sí, mi corazón,*" he said, but his attention stayed on Alejandro. "Where are they?"

Alejandro tipped his chin forward. "Downstairs."

I touched the neckline of my tank top. *Downstairs?* The only downstairs I'd seen was the panic room and storage space, and at the opposite end of the house, the subterranean dining room where the party had been held my first night. "Are they eating?" I asked.

Cristiano laughed, and Alejandro joined in before responding, "No. They may not even have a meal left."

Cristiano's chest pressed against my back. "How'd you pull this off?"

"You've had some bad luck, and it has distracted you,"

Alejandro said. "We thought you needed a win after the past few weeks."

Cristiano slid his hands to rest in the curves of my neck, his fingers stretching over my collarbone. "How many?"

"Four. Once we located the head, the others weren't far behind."

"*Four?*" he asked and released a string of awed curses. "I hoped for one at best."

"One person?" I asked.

"We'll resume our lesson later." Cristiano pressed a kiss to the back of my head and moved his mouth to my ear. "Don't count on me forgetting the position you got me in."

Every day brought more questions, but I was lucky to make it through with even one answer. Who were these people Cristiano had seemingly chased to the ends of the Earth? And what did that family have to do with mine?

"Wait." I turned to face him, grabbing the front of his t-shirt before he could walk away.

He arched an eyebrow at my fist in his shirt, then raised his eyes to me. "Yes?"

"Who are the Valverdes? Why do you need them?"

"I'll tell you everything, but not now." He wiped sweat from his lip and glanced over his shoulder. "First, I need to see what we're dealing with."

I released his shirt and let him walk away. Even though I believed he'd fill me in later, it was still a *no* that transported me back to my first days in the Badlands. I didn't want to return to the moments when my imagination had been left to its own devices, spinning out of control, conjuring up terrible—and ultimately false—theories.

"You said you wanted . . . that we'd do this together," I called after him. "Like my parents."

Cristiano stopped where he was, then turned back. "We *will* do it together."

The drop in his voice registered deep in my stomach, a threat. "Then why can't I come with you?"

"Now?"

"Yes. Now. Show me what's downstairs."

He strolled back to me, his eyes roaming from my ankles to my eyes. "You haven't got the first clue what you're asking to be a part of."

"So tell me."

He massaged his chest. Fisker said Cristiano sometimes got heartburn. He liked his liquor, cigars and cigarettes, and red meat—the constant stress didn't help. I made a mental note to request something light for dinner.

"The Valverdes were around when you were a child," Cristiano said. "Rivals of your father's."

"Some of the old guard, then," I said. Many of my father's original associates had been murdered or demoted, their cartels dissolved, overthrown, or eliminated. My father had mainly survived due to his shift from narcotics into his safer business around shipping logistics.

"Something like that." Cristiano rubbed his temples. "It could be dangerous down there. I'll assess the situation and come upstairs when I know more."

"So you get to pick and choose what I see? How is that a partnership?"

"Partnership? *Mmm.*" He wet his lips, giving me a onceover. "I have to say, I like to hear you own it, my love. I like it very much."

A pleasant warmth traveled up my chest. I hadn't even realized that's what I was doing. The word had just come out. But that's what was developing between us. Cristiano had sought me out to be his queen, and every day, it became truer.

Because what life was there for me now that I'd seen all that I had here?

Now that I'd known a man like Cristiano?

California hadn't been home. It'd been a place to escape my fears and responsibilities. And I didn't want that anymore, which was good—because I'd never be able to go back to that.

Choosing this life left no room for hesitation. Either I was in or out, and Cristiano had to know my decision. "I heard what you said the other night about Mamá wanting me to live honestly," I said. "I don't want to be a victim of my fear. I don't want to be a bystander in my life. I choose this. Whatever's in there, I can handle it."

"I know you *can*, but certain things, you can't come back from. "

He warned me with haunting words, but I couldn't ignore the one truth that had persisted since I'd stepped foot in the church over a month ago. "I can't go back anyway, can I?"

Alejandro whistled for Cristiano.

Cristiano retreated. "Wait upstairs. I'll come soon."

With him, *soon* could've meant minutes or hours.

He turned and strode around the side of the house where the mountainside had the thickest vegetation. I hadn't explored much in that area. I hadn't thought there was anything there but overgrown trees. Now I wondered how it could possibly have a "downstairs."

I returned to our bedroom, turned on the shower, and started to remove my racerback tank when I caught sight of the new definition in my shoulders and biceps. My body was changing. Strengthening. Just like my emotional and mental state.

I left my top on and leaned over the sink to look in the mirror. My first night here, I'd found myself in the ground floor bathroom staring at the reflection of a terrified, angry, and exhausted girl who thought she was headed upstairs to be proverbially torn limb from limb by her greatest enemy.

How much had changed since then. I'd been willfully naïve. Scared to learn truths I'd assumed would be ugly. The result of a lifetime of being coddled by Papá and Diego.

Would I trade the darkness of Cristiano's world to go back to living blindly if I could?

It didn't matter. I couldn't. At least it was honest here.

Steam curled over the shower door. My ponytail had come loose during our sparring and hung over my shoulder. Scars began to take form, a tiny one on my cheek, and a slash under my chin. My cheeks flushed from my morning workout and the running hot water. My eyes had seen things I couldn't forget.

"Certain things, you can't come back from."

What things? I'd already watched Cristiano slit the throats of the men who'd tried to kidnap Sandra. I'd seen the faces of the lost, but not forgotten, taped to a whiteboard, probably no longer waiting for saviors like Calavera. I'd fought off my own attacker. But there was a more horrific side to what Cristiano did. *El Polvo* pouring sand down the throat of his worst enemies. I'd heard of a slow death, but had not witnessed the intricacies and unspoken truths of what it really meant.

Was that what was happening downstairs? A slow death for my father's rivals? An enemy so old and obscure I barely remembered their name? Before the assaults, Cristiano had gone in search of a key to unlock *everything* he wanted. I'd been learning that his unmet need was me. Us. Our partnership. Our marriage. So why had an old guard family stood between Cristiano and me?

My pulse quickened as the puzzle pieces formed a bigger picture. He'd said it had to do with closure. Jaz had said it was proof. And as with everything here, revenge played a part—Cristiano had admitted that our last night alone before he'd left town.

Revenge in my name. In my father's name. Closure for us. Proof. I curled my fists against the counter as the answer formed in my mind.

Papá had told me the morning after the costume party that my mother's *sicario* had been hired by a rival cartel that was no longer in existence.

But maybe they were. And maybe there were *here*.

11

NATALIA

I'd waited almost twelve years for answers about my mother's death, and now, the people responsible were here. Close by. Somewhere under my feet.

Cristiano had asked me to hold on a little longer, but I squirmed at just the *thought* of more puzzle pieces waiting in some cryptic place Alejandro had called "downstairs."

I pushed away from the bathroom counter, turned off the shower, and went to my closet. After zipping a hoodie over my tank top, I tightened my ponytail and headed to the ground floor and around the side of the house where Cristiano had disappeared.

What was I doing? What was I asking for by opening this door that had been locked to me for so long? What if I couldn't handle it?

Cristiano had said I could. But if what I suspected was true, this family was responsible for more than my mother's death. They'd take the blame for the eleven years Cristiano had been on the run. For his poverty and struggle, and the irreparable rift between him and his brother. For bearing the hatred of his mentor and future wife for so long.

And for all of that, they would pay.

Cristiano had exacted torturous death on many an enemy, and there might be no greater foe than the Valverde family.

The farther I walked from the house, the more wooded it became. Dirt began to soften as twigs crunched under my sneakers. Leafy tree tops blocked out the sky. Wings flapped as birds whistled. *Ah, nature—*

With the metal *click* of a gun, I froze.

"*Alto.*" Stop.

I looked around for the male voice but saw nothing— until a nearly completely camouflaged Eduardo stepped out from between some trees. "Natalia?"

My shoulders loosened. "*¿Dónde está Cristiano?*" I asked.

If Eduardo knew where Cristiano was, he didn't answer.

"Get him for me," I said with a sigh. "Now—it's urgent."

Eduardo removed the handheld radio attached to his bulletproof vest. "*Jefe,*" he said into it. "Natalia's here."

Cristiano responded right away. "Bring her down."

Eduardo led me a few meters through the trees. When we reached the mountainside, he pulled on a rock that wasn't a rock, but a steel cover disguising a keypad. He pressed his thumb to a fingerprint scanner, and part of the mountain in front of us slid open like the entrance to a vault.

Dios santo. The door *was* the mountain. I never would've found this on my own.

Eduardo went first, disappearing down a dark stairwell.

My feet wouldn't move, though. Since childhood, I tried not to willingly go down into dark spaces. With the smell of soil, this particular staircase reminded me of the tunnel Cristiano had taken me into.

Unlike that one, though, he wasn't going to leave me down there.

I forced myself to take the first step, then the next, until I stood at the bottom of a stone staircase and before another secure door. Eduardo entered his credentials, and once it opened, he breezed right in without a second thought.

My only company was the sound of my heartbeat. I got the feeling once I stepped inside, I'd come out slightly changed. But I'd learned more during my metamorphosis since I'd arrived than I had years at university, and I took comfort that it was turning out to be for the best—even when it didn't always feel that way.

This was the underbelly of an already gruesome world. I'd spent years running from it, trying to pretend it didn't exist, and distancing myself from my childhood. Yet I was walking into it with eyes wide open now.

It would show Cristiano—and myself—that I was choosing this life. Choosing him. All of him.

And I deserved answers. I deserved the chance to look my mother's murderers in the eyes.

"It's not too late to turn around." Cristiano materialized in the darkness, shadows turning his eyes into sockets.

Awe, and a hint of fear, mingled within me as I stepped into a cool, dimly lit steel room. Little green, yellow, and red lights flashed with the hum of machinery. Not appliances, I realized as my eyes adjusted. Computers and monitors. Combined with the glass cases of books and folders lining the walls, the space looked like a high-tech museum.

And nothing like a place to keep prisoners—but how deep did it run?

I walked farther into the temperature-controlled room.

Eduardo had vanished. "Is this where you store the body parts?" I asked.

"Huh?"

I turned to Cristiano. "Legend has it you keep something from every person you kill and put it on display."

"*Ay. Señor, dame paciencia.*" He ran his hands over his face as he asked God for patience, then laughed. "Another rumor. What kind of unhinged *cabrón* do you take me for, Natalia? I'm no saint, but I don't keep a souvenir from every kill. For one, I'd need a bigger building."

Cristiano smirked, amused by his signature sick humor. In any other scenario, I'd have laughed. The rumor *was* ridiculous to the point of being comical, and of course I'd stopped believing most of what I'd heard about him a while ago. But in that moment, I couldn't get past my nerves.

"Although, I suppose, in a way, these are proverbial bodies," Cristiano added.

"I don't know what that means."

"They're files and records on every operation. Sometimes we have to act fast and on little intel, but we try to be as prepared and organized as possible." He glanced around. "There's a tunnel that connects to the house, but otherwise, this area is isolated for security purposes, and so we can work in peace. We don't want to . . . disturb anyone."

"Disturb them how?"

He cleared his throat, checked his phone, and replaced it in the pocket of his joggers. "I told you to stay upstairs. Haven't you ever heard that expression, curiosity killed the cat?"

Or, *your curiosity is an affliction*, as my father had said to me many times. This ran deeper than snooping, though.

I had to tell Cristiano I knew. I knew what he was

keeping down here. And that I was ready to get my answers, no matter how it would change my life. That was why I'd rushed down here.

Now that I was on the verge, though, the cliff under my feet crumbled more with each step. And since I couldn't see the bottom, I had to assume it was a far drop. In my experience, answers only bred more questions. Retaliation only incited more wars, more death, more revenge. And as Cristiano said—some things, I couldn't unsee.

I swallowed through my dry throat and walked over to a large control panel below a bank of computer screens. Beyond it, a glass window showed a room full of servers. "Is this the security system?"

"One of them, but it's much more than that. Intelligence on organized crime syndicates around the world, everything from narcotics, artillery, black market, prostitution, slavery, money laundering, etcetera." He stepped away, under the dim lights. "We manage data big and small, analyze it for patterns and trends, hoping to tie pieces together, such as how people move, where they start and end up, which mobs are communicating, interactions that seem off. That's just the tip of the iceberg in terms of what's happening out there."

I couldn't keep the awe from my voice. "I had no idea so much went into it."

"Takes a lot of power to reach dark corners. I . . . I don't want to hide these things from you." He pulled on his jaw, something warring in him. He didn't want to keep me out. But he probably struggled with bringing me in, too. "But some of these subjects are closed. *¿Comprendes?*"

Yes, I understood. I recognized resolution in him now. And melancholy. I didn't argue. Things that upset someone like him must scrape the bottom of humanity. I was likely better off not knowing.

My eyes scanned over the shelved and alphabetized binders. Some had people's names, others listed businesses, cartels, or just initials and dates. "Why isn't all of this digitalized?"

"Everything is encrypted, but sometimes, nothing is safer than paper. I assure you, the government has its own hackers, and many officials would like to put a stop to what we're doing."

I frowned. "Helping people?"

"We have all kinds of unlawful ventures, Natalia. They're how we fund our more benevolent ones. Arms trafficking has been very good to me, and I need that income to continue." He massaged the back of his neck. "We have a role. We're the bad guys; the government is the good guy. They don't like when we upset the balance. We're not supposed to do their jobs for them."

"They don't want the press finding out," I inferred. "It would make them a laughing stock."

"The press or other world leaders. Wealthy people, too, who'd take out entire towns to keep the information we have sealed. Fortunately, we don't do what we do for press or for anyone else. But arms trafficking, money laundering, narcotics, freighting—they act as a cover and keep our bank accounts full."

I faced him again. He stood still, hands in the pockets of his joggers, tracking me with his eyes. Cristiano had endless patience. I couldn't imagine my father or Diego walking me through all of this so candidly. They preferred to shield me. To put me in a box. Not Cristiano. For him to tell me not to come down here, it must be bad. I owed him the same trust he'd put in me—I had to include him in my decision of whether or not I was ready to face what lie ahead.

"Are the Valverdes here?"

He glanced at my hands as I twisted my ring around my finger. "*Sí.*"

"Where?" I asked. "What else is down here, Cristiano?"

He worked his jaw side to side before answering, "Every kingpin needs a dungeon, Natalia. It's just the way it is. You'll be glad for it, once you've found out what they've done."

"I already know."

His eyes fell shut. "What do you know?"

"I figured it out. They hired the *sicario* who killed my mother, didn't they?"

He made fists in his pockets and opened his eyes, darting them around the room until they landed on a desk. He strode to it, picked up a two-way radio, and paused. Glancing at the floor, he sighed, shook his head, and said into the speaker, "Make them scream."

My stomach dropped with his sinister command, but Cristiano didn't stop there. He tossed the radio down, went to a closet door, and hoisted a blue bucket with both hands to carry it across the room.

I was about to scold him for lifting things that could threaten his health when he dropped the bucket with a *thud* at my feet.

It was full of sand.

El Polvo. I touched my throat as it closed, as if I was about to learn firsthand his trademark method of delivering death.

A cacophony of deep, guttural screams sounded from somewhere in the building.

I spun, my pulse jumping as I tried to determine where it was coming from. "What is that?"

"*That* is the part of this world you're about to walk into. Are you sure you're ready?"

The yelling stopped, but it didn't halt the shiver working its way up my spine. I'd known this would happen. I had to stay strong. "You're trying to scare me away again, like you did back then," I said. "It didn't work when I was nine. What makes you think it will now?"

"Because you know better."

I studied the man before me. Sometimes, dark things that terrified me became bearable when I shone a light on them—bearable, and maybe even welcome. That wouldn't be the case here, but shadows weren't shields. They wouldn't keep the truth from creeping out, so why not face it head on, when I could control it? "I want answers, Cristiano. Don't I deserve them?"

"Yes, and you'll get them. But tell me the truth—does *any* part of you, however small, still want the life you had in California?" he asked, nodding behind him. "Or do you want what's behind door number two? You can't have both."

"I don't want that life anymore," I said, and it was the truth. What I didn't wonder aloud was whether I was ready for *this*. But I'd learned at a young age, from the man who stood before me—never hesitate, or *bang*! You're dead.

I tilted my head when something occurred to me. "You're giving me a choice?" I asked. "I can leave this marriage?"

He'd never lifted the threats that my family would lose his protection if *he* lost *me*. Technically, I was still his captive as much as his wife. Was he brave enough to let me choose for myself?

His eyes darkened. "If that's what you want, ask for it. See what my answer is."

His answer, I suspected, was no. But Cristiano had often said he knew me better than I thought he did, and now, that was beginning to hold true for me about him. If I asked for my freedom, Cristiano would say no. And he'd believe it. But I knew better. If I truly wanted to be let go, he'd release me.

"I promise you'll get your answers," he said. "I promise your mother's life will be avenged. But you don't need to watch this part."

My heart faltered. So it was true. "They *are* responsible," I said.

"Yes."

I expected grief to hit, but having guessed it on my own, the shock was dulled. Instead, my fingers twitched as fury burned a path through me. "I want to see them," I demanded.

"You have every right to be angry, but that can cloud your judgment."

I pointed to my chest. "It's my choice to make. Not yours. You taught me that."

He couldn't argue that. He rubbed an eyebrow, debating. "If I can't convince you to wait," he said, and paused, "then you should know more before we go in there."

I nodded him on. "I'm listening."

"One of the first missions I embarked on was locating the *sicario* who killed your mother. When your father pardoned me, that should've been enough, but I knew while I still had questions, I couldn't leave it at that." He cracked his knuckles. "Though he may have pulled the trigger, any hitman would off the Virgin Mary for the right amount of money."

I saw things through Papá's eyes now. He'd called Cristiano "ruthless" and "relentless" in his pursuit of the assassin, and I'd scoffed. But he'd been right. "The *sicario* admitted to being hired by a rival cartel—¿*verdad*?" I asked. "That's what my father told me."

Cristiano nodded. "We learned the hit had been ordered by the Valverdes, but it was common knowledge that they'd been out of the game a while. Unlike other federations that crumbled and eroded over time, the Valverdes vanished practically overnight."

"And that was what tipped you off that there might be more to it."

He clicked his tongue. "If there was a puzzle there, I was going to solve it. Especially having you here as my wife and knowing you still thought I'd had a hand in her assault."

I walked forward. "I don't think you killed her," I said, stopping in front of him. "I told you that, and to stop pursuing it."

"You don't think so, no. But you don't *know*, either. And it's been eating me alive."

"What has?"

He frowned down at me. "That over time, my wife may learn to trust me, and maybe even love me—but always, a small piece of her would question that day and what she'd seen." He looked away from me, but not before pain crossed his normally controlled features. "If I can't answer that question for you once and for all, if I can't give you closure, and the safety to give me your complete and unrelenting trust—then I don't deserve it."

Oh. My heart broke for him. From the day I'd arrived, up until recently, I'd been desperately trying to uncover Cristiano's motives for bringing me here. And he'd been showing me them all along. Starting in the church. His proposal, the lasso ceremony, the paperwork to legalize our union, my mother's rosary, the flowers, and his vows—*none* of it had been a mockery. He'd gone about it the wrong way, but that didn't make it less real.

Love and devotion, that he could give and have returned, was the *everything* he sought. The only things he couldn't take, buy, or command. And he didn't think he'd ever truly get those from me until the chapter of my mother's death had been closed. Until he closed it for me.

I stepped into him, placing my hands on his chest. I wanted to take him in my arms and soothe that ache by finally giving myself to him. *Later.* Now, I could only apologize. "*Lo siento,* Cristiano."

"Don't be sorry." He circled my wrists, keeping my hands against his pecs. "You're smart not to trust words, mine or anyone else's." His voice dropped. "You *do* trust actions, though—so I acted."

My scalp prickled. "You brought them here."

"To confess everything. To rid your mind of *any* doubt about me. To assure you that where your mother's death is involved, I'm innocent."

"I know you are. I don't doubt you anymore." I slid my palms higher, relishing the power beneath them. "You never said why they vanished."

"That's what I'm going to find out." He looked away. "You heard them scream, Natalia. You know what I'm about to do. I'll get the information I want, and a confession for you, but it could be days until I do. Be satisfied until then. I'll bring you back when the pigs are ready to squeal."

That was fair. I'd get to hear it from their mouths. But I'd begged for answers so many times. Patience had been forced on me. If I went upstairs, I'd just go back to waiting. And after all these years, I wanted to do something.

"I want to act, too," I said.

Maybe I'd regret it, but my mind had been made up the moment I'd realized who the Valverdes were.

With a short sigh of resignation, he nodded once. "Wait here."

He left me alone in the dark with the haunting echo of grown men's screams. The idea that I thought I could exist on the surface of my internal darkness sounded so absurd now. That I could step on it, walk along it, and never trip and fall. That I could turn a blind eye to the way I'd grown up and to my father's business—and that I expected Diego to do the same.

California had been a bubble. My father had called it like it was—a life there with Diego would never have happened.

It wouldn't have been enough for either of us.

Maybe diving in head first into darkness was equally foolish. But there didn't seem to be any in-between, and I'd learned through Cristiano that ignorance only left me vulnerable.

I went into the closet from which Cristiano had taken the sand bucket. On the shelves sat chains I'd seen used to tow trucks, with massive hooks at the ends. Braided rope as thick as my forearm. A chainsaw.

With a noise, I turned. Cristiano stood in a doorway opposite me. "*Ándale*," he said. "Come on."

I went to him. He nodded for me to pass through first. The door closed behind us with a resolute *click*. Walking through the hallway was like taking a tunnel to Hell. Gone were the steel walls and the comforting buzz of justice at work, replaced with the underbelly of the mountain, wood scaffolding, and masculine, muffled grunts.

The air became dank. Musty. My sneakers chewed dirt on the concrete as we made a right, and then another, until Cristiano opened a door and gestured for me to enter.

As my eyes adjusted, blood drained from my face.

Weeks ago, the scene before me would've been enough to send me running, but not before I'd called Cristiano every horrible name in the book. Now, I understood better.

There was more than one way to make the world a better place. Good didn't always prevail.

Sometimes, monsters had to take the reins.

12

NATALIA

F our shirtless men with duct-taped mouths stared back at me. Flanked by Alejandro and Eduardo, they'd been hooked to the low ceiling by their chained wrists, their toes barely grazing the dirt floor.

Four men, when Cristiano had hoped for one at best.

Four lives hanging in the balance.

Three were around my father's age or older, and the last even younger than I was, possibly still a teenager.

Their bodies seemed mostly unharmed, but bruises darkened their faces. Multicolored confetti underneath them was evidence they'd been tasered.

To my embarrassment, I was too shocked to even move. Knowing these things happened, even hearing them from the next room, was entirely different than witnessing them.

As a rivulet of blood slid from the corner of one man's mouth, the contents of my stomach churned.

But I'd promised myself that I could do this. So when Cristiano said, "*Fíjate bien*"—look closer—I did.

"Read their tattoos," Cristiano instructed.

"What tattoos?" I asked.

Only a few decorated the older men, but they were simply faded sketches that meant nothing to me.

Cristiano guided me forward, staying close enough that I felt his heat even through my hoodie. It wasn't until I was standing within arm's reach of the eldest man that I saw it. Faint, nearly erased ink in scrawling Gothic lettering across his chest. The other two older men had the same word. "Valverde," I read.

"They tried to have them removed. Like cowards."

Two of the four men jerked, their chains and muffled cries echoing around us.

"*Silencio*." Eduardo smacked one in the back with the butt of his AR-15, and they went quiet. The youngest and the eldest of the four both remained still.

"Perhaps they should've cut their names off if they didn't want to be found," Cristiano said, walking toward the men, his back lengthening so he stood at his full height. "They're going to confess their sins. Whatever it takes. I want you to hear it from their fucking mouths."

And if I told Cristiano that I believed, down to my very core, that he was innocent—would he still proceed with whatever he had planned?

I met the pleading eyes of the youngest one. He couldn't have been anything more than a toddler when this had happened.

"What if they didn't do it?" I asked Cristiano.

"I didn't hunt them down to ask *if* they did. I brought them here to find out *why*."

A sense of dread worked through me. For more than eleven years, I'd wished for answers. Now, they'd be granted by the last man on Earth I'd have expected them from. My husband showed me more every day that he made his own destiny, and that I could make mine.

Cristiano paced, pausing in front of each man. "You know why you're here. You ordered a hit on Bianca Cruz. This is her daughter. *My wife.*" He met eyes with one, and the ferocity in Cristiano's gaze made even *my* stomach drop. He shrugged in that menacing way he'd perfected. "The more you cooperate, the faster this will end—but I'm a merciful man," he said in a tone that was anything but compassionate. "I'll let one of you go—the first to confess."

None of them reacted, not that they really could, but their silence got under my skin. The lives of everyone I cared about had been irrevocably changed for the worse because of the men in front of me.

Maybe they needed to be forced to speak.

The thought caught me off guard.

And brought understanding of Cristiano and Diego in a new way. I'd fantasized about justice for my mother's killer, but not in the direct, brutal way that was currently on offer. I'd thought a bullet in the *sicario's* head was a way of evening the score, but that was nothing. It'd been over before I'd even known it was happening, before I'd had a moment to relish the payback.

Cristiano turned to me. "This is where you get off the ride."

That was it? I'd come for more, though I couldn't say what exactly. Was I willing to witness torture? And if so, what holes would it fill within me to watch men crucified for a decade-old crime?

Even as their gazes burned into me, Cristiano and I locked eyes—until the eldest of the four shook his chains. Cristiano turned to him. His gray eyes morphed from dull to expressive as he tried to tell us something from behind his gag.

Alejandro and Eduardo exchanged a look. Cristiano nodded once. "Let him speak."

Eduardo ripped the tape off his mouth. The man stretched his jaw but otherwise seemed unfazed. "*Soy Vicente*," he said hoarsely. "I am—"

"Vicente Valverde," Cristiano said. "The patriarch."

"*Sí*. I knew Costa. I can tell you everything you want to know, since I made the cursed deal myself."

At the mention of my father's name, I stepped forward. "What deal?"

"I must say," Cristiano said, taking my elbow to draw me nearer to him, "knowing your reputation, I thought you'd be the last to crack. Not the first."

Vicente grunted. "I'm not getting out of here alive. There's no point trying to save myself." He twisted in his restraints to make eye contact with the other two men his age, and an agreement seemed to pass between them. "I'll tell you the whole truth on one condition."

Eduardo laughed with such exaggeration, he showed off a missing molar. "He's setting conditions, boss. This should be good."

Cristiano cocked his head at Vicente. "Go ahead."

"Kill me quickly once you have what you want—but spare my grandson and brothers. They're the only remaining members of my family."

Eduardo laughed again, and Alejandro joined in.

"Why would I agree to that?" Cristiano asked.

"My family advised against my strategy. They warned me it could fail and backfire—but I was in charge, and I made the call." With a curt nod, Vicente added, "My grandson was just a boy when this happened. He's only seventeen."

Seventeen? My palms sweat, but I kept from wiping them on my shorts so I wouldn't appear nervous.

"All his life, he's been forced into hiding and poverty," Vicente said, "and he has potential. Let them live, and they would be indebted to you. They could be great soldiers."

"Fuck you," Cristiano said, his back going rigid. "*Tienes huevos*—you have the nerve to ask for mercy? I spent eleven years of *my* life in hiding, and I started them in poverty, because of you."

The teenager twisted in his chains. I wasn't used to seeing such fright in someone's eyes. Most people in this world had already been inured to this kind of thing, but like me, he was clearly in new territory.

"My grandson is fascinated with this world but has never been allowed to be a part of it." Vicente became more animated as his pride shone through. "Instead, he put his energy into computers. He can't fight, I admit. But he can find things on the Internet."

Cristiano wouldn't kill a teenager who'd done nothing wrong. I wouldn't let him. Would I? As my eyes moved between each of them, I couldn't help seeing the poetic justice in taking from Vicente as he'd taken from me.

Cristiano walked toward the wide-eyed teenager and looked him up and down. "What's his name?"

"Gabriel."

"Tell us everything," Cristiano said, turning back to Vicente, "and my wife may decide Gabriel's fate."

Had I been alone, I would've gulped. I wasn't strong enough for that yet—to pull the trigger when there was gray area, even when it needed to be done. Was that what it meant to stand by Cristiano's side? To deal revenge where it was owed, and make decisions that I may never discover to be right or wrong?

It *was* those things, but maybe it was also about knowing when to pull back. There was strength in walking away, and in forgiveness, too.

For the boy, maybe—but not the others.

"Unchain me," Vicente said.

"Keep his wrists and ankles bound." Cristiano grabbed a lightweight, plastic patio chair from one corner of the room and stuck it in the spot where Vicente had been standing.

The old man eased into it, rolling his neck a few times. "Come closer, Natalia Cruz," he said.

My hands tingled. He said my name like *un abuelo* beckoning his granddaughter, as if he'd always known me. Cristiano returned to my side and put a hand to my upper back to guide me toward the old man.

Vicente peered up, looking between the two of us. "When your parents fell, Cristiano, there was nobody to take over the cartel. You boys were too young. I wanted de la Rosa's territories. But Costa had the same thought. So we went to war over them."

"I remember," Cristiano said.

Cristiano's presence, and his big, warm palm on my back, gave me the security to ask questions. "Who won?"

"It's not so simple," Vicente said. "Costa was more powerful, and he succeeded at first, taking jurisdiction over enough turf to push us out—but with his own business expanding faster than ever, and your grandfather no longer around to help, it became too much for him to handle. He started losing control. We got hungrier, fought harder, and at one point, we held the majority. Then we lost it. Back and forth, this went on. An epic turf war that lasted eight years."

My jaw dropped. "Eight *years*?"

I looked to Cristiano, who confirmed the story with a nod. "You were only one when it started," he told me.

"And nine when it ended," I said quietly. Nine years old when I'd looked up from the floor at blood-splattered boots. When I'd said goodnight to my mother for the last time.

"For eight years, I watched my men die," Vicente said. "First, mules, runners, then *hermanos*, cousins, friends, their parents, their children. It had to end. I was losing too many people. My livelihood suffered."

I shifted feet. "How did it end?"

He glanced at the ground, lifting up and resettling in the chair. "Your father's no saint, you know. He has taken out entire bloodlines."

Cristiano slid his hand up to my shoulder. "Answer her."

Vicente raised his haunted gray eyes to me. "It was business. It wasn't personal. Until, of course, it was."

Chills spread down my bare legs. I stuck my hands in the pockets of my hoodie. "What do you mean?"

"Everyone knew Costa had one weakness, and one weakness only. With my cartel dwindling and on the verge of collapsing, I had to make a bold move and take it all, or we'd die off."

I knew what was coming. Despite craving answers for so long, looking brutal truth in the face proved difficult. I wanted to turn away until Cristiano squeezed my shoulder reassuringly, even as his voice carried threat. "Continue," he ordered.

"We took out the hit on Bianca," Vicente said. "We hired the *sicario*, and we saw it through to the end."

His confession thickened the already dank air in the small, grimy chamber. That was it. The final pieces in the puzzle of her death. Nothing all that remarkable. An explanation too small to do her vibrant life justice. A story I'd heard too many times—a grab at power that resulted in lives lost. I gulped around the lump rising in my throat.

"Why?" I asked, hating how my voice cracked. "Why did she have to die?"

"To incapacitate your father," Vicente said simply. "Everyone knew how much he cared for her, and that her death would cripple him. So I formed my plan around that." The chains around his wrists *clinked* as he rested his elbows on his thighs. "Immediately after the hit, we expected Costa to do one of two things. One, he'd fall into a grief so deep, he'd barely notice our invasion until it was complete. And by then, it would be too late."

"And the second?" Cristiano asked.

"Draw him out." Vicente slowly lifted his eyes to my husband, tilting his head as he peered at Cristiano.

When he didn't proceed, Cristiano asked, "Meaning?"

"What would you do if someone took your Natalia from you? How far would you go?" Vicente asked, pausing. "And how easy of a target would you become?"

Cristiano stiffened behind me, taking a moment to respond. "Bianca's assassination would send Costa into a tailspin. He'd lose control," he said slowly, working through it. "React out of passion, not logic—lash out, become vulnerable, and get himself killed."

Vicente nodded. "I admit, I violated an unspoken rule amongst cartels back then—you don't touch a fellow king-pin's family. But I was desperate. I did what I had to do to save my people."

I fisted my hands in my pockets to try to stem the tremble making its way through me. I understood his reasoning better than I should. Being a liability to Cristiano and to my father had almost gotten *me* killed. "Look around," I said. "You didn't save them."

"No. Because Costa *didn't* expose himself to retaliation as we'd hoped. He holed up in his castle to grieve, but he surrounded himself with guards and advisors"—Vicente shifted his eyes to me—"keeping his young daughter close in the aftermath."

Cristiano's hand moved to the back of my neck, under my hairline. I pulled at my collar. Cristiano was sweating, too, but Vicente most of all. "That doesn't explain why you left," Cristiano said.

"Costa's business carried on usual," Vicente said. "It got even stronger, as you both know. And we grew weaker. We'd missed any opportunity to attack, and going up against him at that point would've been a losing battle. So it made sense to pack up what was left of my family and relocate . . ."

"Relocate." Cristiano snorted. "You disappeared, practically overnight."

He nodded. "Because there was evidence tying me to Bianca's murder."

"That was reason enough to flee?" I asked.

"Think of your husband," he said to me. "Of how he'd react in Costa's shoes. If he'd do all this to avenge you mother, what would he do for you?"

I didn't have to consider it too hard. Cristiano had pursued the *sicario* for a decade so he could bring him to my father's feet to get his head blown off.

"I'd weed through every person I had to, yanking out the rotting roots of the cartel responsible—until they were gone," Cristiano said, and under his breath, added, "as I will do to Belmonte-Ruiz."

Vicente nodded. "When I learned the evidence existed, I knew we had to get out of town as fast as possible. If the truth came out, Costa would hunt me, and every member of my family, until we'd been eradicated." He paused for a hacking cough against his shoulder. "It was the right choice. Especially since I heard, later, that Bianca was raped that day. I'm sorry, Natalia. That was never supposed to happen."

I swayed, or the ground underneath me did. I'd suspected that. Truthfully, deep down, I'd known it. Over time, I'd come to understand her ripped dress and the signs of her struggle for what it was. But nobody had ever said it to me outright.

Cristiano held me up by my biceps and said against my ear, "Stay strong. For that alone, Vicente will die. Today, if he's lucky. Or over time, if you decide he's not."

Vicente glanced over at his brothers. "I've told you all I know. I've answered your questions." He turned his face forward. "So will you meet my condition, Natalia? Spare my family. Please. Gabriel is innocent. My brothers opposed the assassination."

Still reeling from everything I'd just learned, my legs threatened to give out. Mercy? He was in no place to ask for it. I was in no place to give it. I'd gotten what I'd come for. What Cristiano had sought for me. *Closure.* But it didn't feel as if anything had ended. I could finally picture clearly what had happened in my mother's final moments, and it sickened me. The fear she must've felt—it moved through me now, leaving my stomach weak and my head swimming.

A stranger in the bedroom she'd shared with my father.

"I'll take her upstairs," Cristiano said, somewhere in the distance. "We won't decide anything now."

"*Claro,*" Alejandro answered.

Cornering her. Violating her.

Before or after he'd raided the safe? And why?

Where had he found her? In her bathroom, by the bed? Had she been in the closet when he'd suddenly appeared from the tunnel . . .?

I let Cristiano guide me toward the exit, unable to see through my haze of mounting questions.

Until . . .

"Wait." I halted before we reached the door, planting my feet where they were. "Wait."

"*¿Qué pasa, mi amor?*" Cristiano asked. "What is it?"

I turned back to face Vicente. Cristiano released me but stayed close. "Only my mother, father, and I knew about the secret passageway the assassin used to enter the bedroom. How did *you* discover it?"

"*Ah.* Well. That part is simple." Vicente's gaze traveled up, over my head, and fixed on Cristiano. "Someone was more than happy to leave the secret door unlocked for us. To carry out the hit, we needed a little help from the inside. And we found it—in a de la Rosa brother."

No. Goose bumps started at my scalp and blazed over my skin. *Cristiano,* my mind said. He'd had some of the highest security clearance at the time. For more than eleven years, I'd blamed him for this crime. I'd had no other explanation. It would be easy for me to slot him into the role as guilty. I turned my head over my shoulder to look at him—my husband.

Cristiano stared back at me. He swallowed but didn't deny it. I was learning to read him better. A blank expression that once might've come off as indifference, was now patience for how long it'd taken me to get here. Anguish that I might not. Struggle not to declare his innocence—and belief in me that I'd arrive at the truth on my own.

My parents had trusted him. He'd been loyal to them. He'd brought me all of this to avenge my mother's death. I could make up some of my faithlessness in him by having confidence that he'd never have cooperated with the Valverdes.

But if he hadn't, that left only one answer. And not only did it turn my life into a lie—it called everything

about me, as a person, into question. My choices, my feelings, my judgment.

The ache of the truth permeated throughout me,
numbing my hands, stiffening my neck as I turned forward
again to address Vicente.

I barely heard myself speak the name that I'd once
revered, but which continued to fall even further from its
long smashed pedestal each day. And now, it seemed, it had
finally hit the bottom.

"Diego."

13

NATALIA

In the dark and dank underbelly of the mountain, Vicente Valverde confirmed the truth. "Diego de la Rosa let us into the Cruz compound," he said from a plastic chair that wobbled on an uneven dirt floor. "But then, he turned my plan against me."

"How?" Cristiano's question rumbled through the small room.

"An assassin only works for the highest bidder. He sold your brother proof that I was behind the murder, and Diego threatened to expose me if I didn't leave." He took a rattling breath as his expression darkened, the first flame of anger I'd seen in him yet. "I should've known if the bastard would betray Costa, the man who'd taken him in as a boy, he'd turn on me, too."

"And us," Cristiano said.

Vicente was only another in the long line of those Diego had wronged.

But at least with him, it'd been business. Not for me. This was deeply personal.

"One of the biggest mistakes I've ever made was

underestimating Diego de la Rosa," Vicente said. "We spread rumors of our deaths and hid our identities so he'd never come looking for us."

"You were a liability to him," Cristiano said. "If anyone found out Diego had helped . . ."

"Diego's life would be over." After another coughing fit, he turned his head and spit in the dirt. "With Bianca's death, Diego ingratiated himself to Costa," he said and wiped the corner of his mouth with his bare shoulder. "He rose in the ranks of the Cruz cartel. Became a trusted advisor. And wrapped his grip so tightly around Costa's daughter that she'd do anything for him—including turn against her father if he pulled the right strings."

My face heated as all gazes turned to me. I'd happily tangled myself in a snake's grip and had never even felt the squeeze. Everyone in the room knew it, too.

Including Cristiano.

I'd been a fool.

With my mortification, tears heated the backs of my eyes. I couldn't stay in that room any longer without breaking down. And I'd never give the Valverdes the satisfaction.

I'd heard enough anyway.

I turned and walked past Cristiano, hurrying down the underground hallway that too closely resembled a tunnel, through the proverbial museum of body parts, and climbed the stairs.

My fists shook. I didn't think of going anywhere, but my feet carried me toward the house.

How could it be? *How*?

Diego had held my hand at my mother's funeral and many times since. He'd picked out my dress for the service and worked with the state to get paperwork in order. Later, he'd helped Papá with the details of arranging the elaborate mausoleum that would become my mother's final resting place.

Maybe my blindness to his true character could've been excused then, while I'd been grieving.

But for the eleven years after? What excuse did I have for that?

I reached for the door handle to walk in the house. My hand trembled along with the rest of me, the threat of sobs immobilizing me. I fought to hold them in. I couldn't break down here, in front of the staff, and where anyone from the Badlands could come across me. They, and Cristiano, depended on me to be strong.

They were fools to depend on me at all.

If I believed this to be true about Diego, then I had to admit a much scarier truth.

I'd been tricked and manipulated to the point I didn't even know what parts of me were real and what had been molded by Diego.

Hands turned me by my shoulders, and arms surrounded me, pulling me to a strong, sturdy chest. The deep, controlled bass of Cristiano's voice hummed in my ear. "You're okay," he said. "I've got you. I'm here."

Instantly, my body loosened, my tears subsiding. I'd felt this sense of security before, breathed in this same masculine mix of sweat and dirt. Unlikely as it'd been, Cristiano's solid body had acted as comfort in the tunnel. I'd clutched his neck, silently begging him not to let go, not to leave me behind.

But that hadn't been the only time I'd been soothed this way.

Days later, Diego had held me in the safety of his arms as we'd lowered Mamá into the ground.

All the while, he'd been responsible. His comfort had

been a lie. Maybe Cristiano's had been back then, too—maybe it was now.

Cristiano guided me up the staircase to the top floor. In our bedroom, he released me to shut the door behind himself. "Natalia—"

"Every *Día de los Muertos*, Diego lit a candle for her," I said. I looked around the foreign room, its quiet fireplace, white gauze curtains, the empty space where the mirror had been, a bar cart where Cristiano sometimes fixed a drink in the evenings. How had I gotten here? I'd been moved into this bedroom like a pawn. "He brought her favorite dessert to the house, and flowers to her as *una ofrenda*." The remoteness of my voice matched my sagging posture, my curled fists. "He listened to me talk about her for hours. He held me as I cried."

"He manipulated you."

Jarred from the memories, I turned to look at Cristiano. "What he did to me weeks ago, he did out of desperation." Even if I found it vile, at least I could understand *why* he'd lied to get me to the church—his life had been on the line. "To trade me for his own safety—that is an act of a desperate man." I turned my body to Cristiano as my voice rose. "But to allow a woman who'd treated him like a son to get *raped* and *murdered* in her own bedroom?" I yelled. "That's not desperation. It's devoid of humanity. Did you know about this?"

Cristiano took my anger without flinching. "I had suspicions—"

"And you didn't tell me?"

"They were baseless," he said. "All I had to go on was the fact that the door had been unlocked. And when I had him alone at *La Madrina*, I could see firsthand how angry he was with Costa—"

"For?"

"For killing our parents."

The answer went down easily, because I'd been over this scenario a million times in my head. Only, it was never kindhearted, gentle Diego who'd been nursing a grudge. It'd been his menacing, ruthless brother.

My body shook so violently, tears almost fell. I bit them back. Vengeance against my father for killing the de la Rosas. I'd been right all along—but I'd never been so wrong.

My limbs weakened with the churn of my stomach. I reached out to steady myself on something, worried I might vomit.

"Come, let me hold you," Cristiano said, stepping forward as he reached for me.

Instinctively, I moved back, my eyes on the ground between us.

I'd once thought him incapable of experiencing pain, but I didn't have to see his face to know I'd hurt him.

He dropped his arm to his side, walked to the bar cart, and poured himself a drink.

Why was I shutting him out? Cristiano was not to blame for this. He was a victim of Diego's machinations, too. I urged myself to go to him. His body, words, and tenderness held comfort.

But so had Diego's. I'd found a home in him more times than I could count, and each time, I was more the fool. Diego was the reason my mother was dead; that made every single touch of his, every word from his mouth, a lie.

My judgment couldn't be trusted.

I'd been emotionally vulnerable when Diego had helped me pick up the pieces of my shattered life following her death. He'd advised my father in his darkest hour and molded me into the girl he'd wanted me to be. Who was to say Cristiano hadn't done the same, purposely severing my relationship with Diego so he could be the one to fill the void it'd left? So he could turn me into his queen, as he often said?

My past had been a lie.

The foundation I'd built my life on had been nothing more than smoke and mirrors.

And it was crumbling under my feet.

My mind replayed one of the few conversations I'd had with Diego about his parents. Maybe the only honest conversation we'd ever had.

"Did you ever think of taking vengeance for their death?"

Diego didn't answer right away. As seconds ticked by, I grew uneasy. There was only one person he would take revenge on. My father.

"In my darkest moments, yes," he admitted.

Diego had played me.

Cristiano was suddenly in front of me, holding out a tumbler with a few swigs of neat, amber liquor. "You're in shock. Drink this. It will help."

I took it from him. Sniffed it. Sipped it, holding it in my mouth. Brandy. I swallowed and handed it back. It would ease the pain for a while, but I didn't want that. I had to feel the mistakes I'd made.

"I know you're hurting. And if it's the last thing I do . . ." He slugged back the liquor and gripped the glass as he said, "Diego will pay for that."

"He said he *loved* me." The words tumbled smoothly over my brandy tongue. "I loved him back."

"If that's all it takes, I will love you too. More than he ever did. More than he ever could."

My heart reached for him. It was incomprehensible how much I wanted that after hating Cristiano for so long. And that after all the ways I'd pushed him away, he was still standing here. "How?" I nearly choked out. How had he not run for the hills yet? "You manipulated me, too. You forced me into this marriage, locked me up in this house, and made me fall for you."

"Natalia. My darling." He took my jaw in his free hand and pulled my face to his. "I fell for you first."

"Then why did you almost die on me?" I gripped his t-shirt to push him away but couldn't bring myself to do it. I'd lost too much already—but with Cristiano, why did it feel as if I had more to lose than ever? I pulled him closer as my chin wobbled. "I hate him. Help me forget. You promised you'd make me forget his name."

Cristiano's expression hardened as he set his jaw and looked away. "And I told you never to come to me again if *he* was the reason. I will not fuck you to make you forget his name."

"Then fuck me so I know *only yours*. I am willing. And I need this, Cristiano."

His chest heaved with an inhale. What was he waiting for? He had his permission. Not that he or anyone needed it. If I could be tricked into sleeping with the man who'd deceived my family in the worst way, and if my mother could be forced by a stranger, then really—what the fuck did any of this matter? What was so special about it?

I took his empty glass, set it on the nightstand, and slipped my hand between us to touch him. My body thrilled when he stirred against my palm. Nothing could soothe me now except this. Except to be taken so hard, I could think of nothing else. "This is what you wanted," I whispered to him. "It's what *I* want."

"I can't," he said, his voice strangled but determined. "Not like this. You're in pain, and you're angry."

"But I'm willing." I fluttered my lashes up at him. "I'm giving you this gift—"

"I won't do it."

Frustration zapped through me. "Then leave me alone!" I screamed as I shoved him. "Get out. ¡*Vete ya*!"

I turned away, fury eating me up inside. How could he turn me away when I needed him?

Did he feel differently now that he realized how badly I'd been played?

I was a traitor to my mother.

But so what? Cristiano had me where he wanted me. Why not take what he'd often proclaimed belonged to him?

When he spoke again, his voice was even calmer against my rage echoing through the room. "You said Diego loved you, but you're wrong, Natalia. Love is *I'd die for you*, not *would you die for me?*" With his pause, his beautiful, unsettling words hung in the air. "Diego had a certain fondness for you, yes, but it wasn't enough. He took your virginity from you after manipulating you into offering it, but I'm going to walk away from you now to show you the difference between his love and mine. To show you that *true love* means putting you first. Always."

His words struck me at my core. Cristiano would do what Diego couldn't—he'd give up what he wanted, what he'd fought for, what would make him more powerful. For me.

"Is that what you need?" I heard the hesitation in his voice. It wasn't easy for him to do nothing when his whole life had been about action. "Space?"

Shamefully, I kept my back to him. I couldn't look at his handsome, pained face and remember that I'd chosen the wrong brother back then—or I'd fall so deep into a black hole of regret, I wasn't sure how I'd get out. "Yes."

"I'll be right downstairs if you need me."

After a moment, the door closed with a soft *click*.

If you need me. Deafening silence remained in his wake.

Nineteen years ago, Cristiano had come to my dad for help. That had ended in a bullet in his parents' heads as he and Diego had watched. What had happened in the eight years since? How had that changed them? Who would I have become if Diego hadn't been there?

I'd let him soothe and kiss and touch, when he'd been the villain all along. And Cristiano had been the hero, showing me respect, even when I'd been a pawn.

I trusted him. But I could trust myself *with* him?

I'd accused him of his brother's crimes time and time again. And even now, he'd taken every hit I'd had to give and come back for more. He hadn't struck back or left me to fend for myself.

Pressure in my chest eased as everything I knew about Cristiano finally became clear. From a young age, he'd defended those who couldn't defend themselves. He'd betrayed his family—an even greater sin in our world than bartering with human lives—and joined ours out of a sense of duty. And he'd been punished for it. Accused of a crime he hadn't committed, driven away, and hunted by the true perpetrator.

Cristiano's truth had fallen on deaf ears. And yet he trusted me to heal him.

I couldn't believe in myself just then, but Cristiano understood that. It was the reason he'd walked away. And that was why I *could* believe in him.

I spun, raced through the door, and down the hall to find Cristiano descending the staircase. "Wait," I said.

He turned back instantly, concern etched in the lines of his face. "What is it?"

I stared at him and saw someone else. I saw *him*. My protector as a child, and my protector now—against enemies who made themselves known and the far more dangerous kind. Those who didn't.

Cristiano was my ally. He was aggrieved.

And he was my husband.

"I . . . I don't need you to walk away to prove your love. I need—"

He strode back up the stairs. When he reached the landing, he opened his mouth to speak, but I was done talking. I gripped his cheeks, pulled down his face, and kissed him with everything I had. He yanked me against his body, one arm strong around my waist, and anchored me as he took a handful of my hair at the back of my head. How could I have ever thought him cold? He was everything warm now as his eager mouth, spicy with brandy, lured me in, our tongues lashing. Then he stopped. Drew back. Slowed the kiss with short pecks from his full lips. His fist in my hair eased, massaging my scalp, then cradling my head.

"*Shh*," he said, brushing his mouth over my cheek, which was wet with silent tears I hadn't realized I'd shed.

I pulled back to look into his eyes. The pain in them, the sheer *relief*, hurt me. Diego had broken both of our hearts, and too many times, Cristiano and I had hurt each other. It was enough. My voice faltered as my tears fell faster. "I—I need you."

"I'm not going *anywhere*. Not now, not ever."

In a moment, I was in his arms as he carried me back to the room, laid me on the bed, and removed my sneakers and socks.

I grabbed his hand as he stood. "Don't go."

He leaned forward and cleared hair from my cheek. "I meant what I said. I'm not leaving your side."

He climbed over me, slipped beneath the covers, and hugged me to his chest. The past hour, the only thing I'd been able to control were my sobs. Knowing Cristiano had me, I released them, breaking down into my pillow as he whispered soothingly into my ear, his hold around me never loosening.

"I let her down," I said through my cries. "I chose the enemy."

"*Shh*," he said, nuzzling my ear. "Take comfort in the fact that Bianca loved you more than anything in the world. And that now we'll all get the closure we deserve."

Closure. This was what Cristiano had risked his life for. To give me answers, knowing they'd hurt me, when nobody else would.

The boy who'd played with my heart was no match for the man who, I was fairly certain, had loved me for a while.

Tears soaked my pillow, but not all of them came from pain as a thought formed. An utter and painstaking betrayal had given me the greatest gift I hadn't even known possible—the permission to fall in love with my husband.

"Thank you," I whispered.

He squeezed me to him. To anyone else, he was a boss, a leader, a killer. To me, he was just Cristiano. Up until very recently, I hadn't let him be that.

My puffy eyes ached. I closed them, suddenly exhausted. He'd known better than I had what I'd wanted and what I'd needed. Finally, they were the same thing. For years, I'd tried to escape the truth, but I was beginning to see . . .

This was my destiny.

I belonged by Cristiano's side.

He was the man I wanted, and now I knew—he was the one I needed.

14

NATALIA

The emotional wreckage of the day before felt physical. It was all around me—and Cristiano and I were a unit in the middle of it. Sometime in the night, I'd shed my clothing and fallen asleep naked in his arms. His body curled around mine so tightly that we were practically one. His muscular legs trapped my thighs, intertwined with my calves. His arms secured my back to his chest, and our linked fingers unbreakable.

Dawn had broken on a new day, and the room around me wasn't the same.

The blues were richer, whites brighter, and the golds glimmered as if they'd just been polished. A breeze fluttered the curtains and cooled my exposed skin as Cristiano's body heated the rest of me.

Cristiano was not the same.

He'd suffered for me and because of me. He would never be innocent, but he wasn't guilty of the one crime that had kept me from trusting him. From falling into him.

Everything had changed.

There were consequences to be dealt, concessions to be made, and wrongs to right—starting here in a bed I had come to know as my own.

I knew what lay ahead. I knew what I had to do.

I wasn't the same.

My decisions were made before I'd even opened my eyes.

I'd fallen asleep in Cristiano's cocoon and had awoken transformed.

"You're up," Cristiano said.

I would've never thought the sound and feel of his voice against my ear could bring such a complete sense of calm and safety. "Stay," I said. "I couldn't say it before, on the phone, but I'm saying it now. Don't leave me. And . . ."

"And what?"

I swallowed. "I'm sorry."

"You have nothing to be sorry for. I do."

That was true, but I'd never expected to hear an apology from his mouth. I shifted under the sheets, and he loosened his grip on me so I could turn and face him. The near-black of his eyes didn't fool me anymore. I saw depth where I'd once seen bleakness. Love where I'd assumed there was hate. And a strength that had always been there. "Why?"

His arms pulled me so close, we barely had to whisper. "I shouldn't have gloated the way I did after I kissed you on our wedding day. I let Diego get to me."

Of all the things he had to be sorry for, that had never even crossed my mind. "You paid the price for it," I reminded him.

"I deserved the slap. The kiss was as real as anything else between us. It should've been our moment, but I let him steal it. I regretted my mistake immediately." He moved a strand of my hair from my cheek. "And the wedding dress. I didn't know it was Bianca's when I ripped it."

"You had it fixed," I said.

"But it will never be the same." Somehow, his gaze darkened even more. "That's all I'm sorry for, though, no matter what kind of monster it makes me. I can't apologize for anything that's led me here. I took you off the course of a life that might've been right for you and brought you down a treacherous road. My dirt road with all its bumps and potholes." He spoke with the satisfaction of a child who'd been caught stealing dessert *after* he'd filled his belly. "I'm not sorry for the things I should regret—the tattoo was fucked up, but every time I see it, I swell with pride to see that you're mine. De la Rosa men are scum, but I have broken you free of one only to chain you to another."

"And you're *not* sorry," I clarified with some amusement.

"To say so would be a lie—I'd do it all over again."

"I have a regret," I said. "Well, I have a few, I think."

He kissed my forehead. "Throw them away," he said against my skin. "They aren't worth voicing."

"I have to say one, then I'll throw it out." Cristiano had demanded one thing of Diego and me before the wedding, and I hadn't given him that. It had to have been important to him. I blinked up at him. "I wish my first time hadn't been with Diego. I thought I wanted it . . . I thought he was worthy."

"I don't give a fuck that he had you first," Cristiano said, shocking me into silence. "It means nothing. *He* means nothing." He ran his tongue along his top row of teeth. "It will be the thing I think of when I finally put a bullet in him, but still, it means nothing."

I couldn't help a small smile. "And if I beat you to it?"

"You have to find him first."

"You don't know where he is?"

He shook his head. "If he's working with Belmonte-Ruiz, then he could be with Max. I hope one leads to the other." His assessing eyes met mine. "But nostalgia is a funny thing, Natalia. If Diego were standing here now, you wouldn't be able to pull the trigger. Too much history there."

Tucking the sheet under my arm, I popped up onto one elbow. "Give me more credit than that. My blinders have been ruthlessly ripped off. I'd laugh in his face if he tried to talk his way out of it."

"And you know he would."

I touched Cristiano's stubbled cheek, running my finger along his square, angular jawline. I'd never denied his beauty, no matter my resentment toward him. Now, I was free to revel in it. I didn't want to wait any longer. "And you know what I'd say to him?"

"Tell me, *mi amor*."

"That his brother fucked me better than he could ever hope to. And that we're sending him to an early grave."

"Then I suppose I'd better fuck you, so as not to make you into a liar . . ." Cristiano bit his full bottom lip, and the small tell of his arousal made my stomach clench. "I've waited a long time for this."

"I know."

"I don't mean sex." He leaned into me until I fell onto my back, and his darkly handsome face looked down on me. He tugged the sheet to my stomach, and I sucked in a breath as cool air caressed my nipples. Licking his lips, he ran a finger between my breasts, eliciting my shudder. "I've waited for you to stop acting like a princess and start thinking like a queen."

"Nothing less would do for my king."

"I wasn't a king until you came along. *Me coronaste.* You crowned me."

I stopped his hand before it dipped underneath the sheets. "You can't just storm the castle walls. You need a strategy."

He moved his hand up to tip back my chin and graze his thumb over my bottom lip. "What should ours be, *mi reina?*"

"Invade, plunder, and destroy until I beg for the king's mercy," I said softly, letting my breath caress his finger. I pushed his chest. He rolled onto his back, and I threw a knee over him to sit astride his hips. "You took me as your prisoner. But you made the mistake of falling in love with me. And when you least expect it, I will claim my throne."

"Nothing would please a peasant like myself more." He gripped my hips and pulled me over his crotch. I inhaled as my naked clit slid along the erection straining his underwear. "But there's more to being a queen than sitting on the king's scepter."

My breasts swayed, and my long hair pooled on his chest. "What then?"

"You have decisions to make. The fate of four men rests in your hands."

I curled my fists on his chest. The whimsy of our dreamy bed and the early morning hours gave way to a brutal reality. Only one man had paid the price for my mother's death. The others awaited my sentence.

What kind of queen would I be? Fair and forgiving or cunning and ruthless?

Cristiano took my right nipple between the tips of his forefinger and thumb. I sucked in a breath when he tugged, and pleasure traveled down my stomach, ending right between my legs. "Even in times of play, you can't forget there are enemies to be dealt with. You're safe with me, but you should never completely drop your guard."

Just like in physical combat, the fight was ongoing.

"Vicente made the call," he said, "but he and his family are nobodies now. They've paid for their mistakes."

I froze, my heartbeat reverberating everywhere from my ears to my pussy. "Are you saying he's not to blame?" I asked, incredulous. "That I should *forgive* him?"

He pushed some of my hair behind my ear, but it fell forward again, curtaining us from the rest of the world— my new favorite thing. "Simply demonstrating that you can rule two ways. With the truth you want or with the facts. And the fact is, you won't gain much satisfaction from killing three old men and an innocent teen."

"So I should let them go?"

"That's up to you. Most men would say kill all four."

"What would you say?"

His eyelids fell as he slid a hand up my spine and applied pressure to my upper back. I leaned in until we were face to face, my breasts smashed into his bare chest, my clit pushing against him at a new angle. "I'm most men."

"No, you aren't. I thought you were the worst of them, but you're fair."

"Is it fair that I'd kill a man for his grandfather's sins?"

The grandson. If Vicente was to be believed, his *nieto*, Gabriel, was smart. And he had his whole life ahead of him. "You would?" I asked.

"We'd be fools to ignore history. There's too much at risk to let any of them live. The betrayal festers—look at Diego."

"Look at *you*," I said, threading my fingers in his hair, putting our lips centimeters apart. I wanted retribution—

not just for myself, but for my husband, who'd suffered—
and it would be so easy to lump Gabriel in with the others.
To turn my cheek as he paid for his family's sins. But I'd be
ignoring Cristiano's history, which was also *my* history.
"You didn't stick by your father out of familial duty likes
others would've. You chose good over bad. Maybe Gabriel
would too."

"True. But here I am, doing everything in my power to
avenge Bianca's death. And I'd do the same for you. The
grandson may not feel resentful now, but that doesn't mean
he won't." His hand dipped to cup my right ass cheek. A
little lower and to the left, and he'd be able to ease the
pulsing ache that'd been growing between my legs for
longer than I cared to admit. "Being a leader goes far
beyond wearing a crown and making demands," he said
with a squeeze. "No decision is ever easy. I'll make this one
for you if you ask me to, but don't get used to it."

He wanted me to stand on my own two feet and take
ownership over this life. If I'd been paying attention, that
was what he'd been asking of me all along. But after years
of trying to smother my curiosity and stay willingly in the
dark, I was done with that. I wouldn't let him decide
for me.

I shifted my weight on him. "I've known what I wanted
to do since I woke up."

"Yeah?" He tilted his head. "Tell me."

"The grandson can live. If you see fit, he can work
here in the Badlands for you." I met his eyes. "The rest can
die."

He stilled. "Natalia . . ."

I made a fist in his hair and stared into his eyes so he
knew I meant every word. "I don't care how you do it, but
finish Vicente and each of his brothers. I want to dump

their ashes at the base of my mother's grave so their worthless souls can spend eternity kissing her feet."

I had watched my mother die, and every single person involved was going to pay.

Including, if I had my way, the son-of-a-bitch who'd ruined my life.

15

CRISTIANO

I had never been more aroused in all of my thirty-four years. I deserved a medal for my abstinence since Natalia's arrival. With the way she was grinding against my dick, and with her order that I execute three men in her name—I was on a rocket ship headed for the moon. She was ready for me; I could see it in her eyes as her hair fell around her face, begging to be wrapped up in my fist.

Even through the haze, though, her pain lived strong. That was fine. Last night, she'd been too deep in it, and it would be a while before it subsided. But now that she'd spent the night grieving in my arms, letting me comfort her, I would give her relief and release.

"It would be an honor to avenge you and Bianca," I said.

She slid her hips back and forth, leaving a wet spot on the crotch of my underwear. "Is there anything you wouldn't do for revenge?"

"You know it's more complicated than that. Retribution can be all-consuming." I struggled to organize my thoughts with her pulsing slit growing greedy for me, but this conversation was important. "I'll never let revenge rule my life as my father and Diego did. That's my promise to you. For me—my wife, family, and people come first."

She hovered her juicy, delicious lips above mine. "I want to know how it feels to come first," she whispered.

With a short growl, I slid a hand into her hair, both pulling it and holding her where she was. "It's a path you can't come back from."

I needed her explicit permission, but I wasn't above playing dirty to get it. With my other hand on her hip, I took a handful of her ass and bucked my pelvis up, ramming my shaft against her clit.

Her eyes rolled back into her head. "Do that again."

Beg. Demand. Tell me to fuck you raw.

It had to be about me and her and nothing else. She had to want this more than she wanted to resist me or hurt Diego. My erection was turning painful, but I needed her to ask, and for it to be *now*.

With a knock on the door, we both froze. "*¿Señor?*" came Jaz's voice.

I closed my eyes and sighed. God, give me a moment of uninterrupted pleasure in this lifetime. Hadn't I earned the exquisite pleasure of fucking my horny wife for the first time? "*Vete*," I called out, sending Jaz away.

"*Es importante*," she replied.

"*Important?*" Natalia scoffed. "No. She has a sixth sense for when you and I are getting close. She wants to come between us. Ignore her."

Whether that was true or not, Jazmín was intuitive enough to know when she was needed and when she should make herself scarce. I took Natalia's ass cheeks in both hands and squeezed hard enough to send the message that this *culo* was mine when I got back—then moved her off my crotch and stood to pull on some sweats. "It could be about Max."

I shoved my hand down my pants and tried to calm my raging hard-on as I crossed the room. I hid it with the door as I leaned my head out. "*¿Qué quieres*, Jaz? It's not a good time."

"Alejandro wants you downstairs immediately."

"*Puta madre*," I cursed. "What's it about?"

She shrugged. "I'm just supposed to tell you."

"Natalia needs me here. She doesn't want to be alone."

"Of course not. She wants you all to herself, even if others need you."

I frowned at her and warned, "Jazmín."

"I'm sorry, but it's true," she said, turning away. "Alejo's waiting for you."

I sighed and closed the door before heading for my closet. "I'm sorry, *mi amor*."

"What is it?" Natalia asked.

I threw on a t-shirt, moving quickly so I could get this over with. "I'm needed downstairs."

"You're needed *here*," she called from the bed. "You always go when Jaz calls."

"I do not. This is Badlands business." On my way out of the bedroom, I stopped in my tracks. The interruption had taken care of my erection, but suddenly it threatened to return. Natalia sat with her back against the headboard, the thin white sheet tucked under her arms, barely concealing the rosy berries begging to be devoured. Her long disheveled hair fell around her bare arms. I'd resisted her for so long, and now that I had her, I was leaving her naked and wanting in our bed?

"*Qué pendejo*," I muttered about myself.

"What happened to 'this is a path you can't come back from'?" she accused. With the vitriol in her voice, I met her glare. "I guess it includes the clause 'unless Jaz needs me.'"

She was pissed, and I was just close enough to the edge to say *fuck it* and get back into bed. Especially considering Natalia's possessive side alone was sexy enough to get me going again. But if Alejandro's news had anything to do with Max, I had to go. And I had to do it now, before I changed my mind.

"I'll be back as fast as I can. *Te lo prometo*." With my promise, I bent at the hip and pecked her hard and fast, before she—or my dick—could protest. "Don't move an inch."

I descended the stairs into the dark basement control center to find Alejandro waiting with his arms crossed over his chest.

"This'd better be good," I said. "You've just put me in the doghouse with Natalia. She needs all of my attention right now."

"She'll forgive the dog if he catches her a rat."

I arched an eyebrow at him as we headed down the hall toward where Vicente and his family remained chained and silenced. Instead, he led me to a different room. Seated alone in the middle was Gabriel, Vicente's grandson, with his hands bound in front of him.

Alejandro yanked tape off the boy's mouth and nodded once. "Tell him what you told me."

Gabriel stretched his jaw but kept his eyes down. "I can help you."

I followed his gaze to a pair of broken glasses on the ground. "Look at me, boy," I said.

He raised his fearful eyes, blinking rapidly and squinting. Perhaps he needed those glasses. "I can help you find Max," he said.

I let my eyes drift over the skinny kid. I was certain I'd weighed more than him at eight years old. "How?"

"My grandfather told you I can find things on the Internet—that's like calling Lionel Messi a good soccer player."

"Lionel Messi, eh? You a sports fan?" I asked, aware of how sinister my laugh sounded as I glanced to Alejandro. "You tore me away from my distraught wife for this?"

"Coding, surveillance, dark web," the kid spoke quickly, tripping over his words, as if begging for his life. "I can do all of it. I built my first computer from discarded parts. The Internet is my sandbox . . . and that makes the world my playground."

"My intelligence team is unrivaled," I said. "They come from all over the world. Beijing, Russia, San Francisco—"

"With all due respect, sir, if that were true, you wouldn't have had a major security breach earlier this month when Belmonte-Ruiz attacked your household."

Alejandro seemed pleased—so, this was why he'd called me down here. I, on the other hand, wasn't so delighted. "How the fuck do you know about that?" I asked, stepping forward.

"All my life I've heard of the guts and glory of my grandfather, great uncles, and the cartel they built. Since we were forced into hiding, I've had to be invisible my whole life. Now, I'm better at hiding than anyone, and I know how to get information. On you, on Belmonte-Ruiz . . . even on Diego." He swallowed audibly. "When I learned he'd blackmailed my family into disappearing, I took an interest in him. I've followed him for a long time."

"Do you know where he is?" I asked.

"No, but give me a chance. I can find him."

"Why should I believe you?"

"Your men learned how to hack, but I never knew a life without it; I *am* it. I never went to school. I only know computers. Let me train with your team, and I will become the best hacker in the world," he said. "Give me a chance to prove myself before you kill me. Let me show you what I can achieve—under your guidance."

From the moment I'd heard Gabriel was Vicente's grandson, I'd known he'd have to die. I wouldn't make the same mistake I'd made with Diego. But I thought of what Natalia had said. I was the other half of that equation. I'd been right by Diego's side and had felt no resentment or anger toward Costa for what he'd done—only gratitude and loyalty.

"Why would I trust you? I'm going to kill the rest of your family regardless."

His fidgeting stopped. "I guess I understand why you have to do it. My *abuelo*, I love him, but he has lived a long life considering his odds."

Spoken like a true math whiz. Logic and reason spoke to this kid. One assassination equaled one retribution.

But then he continued, "And I saw Natalia's face in there. I feel bad. I lost my mom in all of this, too."

Huh. Either there was a heart in that motherboard or he was trying to manipulate my evident soft side for Natalia. "What do you know about Belmonte-Ruiz?" I asked.

"Not much, but I learn quickly," Gabriel said. "I know more about what you do here in the Badlands."

"It's not such a secret anymore. We have our fingers in many, uh, pies, as they say." My finger *should* have been in the most delicious pie right then—I mentally hurried Gabriel along.

"Arms, freight, money laundering—but you also traffic in people," he said, and added, "just in the wrong direction, most would say."

The hair on the back of my neck stood up. Rumors had been spreading about our operation, and that would ultimately hurt us, but there was no way the truth could've already made it to the impoverished corners of Mexico. "How do you know that?"

"I told you—I'm invisible. Your security is top-of-the-line, but I got through. You need me."

That kind of skill was lethal in the wrong hands. But in the right ones, it was an asset. How could I know who this boy was, though? His true intentions? "And what do you think of our operation?"

"You're the good guys."

"We're not," I said, crossing my arms as the fluorescent lighting overhead buzzed. "We've hurt far more than we've helped. If guts and glory are what you want, look somewhere else. We do what we have to so we survive, and to further our cause. It brings no recognition, only enemies from all sides, and that's about to get worse."

"Then you will need good intel, security, and protection. I can help. There are more and more kids like me coming up in the ranks," Gabriel said. "We know technology better than our own faces. But I have something many don't—I've known the worst of this country, and I'm willing to die before I return to it."

That rounded out his third reason for offering help. Logic, heart, and motivation for a better life. *Ay*, and thwarting death, of course. Looking to Alejandro, I cracked my knuckles. "Diego's not the one we're trying to find right now."

"Max," Gabriel stated. "Alejandro told me."

I rubbed the bridge of my nose. My hands were tied. I

had to do whatever necessary to help Max. I'd be a fool to turn down help and a fool to accept it. "You have until my patience runs out to help us find everything you can on Belmonte-Ruiz and Max's current location," I said.

"Yes, sir. Thank you, sir."

I nodded once at Alejandro. "Hand him over to the IT team. Eyes don't leave him for a second. Get him a new pair of glasses. And Alejo?"

"*Dime*," he said, inviting me to continue.

"Don't fucking disturb me again. I don't care if the sky is falling."

Now, I would go fuck my wife.

That was, if I could find her. Because when I returned, she wasn't in the bedroom.

Or the library. Or by the pool.

After I'd been all around the house, I found myself knocking on Pilar's door.

"*Adelante*," came two female voices followed by a bout of giggling, and, "¡*Embrujado*! Jinx!"

I entered the room and found Natalia on the tips of her toes in Pilar's closet, trying to reach a purse on the top shelf—and wearing jeans, socks, and a sweater over her top. Not naked as I'd left her when I'd ordered her to stay put.

I walked in, plucked the bag from the shelf, and handed it to her. "Going somewhere?"

Her fiery eyes met mine a moment before she turned away. "No. We're reorganizing Pilar's closet."

I blinked around the space. It looked as if Pilar had hardly touched a thing since her arrival. "Seems pretty damn organized to me."

"Well, Jaz's method doesn't quite make sense to us," Natalia explained.

"Why not?" I asked.

"Because it doesn't," she snapped.

Pilar's puppy-dog eyes stayed on me, waiting for my reaction—for the explosion. In deference to her history with violent men, I inhaled a breath to control my temper. "I need to speak to you, Natalia."

"After we're finished." Natalia stepped back, pinching her chin as she assessed a row of sandals. "These should really be arranged by heel height."

Ah. This wasn't about Pilar's closet. Natalia was punishing me for leaving her in bed. As if it had been easy for me. As if the thought of fucking her wasn't always top of mind.

I needed to clear my head. I needed the space to think straight. I needed to fuck so hard that there was nothing left in my mind but answers. "Excuse me, Pilar," I said, keeping my eyes on Natalia, "but my wife and I were in the middle of something that needs resolving."

"Oh . . ." Natalia looked over her shoulder and winked. "I resolved it on my own."

If her smirk was any indication, I must've looked as dumbfounded as I felt. The thought of her getting herself off in my bed when that was my job . . .

I stepped up behind her, and by the way she stiffened, she knew I was done fucking around. "March your ass upstairs before I do it for you."

"He expects me to come when he calls," she said to Pilar. "The way he goes running whenever Jaz needs him."

I let a short chuckle free, though I was only amused by the prospect of dreaming up ways to punish her for that comment. I scooped her up, threw her over my shoulder, and gave Pilar a friendly smile. "We'll see you when we're finished. Don't wait up."

To Pilar's credit, for once, she didn't look scared. "Have a good time."

16

NATALIA

Cristiano the Brute dropped me on my feet in our bedroom, seemingly oblivious to my fuming. I'd begun to sweat under all this clothing, but that was part of his punishment for leaving me alone, naked, and more aroused than I'd ever been. "*Pendejo*," I said.

"You're awfully brave to call me an asshole," he said. "Considering you were shaking in your *huaraches* when you arrived here."

"I was not. I stood here, in this room, and invited you to fuck me that first night. You're the one who walked away," I accused.

He didn't deserve that; my gratitude for his restraint during that time knew no bounds. Cristiano could've taken what he'd wanted on our wedding night. How many men in his position would've? I shuddered to think. I'd be a different woman if he had, married to a different man.

But enough was enough. I needed him to finish what he'd started and consummate this goddamn marriage.

"I wasn't going to rape you the way my brother did."

Cristiano stalked up to me, taking my chin in his large paw of a hand and forcing me to look him in the eyes. "And that *is* what he did, Natalia. He said whatever he had to in order to coerce you into his bed. I wasn't going to do the same, and I never will, so you'd better learn how to ask for what you fucking want."

"I *did*. I told you not to leave this morning, but you didn't hesitate a second before running off when Jaz called." Smug satisfaction settled in me at the way he flinched. I'd offered myself to him twice in twenty-four hours, and he'd turned me down both times. The unrelenting need to be relieved by him and only him pushed me to poke him until he reacted. "My husband turns his back on his wife when another woman needs him. Jaz, Tasha, Sandra—is there anyone I come before?"

"How dare you say I haven't put you first!" He took his hand back, towering over me. "Have you wanted for *anything* since you stepped foot inside these walls?"

You.

My desire for him had been simmering since our first dance, I just hadn't wanted to admit it. Now that I could, it overwhelmed me, and I hated that I could be flipped so easily. I trusted Cristiano with my body, but it didn't erase Diego's violation.

"I thought I knew what *you* wanted, but maybe I was wrong," I said, my lips pinched as I dropped my eyes to the bulging crotch of his sweats. "Or maybe I wasn't. There must be some other reason you keep your hands to yourself."

"Watch your mouth, *chiquita*," he warned.

Being referred to as a *little girl* only infuriated me more. I stepped up under his nose. "I think I hear Jaz calling. Perhaps you should run along so I can return to my friend."

"People's lives are on the line. You expect me to laze in bed when they need me and let them fend for themselves?"

"Yes." I was being unfair, but so was he. It wasn't just my heart that had been aching since yesterday, but my body, too. Cristiano had promised to fuck me into oblivion more than once, and he had yet to follow through. Did he expect me to beg for it?

He stepped forward until we were toe to toe, his eyes darkening as his composure fissured. Finally, his anger matched mine. "Heaven's finest symphony is just noise compared to your pleas for me to stay in bed. I couldn't ask for anything more. But understand—you cannot command me. I don't answer to anyone. I have a duty to fulfill."

"You took me, you put me in this role, so, yes—now, you *do* answer to me." I nearly vibrated with rage. "And I won't come second to anyone, especially Jaz. She's trying to come between us."

"Nobody gets between us unless we allow it. And since when do you care?" Heat flashed in his eyes as he tilted his head, provoking me. "Why does my wife suddenly give a fuck where I go and what I do? What could be the reason, hmm?"

"Because . . . because . . ."

Love. That was why.

Because I had run out of reasons not to love him. It had bloomed unexpectedly and brutally. The soil for it had been rich, the foundation laid before I knew what it was to love a man. My mother had trusted him, and so had I. Cristiano had been nurturing that seed all along, and the vines had overgrown my heart without my realizing it.

And he knew it.

"You don't need to pick a fight, *mi amor*," he said smugly. "If you need me to fuck you, just ask—and mean it."

I needed it so badly, I ached with it. I grabbed his cheeks and pulled his mouth to mine. For a moment, he seemed too stunned to react, but then he gripped my hair by the root and backed me up against a wall.

"You thought all these clothes could keep me out, eh?" he said.

"It almost worked."

"You have no idea how wrong you are. Say it," he demanded into my mouth, then yanked my cardigan down around my biceps, trapping me with it. "Ask for it."

My breath stuttered along with my pulse. I was too needy, too aching, too far gone to anything but the carnal pull between us. "Please, Cristiano. Please, will you?"

"Will I what?"

"Do as you've promised. Destroy what's yours to destroy. Take my virginity as it should've been done. Please, fuck me. *Please*."

His hands fisted, tightening my sweater around me. "What a way to ask," he said, his chest rumbling with promise. "You've made it worth the wait. And I'll answer in spades, *mamacita*." He tore off my sweater and shoved a hand down the front of my pants, bypassing the fly, then my underwear. His fingertips slipped and glided against my opening but didn't enter. "Have you been wet this whole time?"

"Since the start," I admitted hoarsely.

His free hand gripped the waistband of my jeans and tugged them higher and higher until the seam of the crotch wedged up against my clit. "How's that?"

Open-mouthed, I gasped as he massaged it back and forth. "Oh. *God*."

He cocked his head, assessing me with complete composure as his chest rumbled with a "*Hmm*."

"What?" I panted.

"I'm deciding what to do with you. Based on how you just came at me, claws out, I think what you need more than anything right now is a good, hard fuck."

The prospect of inviting that from someone like Cristiano both thrilled and scared me—just like everything else when it came to my husband. The last few weeks had been building up to this, a passionate dance, each step becoming easier as we'd each given into faith. I trusted him to hurt me in the ways I needed without going too far.

"I deserve to be punished for how I've treated you. How I've spoken to you," I breathed against him. "Make me repent."

He yanked down my pants and underwear and left them in a heap as he lifted me against the wall. My legs wrapped around him instinctively, like a snake with prey, out of my control, squeezing him closer.

"I'll punish you, Natalia Lourdes, and you'll beg for more," he said, holding me up with one hand and reaching into his pants with the other to stroke himself. "Later, I'm going to ask you to put my cock inside you. I'm going to run my tongue along and inside every part of your body I can reach. But right now, I'm going to shove it inside you, and you're going to let me like the good little doll you are. Understand?"

If I hadn't been pinned to the wall, I might've fallen over with need. Instead, I shoved at his chest, moving him only centimeters. "You don't want a doll. You want the girl who pulled a gun on you. The one you're teaching to fight back."

He trapped my wrists and held them over my head. After locking them there with one hand, he pulled himself out of his sweats, lined his head up with my opening, and started to press inside. "Then it's too bad I haven't taught you how to get out of this hold yet, isn't it?" he asked and thrust his hips forward.

He filled me all at once. "*Fuck*," I cried.

"Yeah, *fuck*," he said, rooting himself there. "*Fuck* you and your too-tight cunt. How's it feel to finally be broken wide open?"

My chest heaved. He quenched a thirst that ran deeper than I'd thought possible. I was full, finally, for the first time in my life, physically—but also emotionally bursting with desire and love and everything else I couldn't seem to get a handle on. "It feels . . ." Even the finest words couldn't convey like the language our bodies spoke. "It feels like we should've done this weeks ago."

"No shit. All I've wanted is to watch your face as I claim you." He used both hands this time to fasten my wrists above my head before he drew back and impaled me again. "As your pussy yields for me, then sucks me deeper."

"*Ay, Dios m*—" I cried. "Oh . . . my . . . G—"

"Who are you talking to, *mi vida*?" He took my mouth for a hard, wet kiss as he moved in and out, making sure I felt every ridge and vein of his shaft. Trapping my bottom lip between his teeth, he pinched it until I moaned, then released it. "Nobody's as divine as you," he professed. "You're the goddess in the sky the rest of us appeal to. Who could match you?"

"You."

His tongue ran along my lip to the corner of my mouth as his hips picked up pace. "Does it hurt?"

It was a simple question with myriad answers. Was pain always bad? Could it feel so good that it hurt? Was I allowed to crave physical agony to incarnate my soul-deep yearning for him? "Yes," I said as my pussy contracted around him and my legs pulled him even closer.

He pulled out until I had to engage my thigh muscles to keep from slipping down the wall. "I could be gentler," he said. "Treat you like a real doll. Like you can't handle it."

"I can take it. I want it to hurt, and I want you to make it better." I met his gaze, the evident need in his eyes. Not to push me up against a wall—he could've done that any time. But a need to fill me in ways nobody else could and master this domain. To *finally* have me willing. I freed my wrists from his grip, hugged his neck, and pressed my forehead to his. "I know it hurts you, too."

Something passed over his face. He leaned in, and I drew back, keeping myself just outside his reach. With a growl that reverberated in my chest, he captured my mouth for a punishing kiss, the kind I'd expect of a deadly, passionate, dominant kingpin.

Without disconnecting, he carried me across the room and lowered me until just my upper back hit the mattress. Holding my hips up, he brought them to meet each of his hard and fast thrusts. "Watch how your pussy takes me, Natalia—every inch," he said, reaching out to press his thumb in my mouth. I automatically sucked. "I'd promise that by the time I'm through with you, you'll be ruined for anyone else—but I'll *never* be through with you." He removed his thumb and bent forward to pinch my chin and keep my eyes on him. "And if that scares you—good."

I arched my back as his relentless drives hit me deeper and deeper. Warmth coiled in my core, another aching knot in me that Cristiano had inspired—one only Cristiano could relieve. "I'm not scared," I said.

He slid a hand under the hem of my t-shirt and spread it over my lower tummy as it trembled. His thumb dipped between my folds to my clit. "You were."

"I was."

"But now, you'll take everything I have to give."

"How much more could there be?" I breathed as my muscles quivered around his cock.

"I can get deeper—so much deeper," he promised. "But I need you to come for me first and loosen up your cunt." He took my waist, his grip so tight that his fingertips almost met as he lifted me higher. Pulled me onto each thrust. Fucked me so hard his balls slapped against my ass cheeks. "Give me that nectar only good enough for a god; let an unworthy man into the depths of Heaven."

I shivered with his words. This was what I'd always needed. Not to be coddled and pacified with Diego's flat, emotionless, stupid-as-fuck poetry. I'd take the raw and profane from Cristiano over lifeless prose any day. I'd take his fast and hard screw over Diego's sniveling lovemaking.

I closed my eyes so I could feel every sensation as it washed over me, every nuance of Cristiano's demanding fuck.

"Eyes open, Natalia," he said. "I know you're afraid of the dark, but in my bed, you'll face me."

I flitted my lids open to the beastly devil above me. The monster under my bed that had crawled out and mounted me. The one who knew my deepest fears and conquered them with me.

I shook with the force of a sudden, foundation-splitting orgasm. He held me in the safety of his black eyes as I found rapture—not in the heights of Heaven but in the depths of his hell.

"God. *Fuck*." He stilled and groaned up to the ceiling. "You're holding onto me so tight, it *might* be enough to keep me out of your ass for a few days."

I released a quivering breath as the aftershock of my orgasm rolled through me. *Now*, I was scared. I had come for the devil and enjoyed every second of it—and now I feared I'd give it to him any way he asked.

He pulled out of me, his cock hard, throbbing, nearly purple between us—and covered in me. Before I could even register it, he leaned forward and ripped open my top. "Flip over," he demanded, urging me onto my stomach faster, discarding the ruined shirt.

His hands spread over the base of my spine and glided to the clasp of my bra. He got it open, smoothing his palms up and down my back. "*Qué buena estas.*"

I wasn't sure I felt *sexy* in that moment, bent over the edge of the bed, my ass in the air, wide open to him. The thought of taking him back there inspired more nerves than excitement.

He slid his slick shaft between my cheeks and the veiny, soft skin rubbed the raw bud of nerves at my opening.

"You got quiet," he said, and I could've sworn I heard a smile in his voice.

He was enjoying this, the way my body had gone as tense as the strings of an over-tuned guitar. With the curtains open and the sun streaming in, fucking like this in broad daylight felt *obscene*. "Not my ass," I said, pressing the side of my face into the mattress. My voice pitched as I said, "I can't . . ."

"Not your ass," he agreed. "It's not ready yet. I want to play with it first. Get to know it. Introduce it to my fingers. My tongue."

I fisted the sheets, glancing back at him as my face flamed with heat. "You wouldn't."

"Oh, I would, *mamacita*. And I will." He drew his t-shirt over his head, stripping down at lightning speed. "But understand one thing. When we do get there, I'll never hurt you that way. Not ever, Natalia. When I take your ass, it will be to send us both to the moon."

I closed my eyes, and instead of fear, satisfaction washed over me. I'd spent so long fighting to distrust every word out of his mouth, especially when it came to the pain he could inflict. I chose to believe him now.

"Your pussy, however," he said, spreading my lips with his thumbs. He slid inside me from behind, his complete, staggering length impaling me slowly, until I'd taken him to the root. "That, I will use until I've filled you up with enough cum to make up for each night I've missed as your husband."

The bluntness of his words cut through my haze. "But I could get pregnant!"

"*Me vale verga*. I don't care. It's too late. It's already leaking out of me. And your sweet, thirsty pussy will swallow everything, won't it?"

I had never wanted anything so badly in my life. I knew no other response except one. "Yes, sir."

"Obedient little bride."

He put one foot on the mattress, held down my hips, and drove into me so deep, I whimpered. "That's it," he said, his voice full of gravel as he hammered me. "I can feel the end of you now, and I'm going to fuck you there until even that gives."

My face flushed. The utter and complete fullness of my pussy, the feeling of being more him than me in that moment, tapped into my basest needs. The pleasure intensified as he drilled away until all I could do was scream. I'd never heard myself do such a thing, but I was too gone to be embarrassed that my cries nearly shook the walls. "Yes!" The only words I could form spilled from me. "*Yes, papi. Por favor*—please."

I wanted his release as much as my own and I even tried to meet his penetrating thrusts as I was pinned down.

Relief came quickly. He ground me against the mattress over and over until I came again.

My fatigued muscles shook as I relaxed into the mattress. Cristiano took me until the very end, until he delivered on his promise and erupted into my wilting body, breathing life back into me.

17

NATALIA

Cristiano sat squarely in front of a large, majestic, burgundy velvet tapestry with golden thread that hung on one wall of the main room. At the head of the dining table, the open floor plan allowed him to see through the house, down the hall, and almost to the entryway. I couldn't help thinking he'd designed it that way.

Remnants of our small feast, prepared in honor of a visit from my father, littered the table. Papá had been quieter than usual since we'd returned from a horseback tour of the Badlands. We'd invited him to stay for a few days so we could introduce him to the business he'd become a part of with our . . . *merger*.

And, in a way, it'd been an introduction for me, too. We'd made our way through the town square where Cristiano had bought my sandals, *click-clacking* down the road on our horses. From the outside, who would've thought the Badlands would have something as quaint as a Main Street? There were also fully functioning farms to keep residents fed—and even a distillery to keep them in good spirits. Doctor Sosa, who'd tended to Cristiano and me after Belmonte-Ruiz's strike, ran a decent-sized medical clinic where she regularly saw patients.

It awed me how well they operated as a society.

I couldn't quite read my father's reaction, though. Today, he'd learned the truth about Cristiano's business— that Calavera was involved in the flesh trade, but instead of trafficking in people, he was saving them.

Seated to Cristiano's right, I took the last bite of chicken *mole* I could possibly stuff into my stomach and deflated against the back of my seat, covering my tummy. "I'm so full."

"It was an excellent meal, Pilar," Papá said from across the table. He always sat at the head, but there had been no confusion over who belonged there in Cristiano's home.

In *our* home. I suspected it would be a while before it really began to feel like mine. I hadn't picked out any of these things, or, like Cristiano, overseen its construction from the ground up. It was the people who felt more like home than the Badlands.

It was him, Cristiano.

"Should I get the dessert?" Pilar asked and dabbed her mouth with a napkin. When she stood, Alejo and Barto did, too. Her face reddened. "Oh, no, don't get up. I can handle it."

The men exchanged an unfriendly glance. Over Pilar? She and Alejandro had become close spending time together here at the house, but Barto had known her for most of her life as my friend. He'd been quieter than usual tonight, his eyes roaming the room and the company. He was obviously uncomfortable as a guest in the Badlands despite Cristiano's invitation.

As Pilar exited the room, Jazmín entered with a tray of tall shot glasses and a liquor bottle that looked more like a piece of art. A pewter mermaid embraced the tequila, her tail gracefully wrapped around a decanter topped with a skeleton.

"This is a two-thousand-dollar bottle of tequila," Papá remarked as Jaz poured each of us a shot.

"It's aged three years in French oak barrels right here in our region—only a hundred bottles were produced," Cristiano said. "*Sirena del Deseo.*"

"Mermaid of desire," I translated. Our eyes met. Cristiano and I had snuck down to the strip of beach below our balcony earlier. "*Mi sirenita,*" he'd called me—*my little mermaid*—as we'd swum and danced in the ocean, then fucked under the hot Mexican sun.

As Jaz distributed the drinks, Cristiano brought the back of my hand to his mouth for a kiss. "With the decanter, the artist tells the love story of a Mexican warrior who traveled to the very depths of the sea in search of his beloved mermaid."

"How romantic," Pilar said, crossing the room from the kitchen, her hands full with a cake. Behind her, one of the kitchen staff carried in a stack of plates and silverware. She set toothpicks on the table near Cristiano.

"Ah, Pilar's famous *tres leches* cake," my father commented.

She blushed, handing him the serving utensil. "As our guest, you get first slice, *señor* Cruz."

"I don't think the tequila is meant to be romantic," I said, back on the decanter. "The warrior on top is a skeleton."

"It *is* a love story, but a tragic one," Cristiano said, "as he did not survive his quest."

The warmth of his palm against mine did nothing to stem the trail of chills up my arm, nor did the graveness of his frown.

When we all had tequila and cake before us, I asked, "What's the occasion?"

Cristiano's mood lifted with a smile. "Do I need one to celebrate my wife and her family? *Salud.*"

We each raised our tequilas with a "¡*Salud*!" and sipped.

"Though, if my calculations are correct," Cristiano added, lowering his glass, "today *does* mark six weeks since we stood in the church and said our vows."

My eyes stayed locked with his. "Six weeks and a lifetime."

"Give your husband a kiss to celebrate," he said.

I pursed my lips, but not for a kiss. Everyone was watching, and Cristiano knew it. "When we're alone."

"No. Now." He leaned over. "Come. *Un beso.*"

Drawn to him like a magnet, I inclined forward to meet him, balancing on his thigh as my mouth found his, the full, warm lips all at once new and familiar. I curled my fist against his leg. I knew him intimately and still had so much to discover. But I drew back quickly when I remembered we weren't alone, lowering my eyes to the table as I blushed.

"What happened to your neck?" Barto's abrupt question and hardened tone made my eyes jump to his. "That looks like the beginning of a hypertrophic scar."

I covered the ugly imperfection as Cristiano and I exchanged a glance. I didn't want to lie, but we hadn't broached the subject of Belmonte-Ruiz's strike with my father yet. The scar wasn't overtly noticeable, but had started to become pink and raised. I'd originally put on a turtleneck for dinner, but on such a warm June night, Cristiano had said it looked suspicious—before reminding me to wear the symbol of my survival with pride.

"It's nothing," I said with my first bite of cake.

"She fell into a mirror," Pilar volunteered. "It broke."

Barto snorted, his knuckles whitening around his fork as he turned his glare on Cristiano. "She *fell*? You expect anyone to believe that?"

"Barto," my father warned, then turned to me. "Is that true?"

"She can't be honest," Barto said. "If she is, she may 'fall' again. Or maybe it will be Pilar this time."

His statement hung as eerie silence descended over the room. All eyes drew to Cristiano. He ate a chunk of his cake, chewing slowly before swallowing it down with a gulp of tequila that must've cost thousands of *pesos*. Looking at Barto, he leaned back in his seat. "Fuck you."

Alejandro grabbed Barto's arm as he tried to stand. "*Tranquilo*," Alejo said. "Relax, friend. Cristiano hasn't laid a hand on Natalia, and he never will."

"Why should I believe it?" Barto asked.

Cristiano sucked his teeth. "Natalia and I need to speak to Costa in private."

Alejandro and Pilar stood with their dishes, but Barto stayed where he was. "I'm here to protect and support Costa," Barto said. "You can say anything in front of me."

"That was an order," Alejandro said, looking down at him.

Barto fisted his napkin and rose to his full height, eye to eye with Alejandro. "I don't take orders from him. Or you, *pinche pendejo*."

"Please, stop," Pilar said, touching Barto's forearm and drawing Alejo's gaze there. "Alejandro is not an eff-ing a-hole, and I know you're just being protective, but we're all on the same side. Cristiano has been good to Natalia."

"Thank you, Esmeralda," Alejandro said, and Pilar blushed at her new name.

Barto's brows drew together. "Esmeralda . . .?"

Cristiano addressed my father. "You can fill Barto in on everything later."

Papá nodded once. With the dismissal, Barto threw his napkin on his plate of half-eaten cake and strode from the room with Alejandro and Pilar behind him. The last thing I heard was Alejandro's taunt. "Try to keep up, Barto. Pilar goes by Esmeralda now."

When we were alone, my father licked his fork clean. "Pilar really is a good baker, like her mother." He sighed, setting the utensil on his plate as his expression cleared. "It's a lot to take in, Cristiano, everything you showed me here."

"It's truly remarkable, isn't it, Papá?" I really wanted him to like it here—to be as impressed by Cristiano as I was, and to feel welcome to visit whenever.

"I would feel a little claustrophobic," he said.

"Beyond the walls, you have open desert on three sides and the whole sea behind you," Cristiano pointed out.

"What good is that?" He shrugged. "The ocean traps you in."

"No, *señor*," Cristiano said. "We have a small naval fleet so that makes land, air, and sea wide open to us. The ships are stored inside the mountain, where we've hollowed it out." He winked at me. "Did I mention there are jet skis?"

I suppressed a smile. No, he hadn't. I discovered more of the Badlands' secrets each day and had just learned about the mountainside that afternoon—but there'd been no mention of watersports. Was there anything they hadn't thought of?

"What I love, is that it's self-sustaining," I told my father. "The woman who made my wedding rings, Teresa, is also an electrician thanks to education she received after her arrival. Another couple makes the smoothest tequila from blue agave grown right here."

"*Está buenísimo*," Cristiano agreed. "So good, we keep it on hand here."

"Everyone has been trained in a trade or skill," I said.

"That's intentional." Cristiano spun his tumbler on the table. "It gives me pleasure to see them well-fed, healthy, and happy, but should the Badlands dissolve tomorrow, its people would survive. And if something happens to me, Max knows . . ."

He stopped.

It wasn't the first time Cristiano had referred to Max as if he was still around. And without fail, I'd see the moment Cristiano realized his mistake, pain flashing across his expression. As I'd learned with my mother's death, one way to help ease grief was with memories. Max wasn't dead that we knew of, but I was pretty sure Cristiano believed he wasn't ever coming home. I couldn't personally think of an instance in which a cartel had captured and then released a rival.

I covered Cristiano's hand with mine. "How did you meet Max?"

"Like everyone else," he said, blinking his dim gaze to me. "Each of us, down and out, were looking for a leg up. We made our own leg up and then helped the other. In the early days after I'd left the compound," he said, looking to my father, "I'd gamble. Turn twenty *pesos* into forty, forty into a hundred."

I eased back against my seat with my tequila, content to learn something new about Cristiano's past. "I didn't know that."

With a nod, he continued, "Max was also scraping by. One night, I lost nearly everything. He'd had a winning streak. He let me stay with him until I was back on my feet, and when the tables turned, and he needed me, I was there. It's been that way ever since."

"So how come he wasn't—*isn't* Lord of the Badlands?"
I asked.

Finally, I got a smile from Cristiano, albeit a crooked
one. "Diplomacy doesn't suit him. He'd rather do what
needs to be done."

"*Ay*, and *you're* diplomatic?" I asked.

With a chuckle, he raised his glass. "To Max. Ugliest
son-of-a-bitch I ever saw but with a beautiful heart."

The three of us clinked glasses again. "Your cama-
raderie, your operation—it's like nothing I've ever seen in
my lifetime," my father said. "But what's perhaps most
impressive of all is that you've managed to keep it a
secret."

"The secret's getting out," Cristiano said frankly. I
knew it was anything but easy for him to say, but he wasn't
one to sugarcoat things. He cleared his throat. "There was
. . . an attack."

My father's dark, bushy brows lowered as he set down
his shot glass. "Here?"

"*Sí*. And Natalia was a target."

"*¿Qué?*" His voice, which had become more sonorous
with age, was the only one I'd heard go deeper and gruffer
than Cristiano's. "When was this? Why didn't I know?"

"I'm fine," I said. "Cristiano was the one who got hurt,
but we couldn't say anything because nobody outside of
here could know he was injured."

Papá leaned over the table, his hands two fists on the
wood surface. "When was this?"

"About a month ago," Cristiano said.

"A month! You should've told me as soon as I walked in
the door." He slapped the table. "*Sooner.*"

"Your blood pressure, Papá," I said.

He drew back. "Eh? What about it?"

I had no idea of my father's vitals, that wasn't something he was inclined to share with me. But it sounded like the right thing to say, and he looked confused enough to forget his anger for a moment.

Apparently, the art of distraction worked in more scenarios than hand-to-hand combat.

"Is that where you got the scar?" he asked me. "You lied to Barto."

"Because I knew how he'd react."

He waved a hand dismissively, sat back in his seat, and pinned us each with a look. I couldn't help feeling like a student in the principal's office. "What happened?"

My father listened silently and unflinchingly as we told him the details of the strike, right up to the aftermath, including how Alejandro and his team had been out in the field, but had come up empty-handed so far.

"Are you asking for my help with an army?" Papá finally asked.

"No—this leads me to other news," Cristiano said. "I mentioned I spoke with Natasha Sokolov-Flores at Senator Sanchez's event. You know how powerful her family is. Together with Alejandro, they were able to find Vicente Valverde."

At the mention of his old enemy, my father's face changed, his only reaction in minutes, aside from asking for clarification or sipping tequila. "Vicente Valverde is *dead*." He looked to Cristiano and laced his fingers on the table. "I would've hunted him down and killed him after what the *sicario* told us, but many confirmed he died of a stroke."

"A stroke of good luck to get away with it so long, perhaps," Cristiano grumbled. "But his luck has run out. Vicente is very much alive and waiting to see you."

He stilled, his wrinkles easing as a frown slowly overtook his face. "What are you talking about?"

"The Valverdes vanished too easily," Cristiano

explained. "I wondered why, and simply bringing you a hitman wasn't enough." He extended his arm toward me on the table. "I wanted you both to be able to face those responsible for Bianca's attack, and now I have brought you all but one."

My father's weighty stare shifted from my husband to me and back. "Let's move somewhere private, Cristiano. Bring those Honduran cigars you've been going on about."

Cristiano shifted in his seat. "Natalia already knows everything."

"We shouldn't discuss such violent and traumatic things in front of—"

"I've faced Valverde myself," I said. My father needed to start understanding I wasn't Cristiano's cartel princess. Like my mother, I was learning how to be a partner in this. "I've seen his battered face, heard his vile excuses and admissions—including, for the first time, that my mother was raped. I knew it happened, but nobody ever told me. I had to wonder for years, then hear it from Vicente Valverde."

My father's face paled. "Why would I tell you that? Learning of Bianca's final moments nearly finished me all those years ago. I kept it from you to protect you."

Cristiano flipped up his palm on the table and gestured for mine. I took his hand. "She's tougher than you know, *don* Costa," he said. "Keeping her in the dark does nothing but harm her."

"I defer to you as her husband, but I can't say I agree." Papá stuck both elbows on the table and pinched the bridge of his nose. "No child should hear such things about a parent."

"You didn't shield Bianca from the horrors of this world," Cristiano pointed out.

"And as I've told you," Papá snapped, "look what happened to her."

"It didn't happen because you included her in your business," I said softly. "And it wasn't because you didn't protect her. You couldn't have stopped it."

"You don't know that."

Cristiano and I exchanged a glance, speaking to each other without words. There wasn't much left to say except for the final bit of news I doubted either of us wanted to break.

My father heaved a sigh. "Tell me you've brought me this information about Valverde so I can act on it. Now. Tonight."

"You can act tonight," Cristiano said gravely, nodding slowly. "I'll take you downstairs to them when we're through here."

"Them?" he asked. "How many?"

"Three plus a grandson, Gabriel Valverde. That's all who remain of the family. But we've decided to spare Gabriel's life."

"*Jamás*," Papá said, shaking his head vigorously. "Never. No."

My mouth popped up. "You haven't even heard who he is."

"What's there to know? He's a Valverde. Their blood-line ends now."

I shifted in my seat. "But—"

"The answer is no." His gaze darkened on Cristiano. "If *any* man had *anything* to do with Bianca's murder—"

"He's not a man." I swallowed. My father and Cristiano's presence dwarfed me, but it couldn't mute me. "He's only seventeen. And he was a child when all of this happened."

My father looked to Cristiano "You can't allow it."

Cristiano's gaze drifted to the plate of crumbs before him as he flexed and curled his hand on the table. I could almost hear the wheels of his mind in motion. I'd made myself clear about Gabriel. What was there to think about?

"It's Natalia's call," Cristiano said finally, "and the queen has decided to let him keep his head. I support her completely."

"Natalia is too merciful"—he frowned at me—"I'm sorry, *mi amor*, but this is a man's domain. If you want to be a queen, step up and—"

"I *am* being a queen." With the weight of a proverbial crown, it took a little more effort to sit up straighter, but I did. "We don't kill the innocent. Not every conflict is resolved with vengeance and violence. I learned that from you. *You're* merciful. You're fair. You showed Cristiano mercy when he was a boy, and look who he is now."

"It's a mistake," he warned.

"But it's mine to make."

"The boy is a computer whiz," Cristiano cut in. "He's only been with us a week, but Eduardo reports he's as talented as he claimed. He could have a lot to offer."

I hoped that was true. I wouldn't know if I'd made the right decision until—*unless*—Gabriel betrayed us. I was getting a crash course in the reality that my decisions no longer affected only myself, but my husband, and an entire town, too.

Cristiano's expression soured as if he were about to endure a tooth extraction. "Enough of that." He looked to me. "Tell him."

Me? The nape of my neck got clammy. And for a moment, I understood all too well what my father had just been saying. I wanted to protect him from Diego's gutless betrayal, from the news that he'd not only trusted an enemy for so long, but had kept him close.

I could ask Cristiano to tell him for me or have him take Papá into the basement to hear it for himself, the way I had. But Cristiano's gaze challenged me. Showing strength when others needed it was part of my role.

I stood and rounded the table to sit in the seat next to Papá. When I reached out, he opened his hand, took mine, and brought my palm to his lips for a kiss. "*¿Qué, querida?* What's wrong?"

"You warned me about Diego."

He flinched back. "Yes, and finally, he's out of the picture. Why are you bringing him up?"

"I should've listened—but even if I had, it would've been too late." I paused to think of the best way to put it. I could soften the blow with gentle delivery—or, I could make my father hear me by speaking his language. "He fucked us over."

Out of habit, I expected him to comment on my language, but he only gripped my hand more tightly and scowled. "Explain. Now."

"The Valverdes acted out of desperation to salvage their cartel. But they had help. From Diego. And *he* was not a desperate man, but a vengeful one."

My father's eyes bulged in a way I'd never seen. I could always tell his anger by the way his gaze narrowed, over-shadowed by his heavy brows. This was something more. "Diego . . . *helped?*"

"He's the one who let the *sicario* into the house, tampered with the compound's security system, and gave him the codes to the safe."

My father had learned the necessary art of hiding his reaction, but it didn't come naturally to him. Currently in safe company, his face turned cherry red as his hand shook holding mine. "I shouldn't believe it so easily." His low, deep voice reverberated through the room. "And that says everything. Bianca warned me."

I squeezed his clammy hand. "He fooled *everyone*. Except maybe her."

"Why?" Beads of sweat formed on his upper lip. He shook his head. "I already know. His parents' execution. Bianca said he harbored resentment over it. And I, always priding myself on being a good judge of character . . ."

"You are," I said. "This doesn't change that."

"He fooled me, too," Cristiano offered, his tone solemn. "And I was his *brother*."

I didn't miss his past tense reference. I glanced to Cristiano, eager to go to him. That Diego had hurt my husband and father so deeply lit embers of rage in me. I wanted to be fair and just, but did that mean I couldn't also be ruthless when the time came? If I had Diego here in this room, would I try to hold Cristiano back, knowing the damage he could do? Or would I let loose the beast?

Part of me wondered not just about Cristiano . . . but also what *I* was capable of in the name of revenge, especially for those I loved.

"Diego's a liar and a coward who'd commit any sin to serve his own best interests," I said. "He killed *mi madre* to avenge his parents, yes—but he also knew it would cripple you and give him the opportunity to stay by your side as you grieved."

I let my father work through the equation on his own until his head bobbed up and down. "To gain my trust. To advise me. To infiltrate the Cruz cartel—so he could someday make it his own to replace the legacy he feels he's owed."

Cristiano stuck a toothpick in his mouth and sat back. "I'll let Valverde fill you in on the rest," he said. "How

Diego ruined and exiled them, and how he'd planned to turn Natalia's love against you—until I came along."

"*Qué cabrón*," Papá uttered. "I'd never have allowed that fucking bastard to do it."

I wished I could agree with him and promise my father he would've always known my deepest loyalty. But if Cristiano hadn't returned, I'd still be under Diego's spell. After everything I'd already fallen for, would I have allowed him to eventually oust Papá?

I glanced at my hands. "I thought I loved him, and it blinded me."

"You *did* love him." Cristiano lifted his eyes to me as he struggled to add, "It's okay to say. It was real for you."

For *me*. That made things all the worse. Pretending I'd been tricked into false feelings would be easier than admitting I'd opened my soul to an enemy.

"You see now the man Diego is," Cristiano said. "That's what matters."

"I warned you I'd have to kill him if he broke your heart," my father said.

I nodded. "You did."

One corner of Cristiano's mouth twitched as he suppressed a grin.

"That gives me two reasons to put his head on a stick and send it down Main Street on a parade float," Papá said, rising from his seat and towering over the table. "Now tell me where to find him."

"I wish we could," I said.

"Nowhere is safe for him now. *Barto!*" Papá called.

Barto entered the dining room at once.

As Papá debriefed him, I met Cristiano's searching eyes. His hungry gaze followed me around the table as I went to him. He pulled me into his lap before sliding my cake in front of him. "You didn't finish your dessert."

I put my arms around his neck. "I'm stuffed. I can't eat another thing. If you want it—"

He stabbed his fork in it, picking up nearly half the slice, and shoved it into his mouth.

I blinked at him. "A full-course dinner and dessert wasn't enough?"

"Never turn down food," he said through his chewing.

I hadn't seen him devour anything with such fervor since he'd eaten my *panocha* on this very table. The man was insatiable—and he'd been right about taking my virginity. Anything I'd experienced up until meeting Cristiano's rooster was forgettable.

Papá cleared his throat, and we each turned to him. "I take it the marriage has been consummated."

"*Papá.*" My cheeks flushed as my arms tightened around Cristiano's neck. "That's none of your business."

"It is my business," he responded, his eyes on Cristiano. "I promised I'd make your husband pay if he harmed you."

"Does she look harmed?" Cristiano asked. "I said she'd be loved, treated well, and protected here. I'm doing my best on all fronts."

I was treated well, and I was protected as much as anyone could be in our circumstances. But was I loved? Warmth pooled in my tummy as I studied, up close, Cristiano's dark, angry stubble, the hollow of his cheek, and the fine lines around his devastatingly shrewd eyes.

Was love something he could voice when he felt it, or would he need time?

"Things have obviously changed between you," my father said. I turned back to find him staring at me. "I guess knowing the truth has made a difference in how you view your new husband, *mija.* Yes?"

"*Sí, Papá,*" I agreed. "Surely there were better ways to

go about making me his wife . . ." Cristiano had the decency to like contrite—even though he'd made it clear he had little to regret. "But I have a lifetime to punish him for it," I added.

Cristiano's mouth slid into a sinister grin. "A sentence I will gladly serve."

"I expect grandchildren soon," my father said in a good-natured tone that made Cristiano and I raise our brows at each other.

I turned my head to Papá. "Why . . .?"

"Do I need a reason?"

A surprised laugh escaped my lips. I tried to stand, but Cristiano's arms tightened around my waist.

"With this news about Diego," my father said, "I can't help but think of family. Of what he cost me. Of how Bianca would've loved a grandchild, especially since it would be from Cristiano, whom she cared for."

With my mother's approval, even from beyond the grave, my heart fluttered. I leaned in and rubbed my cheek against Cristiano's. "It's a nice thought, *Padre*," I said. "One day. We have time."

Cristiano was uncharacteristically silent on the subject. He had only one thing left to say as he patted the outside of my hip. "Go on to bed—I'll be up shortly. Your father and I have business downstairs."

Business was all I needed to hear.

The time to eat, drink, and be merry had passed. Now was the time to kill.

18

CRISTIANO

Maybe it was all the time I'd spent on farms today that'd turned me into an animal tonight. Maybe it was weeks of sleeping by Natalia and thinking of nothing but all the ways I wanted to take her. Or years of wondering about her life—if she'd flourished or had resorted to simply existing following Bianca's death, and whether she'd still been blindly devoted to my brother or if it was more nostalgia than anything keeping them together.

It didn't matter. Tonight, I'd embrace the animal. I'd proverbially lain her mother's murderers at my wife's feet. I'd slit three more throats in Bianca's name.

On our bed, gripping Natalia's hips with more strength than I meant, I pounded into her from behind like a dog mounting his bitch. I'd never been more grateful to have soundproofed a room. I must've known I'd end up marrying a screamer.

I wrapped Natalia's long, dark hair around my wrist and pulled so her head drew back. I liked her from this angle, on her hands and knees, but I missed her face. Especially when it was screwed up in pleasure.

"Faster, *harder*," she cried.

Was she serious? I'd never fucked like this in my life. If I went any faster, she'd end up in the next room. If I went any harder, she'd suck up my balls.

I slowed down instead, and after a few deliberate pumps, curved my hand around her ass. "For so long, you treated me like your own personal monster," I threatened, grabbing a fistful of her ass. "Now, while I'm filling you, I want to hear you say you're my wife."

"Or what?"

She wanted to play. So did I. Natalia had poked the beast before, on our wedding night, when I'd bent her over the side of my bed and threatened to wreck her. Her pussy had left a wet spot on the tip of my dick. Maybe a week later, I'd given her a chicken dinner when I'd jammed *El Gallo* down her throat—and she'd cleaned her plate. She possessed a darkness that extended into the bedroom. Lucky for me.

"Say you're my wife, or I'll spank your ass."

She bit her bottom lip and deliberately didn't respond.

I forced myself to withdraw from her, painful as it was to lose her warm, wet heat.

My palm landed with a sharp slap on the outer curve of one cheek, and she gasped. The shock on her face alone was enough to make my dick jump. I kneaded the meat of her ass, then lined up my hand in the same exact spot.

She dropped from her hands to her forearms, pressing her head into the mattress.

"Get back up," I said.

"And if I want more?"

Beautiful. I spanked her twice with enough precision and force to make it sting. After a moment, my handprint bloomed on her skin. Maybe *that* was what I should've tattooed on her, because I'd never seen anything so fucking hot.

Or had I?

I lined up my throbbing head to her wet slit and thrust inside her. Her answering moan was almost as sweet as her candy pussy. Now that my cock filled her up, my handprint looked even better.

I took her elbows and pulled her upright. We both groaned at the new angle. I was fucking *deep* now. I kept her arms in a firm hold, using them as leverage to drive into her. "You're trapped now, eh? This greedy little pussy belongs to me. *Say* it."

She arched her back, dropping her head onto my shoulder. "It's so . . ."

"So what?" Buried to the root, I nudged her cervix with a few short thrusts, and her tits bounced toward the ceiling.

"Is it possible to feel it in my stomach?"

I could see her better now. I wanted her mouth, her exquisite eyes on mine, and to see her delicate features shatter with her orgasm. "You're the most perfect thing I've ever laid eyes on." I captured her earlobe between my teeth. "But if you don't call yourself my wife, I'm going to come in you and stay there until there's no question you'll get pregnant."

She shuddered. In so little time, I'd come to known that specific tremor as the first quakes of her climax. "I don't want your baby."

"I don't care." I circled my hands around neck, pulling her back against me. "Look at me and say it."

She could barely turn her head in my grip. I'd never put my hands around a woman's throat this way. I wanted to scare her. I wanted her fear and her orgasm. Her ever-mesmerizing violet eyes found mine, and in them, *I* found clarity. Determination. Devotion. "I'm your wife," she said levelly. "I'm yours. And you're mine, *husband*."

My ears rang with my impending eruption. I was holding her too hard, rutting into her, trying not to bruise her delicate neck as her cervix took a beating. I only loosened my grasp when I heard the word *stop*. I forced myself to slow down long enough to make out what she was saying.

"Don't stop," she cried. "God, *Cristiano*. Please don't stop."

I fucked her to quiet her. She was a screamer up until the final moments, but her orgasms silenced her. When she went mute, she was close. She opened her mouth and gasped for air, dropped her head back against my shoulder, and submitted to her climax.

The moment her pussy gripped me, I was a goner. I released her neck and hugged her close as she milked me until I erupted.

As she went flimsy in my arms, I eased her onto her stomach, propped myself over her, and pumped slowly, keeping my promise. I spurted every last drop into her, and when I was done, I stayed buried inside her, plugging her up.

"We never talked about this," she said quietly.

"What are you referring to?" I asked, even though I knew.

"What do you *think*?" she asked with that bit of sass I loved. "You know I'm not on birth control."

I withdrew and sat on the backs of her thighs, prying apart her sweet pink pussy lips. "You just look so *fucking* good filled to the brim," I said. "You should see how my cum looks inside you."

"You know what happens when you do that, though, don't you?"

I couldn't help my laugh. "I've heard."

I moved off her to lie by her side, brushing her hair off her face. "At your age, you're extremely fertile."

"Are you fertile *at all* at your age, old man?" she asked, batting her lashes at me.

I balked. "Thirty-four? Sorry to break it to you, but I'm in my prime. We could already be pregnant."

"You say that so easily, like you're letting me know you're going out for *conchas* and coffee." She took her gaze from me, looking at nothing on the bed between us. "We just started doing this, Cristiano. Is it a good idea—"

"I love how you say my name," I told her, suddenly unable to think of anything else but kissing her. "Come here."

"I can't move an inch. After horseback riding, plus training to fight off predators during the day and giving into one at night, I'm so sore."

I'd worked her every muscle the past week. I wanted her strong and satisfied at the end of each day. "We'll stop the training," I said, massaging her shoulders with one hand. "If by some crazy chance you *were* pregnant—"

"I don't *want* to stop," she said, closing her eyes with a contented sigh. "I like it. I'd rather be prepared than pregnant."

We should've had this conversation already. I'd just barely stopped to think about it. I wanted to be inside her all the time. To come as deep as I could. To see my child growing in her belly. "Do you not want a baby?"

She opened her eyes to study my face and grimaced as she got up on one elbow. "Not yet. This has all been so . . ."

"So what?" I asked quietly when she didn't continue. "You can be honest."

"So fast. I'm grateful for it, but sometimes I still feel shame." My stomach clenched before she added, "Ashamed at how happy I am. I spent so long viewing cartel life as evil. You're supposed to be the devil. I feel like I'm living someone else's life."

Alarmed, I also got up on my elbow. "What does that mean?"

"Just that everything flipped so quickly. And at the same time, it didn't. I've always felt something strong between us. At first, I thought it was just sexual chemistry. And hatred. A twisted kind, where I also couldn't stop thinking about you." Her eyes darted between mine before she rolled onto her back and looked at the ceiling. "I'd wonder if I was betraying my former self, but after Diego's manipulation I don't even know who *I* am. So what if *none* of this is real?"

It pained me to hear her question herself. Was this what had been running through Natalia's mind since that day with the Valverdes? She'd just assured her father that Diego had fooled all of us, and it didn't diminish Costa's judgment of character.

"I would rid that shame for you if I could." Her hair splayed over the pillow, and I picked up a handful of silky strands to run them through my fingers. "But you will overcome it in time. His betrayal is still raw. In the meantime, I ask that when you can't trust yourself, trust me to know who you are. And you're right where you're meant to be."

She turned her head to me. "How do you know?"

"When I returned home from eleven years away, I saw what you didn't. That Diego was fooling everyone. And that he had you in his grasp. I went to great lengths to get you out, did I not? I knew. Trust in me. The path wasn't clear or easy, but I had faith we'd end up here."

"Here," she repeated. Simply. With no inflection or enthusiasm.

Natalia had given me no indication recently that she wanted to be anywhere else. But if the truth of Diego's deception had her doubting herself—if it had changed something for her . . .

I swallowed, trepidation sinking in along with a question I needed to ask. I'd faced many fears in my life, and I'd always come out stronger. But not since I was a teenager, standing before Costa, had I been confronted with the fear of willfully giving up someone I loved.

"Right before you confronted the Valverdes and learned the truth, you told me you were done with your old life. Has that changed?"

Her answering silence made me sweat. How tragically ironic it would be. I'd fought hard to bring her the Valverdes so she could finally release any doubts about me and let herself fall for me completely. But she'd begun to fall already. What if learning she couldn't trust her judgment would have her doubt us? Doubt *me*?

"I want to be here more than anything, but . . ." she said so slowly, it hurt.

My heart pounded just as hard as it had during sex. I wasn't sure, if faced with the decision, that I could let her go. Now that she'd glimpsed the life she could have with me, the right thing would be to release her and let her decide for herself.

But then, the right thing would've been not to take her in the first place.

"But can you understand why it's hard for me to admit that?" she said. "That I *choose* this?"

She chooses this. That was what I needed to hear to assuage my fears—for now.

"Is it possible that even when I didn't trust you, I did, deep down?" she continued.

"Yes. It'd been my job once to watch over your family."

"The day my mother died shook our foundation to the core, but maybe it never broke." She cupped her hand to my cheek, and I leaned into it, rubbing my stubble over her palm. "I love it when you do that," she said. "It makes me feel as if I've tamed a beast."

"You'd call what we just did tame?"

She smiled. And then, "I trust you."

Ah. There it is. Because I'd never felt such contentment, I slid my hand under her hair and bent to kiss her. And yet, in the back of my mind, I understood that I was as terrified as I was fulfilled—Natalia and her love came with even greater fears.

The fear of losing her would only grow as our relationship deepened.

"You're the *everything* I went in search of," I said against her lips. "That loyalty and devotion you showed Diego as a nine-year-old girl—I craved it. The love between your parents—you were a true family." I scanned her face closely. I didn't even want to blink. "Once Diego offered all of that to me, I wanted it so fiercely, I was willing to break all my rules to have it. To have you."

"That's why you were so insistent I come to you willingly. You wanted me to choose you. And I do."

"All that I did, I did with the knowledge that I could give you everything you ever desired."

"And if I desire freedom?"

I paused. The one thing I could give her that would destroy it all. "Then ask for it. See what my answer is."

I didn't know my response, but my gut reaction was

never. If you love someone, set them free—fuck that. I wasn't the type to crush something I coveted before I'd ever let it go—except maybe when it came to her.

Fortunately, she didn't ask.

"My father told me once he wanted me to marry a 'great' man—not a good one." She inhaled audibly. "Now, he demands grandchildren—he must think you're great."

I'd always believed Costa was a great man. To have the sentiment reciprocated after growing up with a snake for a father meant more than Natalia could know.

"I want a family," I said, "and we'll grant Costa his demands—but you're right. It's not the time. I should be more careful, but with you, and only you, I seem to lose control." I ran my knuckles over the goose bumps on her arm. "The time for a child will never be right when everything around us is a threat, but until we've dealt with Diego and Belmonte-Ruiz, we'll wait."

"Agreed." She reached out and touched one of the wounds on my abdomen with a warm, soothing palm. "You didn't hold back anything tonight. Do you feel all right?"

I'd been riding horses, lifting boxes, and riding and lifting my wife any chance I got. "I'm fine."

"You think you're invincible, but you're not, Cristiano." She turned onto her stomach. "If I'm going to stay here with you, then I need you to stick around."

"I'm not going anywhere," I promised as my eyes jumped to the perfect curve of her ass under the white sheet.

She shut her eyes and moved her cheek against the pillow. After a few moments, she said, "Cristiano?"

"¿*Sí, mi amor?*"

"Did you bring your gun to bed?"

Ah, the one cocked, loaded, and prodding into her hip. "I don't control when the rooster crows."

"I meant what I said." She heaved a sweet sigh. "You've wrecked me. I literally cannot move."

"You don't have to. In fact, it would be better if you don't."

"Why?" she asked.

I slid the sheet down to her thighs, then linked a leg through one of hers and drew it open. Salivating at the sight of her smooth, taut ass, I said, "I can break you in just as you are now . . ."

She laughed softly. "You're like a dog with a bone."

"Indeed." I slid down in the bed to get closer to her, ran my hand up her back, and whispered in her ear. "I have to get it out of my system. This overwhelming need to fuck you raw. Then we'll make love, I promise."

"Cristiano, my sun, moon, and stars," she said, her eyes still shut. "We have already made love."

"I know. But I mean in a way that changes us each to our cores. I'm holding back so I don't scare you."

Her lids fluttered open. "You already scare me. Don't you see how I reacted to the idea of you putting yourself in danger again? What if I let myself . . . and then I lose you?"

I inhaled and tried not to read too much into what she *hadn't* said. "What if I lose *you* now that I finally have you?" I said. "Does that mean I shouldn't even try?"

"Try what?"

"To love you or anyone. Nobody in my life is safe. Nobody ever will be." I traced the faint tan lines on her ass cheeks from our afternoon at the beach. "Do you think your father regrets loving Bianca? He doesn't."

Her shudder, and the look of satisfaction on her face, nearly set off the gun between us. That was my cue to go.

Slowly, I withdrew from her and stood.

She lifted her head. "Where are you going?"

"I'm going to shower and jerk off, or else I won't be able to sleep."

"What about me?"

"You're sore. And tired—I hear it in your voice. Get some rest. If I wear you out, I may not be able to enjoy you in the morning. I'll finish you off then."

She rested her cheek back on the pillow as I went and flipped on the shower. Seconds from now, in my fantasies, I'd be balls deep in Natalia's asshole.

But as I stepped under the stream of water and took my dick in hand, that wasn't where my mind went. Instead, I saw Natalia pregnant with my child. No question I was a sick fuck for getting hard over that, but *El Gallo* wanted what *El Gallo* wanted. God help her when she really *was* expecting—I already knew I'd be an overprotective mess.

It was everything I wanted.

I flattened a hand against the tile wall and was about to stroke myself to Heaven when a small, tentative hand beat me to it. I looked over my shoulder. Natalia placed her cheek against my biceps and smiled up at me. My body shielded her from the water, but her wet palm glided along my shaft.

"I thought you couldn't move," I said.

She stroked me gently, almost as if offering comfort. "You have already changed me to my core, Cristiano. And I love you."

Something broke loose in my chest. I hadn't expected . . . not yet. Even though I already knew she loved me, there was nothing like hearing it. Even though I'd kept the faith that she one day would, I almost couldn't come to terms with my luck.

Warmth coursed through me. Warmth, and gratitude. I

turned and took her face in my hands, suddenly over-whelmed. "You . . . I love you, too, my Natalia."

I couldn't express the magnitude of it with words beyond that, so I told her with my kiss—and she responded, her soft, plush lips taking every firm peck I had to give.

19

NATALIA

As water soaked my hair, Cristiano backed me up against the shower wall and slipped a hand under my thigh to lift my leg. He slid inside me and rooted himself there, stilling as we kissed, becoming a part of me in irrevocable ways. His fingers curled into my hair. With my arms wrapped around his neck, I pulled him closer.

He slid in and out slowly, hitting me in a new spot, one that sent deep, satisfied rumbles of pleasure through me. I was already swollen, sensitive, and throbbing from my last orgasm, raw and aching.

I hadn't known the meaning of lovemaking until this moment—I hadn't known the meaning of *love*. I'd been foolish to think I had. I didn't *want* to love Cristiano. It scared me, especially when I'd so recently feared him. Knowing him this way, when he could be taken from me, was more terrifying, though.

Everything he wanted to accomplish, everything he wanted to protect . . . I admired him for it, but it also put him in danger every day.

And yet, in a world of machismo and courage, Cristiano's words earlier were the bravest I'd ever heard. Not just loving someone he could easily lose, but *wanting* love. Seeking it out.

I wasn't as brave. Something told me that losing him would devastate me. And losing Cristiano was even more likely to happen than falling in love with a man I'd once wholeheartedly hated.

But it was too late now.

Cristiano groaned, moving into me, our slick bodies slipping against the other. He drew back, his expression pained as his eyes met mine, and his thrusts grew hard and firm, instead of fast and fevered like earlier. Water beat down on us, dripping from his nose onto me.

How could I love him so fiercely in so little time? And feel it returned without condition?

Our mouths met, savoring the taste of each other. "Don't come inside me," I said.

"I have to. I want to, Natalia."

"But I want to taste you." I pushed his chest, and he withdrew, his cock at full attention and bobbing between us. I got to my knees, took him in my mouth, and showed him my hunger, my desire to watch him unravel. With a hand in my hair and a groan on his lips, he spilled into my mouth without so much as a warning.

We exited the shower, and after toweling off, I slipped my wedding rings back on as he took his razor from a drawer.

"You're going to shave?" I asked.

"If I don't, it'll be twice the length by the morning. You'll wake up next to a wild animal."

"Imagine," I said sardonically, as if I wasn't at the mercy of one every night. I rose onto the tips of my toes for a quick kiss, then ran a finger over his chin. "Sometime, when I'm not so tired, I'll shave it for you."

"Sometime," he agreed. "When I'm a hundred percent sure I can let you near my throat with a razorblade."

I laughed. "A wise man once told me one-hundred percent confidence is a death wish."

As I turned to leave, he took my forearm, drawing me back in front of himself. He pressed his lips together, hesitation in his eyes.

"Is something wrong?" I asked.

"I want you to make me a promise."

A breeze passed through the room, or perhaps it was just the chill of his grave tone that made my hair stand on end. "What?"

"If anything ever does happen to me, Natalia—and it could—tell me you'll go on to live a full life. If your place is here, you'll take the reins. You will be ruthless and gentle and prevail knowing you have my blessing from beyond. And if you choose another life, you will relentlessly pursue happiness."

"I don't want to think about that." It hit too close to home. *Of course* I knew anything could happen at any time—it had to my mother. Death had almost caught Cristiano and myself. I was raw, physically and emotionally, both fucked and made love to tonight. And I'd conceded any last shred of resistance I might've had so I could love Cristiano with all of myself.

It was the greatest risk I'd ever taken because of how closely death hovered over him, and—

You will die for him, your love.

The soothsayer's words shivered through me for the first time in a while. What was Cristiano saying? Why was he bringing this up now?

Because love wasn't just a slippery slope; it was driving

with no brakes and trusting you'd be safe at every hill, valley, and sharp turn. And Cristiano wasn't used to being at the mercy of anything.

"You *have* to think of this," he insisted. "It's part of being a ruler. You need to promise me you'd pick up and move on if you had to." He took my hand in both of his, bringing it to his unshaven mouth, scraping my skin as he kissed it with reverence. He put it to his forehead, as if in prayer. "*Por favor*, Natalia. Give me some peace in the afterlife. Tell me you'd continue on, and pursue happiness, if I were gone."

"Fine," I said, irritated that he was pushing this on me when I'd like to live just *one* day without the anxiety that I might lose everything I'd just found. "But give me the same gift of peace. If Belmonte-Ruiz had succeeded in killing me, you would've gone on. You *will* go on."

Calm pervaded him, and his oft-black eyes were closer to melted-chocolate brown just then. "I can't make you that promise," he said, the heavy words landing at our feet.

I balked. "You just made *me* say it. Why can't you?"

"Because I will follow you."

Frowning, I shifted and placed my other hand over his —so we made a fist like a heart. "What do you mean you'll follow me, Cristiano?"

"Into death."

With a sinking feeling, my eyes fell to our grasp on each other. I could barely wrap my head around what he was saying. I squeezed his hand, more out of a need to hold onto something rather than to offer comfort. "Don't say that. You wouldn't . . ."

His chocolate-brown gaze hardened to an opaque, unreachable void. "Nobody would get away with hurting you. I'd raise hell to avenge you, and if that meant risking my life to achieve it, I wouldn't hesitate."

"Cristiano—"

"I wouldn't be allowed in Heaven, but I swear on all that's holy—I'd rattle the gates until they let me have you."

Goose bumps sprang over my skin with a new kind of dread. He *meant* it—and there was no changing his mind. My death would mean Cristiano's.

I *could not* die for my love—or I would take him down with me.

Sometime around dawn, a firm, wooden knock came on our bedroom door. Cristiano left the warmth of our bed, and as I began to drift back to sleep, he roused me.

"Come," he said, a thread of panic in his voice. "Get dressed."

"What?" I opened my eyes and blinked away sleep. "What's wrong?"

"It's Max."

We got dressed in a flash, and I tied my hair up into a bun as Cristiano and I hurried down to the ground floor. He opened the front door for me, and we stepped outside.

Dawn broke on the bruise-colored mountains, the trees lime green as the rising sun hit their leaves. The peaceful vista of the sprawling, sleeping Badlands was disrupted by a revving engine. One of the security vehicles always posted at the Badlands' front gates barreled up the side of the mountain.

I shielded my eyes, squinting ahead. The truck kicked up a dust cloud as we walked down the front steps. When we stopped at the end of the drive, Alejandro, Eduardo, and Barto appeared next to us.

"Is that . . ." Alejandro started.

The car stopped, and one of Cristiano's uniformed

gatekeepers jumped out of the driver's side before hurrying around to the side door. "¡*Ayuda!*" he called for help, then wrenched open the door. As the passenger stumbled out, all four men sprinted forward.

The sun peeked out, shining down on the man as if he'd fallen from the skies. Dragging a foot and with a swollen face the color of the purple mountains at his back, he was almost unrecognizable. Except for the glass eye. "Max," I whispered.

He fell to his knees and curled his fingers into the grass. Cristiano reached him first and fell to Max's side.

I glanced over my shoulder. My father stood in the doorway along with half the staff, hands over their mouths. "Call Doctor Sosa."

Max pushed himself off the ground to sit back on his heels. "*Agua,*" he pleaded.

As I walked forward, I called back, "And get water —now!"

"You escaped?" Cristiano asked as I reached them.

With a grimace, Max shook his head. "They . . . let me go," he rasped.

Cristiano glanced up at me. "But why?"

"Truce," Max said hoarsely.

Truce? I was immediately doubtful. That didn't make sense. "Why would they ever call a truce?" I asked.

Max's face contorted as he swallowed and formed fists against the ground. "Leave their business alone."

"Why would I?" Cristiano asked. His anger sent a tremor through the air. "Because they returned a man *they* took? And tortured? I have even more reason to destroy them."

"They'll get out . . ." Max said. "They'll stop."

"Stop what?" I asked.

"Trafficking."

Cristiano froze. He hadn't expected that answer, and neither had I. It was what he'd wanted—to end their business. But could we trust that information? Concern also registered on Cristiano's face.

Jaz delivered a bottle of water and stood back, crossing her thin arms over her stomach. Max drank it down in one go, tossed the empty plastic aside, and tried to get up.

Cristiano rose and helped him. Watching Max struggle to stand on his own two feet was painful to watch, and Cristiano must've felt the same. "There's no truce," he said. "BR will pay for this, my friend. They've done too much damage—"

Max held up a hand to stop him and wiped his mouth on his sleeve before accepting another water bottle. As he cracked open the twist top, he managed, "Diego."

The name sent chills down my spine. Instinctively, I reached for Cristiano as he opened his arm and pulled me to his side. "He had a part in this?" Cristiano asked.

Max started to nod, then coughed and sputtered, turned away, and puked.

Cristiano looked at Alejandro. "Find Diego and execute him. *Now*. Throw him over a cliff for all I care. I no longer need to watch the life drain from him." Cristiano lowered his eyes to mine. "Do you?"

I shook my head. "I just want him gone."

"My wife demands his death," Cristiano said. "So kill him—and make it swift."

Max, panting for breath, cringed as he hunched over, his hands on his knees. "We—we can't kill Diego."

"Why not?" Cristiano ran his tongue back and forth over his front teeth. "Give me one *goddamn* reason I shouldn't—"

With great struggle, Max lifted his head. "He's already dead."

20

NATALIA

Max lay in a dark guest bedroom, freshly bathed and gripping a bottle of painkillers. The nurse Doctor Sosa had arranged for us placed a damp towel over his swollen eyes, careful of his cheeks marred with cuts and bruises. He thanked her.

Clutching my mother's rosary, I fell into a chair and pressed my thumb to the crucifix.

Diego was . . . dead.

What was I supposed to feel about it? Triumph? Pity? He could've had love, and offered forgiveness. Instead, he'd chosen hatred and revenge—and it'd been the wrong path. Nostalgia tinged my relief that he was gone. There'd been good times. Genuine moments of laughter and fondness. Riding the property line on our horses, racing from one end of a fence to the other. In my mother's art studio, turning our yellow-painted handprints into chickens by adding red feathers and beaks to the thumbprint. And taking turns with the telescope, pointing out constellations to each other. I remembered his wide smile, patient eyes, and his concern for my wellbeing whenever we'd spoken on the phone—but was any of it real if it'd all been built on a lie?

It didn't matter anymore. He was out of our lives, and that was the way it had to be. I'd thought maybe I'd want to face him at the end, even taunt him—but I didn't need it. It was enough to know he was gone.

Max removed the cloth and set his pills on the night-stand. The nurse helped him ease into a sitting position, then arranged his pillows against the headboard.

"How do you feel?" I asked.

"Sore," he answered, "but grateful to be alive."

At the rasp in his voice, the nurse refilled his water from a pitcher on the nightstand.

Worry etched lines around Cristiano's eyes as he dismissed her with a nod. "What happened?" he asked when we were alone.

Max looked at me and then picked at a blackened fingernail. "I'll tell you everything later. For now, the thing to know is that Belmonte-Ruiz put Diego in the ground."

"Are you certain, Maksim?"

Even with Max's puffy eyelids and the bloated, Byzantium-purple welts around his lips, I could see his expression tighten. "I saw it with my one good eye. Diego is gone."

"I want to say I'm not surprised," Cristiano said, looking from me to Max. "But I knew, in the church, that when I turned my brother free, he wouldn't make it as long as I had out in the wild. I underestimated him, but in the end, I was right."

"How'd it happen?" I asked.

"When I learned Diego was dead, I said I wouldn't deliver the message to you unless I could be sure. They allowed me to see the body before they disposed of it. Diego was cold and lifeless in a body bag. Involuntary overdose . . ."

The hair on the back of my neck rose, and I crossed myself. Even as my stomach somersaulted at the thought of my childhood best friend's decaying body, I welcomed the confirmation of his death.

Cristiano covered his mouth with his fist. "Reason?"

"An offering to make peace with you and Costa," Max explained, "but there's more to it than that. From what I gathered during my time there, Diego was costing them money, making promises he couldn't keep."

"Like with the Maldonados," Cristiano said. "History repeats itself. Diego never learns. What kinds of promises?"

Max's face contorted as he shifted. I stood to help him fix his pillow. "My guess?" Max said. "Based on what I picked up from the guards and other prisoners—Diego told BR he could get you working *for* them, not against them."

"Why the fuck would I ever work for them? No dollar amount could convince me, nothing on the planet would —" Cristiano ran his hand down his face as he shook his head. He sighed. "Natalia."

"What?" I asked.

Max nodded up at me. "I heard about the security breach here the same night they attacked us at the hotel. Could they have been trying to kidnap you?"

"*Sí*," Cristiano said through his teeth. "They would take my wife. For payback *and* for strategy."

"Strategy?" My palm ached as the ruby and pearl rosary beads dug into it. I looked between the two of them. "To do what with me?"

Cristiano had ensured the world thought I was nothing to him. Only few people understood, from the beginning, that the opposite was true. Diego had been the first. He had set all this in motion.

He had gone to Belmonte-Ruiz and told them what I was worth.

And how to get me.

My nostalgia vanished as I was reminded how conniving Diego had been all along.

My throat closed as I realized the answer to my question was obvious given what their business had been built on. "They would've sold me."

"No," Cristiano said. He paced Max's bedside, massaging his jaw. "That would've only started a war between us, and it wouldn't have benefited Diego at all. He's always thinking of how to come out on top. If I were in his shoes, my need for control would win over pride."

"I don't understand," I said.

"If they were able to hold Max just outside my grasp, they could do the same to you. I'd be forced to cooperate to keep you safe."

"Cooperate . . . how?"

"Our infrastructure when combined with Costa's shipping solutions spans not only the Americas, but Europe, and parts of Asia, too," Max explained. "Working with us could grow their business overnight."

Cristiano nodded and finished Max's thought. "But after the lengths I've gone to just to handicap them, they must've known I'd never agree to partner up—not for any amount of money."

My fingers went cold as I put the pieces together. "They wanted you to traffic people."

Cristiano dropped his arm to his side. "Diego knows there's nothing in the world that could get me to do it."

"Except for the one weakness he's exploited before," Max said.

Me. I was the weakness. The little girl he'd been charged with protecting. And then, when he'd come back to town, I'd become a whole other kind of weakness. Cristiano had confessed more than once that he'd done all this for selfish reasons. Because he wanted love. *My* love. My family. He wanted me.

And he'd been willing to let Diego live in order to have all of it—giving Diego all the ammunition he'd needed. He'd planned to use me as leverage to turn Cristiano's life into a living hell. To force Cristiano to do the one thing he'd sworn never to do. What he'd built a whole life around preventing. And in the process, Diego would have gotten more control, more wealth, and turned the knife in his brother's back—all at the same time. And what would've become of me?

I would never find out, and for that, I thanked God for keeping the devil safe. And I thanked my devil for protecting me.

When I caught Cristiano staring at me, his face etched with pain, I crossed the room to him and cocooned one of his enormous, mighty hands in both of mine. What would it have done to Cristiano to have to decide between me and the lives of many innocent men, women, and children? I recognized the tormented look in his eyes for what it was. He was beating himself up for not knowing what he would've chosen.

I put my mouth against the warm, sinewy back of his hand and swallowed to control the emotion in my voice. "You would never have gone through with it," I assured him. "You're too good of a man. You would've let me go in order to save them, and it would've been the right choice."

"Too good of a man?" he repeated. "You know what I am. I could never let you go, and that makes me the kind of monster I've been fighting against."

I shook my head and clenched my teeth against a wave of tears. It was too horrible to even think of. Cristiano would've done the right thing. "It doesn't matter. You'll never have to make that choice."

He wrapped an arm around my shoulders and pulled me close. I turned my cheek against his chest, and he covered the opposite one, holding me there. "Diego got off easy if he'd promised them he'd deliver me," he said, his voice rumbling against my ear.

"Yes," Max said. "But if you don't stop fucking with Belmonte-Ruiz, they'll always be an enemy."

"I want to believe the possibility that they'd stop," Cristiano said. "But why would they? Their entire business is a trafficking ring."

"They have something going on the narcotic side," Max said. "All I know is what I picked up here and there, but perhaps the informant Alejo uncovered can find out more."

"If it's not trafficking, it doesn't matter," Cristiano said. "Let them have their drugs. They can even get into arms and try to steal my territories for all I care. As long as they move on."

I turned my face into Cristiano's palm and kissed it, grateful for its comforting warmth, before pulling his hand away. Max had to be exhausted. We needed to let him rest. But first, I had to ask. "You'd accept the truce?"

After what he'd been through, I'd expect him to say no. He had all the reason to want to strike back. But he only narrowed his eyes and said, "It's not my call alone, but if I set aside my own personal vendetta . . . they made two offerings in good faith—taking Diego's life, and sparing mine. If *they* stop because *we* do, then we all get what we want."

Cristiano nodded. "Do you agree, Natalia?"

It felt like the end. Diego was no longer trying to hurt us. Belmonte-Ruiz wanted us off their backs, and in exchange, there would be a little less suffering in the world. That was what Cristiano had aimed for. I nodded. "I think if it's true . . . we should accept."

Diego was gone, and the only regret I felt was that he hadn't been able to overcome his own demons to make something of his life. But if he had, I may never have known the love rooted deep inside me for his brother. I was glad, if it had to be us or him, that Cristiano and I were still standing.

I twisted to wrap my arms around Cristiano's neck. "It's over, *mi rey*," I said with a genuine smile. "My king."

He searched my face with dark, skeptical eyes. Cristiano had spent eleven years waiting for this moment, and it had eluded him more than once.

I gripped his neck, ran my thumbs up the hollows under his cheekbones that always made him look so grim, and reassured him. "It's *over*."

Months of danger and strife had ended. And yet, I wasn't sure it was a history I'd trade for an easier one. It had prepared me. Educated me. Fortified me. And it had brought me Cristiano.

Together, we would walk into the future stronger than ever.

21

NATALIA

F*ive Months Later*

Cristiano and Papá waited for me downstairs so we could leave for the Day of the Dead parade, but I wanted just a few more moments to myself on the balcony of my old bedroom. The mariachi music seemed fainter now than it had in my childhood. I remembered dancing to it, skipping through the house as I'd hummed to myself, my worn leather sandals clicking on the tile.

I returned to my bedroom and checked my outfit once more in a floor-length mirror. Today, my colorful, off-the-shoulder dress—an explosion of marigold-orange, fuchsia, and rose-red against bone—was a tribute to Mamá as I'd stand by my father while the town honored him with a ride on the final float.

Strong arms slipped around my middle, and I met Cristiano's molten-brown eyes in the reflection. "Even more a symphony than usual in this dress, and music to my ears," he said in my ear. "You look beautiful. You look like *her*."

In a suit and tie, he was handsome as ever. I covered his forearms with mine, lacing our fingers together. "She should be here with us."

"She is." He kissed the back of my head. "Today, we'll go to the *Día de los Muertos* parade and celebrate her life."

"With the whole town," I added.

"They adored her, as they do you," he said, resting his hands on my waist, fingers inched inward . . .

I inhaled and shivered as a chill ran up my spine.

"Cold?" he asked.

No. It wasn't that. Did he know? Could he sense what grew under his fingertips? I adjusted my crown of red roses in the reflection. "With your hands on me? *Jamás*. Never."

It was true. Cold was one thing Cristiano and I would never be. With Cristiano, there was only warmth. Contentment. Even when we fought, fire burned between us.

I wouldn't have it any other way.

Life was as lively as ever at the Badlands, but it'd been relatively peaceful since our truce with Belmonte-Ruiz.

I had everything I could possibly ask for—a community that kept us both on our toes. My husband's and my father's fruitful businesses. My family in good health. A full and promising future.

A loving husband.

And the blessing of his child in my belly.

I'd first suspected I was pregnant last week, after overwhelming nausea three days in a row, but I'd wanted to be certain before telling Cristiano. It was nearly impossible to do anything in the Badlands without him finding out, so I'd snuck away to see Paula at the medical clinic before we'd come, and she'd confirmed it.

We were having a baby.

My heart fluttered thinking of the sonogram tucked away in my purse downstairs. Cristiano would be nothing but thrilled to learn the news, but still, nerves edged my excitement.

Especially on the anniversary of my mother's death.

It wasn't the life I'd imagined for myself. To be a cartel wife, married to a narco king, and a mother by the age of twenty-one. Cartel queens and kings fell all the time, and where did that leave their princes and princesses? Cristiano and I knew all too well—once upon a time, we'd been them.

It was a great responsibility—one neither of us would take lightly. It came with risk. Already, fear bloomed in me in a new way knowing what I did of this life and what emotional attachments could mean. Cristiano and I had both lost parents early on. I didn't want that possibility for my child, but it was the life we led, and that wouldn't change.

And I had the greatest man in the world to lean on. I would be that same support for him.

As he did everything else with unrivaled passion, fervor, and heart—so would he do fatherhood. This child would know the deepest love from both its parents.

"Ready to head over to the parade?" Cristiano asked.

I nodded. First, we would celebrate my mother's life, along with everyone expecting visits from their loved ones on this, the Day of the Dead.

And then we would rejoice in the gift of life growing inside me.

———

We rode through the parade on the last float, the grand

finale—a skeleton in a tuxedo with a cigar stuck in one side of its mouth, surrounded by live roses and marigolds. Cristiano and my father each puffed on his own Montecristo as Papá grumbled about the obligation of his presence, even as he waved and smiled. Secretly, he was pleased by the honor.

Sugar skulls in white and black danced around us, while ladies dressed as *La Catrina* twirled in colorful dresses, and masked men on the floats gestured with both hands to get the crowds to cheer.

We crawled along the main road of shops, fruit carts, and *mercados* advertising cigarettes and Coca-Cola.

"I'm going to send the kid to get me a mezcal," my father said as fine, white, cinnamon-scented cigar smoke wafted into the wind.

"Gabe is working," I reminded him.

"He's hopeless with a rifle. Should've been Barto up here."

I glanced down at Gabriel Valverde, his gun at the ready as he rode on the lower tier of the float. Cristiano hadn't protested when I'd been asked to join my father in the parade, but even though things had been peaceful for a while, being out in the open at any time made him anxious.

"I'm trying to build Gabriel's confidence, and Barto has no shortage of that," I said, smiling down at where Gabriel was stationed, out of earshot. "He's improved a lot. Can't you see how much stronger he looks?"

"The kid is a genius." Father had been reluctant to accept a Valverde in his life, and still wouldn't call him anything other than "kid" or "boy," but at least he recognized his talent. "He should be in front of a computer. You need his brain indoors, not splattered all over a *papier-mâché* skeleton."

He had a point.

Both Barto and Cristiano had made the same argument—and even though it'd been the only thing they'd agreed on in a while, I'd put my foot down. The parade was the perfect opportunity to show Gabriel how much I believed in him. With Barto somewhere patrolling the street, every overprotective man in my life was within a fifteen-meter radius. I'd never felt safer.

A cold drink *did* sound pretty good, though, considering my stomach had been so uneasy. "I'll go get you the mezcal," I said. "An iced *horchata* sounds perfect anyway."

"Better than a warm Coca Light?" Cristiano asked. "Since when?"

My cheeks warmed. My body was experiencing new and unusual things. "Just a craving for something different," I said.

"Oh . . .?" He arched an eyebrow. "A *craving*?"

I raised to the balls of my feet and kissed his cheek before he could follow whatever train of thought was forming in his mind. This moment was about Mamá. We'd have ours later. "I'll be right back."

"You stay here." He reached by me to put down his cigar. "I'll go."

"Relax. Enjoy your Cuban," I said and gave him a scolding look. "It'll be the last one you have for a while."

When I'd learned of Cristiano's heartburn, I'd made him stop smoking, limited him to a couple drinks a week, and had been working with Fisker on healthier meal recipes that didn't make Cristiano want to skip straight to dessert.

But it was a special day.

I picked up my purse from where I'd stowed it, put it over my shoulder, and started to walk away when a hand at my elbow drew me back. I turned around to reassure Cristiano I'd be fine, but when I met his eyes, there was only a spark of excitement in them.

He raised them to the sky. "Look."

A small kaleidoscope of monarch butterflies fluttered over our heads. "Papá," I called, and he ambled over to us, following our gazes.

The monarch migration passed through during early November—like now, on All Souls' Day, when the deceased came to visit the living. That was why monarchs were believed to hold the spirits of the departed. It happened every year, but it was never any less special to believe Mamá was with us. On my wedding day, I'd thought her presence a warning. I now knew it had been approval. Today, she returned to bless me and my unborn child.

"*Te extraño mucho, Bianca.*" Telling her he missed her very much, my father smiled, flicked ash from his cigar onto the live marigolds surrounding us, and walked away.

Cristiano took his Montecristo from his mouth, pulled my face to his with one hand, and pecked my lips.

I walked around to the rear of the float, waving back at the throngs of parade-goers. With the *rat-a-tat-tat* of poppers that sounded too close to gunshots, the crowd inhaled a collective gasp. I descended the stairs of the float and hopped off, into the street.

As I made my way through the crowd toward a drink vendor, a dancing skeleton bumped into me so hard, I stumbled in my high heels. Instead of trying to catch my purse as it fell, I covered my stomach. Once I'd righted my footing, it hit me for the first time that my body would change—as would the way I treated it. I'd have to be more careful everywhere I went—and definitely no more training.

I squatted and picked up the envelope with the sonogram first, then bit my lip to hide a smile as I tucked it into a side pocket.

As people walked around me, I shoveled my things back into my handbag. I searched the street for my cell phone, then checked to see if it was still in my purse. Unable to find it, I stood and turned, my gaze landing on a mariachi in the crowd with a familiar pair of eyes.

A piercing gaze that sent a chill straight down my spine, then vanished under a sombrero as the man disappeared back into the crowd.

Diego.

No. Diego is dead.

I took a deep breath to try to calm my thumping heart. It wasn't possible. My current condition was doing things to my brain, and my emotions were overwrought from being back home on the anniversary of Mamá's death. I rubbed my temples, took a few more steps, and crouched again to try to locate my phone.

Mariachi music started from somewhere. I'd been hearing it on and off all day, but now that Diego was on my mind, it took me back to my parents' room on this same morning twelve years earlier. The haunting echoes of the music through the house. The fan rotating with a breeze from the open windows, casting shadows over Mamá's body on the tile floor. Diego running in, his gun drawn, acting surprised. Cristiano's forearm a bar around my waist as his hand clamped over my mouth.

A bout of nausea hit me. Something didn't feel right. I got back to my feet and started back for the float when I noticed a man in a ski mask walking toward me.

Fuck. I willed my breathing to slow so I could think. We had no enemies at the moment, but as Cristiano said—the fight was never over. I couldn't be too careful. I ducked left and hid in a group of dancing women while maneuvering my way back toward the float. They spun, their skirts blending together into reds, greens, and purples.

I surveyed the crowd and sucked in a breath as Diego's face flashed by.

No. It wasn't . . . it couldn't . . .

I stepped up onto a curb and furtively searched the throngs of people, but I didn't have to look long—his height set him apart. He removed his sombrero and shook out golden-brown hair. It *couldn't* be him. And yet, Diego's mannerisms were seared into my memory. As long as I lived, I'd never forget the way his long fingers tracked through the strands of his hair. He palmed the sombrero the way he had his cowboy hat at the costume party. As he started to turn toward me, I noticed a bolo tie—but I wouldn't wait to see if it bore the de la Rosa family crest.

I ran, sprinting through the crowd, pushing people aside.

A man in chalky white face paint and blackened eye sockets stepped in my way, and I stopped short. The skeleton that had bumped into me earlier. I whirled to go another way, but the ski mask closed in from another direction.

I had a knife in my purse. I reached in and grabbed it as a voice said in my ear, "If you make a scene, your daddy gets a bullet in the back. Then we start shooting up the crowd, Natalia."

My scalp prickled, air sucking from my lungs. "Who are you?" I asked. "Belmonte-Ruiz?"

He didn't answer.

My palm sweat around the handle of the knife. I needed to fight back—but as of this morning, physical violence had taken on a new meaning for me. Since my arrival at the Badlands, Cristiano had impressed upon me that I couldn't ever be afraid to get hurt. I wasn't. But now that I was carrying his child?

That was different.

I had to protect my body at any cost.

I'd hesitated too long.

He grabbed my handbag and the knife with it as more armed men dressed in black and in face masks appeared all around me, closing in. With a screeching sound, yelling started. A white van barreled toward us, sending people jumping out of the way.

I opened my mouth to scream, and a damp towel covered it, suffocating me with a sickly-sweet reek. I held my breath, fighting not to inhale. I was surrounded. My vision blurred with little bursts of light. Not even the tight hold on me could disguise the feeling of my lungs caving in. Nor could people's screams and mariachi music drown out one single word in my ear as the world around me faded to black.

"*Princesa.*"

22

NATALIA

My head lolled somewhere soft, but the backs of my eyeballs throbbed. Lying on my side, my body jostled with the whir and hum of an engine.

My baby.

My eyes flew open to dark nothingness. I went to cover my stomach, but my elbows were bound behind my back and had been long enough that I couldn't feel my hands.

"Sleeping Beauty stirs." The voice sounded both muffled and directly above me and its familiarity tugged me from my dull consciousness. Aching shoulders. Burning throat. My cheek scratched against burlap. I was . . . on a lap?

"We didn't even get to the part where the prince kisses you," he added.

Diego.

My heart lurched in my chest as my entire body stilled.

On All Souls Day, Diego had risen from the dead. My head pounded with pain and questions. *How* was he still alive? Where had he been the last several months? What did he want with me?

Traces of earthy soil and pungent gasoline mixed with Diego's familiar smell. *Never get in the vehicle.* It was rule number one around here. I had no idea how long we'd even been driving, but a victim in a van was as good as dead.

Then again, it seemed death wasn't always permanent.

"You were . . ." My vocal chords protested from whatever he'd used to knock me out. "You died."

"Not yet. Not without you." The sack lifted, and my skin cooled as I blinked open my eyes to two armed skeletons in face paint across from me. We rode in the back of a gutted, windowless van with a bench along each side panel. The man who'd helped corner me laid his gun on his knee, and it pointed directly at me. One major pothole and I could be done for.

I shifted, turning my face up to see Diego looking down at me. His golden-streaked, cocoa-colored hair fell around high, regal cheekbones. A black shirt with dust on the collar lent masculinity that offset features pretty enough that he could've been a movie star. I saw the same patience and kindness in his mesmerizing green eyes as I had many times before, but now, I could only interpret it as an act to get what he wanted.

I could act, too, though.

He stroked my hair. "I promised I'd come back for you, didn't I? I risked my life to get you away from him."

Him.

They could've hurt or taken Cristiano, too. Everything had happened so fast. My throat thickened with emotion. "Where is he?"

"You're free of him now, *muñequita.*"

Muñequita—his little doll. Fury snuffed out my confusion as a million rebuttals raced through my head. I could never be, and never *wanted* to be, free of Cristiano. He was my husband, my rock, and my future. He was ten times the man Diego would ever be—and he'd never treated me like a helpless doll.

But I had to think straight. To be smart, like the queen Cristiano demanded I be. One worthy of standing at his side.

One thing he'd imparted: if I'd failed to incapacitate a captor, as I had now, I should act compliant, even if it felt unnatural, until I had an escape plan in place.

I couldn't act recklessly or out of emotion. Raging at Diego wouldn't get me anywhere, especially while I was tied up and at his mercy. While I carried our baby, my body was my priority.

There had to be some part of Diego that cared for me; it couldn't have *all* been a performance. Cristiano had called it fondness. Diego had spent day in and day out by my father's side, picking up my calls, and listening to me go on for hours about school, or how I missed him or my mother.

I couldn't be the girl I was with him anymore—even if I wanted to be—but I could act the part. Cristiano had tried to warn me early on that this was a game, and I had to compete.

I steadied my breathing. "Everything hurts," I said softly.

"I'm sorry we had to ambush you like that," Diego said. "I couldn't be sure you wouldn't scream or fight back. I'm sure my desperate brother has tried hard to convince you that you *want* to be in the Badlands."

"I've had to make my life there bearable." The lie soured on my tongue as it came out, but it wasn't hard to sound convincing. After all, before I'd loved Cristiano, I'd fought against anything to do with him. "But that doesn't mean I forgive you for trading me to him."

"I *didn't* trade you. I let him think he had you for a while so I could ensure our survival—and it worked, didn't it? We're both still standing."

That he should live while the heavens had taken Mamá . . .

I inhaled through my nose to control my urge to unleash on Diego the way I'd fantasized. "I'm really uncomfortable," I said. "Will you *please* untie me?"

His eyes roamed from my face down to my breasts, stomach, and thighs. "You look different," he said. "Leaner. Stronger. How do I know you won't try to fight back?"

"Fight *you*? Even if I knew how, I wouldn't do anything that stupid. You can easily overpower me." He'd always treated me like his breakable princess, but he was right—I *was* stronger. And with enough time, I could free my hands from almost any binding. Solomon and I continued to train almost daily, and Cristiano especially liked Solomon to put me through potentially life-threatening scenarios. It had been a rigorous few months.

At least, up until last week when I'd started faking a wrist injury until I could go see Paula at the clinic for a pregnancy test.

"I didn't do anything at Cristiano's house but ride my horse and play soccer with the staff to keep myself occupied. And anyway," I added, nodding across the aisle of the open van, "I can't exactly fight back with guns trained on me."

Diego clucked at the man with the 9mm on his knee, and he holstered it. "They're overly cautious," Diego explained. "They think this is a kidnapping, not a rescue."

Diego no doubt picked his words carefully, hoping

they'd influence my point of view. This wasn't a *rescue*—to him or to me.

Diego wanted me alive for a reason, which meant he needed me.

I was leverage against Cristiano and my father—but to what end? He'd obviously joined forces with some federation, most likely Belmonte-Ruiz. Which meant after five months of silence, they'd broken their truce. If it had ever been real.

Diego took a knife from the leg pocket of his utility pants, flipped it open, and cut the restraints at my elbows. I rolled my shoulders forward, stretching my arms as I sat up slowly.

I could see him in all his glory now. Tall, muscular, with the baby-faced version of Cristiano's brutally beautiful face. It was Cristiano's black hair and eyes, his hollowed cheeks and high cheekbones, that made him too much for the silver screen. The world probably couldn't handle it, sadly for them.

I tried tapping into that attraction for Diego again. "Where have you been?" I asked. "In the church you said you'd come back for me. You didn't."

"That's why I'm here now." He took my hand, bringing it to his mouth. "Poor girl. You've always had someone to rescue you. Me, Barto, Costa, Cristiano. And yet, we've all hurt you, too."

"The Diego I knew would never hurt me." I took back my hand, rolling my wrists with exaggeration, hoping to lean in to the frailty he expected of me.

"I'm not the one who changed. My brother did." He put his knife away. "First, Cristiano took my parents from me. Then he took you and Costa. He made the first move —I'm just playing the game."

Diego believed *he* was the one who'd been wronged.

He'd have carried on his parents' gruesome business without hesitation despite all the lives it would ruin.

Max wouldn't have lied to Cristiano. Since his return, he'd been as loyal as ever. If anything, he was *more* protective of us. So there had to be another explanation for Diego's sudden return. "Max saw you in a body bag."

"I know. As I said, I risked my life for you—I almost died that day."

That day. I remembered it well—at least, the moments when Max had come stumbling home to us and broken the news. Diego had put Max, Cristiano, my father, my mother, and myself in harm's way too many times. I licked my lips, finding my mouth dry. "How'd you do it?" I asked. "And why?"

"Cristiano would always be a threat to me. I needed him to believe I was dead."

The road turned bumpy, and I steadied myself on the van's side panel, suddenly overwhelmed with nausea. "Why?" I asked.

"So Cristiano would drop his guard while Belmonte-Ruiz and I formed a plan to get you out."

So this *was* the work of Belmonte-Ruiz. "What about their truce with—" I stopped before I could say *us*. I needed to use language to my advantage, too, and separate my interests from Cristiano's. "With Cristiano and his cartel?"

"A ploy to buy us time while we got things in place."

"What things?" I asked.

Diego pushed up the sleeves of his black Henley. I'd told him on many occasions how strong and sexy he looked in the ribbed, long-sleeved shirt. Had he worn it to remind me of that, the same way he carefully chose his words?

"It's complicated," he said, "and not anything you need to worry about. Just cooperate, and you'll be fine."

Don't worry. Diego's mantra when it came to me. Diego asked for my trust in him, which meant he believed I was still foolish enough to give it. And why shouldn't he? He couldn't know the woman I was now. How I'd grown. The depth of love I possessed for my husband, and the lengths I'd go to to get home to him.

Was he safe?

The road had smoothed, but my nausea returned.

Had they ambushed him, too? God. Let him be safe.

I put my face between my knees as I had the urge to vomit.

"Is it morning sickness?" Diego asked.

My heart plummeted to my feet. Blood drained from my face as I stared at the muddy floor of the van. My red toenail polish, too happy for the moment, burned my irises. There was no *possible* way he could know I was pregnant. *I* hadn't even known until yesterday, and my stomach was nothing but abs after the workouts Cristiano had put me through.

I raised my head. "What?"

"I saw the sonogram in your purse." He furrowed his brows. "I'm sorry, *princesa.* To think of Cristiano's hands on you . . . it kills me. The things you must've endured with him."

As he spoke, a red film covered my eyes. If Diego knew I was pregnant, he could—*would*—use that against me. Against Cristiano.

Fucking bastard.

Diego thought I endured Cristiano's sexual advances instead of welcomed them. He assumed the pregnancy was against my will when it was the happiest news of my life.

It wasn't the truth that mattered, though, but what Diego believed.

I suddenly understood all too well the position Cristiano had been in since our wedding day. Those who knew our weaknesses could exploit them. That was why, early on, he'd let the world think our marriage was only for show.

It was why I couldn't let Diego know I'd do anything possible to save my baby.

I resisted the urge to pull my knees to my chest and sat up instead. "I didn't ask for it," I said simply. "The baby. The world doesn't need more of someone like Cristiano."

Diego tilted his head at me. "You don't want it?"

A pit formed in my stomach. On Our Lady of Guadalupe, I wouldn't wish away my child. I *couldn't*. But as Cristiano had taught me, it could be the best way to protect it.

I glanced at the ground, shaking my head. "No."

"No?" he prompted. "No what?"

"I . . . I don't want the baby."

Diego quieted. My stomach churned even more for the lie as it settled between us. I felt sick. How could I say it?

After a few moments, he replied, "You're lying."

My eyes fell shut. *He* was calling *me* a liar? "It's the truth," I said, but I didn't sound convincing even to my own ears.

He shook his head slowly. "You forget how well I can read you. You want the baby. I have to assume you want Cristiano, too, then—which is a problem for us."

I gripped the edge of the seat.

I didn't want to cooperate or comply. Or malign or dismiss the most important man in my life. Or to pretend as if Diego hadn't betrayed me in the worst possible ways.

I bit my bottom lip until it smarted. I *had* to hold my tongue. Information was power, and I needed to withhold it as much as I needed to get it. I couldn't reveal that I knew his crimes, his scheming, the mask he hid behind, the fact that he'd . . . he'd . . . unlocked the tunnel and as a result, my mother had—*fuck*. Fuck him. *Fuck* him.

"I can see you're upset, Tali. Tell me what's running through your mind—the truth, though. No more lying."

"Yes, I want the baby," I admitted. "I thought you'd think I was a traitor if I admitted it. It doesn't mean I care about Cristiano—"

"Another lie."

I couldn't do it. I couldn't sit here and pretend he hadn't done this, or that I would betray Cristiano. I'd been innocent and naïve with Diego my whole life, and where had it gotten me? *Here*. For months, I'd lamented that I'd never gotten to hear Diego confess. I'd been given a second chance to face the man who was, in my eyes, my mother's true murderer.

I lifted my head. The words tumbled out, leaving a metallic taste in their wake. "I know what you did."

His expression eased. After a few moments of strained silence, he asked, "What are you talking about?"

"Exactly what you think."

Once I revealed what I knew, there was no turning back. It would permanently put us on opposite sides. But I had to do it. For myself. For her.

"I heard it directly from Vicente Valverde," I said, my jaw tingling with disgust and contempt. "You let them in the house, and then ran them out of town. *You're* responsible for my mother's death."

23

NATALIA

At the mention of the Valverdes—a name Diego had probably never expected to hear from my mouth—he went completely still. He didn't blink.

The shift was palpable, and for a moment, I wondered if I'd just sealed my fate. I was no longer the damsel in distress he wanted me to be.

But I'd been holding it in for months with no guilty party to accuse face to face. Now, I'd redeemed some small part of what Diego had stolen from me, from my mother and father, and from Cristiano. He now knew that in my eyes, he'd never be the hero again.

And that there'd never be a greater villain to me than him.

"Why'd you do it?" I asked. I knew why, but he should have to say it.

He looked across the aisle of the van at the two Belmonte-Ruiz men. Their expressions hadn't changed. I doubted they gave one fuck about this conversation.

"Costa owed me two lives for taking my parents," he

said. "When the Valverdes came to me, I saw my opportunity. I took it. Bianca paid the price for what Costa did,"
Diego said slowly, as if carefully choosing his words. "I'm
sorry it hurt you, and I'm even sorry she had to die."

"How can you say that when you were the cause of my
hurt and her death?"

His forehead wrinkled with concern as he looked at his
hands. "I cared for Bianca—as I care for you. Falling in
love with you happened both slowly and overnight. It hit
me hard. I *still* love you." He splayed his hand to remind
me of the tattoos between his fingers—the roses with his
family name on one, and on his ring finger, our initials. "I
always wanted us to do this together."

I clenched my teeth. *Screw you.*

I wanted to spit at him, headbutt him, kick him in the
balls. But I didn't bat an eyelash. "Do what together? What
do you want me for?"

"Costa would've lost the Cruz cartel if not for me,
Talia. After your grandfather passed, and before I stepped
into an advisory role, Costa could barely control what he
had—that's why the Valverdes tried to take it." He sighed,
propping his elbows on his knees as he rubbed his face.
"But under my helm? It *flourished*. It was *mine* to take over
one day—it only made sense that you and I would run it."

"What about my father?" I asked.

"Once you and I were married, he'd have understood
it was time to step down."

"And if he hadn't?"

"He would've." A threat. "If Cristiano hadn't reen-
tered the picture, that's what would've happened," Diego
said. "We took a little detour, but we'll end up in the same
place."

As Cristiano had said, Diego would've taken over by

any means, and the course he'd have chosen was using my love for him against Papá.

And if Diego still saw me in that role but knew I wouldn't cooperate—what were his plans then?

"Where?" I asked through a swallow. "Where will we end up?"

"At the head of the de la Rosa and Cruz cartels." Diego linked his hands between his knees and glanced over at me. "And now, you'll help me get Calavera, too. Costa still owes me a second life, but I'll take the next best thing —his cartel. His daughter. Cristiano's wife. If you can get past all this, we can do it as a team again—"

"You lied to me. You kept me in the dark." The van jostled as we hit more unpaved road. "That's not a team."

Diego kept his eyes down as he flexed his hands and massaged one palm. "The secrets surrounding Bianca's death always weighed on me. I know my involvement hurts you, but you'll move past it. And when you do, we'll get everything we always wanted. The fortune, the business . . ." He glanced up at me. "Over time, once you forgive me, maybe we'll even get more of the romantic nights like our first."

My stomach roiled. How *dare* he call that night anything but it was—a violation. It made me sick. God willing, I'd never think of that night again and how stupid I'd been to fall for his empty words. "You *stole* my virginity."

"You gave it to me." He reached out to touch my face, but I flinched back, and he dropped his arm. "You're right to be upset. I just couldn't bear the thought of watching you marry him without having *any* piece of you to myself. It meant so much to me, Tali."

Bile rose up my throat, and this time, it had nothing to

do with the road. *It means less than nothing to me*, I wanted to tell him. *Cristiano fucks me so much better.*

I would've said it if I was only responsible for myself, but I couldn't risk provoking him.

Diego sighed. "We should arrive soon."

"Where are you taking me?"

"We have some things to figure out."

Some things. I had an idea of what he meant. "Cristiano won't cooperate," I said bluntly.

Diego's eyebrows rose. He didn't respond at first, as if deciding whether I actually knew anything.

I might, if his plan was the one Cristiano, Max, and I had pieced together months ago. Belmonte-Ruiz hadn't killed any of us when they'd had the chance—that was no coincidence. Diego had intended to use me as leverage to force Cristiano into helping Belmonte-Ruiz expand their human trafficking ring.

But that would *never* happen.

Cristiano knew my wishes. I would not allow him to put his soul and others' lives at risk for me. Diego was delusional enough to think he could pull this off, and I'd come to learn that Diego's delusions were extremely dangerous —and for Mamá, they'd been fatal.

"My brother has pissed off a lot of people; I'm not the only one who wants to see him dead," Diego said finally. "If anything, my plan is the only thing keeping him alive— at least, for as long as I need him."

The vehicle hit soft ground and slowed to a stop. Diego patted my knee, shrugged into a jacket, and passed me the burlap sack. "Put it on."

He helped me from the van. The sun never hit my face, and the temperature had dropped, but the sack let in enough light that I could tell it was still daytime. We walked up a small hill, and I struggled for breath, as if something sat heavy on my chest. My dress brushed the ground as dense dirt gave under the spikes of my heels.

Once my shoes hit firmer ground, and the fresh air turned stale, Diego said, "You can remove it."

I pulled off the sack. We stood in a sprawling, one-story concrete and brick warehouse, surrounded by wood pallets and a forklift, steel shelving with plastic bins, gas cans, and crates. I searched for any potential weapons. Petrol and wood to burn the place down. Scissors at a workstation near a conveyor belt. If he didn't tie me up, I could sprint for the fire extinguisher against one wall. Incapacitating *him* would require little mobility and even less creativity— but what about the other men?

Diego took me to a windowed office in one corner of the warehouse. He handed me a key and said, "Unlock it."

He didn't want to turn his back to me. With the truth about my mother out there, I'd lost at least some of the trust he might've kept. I took the single key. *I could jam it in his eye.* Slipped it in the lock. *But that's not strategic.*

He definitely had a gun on him—he'd be stupid not to. It was most likely somewhere around his middle.

I held my breath as I opened the door.

Diego took the key and the sack from me and gestured for me to pass through, then at a metal folding chair against the back wall, under a domed floor lamp. "Sit."

He walked to a desk of computers across from the seat. Above it was a bank of monitors—security footage of the inside and perimeter of the warehouse.

"What is this?" I asked, trying to distract him as I noted my surroundings. Empty buckets in one corner. A stack of bricks in another. A file cabinet. Even the lamp and chair could act as defense weapons. Anything that wasn't bolted down. My purse was nowhere in sight.

"We're just going to let my brother know you're safe."

"Why?" I asked as I walked to the chair.

"Hands behind your back."

I held them together in front of me, hoping he wouldn't think anything of it. Easier to escape that way.

Diego eyed me up and down. "I said *behind* you."

"Does it matter?" I said but obeyed, mentally preparing myself for the most difficult restraints. However he bound me, I could get out of it. I'd practiced countless times. But some scenarios were worse than others. For handcuffs, I could try to find a prop on the desk in front of me, but I'd need time alone. All my sneakers at home had Kevlar laces that could cut through zip ties or rope, and some even had universal handcuff keys strung on the laces for this purpose—but of course, I was in heels today.

I'd have to find another way.

When I heard the screech of duct tape, my fraught nerves settled slightly. Of everything he could've chosen, that was on the easier side to escape. I might even be able to do it with him in the room. He had little faith in me and hadn't even bothered to try very hard.

It would be his mistake.

I made two fists to give myself more wiggle room as he taped my wrists good and tight.

But not tight enough.

"I'm sorry if that hurts," he said. "It's partly for show, and partly because I'm not sure I can trust you right now."

A genuine apology. In his voice, I heard the boy I'd once loved. I tried to see Diego the way I had before—as a creative, smart, level-headed man I'd aspired to spend the rest of my life with. He'd said he'd loved me, and I still believed he'd thought he had. Perhaps selfish love was the most he was capable of, but Cristiano's selflessness and had taught me love's true meaning.

His words came back to me now.

Love is, "I'd die for you."

Not, "Would you die for me?"

A lump formed in my throat. Not for myself, but for what Cristiano must be going through. For me to disappear from right under his nose would devastate him. He'd blame himself. He'd suffer.

If *I* could manage to tap into better times during a situation like this, then Diego could, too. "How'd you do it?" I asked as he ripped off the tape and patted it into place.

"Do what?" He came around to stand in front of me, surveying his work. He held up the tape. "I won't bother with your mouth, but don't scream. The only people who'd hear you would enjoy it and might come sniffing around. I'm only one man to defend you."

I refrained from shuddering. Again, his words were intentionally chosen to rattle me. I wouldn't let them. "How'd you look me in the eye every day?" I asked. "You watched us bury her."

He set the roll of tape on the desk and took the small white envelope with my sonogram from his jacket pocket.

My pulse jumped at the sight of it—but I forced myself to school my reaction.

"It's in the past, Tali. No point in reliving it. Just know, I'm sorry it happened the way it did." Diego sighed, as if truly regretful. "And for Cristiano to be accused of violating a woman who'd acted as a mother to him? A man like him, a known rapist? It must've torn him apart. I can't imagine."

My breath caught in my throat. He *could* imagine, and it pleased him. Maybe Diego *had* known his older brother had tried to shield him during his youth from their parents' business. Yet, somehow, he saw that as betrayal. "How can you say it like it's nothing?" I asked. "She was abused because *you* let the *sicario* in."

"There's no way I could've known it would happen that way." Diego stared at me, his green eyes sorrowful. "Bianca didn't deserve it, but your father did. And he deserves what's coming even more."

My throat dried. Diego could easily rip out the hearts of the two men who'd killed his parents—because he had me. "What's coming to him?" I asked so softly, I wasn't sure he'd heard.

He came and squatted in front of me. The fact that he had the nerve to look me in the eye told me that he'd convinced himself he was the hero of this story.

"My problem is only with Cristiano and Costa," he said.

"Then it's with me, too. They're *mi familia*."

"They can't walk away from killing my parents and destroying my family's business," Diego said. "I'm going after what rightfully belongs to me. Can't you understand that?"

I tried with everything I had. If I could not only understand but love Cristiano after years of loathing him, it shouldn't have been difficult to see the point of view of the boy I'd worshipped. My father had made both of them witness their parents' murders as a warning—loyalty would be rewarded, dissention would cost them their lives.

Cristiano and my father had decided Diego's fate for him. Instead of inheriting the legacy his family had built, Diego would forever be a charge, second in command, "just another worker" as he'd once bitterly referred to himself. He'd lost his family and his empire, as had Cristiano—but at least Cristiano'd had a say in it.

But all of that was erased by the deliberate, calculated betrayal that had cost my mother her life. Diego'd made that choice when he could've easily gone to my father and saved her. So no, I couldn't understand.

My jaw ached, molars grinding together. "You should've known, no matter how much I loved you—I would've never stood by your side and played with people's lives."

"You would've. You will," he said resolutely. He held up the small envelope, then tucked it into the neckline of my dress, over my left breast. Close to my heart. "Just remember this if you're tempted to do anything stupid."

I'd been grateful for the duct tape a moment ago, but suddenly, it was excruciating that I couldn't lash out at him or cover my stomach to protect what'd only just begun to grow inside me. "Cristiano won't play your games. He knows I'd rather die than let that happen."

"It's not your choice." He checked his watch, then walked to one of the large windows to look into the warehouse. "Costa, Cristiano, and I each love you, but we've all used you as a pawn."

While his back was to me, I glanced at the surveillance screens. Two men guarded the inside of the warehouse, though I couldn't tell where they were in relation to us. Two more milled out front, while one stood at the gated entrance. *Five.* Numbers six, seven, and eight held assault rifles and walked the perimeter, which was surrounded by large trees.

"Cristiano will comply," Diego said, still looking off into the distance. "He loves you, and he of all people knows that being with me is a fate far better than the hell I could arrange for you."

It took a moment for his threat to sink in. He could sell me. As his father had Angelina. I didn't want to believe he was capable of it, but the truth was, I didn't know the level of depravity I was dealing with. And the worst part was that Diego knew exactly what a threat like that would do to

Cristiano. It may even be enough to convince him to cooperate.

With a series of *beeps*, Diego took his phone from his pocket and hit a button to speak into it. "*Bueno.*"

"*Listos,*" came a man's voice through the speaker.

Ready.

Diego returned to the computer beneath the monitors and the security footage flickered off.

My insides twisted. Something was happening. "What are you doing?"

"Don't worry. Cristiano will cooperate to keep you safe." Diego opened a closet and removed a tripod. He set it up behind the desk, in front of the control panel. Next, he took a smartphone with a bulky case out of a desk drawer and swiped his thumb over the screen. "Knowing I have you will torture him. You saw the way he tried to feed me to the Maldonados. I couldn't let that go, Natalia—you know that. Cristiano deliberately provokes his enemies, and he shouldn't be surprised when that comes back around to him."

I couldn't argue that Cristiano was a good man, or even deserving of what he had. He, like Diego, my father, and myself, had committed many sins. But I loved him for who he was, flaws and all. I couldn't ask for a better partner or for a better father to our future child.

When did one become a mother? I wasn't sure, only that I already felt extremely protective. Maybe it had to do with what lay ahead more than anything. Since I'd suspected the pregnancy, I'd started to envision a new life with Cristiano. Our latest adventure—parenthood. Gruff, rough-around-the-edges Cristiano cradling a newborn son in both hands. Me, passing on the lessons I'd learned to a daughter and thereby honoring her grandmother and her father, who'd both taught me strength.

I had to do whatever I could to protect that.

Survival, no matter what.

Red lights flickered on the TV screens directly in front of me. Images flashed on and off.

Diego hummed with satisfaction, screwed the smartphone onto the tripod by its case, and stepped back before he spoke into his own phone. "We're connected. Put them through."

"What is this?" I asked hoarsely, but I wasn't sure I wanted to know.

He aimed a small remote at the smartphone and pushed a button. "We're streaming. Look into the camera and say hello to your husband."

24

CRISTIANO

I t took me a moment to register what I was looking at.
A well-lit office. A metal chair in the center. My
wife.

Blood rushed in my ears. My heart thrashed hard
enough to deafen and disorient me.

My team and I had scoured the abandoned parade.

As soon as guns had come out, people had cleared the
area quickly, except for a few bodies in the middle of the
road who'd possibly tried to stop *them*. Who were *they?*
Who'd taken my wife? All anyone could tell me was that
men in black, some costumed, had put her into a van and
vanished.

Just like that.

Costa's and my choppers had been dispatched but had
yet to find anything.

I'd trampled fallen crepe streamers, glitter, and plastic
plates and forks looking for a clue—*anything*—until we'd
received word that her abductors wanted to make contact,
and we'd rushed back to the Badlands.

Now, Costa and I stood in the basement control center

as Gabriel patched through a live video feed to our security monitors.

Natalia.

Her dress, colorful against a gray backdrop, remained intact—*gracias a Dios*. There were no injuries that I could see. Her hands appeared to be bound behind her back, but she wasn't gagged.

"Natalia, *mi amor*," I said, surprised at the even, calm tone of my voice. I may have learned to keep my composure in a threatening situation, but this was something else entirely. This was my entire fucking life. "Can you hear me? Where are you?"

She nodded almost imperceptibly, but her eyes shifted to the side of the camera. She wasn't alone.

I prayed she'd been taken for ransom by some recklessly stupid faction and that Belmonte-Ruiz hadn't broken their truce.

But why should the devil's prayers be answered?

"Brother."

Chills spread over me at the all-too-familiar voice. One I'd never mistake. One I never thought I'd hear again.

A face resembling my own filled the screen, but it might as well have belonged to a stranger. My brother. *Diego.*

What the fuck. He was alive. Everything in my body ceased to function. I froze, and it was a good thing. I never wanted Diego to think he'd caught me off guard.

He blocked Natalia as he looked from me to Costa and back. "Good. You're both here."

My hands twitched with the urge to reach through the screen and wrap my hands around his neck, tighten them slowly so he'd experience the crush of every delicate bone, the collapse of his windpipe—

"You don't know what you're doing, boy," Costa said

from beside me, his voice reverberating through the room. If he was shocked to see his former charge, he didn't show it. "Let her go. She doesn't have anything to do with this."

"She has *everything* to do with this." Diego retreated until Natalia came back into view. She focused her eyes above the camera lens.

On me?

"Natalia."

She closed her eyes, swallowed, and reopened them. I couldn't miss the fire in them as my own stare bored into her.

You've got this, I silently told her. *Be strong. We'll get you out of this.*

"This will be easier for all of us if Talia's alive," Diego said, removing a gun from the inside of his jacket. "I love her and don't want to hurt her. But let's get one thing straight—I will put a bullet in her pretty face if I have to, so don't do anything I don't explicitly instruct you to."

Rage burned up my chest like heartburn of days past. Days *past*—since Natalia had decided to change my lifestyle. She wanted me healthy. That was my fucking wife, taking command of me when I'd never let anyone tell me how to live. Anyone but her. The love of my goddamn life.

My throat closed. I breathed in and out, willing my fury away. Anger would only blind me.

Focus.

Diego *had* loved her in his own selfish way. I believed when he said he still did. But she was more than that to him. She was my weakness, and Diego had always known it.

I had to trust Natalia could get herself out of this after all the drills we'd run, the moves she'd perfected, and the countless hours I'd spent punishing her and myself for the fact that a man had come too close to taking her from me months ago.

A roll of duct tape on the desk gave me hope—she'd be able to free herself if that was what he'd used to bind her hands.

And I didn't miss the way Diego *stupidly* turned his back to her.

He trusted her—that was good. But even better—he didn't seem to consider the possibility that she *could* fight back. He'd never seen her as anything other than precious. Breakable. Compliant.

But she was none of those things, and if she ever had been, it'd been a product of her environment.

She could take him on.

She *had* to.

She just needed to free her hands, and *I* needed to keep his eyes on me and off of her.

Reluctantly, I tore my gaze from her and returned it to Diego, who was watching me with a hint of a smile. He knew this was killing me. "What do you want?"

"It wasn't so long ago that I asked you the same thing." Diego put a hand in his pocket and inspected the other, running his thumb along a tattoo on the inside of his ring finger. "You and I stood across from each other in your office as you stripped away my options until there was only one left—submit to the Maldonados and face death."

Aren't we a little old for story time, Diego? I bit my tongue. I could think of a thousand responses that would bruise Diego's ego as I slowly worked my way under his skin. I had rattled him before, like that day at *La Madrina*. But Natalia could pay the price for provoking him. I had to grin and bear it.

"You thought you had me," Diego continued. "You

should've known not even my death would end this. Aren't you curious how I'm still alive?"

"No," I said. "I don't give two shits about that or any other lie you've spun to justify the way you are." Natalia jerked silently behind him. She was working her hands free. As Diego started to turn, I said, "Why are you doing this?"

There were plenty of things I wanted to say to him for his involvement in Bianca's death, but none of it was more important than holding his attention. Keeping it off Natalia. Keeping her safe. And *finding* her.

Gabriel, Max, and Alejo monitored everything from the next room, searching for clues on the screen that might indicate a geographic location, listening for any valuable information Diego might slip up and reveal. He wasn't stupid enough to make a traceable call, but this connection was all we had.

Diego crossed his arms over his chest. "I've never met a man more willing to betray family—or turn his back on the world he was raised in. Everyone now knows you as a traitor. You continue to bring shame to our name long after our parents' death."

Good. I could think of no greater compliment.

"For Cristiano, blood doesn't make family," Costa said, seething beside me. "His loyalty to me has stood the test of time and circumstance. He is *mi familia.*"

I put my hand on Costa's elbow to show my gratitude but also to warn him to control his reaction. It was torturous not to look at Natalia every few seconds, but if I did, Diego might, too.

"Costa," Diego said, shifting his attention away from me, "you would've crumbled without me. Your cartel is what it is because of *me.* You were inconsolable after Bianca's death, but I propped you up. After that, you only kept up with demand and the new order because of the technology and fresh ideas I introduced." Diego leveled his unblinking stare on Costa. "*I* oversaw the development of our advanced tunnel system into the States myself," he said simply. "*I* made most of the connections we needed at the border. I know your business better than anyone." He stuck his hands in his pockets and shook his head. "And without so much as a second thought, after twenty years of loyalty, you kicked me out of the home where I'd spent the majority of my childhood."

"Loyalty?" Costa boomed. "*You killed my wife.*" Costa barreled toward the camera, gripping it with both hands. "Your betrayal cost us everything, and *me las vas a pagar*—I will rip your balls off for it," he said, spittle covering the lens. "I won't let you take my daughter, too."

Diego ran his tongue along his upper teeth. He'd finally gotten the reaction he'd come for.

"You've only paid half the price for killing *both* my parents, *don* Costa," Diego responded coolly. "An eye for an eye means you owe me a life still."

"Then take mine," Costa said.

"Too easy. I'm willing to negotiate, though. I won't kill Natalia as long as you do what I say." He glanced at me. "I should like to have her by my side in this next venture."

Over my dead and rotting body. My hands throbbed from clenching them, but I couldn't get myself to release my fists. Couldn't let my anger drown out my reason. Revenge blinded Diego to the fact that Natalia was not the weak girl she'd once been. I couldn't let it distract me, too.

She needed my entire focus.

Keep her safe. Get her the fuck out.

I glanced over my shoulder as Maksim entered the room. His haggard face turned sheet-white as he crossed himself and uttered something in Russian. "I saw your corpse," he said to Diego.

"You saw what I wanted you to see." Diego cleared his throat. "Get out."

Max and I met eyes briefly. Did he know anything? Not yet, it seemed. He walked out.

"How'd you learn about the tunnel in my home?" Costa asked, his tone level now. "Nobody knew but Bianca, Natalia, and me."

Diego glanced briefly at the ground and back up. "With an abundance of patience. I watched. I waited. I learned the security codes, I learned about your underground secrets. I left the door open for the *sicario* when I knew you'd be out of town."

"What about the safe?" I asked.

Diego smirked. "The valuables and cash in there totaled well over a million dollars. In exchange for the contents, the hitman provided me a weapon, bank account transfer info, and hidden camera footage linking Vicente Valverde to Bianca's murder."

"Which you used to run them out of town," I said. "And Natalia was supposed to be at the parade, but what about me?"

"I was as shocked as both of you when I walked into the bedroom. I knew what was supposed to happen, but seeing her there was still difficult." He paced to one side of the room, glancing through a window into the warehouse, then turned to me. "You found Bianca, Cristiano, and I found you, gun in hand," he said. "It wasn't part of the plan, but it worked out well. I would've killed you if I could've. Either way, I would've been the hero."

Natalia stilled. Her lips twitched. She wanted to speak. To rail. To protect *me* when she was the one in danger.

Stay calm. I had to will it to her without looking at her for more than a couple seconds.

It couldn't be easy for her to hear all this, but she needed to keep her mouth shut and focus on escape.

"Get to the point, *rata*," Costa said on a growl. "Why are we here?"

Diego's jaw ticked. He didn't like being called a *rat*, especially by the man who'd murdered his parents. Costa needed to stop poking him. If Diego took his anger out on Natalia, I *would* find a way to get in that room, even if it meant climbing through the camera lens. But his pinched expression quickly returned to neutral.

"You work for me now. Comply, and Natalia will be safe. She's angry with me now—I have you to blame for that, brother." Diego rolled his shoulders. "But once your spell has worn off, we'll return to the way we were. If you care for her, too, you'll accept it, because she'll be happy here. She will be loved—by me." He bit his bottom lip and added, "Every night, to make up for all the time you stole from us."

No.

My heart pounded as I fought off the image of them together.

Don't react.

This wasn't about me.

I wiped beads of sweat from my upper lip. I had to focus on her, but she seemed so far away. I couldn't see her as well as I wanted. I didn't know if she sweat, too, or if she shivered instead. If her rage heated her, or if icy hatred took over. She needed me. My warmth.

My breathing grew more ragged. *Don't think of Diego's hands on her.*

Did she feel strong? Or did she struggle to separate the person in front of her from the boy she'd known?

"We'll get to her before you ever touch her," Costa said. "I promise you that."

Whether he promised Diego, Natalia, or me, I wasn't sure, but he was leveling threats that could only hurt us. I looked over at him. His corded neck and beet-red face said it all. He was trying to fight off the same images as I was.

"*Tranquilo*," I said to him under my breath to remind him to stay calm, but he kept his eyes laser focused on the screen.

"Is it worth losing Natalia?" Diego asked, his nostrils flaring. "Because if I hear even a whisper that you're trying to find our location, I will take her life, and then you and I will be at all-out war. Your armies together are strong—but Belmonte-Ruiz's is now three times the size it used to be, and it's growing every day as word spreads about how you're working for the wrong side."

I didn't doubt that now. I hadn't blindly trusted Belmonte-Ruiz's truce, but the more time that'd passed, the less concerned I'd become. They'd held up their end of the bargain by moving on to other ventures. Our informant had been killed; we hadn't replaced him. And foolishly . . . I'd wanted to believe we could all live in peace. Because Natalia and I were ready to start a family, but we wouldn't during a war.

I hadn't realized we were still in one. I should've fucking paid closer attention.

"So you want Cristiano's global network and my shipping infrastructure, eh?" Costa said. "To distribute on a larger, more international scale. Is that right?"

"Everyone will benefit, even both of you—which is generous on my part considering the rules of this world."

"Which are?" I asked, even though I knew. Even though I didn't give a *fuck*.

But I asked to keep him talking. Natalia was squirming now, definitely close to freeing herself.

"The rules mandate that I kill you for your sins against my family," Diego said. "But I'm willing to take another form of payment. We're developing a new drug and want to explode onto the market. We can mostly handle North America, but we need both of you in order to take Europe, Asia, the Middle East. Your income will double."

I watched Diego's face closely as Costa grunted. "Then why blackmail us?" he asked. "Make a proposal, and my partner and I will discuss it. I won't do business with you while you've kidnapped my daughter."

"Because Cristiano's answer will be no." Diego strolled backward. "He needs motivation."

My chest locked up as he rounded Natalia's chair and set his hands on her shoulders. Touched her. Massaged her. My body shook with an impending explosion. I finally let myself look at Natalia for more than a few seconds. I tried to draw from the strength in her eyes. *She* was trying to soothe *me* when it needed to be the other way around.

I love you, I said with my gaze. *I'm coming for you. No matter what.*

I inhaled through my nose. I needed a level head—and to keep his eyes on me. He stood behind her. If he saw her restraints broken or even loose, that could only make things worse.

"Narcotics   distribution   is   what   Belmonte-Ruiz demands in exchange for all that you've cost them," Diego explained. "But then there's what I want."

What had Diego desired from the start?

Revenge. Legacy. Power.

And at any cost.

I crossed my arms. "Nothing will bring our parents back to life, Diego."

"You're wrong. Belmonte-Ruiz is the most successful human trafficking syndicate in the country. With their approval, your help, and my guidance, the de la Rosa cartel will scale that business to an international level—like our father would've wanted."

It was as Max, Natalia, and I had guessed several months ago. He asked me to play God. To enslave, torture, and break innocent people. To relinquish the code I lived by. He asked of me the *one* thing I couldn't give him. That was why he had Natalia. "I won't do it."

Diego squeezed Natalia's shoulders. "Then Natalia will pay the price," Diego said, "and if you think that means death, it's far too easy."

I stilled. "You care about her too much to sell her."

"That's why, unlike you, I'm trying to keep her safe," he said. "But maybe our father had it right when he sold Angelina."

My chest tightened at the mention of her name. Diego had been too young to be part of that and knew only what I'd told him during our time as young adults at Costa's ranch. I'd been vulnerable with him. Revealed how I'd still thought of Angelina, and wished I'd had the means to find her.

"Sometimes, if you want to learn to be ruthless, you have to start by ripping out your own heart," Diego said calmly. "I'd rather not do that by giving up Natalia, but I will. You understand." Diego addressed both Costa and me. "You taught me early the dangers of emotional attachments."

My lesson had been Angelina. Diego's had been witnessing not just a father's death, but a mother's, too.

It had changed us both in very different ways.

"Bianca suspected," Costa said. "She had a feeling what you were. *Are.*"

"Regardless." Diego shook his head. "You went to extreme lengths to see me suffer, and make no mistake I want that for you, too." Diego slid down the elastic of Natalia's off-the-shoulder dress, rubbing her bare biceps as a rock hardened in my stomach. "We'll grow our business with or without you, but we can do it exponentially faster with your help." He paused. "You'll never have to come face to face with the lives you buy, sell, and trade—they'll always be nameless, faceless strangers. But Natalia?" He glanced at the top of her head then back up. "By tomorrow, she could be on a yacht in the Mediterranean, at the mercy of a sheikh so powerful that nobody, not even you, can touch him. It's your choice which hell you want to live in."

My blood boiled. This was the chance I'd taken when I'd followed two paths that should never cross—angering dangerous people by disrupting their systems . . . and falling in love. I wouldn't trade the impact we'd made or my love for Natalia for anything, but *fuck* Diego for knowing exactly how to manipulate me.

My fury had coiled too tightly. I slammed my fists on the desk under me and sent everything flying. "I should've murdered you when I'd had the chance."

"I don't think anyone would disagree on that point." Diego patted Natalia's arm, smiling at me. "So, do we have a deal, partner?"

Natalia shook her head as she mouthed, "No."

Diego was just demented enough to follow through with his threat against Natalia. I had no choice. Whatever Natalia asked me to do or not do, I wouldn't put her in harm's way if I could help it.

Diego flattened his hand on Natalia's chest and slid it down until it breached the neckline, over her breast.

No. Motherfucker. No—

He flicked a white envelope from her dress. "If you need another reason to comply, let this be it." He tore it open and pulled out a black-and-white photograph.

I squinted. *What . . .?*

As the image before me took shape, my throat went bone dry. It couldn't be.

"What is it?" Costa asked, his eyes narrowed.

My mouth moved, but my ears rang so loudly, I never heard myself say it. "A sonogram."

"What?" Costa roared. "*Vete a la chingada.*"

He cursed Diego, while I couldn't even form a word.

News I'd yearned for over the last few months, I suddenly wished away. I should've been elated. Instead, I prayed to the Virgin Mary that it wasn't true. My knees buckled as a fear I'd never known weighed on my shoulders. It couldn't be. If I let myself believe it, I would either rage or crumble, and neither reaction would help Natalia.

They were lies.

Diego had planted the image to unnerve me. To get me to agree to his terms. It wasn't true. There was no baby . . .

I held onto the desk and looked from him to her, the only one who mattered here. I met her anguished eyes. Her lips pressed so hard together, they were white—I knew that look. She was doing everything in her power not to cry.

My vision blurred. The ground underneath my feet rolled. It was true.

It would explain why she'd invented a wrist injury last week to stop our training. And why she hadn't fought back when Diego had taken her from the parade.

It was the one mindset I'd never thought to prepare her for.

She was worried for her condition.

I thought I'd done everything I could to equip Natalia, but this was a situation none of us had ever faced. I'd failed her. I wanted to turn away so I wouldn't break down right there, but I couldn't let Natalia think I'd left her alone in this for a second.

We were in it together.

I limbered up my shoulders as if preparing for a boxing match. "Fuck you," I said.

Diego responded as I wanted, coming out from behind Natalia's chair to look at us straight on. "Is that a yes then?"

Natalia's head whipped up. "Don't do it, Cristiano," she said, choking back her tears. "Those people need you. It's everything you've worked for. Don't make the deal."

The thought of betraying those I'd helped, and those I might still help, chilled my insides. It wouldn't be forever; it *couldn't* be. I'd find a way out. But every life mattered. If I didn't believe that, I would never have taken on the thankless, impossible mission to try to make a dent in the sex and forced labor trades.

If I did this, I'd go from savior to enemy.

I couldn't ruin countless lives to save one, could I?

To save *two*.

The fates of my unborn child and my wife were in the hands of a man who'd spent twenty years waiting to see me suffer.

Natalia's eyes pleaded with me not to do it. But didn't she know I could never walk away from the love of my life? From our baby? That I would do *whatever* it took to keep her safe? Even if it meant breaking all my rules and becoming the worst version of myself . . .

My father.

I nodded once. "You have a deal."

25

NATALIA

"You have a deal."

Cristiano's words hung in the room.

My heart broke knowing what it had cost him to agree to the arrangement. He'd call into question more than a decade of work. And going forward, every day, he'd die a little inside aiding a true monster—because I was in its grip.

Except I wasn't. I was going to save him—*us*—from that pitch-black future.

While Diego had listed his demands to Cristiano, I'd put everything I'd had into getting out of my restraints—and I'd succeeded.

I'd freed my hands.

Now, I had to free myself—and my husband and baby.

My throat went completely dry. I couldn't lose my nerve now. There was no time to strategize, and yet, one false move could cost me everything.

I had to act before he turned around and saw I'd gotten loose.

He'd replaced his gun inside his jacket. I had to make

sure once I was up, he didn't have even a second to reach for it.

My eyes darted around the room and landed on the stack of bricks against one wall. They were the closest thing to me that could do serious damage. It had to be that, and it had to be now, while Diego distracted himself with the logistics of their deal.

"One week?" Cristiano asked in response to something Diego had said. "It's impossible."

"You'll find a way," Diego said.

My heart pounded as I silently removed my high heels.

"I don't do business with traffickers. I need—" Cristiano's voice faltered when I stood, but his eyes stayed trained on Diego. "I need time for my connections to . . . to build me a new network."

"That would take too long," Diego said.

In bare feet, I tiptoed to one corner.

Diego turned his head slightly, and Cristiano said, "Come on, *cabrón!*" so loudly, Diego's head snapped forward again. "Do you want this done sloppy," Cristiano said, "or do you want it done *right?*"

Diego seemed to consider the question. He actually meant to go through with this—to build a new cartel at any cost.

And whether it was Diego's true motive or just icing on the cake—he believed he'd now be the *only* person in the world with any power over Cristiano de la Rosa.

But didn't he know that title belonged to me?

Only I could tame the beast. Today, tomorrow, and forever. Cristiano was *mine*.

I couldn't wait any longer.

I used two hands to pick up a brick from the top of the pile. I tested its weight. Heavy. Solid. I raised my eyes to the back of Diego's head. At least I wouldn't have to look him in the face. My childhood best friend. My first love.

I shut my eyes briefly, opened them, and ran forward.

Don't hesitate. Don't—

Diego spun around. I hefted the brick across his face. *Smack.* Blood splattered. His body flew to one side as his guttural shout filled the small space.

My stomach heaved as I froze.

Tell me you love me, Talia.

Tell me you're still my girl.

"It's not over!" Cristiano's shouting jarred me.

Diego was still on his feet, doubled over as he spit out a tooth. He rushed at me. I stumbled backward, tripped over the lamp's cord, and dropped the brick as I threw my hands back and caught myself before my ass hit the floor. I used my momentum to push off the ground and spring back to my feet.

I *refused* to go down, especially because of Diego.

He came at me again, leaning to one side, struggling to focus his eyes.

I picked up the metal folding chair and raised it over my head. I brought it down as hard as I could, but he blocked my blow, grabbed the seat, and used it as leverage to fling me into a wall.

As my head knocked against concrete, I shook off a bout of dizziness.

"Talia—" Diego coughed, blood streaming from his head as he tried to grab me.

I ducked out of the way, snatched the brick off the ground, and whirled around.

This time, I aimed not for his head but for his *brain*.

The brick *thudded* against his skull. He staggered back, his eyes pleading with me, then fell to his knees. I kicked him onto his back, jumped on top of him, and lifted the slab again.

He was hanging on by a thread.

I just had to do it one more time.

Don't look at his face.

He groaned. My eyes jumped up. Covered in blood, his head dropped to one side, eyes half-open. I'd crushed one of the high cheekbones that made him so beautiful, one I used to touch with reverence.

"When I go, you'll be my side, okay?" he said. *"I'm with you, life or death."*

"Life or death," I'd responded.

I had so much more to live for now, and everything to fight for. It was me or him.

I slammed the brick down. His skull collapsed. His eyes remained open but distant. One socket had caved in.

My chest seized. Breath halted. Throat closed, cutting off my air.

I shook, and my hands loosened around the weapon.

But there was no time to panic. It wasn't over—the fight was *never* over.

I jolted into action, frisking his legs until I had his folding knife. Sticking it between my teeth, I found the gun tucked into his jacket pocket.

I got to my feet holding both weapons. Ears ringing, I turned around. Cristiano's beautiful, ashen face filled the screen.

Home.

I stumbled toward him. "Cristiano." My strangled voice sounded far away.

"I know, baby. I know," he said, his jaw set, eyes shrewd as they darted around the room, then refocused on me. "You did good—but you're not done yet."

My heart raced. I willed it to slow and pulled myself together. "There are at least eight men outside with guns."

His eyes quickly scanned my face before he turned his head over his shoulder and called for Gabriel. "I'm coming for you," Cristiano promised me. "Do you know where you are?"

I shook my head. "Some kind of huge warehouse."

"Get out of that room. Find a place to hide until I get there."

"There are too many of them."

"Listen, *mi amor*." The calm in Cristiano's voice settled my nerves. "Turn around and cut Diego's throat so you *know* he's dead. Don't use the gun unless you absolutely have to. Check his body for a different phone, then hide and call me from it so we can try to trace it. If you encounter anyone—fight, Natalia."

I would fight. I *had* already. But me, with a knife, a pistol, and a baby to protect against *all* of them and their rifles?

"I . . ." I held the weapons to my queasy stomach as my voice broke. "The baby. It's true."

Cristiano gritted his teeth and swallowed. His father had warned him young never to form emotional attachments that could be painfully severed. This was the price of love. I couldn't let him regret it.

"Mindset, Natalia," he said firmly. "*You* are the White Monarch. Don't you see that? You're the weapon, the survivor, the killer. You can do this."

I had no other choice. I sucked in an inhale and nodded hard. "I couldn't see anything as we came in—but the air pressure here is low. Thin," I rushed out. I glanced over my shoulder, unnerved by the silence of the warehouse. "It's like a forest. The ground is soft, lots of big trees—"

"What kinds of trees?" Gabe asked, entering the frame behind Cristiano.

"I don't know. Pine? It's dry—except, it almost sounded like it was raining outside. But it definitely wasn't."

Cristiano glanced back at Gabriel. He nodded slowly, his eyes on me, but his thoughts somewhere else. "The monarch butterfly migration," he said finally. "Must be. Their colonies cluster together in certain winter habitats. The oyamel fir only grows in high altitudes. There are so many butterflies, their wings sound like a rain shower."

"God's messengers," I whispered. They were here.

"*Sí*. You're protected," Cristiano said and turned back to Gabriel. "Do you know where she is?"

"These forests are small, and may be designated reserves, but Belmonte-Ruiz's tunnel system runs right underneath that area with an entrance at the nearby Acapulco port." He pinched the bridge of his nose, talking to himself, as if working through it. "It would make sense that they'd managed to build an operational facility there."

"Where?" I asked.

"Under the cover of the Sierra Madre del Sur mountain range." Gabriel met my eyes and nodded. "I know where you are."

One moment, Cristiano's beautiful but drawn face looked back at me, and the next, I was alone. Cristiano was on his way. The TV monitors went dark, the warehouse office deafeningly silent. Diego's blood covered my shaking hands. He'd lost, but what had I won? Wanting him dead wasn't the same as committing the act. He was only the second person I'd ever killed, and at one point in time, I'd loved him more than anyone.

I made the sign of the cross, part of me hoping Diego found peace in the afterlife while I also damned him to Hell.

He was dead, and to make sure of it, I would cut his throat.

And then I'd have to prepare for the possibility of defeating a troop of armed men.

I went to the desk, grabbed the computer mouse, and clicked on the CCTV program. A minimized window opened with a grid view of surveillance from different cameras. This time, it didn't broadcast to the overhead monitors. I squinted and quickly re-counted the guards. The two in the warehouse were the greatest threat, but I only spotted one now as he leaned against a metal shelving unit, scrolling through his phone. I leaned forward, searching each display. Where was the other one? And where in relation to the office were—

My forehead slammed against the computer screen, blurring my vision. Something pinched my upper arm. A fist in the back of my hair yanked me to the ground.

On my back, the room spun so fast, I gagged. Diego stood over me, skull bashed in, blood dripping into his eyes, onto my dress.

My head pounded, my eyes crossing as vomit rose up my throat. I forced it back down. *Don't lose consciousness. Stay here.*

He was half-dead. I needed to get up and finish the job, but my limbs suddenly felt as if they weighed hundreds of kilos.

Diego's wobbling legs gave out. He sank to his knees and fell on the ground next to me. My attention drew to pain in my upper arm where I'd felt the pinch just now. It smarted as if I'd been stabbed with a small blade.

I struggled to lift my head. A syringe stuck out of my biceps. And Diego had his thumb on the plunger, pushing down on it, grimacing as if it took all of his effort to empty it into me . . .

Moving in slow motion, I reached over. He was losing consciousness, and I managed to wrestle the syringe from him and yank it out. "Wh-what is that?" I asked, my voice sounding far away.

His eyes drifted to the ceiling. As sweat trickled down his temple, he wheezed in such a painful sounding way that I felt it in my own chest and throat. "You're . . . coming . . . with me," he said and started to convulse.

My lips tingled so strongly that I had to suck in a breath. A strange but not unpleasant prickling sensation moved down my jaw. Arms. Fingers.

Numbing me.

"What . . . what's happening?" My lethargy glued me to the ground. I couldn't even turn my head away, and I was forced to look at him. "What have you done?

Diego stilled. His chest sank. His gaze went distant—as my mother's had in her final moments. Life drained from his eyes as he said, "*Escalera al Cielo.*"

And then he was gone.

Stairway to Heaven. The memory came back in pieces. Diego humming Led Zeppelin. His casual reference over Coca Light that Juan Pablo Perez, the chemist from Nogales, was developing a new drug. Puffer fish toxins . . . sedative . . . a slowed heart rate . . .

A round-trip ticket to Heaven. The most elusive and euphoric high.

But with the wrong dosage, the stairway home vanished. Heaven became the final destination.

Mustering all my energy, I lifted the syringe in front of my face and tried to focus my blurring vision. Almost . . . *empty*? No. God, no. If he'd overdosed me, I'd die right here on this floor. Tears filled my eyes as fear tremored through me, then fizzled with the onset of such intense happiness, I had the urge to smile.

I needed to turn over. Get up. Crawl if I had to. But my body betrayed me. Exhilaration and satisfaction mingled in my stomach like a groundswell, rolling through each of my limbs, warming my face.

Hide, Cristiano had told me. I couldn't lift a limb. I slid on my back toward the desk. My arms and legs became noodles, loose and droopy, fatiguing with the effort.

My nerves vibrated. A pleasant hum took over.

I had to keep going. Escape. Hide. *Fight*.

But I could only sink into the ground, as the sky pulled me up, up, up—and away.

26

CRISTIANO

Max took the forest's rough terrain as rapidly as he could, but every minute that passed felt like an hour, and we might as well have been moving in slow motion. As dusk began to fall, we crawled up an embankment of boulders. I braced myself against the roof of the Humvee to keep from smacking my head.

Alejandro had a map spread out over the center console between the front seats as Gabriel directed us over speakerphone. Alejo removed the flashlight between his teeth and yelled over the scrape of the truck's skid plates against rocks. "Repeat that."

"If my"—Gabriel's voice cut in and out—"are correct, you . . . close." The bouts of static over the line had gotten worse the farther we strayed from civilization. The kid had been directing us along the red-marker line he'd drawn on the map to indicate Belmonte-Ruiz's network of tunnels, but it seemed we were about to lose contact. "Three clicks."

Three kilometers? "Until what?" I demanded.

No answer.

Max straightened up. "Are those tire tracks in the mud?"

Could've been that, or nothing at all. "It's getting dark."

"Look for . . ." Gabriel said. "Trees——"

"A spot where trees have been cleared." I pointed through the forest toward a muddy path just big enough for a car to pass through.

Max ramped up his speed, barreling down the makeshift road. I rolled down my window and gestured ahead for Eduardo and the men in the vehicle behind us.

I mashed my teeth together for the thousandth time since we'd left the Badlands. I had to believe there was an explanation for why Natalia had never called from Diego's phone liked I'd instructed her to. Dead battery. Broken phone. No service.

Any moment now, I'd have her back in my arms. She'd survive this. I knew it in my gut.

When I'd returned earlier in the year, I'd watched Diego overlook and manipulate the best thing in his life. And so, I'd taken her from him. And nurtured her, watched her grow and change, from a girl to a woman, from my captive to my wife, and now, the mother of my child. Diego had underestimated Natalia for the last time, and today, she'd prevailed.

She'd finish this. I'd trained her well. I trusted no one more than my men, and together, we'd taught her how to stay alive. She'd hang on until we got there. And then we'd torch the motherfucking place to the ground.

"You have to be close." Gabriel's voice came through clearly. Alejo and I exchanged a look. The static was gone. We were near a cell tower. "This area is super isolated," Gabe said, "and could serve as an entrance or exit to an underground passage."

Max looked over his shoulder. "If you're leading us into a trap, you should know that you wouldn't be the first. You wouldn't be the last, either."

I didn't condemn Max's skepticism. Of all the crazy shit that'd crossed my mind in the past several hours, wondering if Gabe could be setting us up was a mild thought. Gabe had done everything asked of him, though. He enjoyed both being behind the computer *and* his lessons with Solomon. But Diego's patience for revenge had been never-ending, and he'd fooled just about everyone, even me for longer than I cared to admit.

Gabriel was deep enough inside our systems to do serious damage, but Natalia trusted him, and now, he was my only hope. I nodded Max on down the route laid out for us toward a destination none of us were even sure existed.

From the backseat, Alejandro passed Max and me our artillery and loaded himself up next. Maksim accelerated toward a chain-link gate surrounding a brick structure.

"Take it down," I ordered.

The hand of the speedometer flew higher as we rushed the gate and crashed right through.

I waited for gunfire. Warning shots. Bullets to pepper the side panels or shatter the windshield's exterior glass.

Nothing.

Silence.

Max didn't screech to a stop until we were meters from the door to what looked like a warehouse.

I opened the door, using it as a shield as I surveyed the area.

"Maybe the tire tracks in the mud were going, not coming," Max said when nothing happened.

Or maybe we were in the wrong place.

Fuck. I had to get inside.

Alejandro opened his door. "We've got your back," he said. "Go."

With an assault rifle strapped over my bulletproof vest, I pulled out my .45 and sprinted the short distance to the entrance. I shot the lock. Kicked open the door. Ducked inside.

The expansive, well-lit space stood deathly still. Utterly silent.

Just me. And the pounding of my heart.

What if Natalia wasn't here? What if she'd never been?

No. She was here—hiding, like I'd told her. She had to be.

I strode past a conveyor belt toward rows of metal shelving, glancing down each aisle as I called out her name. When I'd made a partial circuit of the perimeter, I started through the stacks. Kicked aside random bins. Concealed the panic in my voice as I said her name so she wouldn't hear my fear.

"Natalia."

Nothing.

"Natalia."

Silence.

"Natalia! Goddamn it!"

A windowed security room sat ahead in one corner, lit by computer screens. Gun drawn, I strode toward the open door. I was greeted by the gentle hum of equipment.

And a dead body.

Diego.

Even with his face smashed in and blood smeared everywhere, I recognized my brother. Was I supposed to feel something? I couldn't muster anything except relief to find we were in the right place.

But where was Natalia?

Hiding? Taken?

My throat began to close, and I struggled for air.

I turned to resume searching the warehouse when my eyes snagged on a pair of bare feet sticking out from behind the desk.

Toenails the color of the polish Natalia had waved in front of my face two days ago, begging for a pedicure. I hadn't been able to say no. I'd do anything for those toes.

I took a step forward.

Anything for the slender calves I ran my mouth along any chance I got.

For the hips that swayed against me when we danced. That kept my gaze whenever she left a room. That would bear my child.

A buzz started in my ears. My boots grew heavier with each step. Pressure weighed on my chest. No breath entered or left my body as I rounded the corner.

Arteries of black hair over the concrete ground reached from her pale, heart-shaped face. Eyes shut in peaceful rest. Slightly parted lips—pink and smiling that morning, now an alarming, icy blue.

My handgun clattered to the ground. I dropped to my knees and shook her by the shoulders. "Natalia. Wake up, *mi amor.*" I'd just held her in my arms as we'd celebrated Bianca's life. She'd been warm. Glowing and beautiful. Growing with life, I now knew.

"We have to go. Get up!" I gripped her hand in mine. Cold. Limp. I held it to my collapsing chest and pressed my other fingers to the pulse under her jawbone.

No heartbeat.

That wasn't possible.

It couldn't be right. I was just too panicked to find her carotid artery.

I forced myself to exhale. Slid a hand under her head.

Pulled her delicate frame into my lap, put my ear to her chest. Listened.

But she'd fought. She'd won. I'd seen it with my own eyes.

Natalia would not lose this battle. She was too strong, too good, had too much left to offer.

I waited with my cheek against her chest. And waited. Her body vibrated under me. Her heart or mine? My own beat so strongly, I couldn't hear anything else. Just silence.

Dead silence.

I couldn't breathe. Air became water, thick and slow, drowning me. "Wake *up*, Natalia."

But her body didn't lie. Her chest was a cavern. Mine hollowed out. My ribs caved in as my heart struggled, pounding hard and full of rage. "No," I begged her. "No, no, no."

How? I ripped off my guns and bulletproof vest, kneeled back, and drew her body against me. There was a new gash on her head, but it'd barely even bled. No strangulation marks. No other wounds.

I choked back an angry sob and yanked up her dress but only found smooth, untouched skin everywhere. No gunshot, injury—nothing had killed her. Why wasn't she breathing? Why didn't her heart beat?

The useless muscles I'd built to protect, defend, and support held her up but could do nothing else. Hope drained from my body.

Clenching my aching jaw, I placed her on the ground, put the heels of my hands between her breasts, and pushed on her chest once, twice, three times—over and over, then stopped to check for a pulse. Cupping the top of her head, I tilted back her chin and put my mouth to hers, breathing into her, willing her to life, calling her back from death's doorstep.

I should've never let her leave the float. I'd let my guard down. I'd turned my back, thinking Diego was dead. That Belmonte-Ruiz had moved on. I hadn't trained her how to fight in case she ever got pregnant—why hadn't I thought of it? Why hadn't I gotten here faster? What had happened between our call and now?

"Come on, Natalia." I returned to chest compressions. "You promised to come home to me—"

Nothing. No soul left in her. I didn't want to admit it, but I'd known it the moment I'd seen her.

She was gone.

My unborn child gone.

My life . . . gone.

Boots pounded the pavement of the warehouse, drawing closer until they stopped behind me.

"Cristiano," Max said, his voice breaking as his foot-steps resumed. "Come on. We can't stay."

I sat back, staring at her. I couldn't move. Couldn't . . . anything. I'd rushed into this warehouse certain I'd come out with Natalia—not in my arms but by my side.

"Cristiano."

I ignored Max. Someone had to pay for this. Now. Today. "Where are they?"

"Belmonte-Ruiz isn't here anymore. They must've found the bodies and left. But they could come back any minute—"

I gritted my teeth. "I want to be here when they do."

"Then you'll leave in a body bag." Max had my shirt in two fists before I knew it, yanking me to my feet. "Put your vest back on." He shook me as his eyes burned with—what? Fear? Anger? Grief? "Pick up your wife and take her home. Give her a proper burial. You owe her that and so much more." He shoved me away. "Do you want them to carry her corpse out of here with yours?"

Yes. If it meant avenging her, then yes. I shut my eyes, but I still saw her lying on the ground.

"Look at her, Cristiano," Max ordered. "*Look at your wife.*"

I couldn't. I couldn't face it.

"Will you abandon her here?" he asked.

Abandon? Never. No. I couldn't do that to her.

She needed me—even in death. I had to get it together and take her body home, somewhere safe. I called on strength deep within and forced myself to turn back to Natalia.

The starkness of her lifeless frame was no less shocking. My pulse vanished; my blood ceased to flow.

"How'd this happen?" Max said, searching the ground. "She was alive when—"

"I don't know." It didn't matter. I stared at her. All the lives I'd taken, and I'd never seen anyone so still. So unresponsive. Maybe, since Bianca, I'd never cared enough to look.

"Pick her up," he said.

For once, I had no idea what to do—so I listened to Max.

I lifted her body to my chest as I stood and walked out the building, into the dark, to the forest.

I paused at the door to the vehicle as a breeze moved through the leaves of the trees.

Not leaves. Not a breeze.

Butterflies.

Overhead, thousands of monarchs covered the firs, fluttering their wings. Natalia had found comfort whenever one was near, thinking it was the departed soul of her mother returned to check on her.

But not me.

I had faith in very few things, and in even less now.

"*Fuck* you." In my arms, Natalia was simultaneously deadweight and light as a sparrow. "Fuck you for taking her from me."

Boots sounded behind me. Max and Alejandro appeared at my side. "Oh, God . . ." Alejo said. "No."

"Get in," Max said. "We're in enemy territory. *Get in.*"

I carried Natalia into the backseat, cradling her against me.

I'd done everything in my power to bring Natalia back into this life. I'd promised her my protection. I had failed her. I should've left her alone. Costa's words about Bianca's death many months ago rang through my ears.

"I wouldn't wish my pain or guilt on any man."

I understood now. Bringing Natalia into this world hadn't just risked her life but mine, too. Maybe Costa was strong enough to live without Bianca, but I wasn't without Natalia. If that made me a coward, then I was one to my core.

As we pulled away from the warehouse, I put my face to Natalia's. I kissed the dried tears on her cheeks, her wet lashes and cold lips. A sigh escaped her, and I swallowed it. Even death's rattle came soft and gentle from her sweet mouth.

"Heaven or Hell, I will find you," I whispered to her. "I will make Belmonte-Ruiz pay, and it will be the *last* thing I do before I join you."

A sense of calm fell over me knowing I would be with her again soon.

27

CRISTIANO

I stayed at the back of the dark chapel that anchored the Badlands' town square. Somewhere in the hours between midnight and dawn, Max, Alejandro, and Eduardo lit candles and prayed at the altar where Natalia's body had been laid. Already, her father, Barto, and Pilar had been to see with their own eyes. Tomorrow would be the *velorio* before Natalia's burial, but I could not bring myself to celebrate life as was accustomed at our wakes. I would say my good-byes tonight.

Max rose first and put his phone to his ear to answer a call. Even God's house was not exempt from the demands of work. Maksim looked down the aisle at me, nodded, and came in my direction. "*Gracias* for the update," he said, hung up, and addressed me. "We need to speak."

"Not now," I said, my eyes burning as I stared ahead.

"It needs to be now. Lives are at stake. Put your grief aside."

Impossible. I would never know another moment without it. To have loved and been loved by Natalia was all I'd ever needed, even when I hadn't known it.

I couldn't bring her back.

"You still have other lives depending you," Max said.

I swallowed and turned my focus to him. "What is it?"

"We always knew there would be a price to pay for what we do," Max said.

My heart lurched, forcing its presence on me even after it had been torn out. I scowled. "I've paid it."

"The lives of your wife and child might've satisfied Diego, but their deaths mean little to Belmonte-Ruiz." He paused as Alejandro and Eduardo approached, then said, "They're coming."

That was to be expected. I was weak now, and I'd derailed yet another of their deals, one they'd spent months preparing for. "How far?" I asked.

"They should be here by dawn."

"Dawn is now," I said.

"Not quite," Max said. "But soon."

"How many?" Alejo asked.

"Enough. Belmonte-Ruiz has enlisted several other federations to join him, trading strategy for a massive army and sheer brute force to storm the Badlands . . . and cut off Calavera's head." He looked to one side as his nostrils flared. "They want the entire country to know you're done."

Diego had once again promised someone more powerful than him things he couldn't deliver. And he'd paid the final price.

But I hadn't.

Belmonte-Ruiz's thirst for blood and vengeance would not be satisfied while I was alive. I had stolen from them. Killed their men. Cost them business and money. I'd made enemies of several cartels by making them look the fool too many times. And I'd gotten away with it.

Until now.

"Someone give me a cigarette."

"You quit," Alejandro said.

"For Natalia. For my future. I have neither now." My palms sweat. I ached to hold Natalia. It would be the last time. How could it be that I wouldn't be able to touch her when I pleased, take comfort in her presence, her love? I turned my back to her body, glowing in the candlelight as it waited for me at the end of the aisle. "Let me kill myself as slowly or as quickly as I see fit. Give me a fucking cigarette."

Eduardo offered one up with a lighter. He'd always been a man of vice. I lit the thing and took a comforting drag.

"You know the exit plan," I said to them.

"It's already in motion," Max replied.

I nodded. For them to begin evacuations without consulting me had to mean it was truly the end. I exhaled a cloud of smoke. "The fleet is ready?"

"We've already sounded the alarms. People are boarding. They'll have food, water, and money—enough to get them on their feet wherever each person settles."

"There's another option," Alejandro said, gripping his cell at his side. "I could call back the heads of every household. They're armed. We can fight."

"Belmonte-Ruiz has spent the past several months galvanizing others that believe us to be traitors. They have the numbers," Max said. "It would be a battle to the death."

"We're prepared for that," I said, holding out my cigarette as I took in the peaceful nave of pews around me. Everything I had built. "But we will lose—if not today, then tomorrow."

"We're prepared to lose as well," Max said.

Alejo and Eduardo exchanged a look, then nodded.

We'd always been prepared to die for this. And for the possibility that there'd come a time to leave the Badlands behind. I'd never doubted my men's loyalty, but to hear them stand up and say they'd run into a losing battle only reinforced that every decision I'd made up until the parade yesterday morning had been the right one.

But I'd taken my eyes off my wife, and now I would pay the price.

We wouldn't fight. I had other plans.

"They won't stop until they get to me," I said, and added with finality, "Get everyone out."

Nobody spoke for a moment. This was where it ended.

"You have served them well," Alejo said. "And you've equipped them. Everyone in these walls will survive outside of them because of you. Many of them are only alive because of you."

I nodded once. "Time's not on our side—go."

"And you?" Max asked.

I looked at the cigarette in my hand. It should've been a cigar enjoyed in celebration of good news. Of my first child on the way. Of the goodwill God had placed upon my wife and me.

Instead, I raised it toward the heavens before ashing it out on a pew. My life had been taken from me. There was nothing more for me here. "Once everyone is out safely, meet me back here," I said to Max. "And bring Barto. Just the two of you. Until then, I'll be alone with my wife."

28

CRISTIANO

Dressed in a white satin nightgown, Natalia glowed at the end of the aisle in the dim chapel. Flickering candles made shadows of her body on the wall behind the altar. I walked toward her and ascended the steps to where she'd been laid on a bed of handmade blankets and cream silk sheets and pillows. The candlelight brought color to her cheeks, creating a painful illusion of warmth and life.

I looked down on her. Hands folded over her stomach. Her dark thicket of hair around her pale face, arranged by Pilar to fall in curls over her slender shoulders.

I touched her cheek. Impossibly soft and smooth. Thumbing the corner of her mouth, I bent over to press my lips to hers—and stayed there. I couldn't bear to pull away.

Wetness dripped from my eyes to her cheeks. What was this? The last time I'd cried, I'd shed one tear for Bianca's death, and then I'd had to run for my life. Now, tears flowed down my cheeks, dropping onto Natalia's lifeless lips.

I gripped the sides of her face, kissing her forehead, the corners of her mouth, remembering how they'd twitched early on when she'd fought her feelings for me. I sat on the makeshift bed and touched her hair. The tattoo on the back of her shoulder. I took her hands from her sides to bring them to my mouth, breathing on them long enough to actually *warm* them.

My mind played tricks on me. I was going mad. Perhaps I'd already gone. There was no question—without her, my mind would surely go.

"I love you, Natalia Lourdes," I said. "*Mariposita*. I'll love you always."

I lowered her hands and kissed the fabric over her stomach. An all-too familiar metallic smell filled my nostrils. I pulled up her dress to find blood between her legs.

Fuck. I fisted the satin.

Was it not enough to lose her? I had to witness my dead wife's miscarriage?

I no longer wished for Natalia's life but for my own death. And I couldn't rely on anyone but myself to grant that wish. I buried my head against Natalia's womb, gripping her sides as a sob wracked my body.

There was no God. No Virgin. They would not take my wife from me and let me glimpse for a moment the family I could've had. They would not show me pure love only to sever it from me so suddenly and viciously—no higher power could be so brutal, not even to punish a man like myself.

Exhausted and emotionally wrung out, I drifted in and out of consciousness.

I wasn't sure how long I'd slept when the *click* of the chapel's heavy front door roused me. Max and Barto stood at the entrance. I rose to meet them halfway down the aisle.

Barto's eyes stayed narrowed on me. "You asked for me?"

"Is everyone out?" I asked Max.

"Every person. Every animal. Only we remain— Alejandro, Eduardo, Pilar, Jaz, and Costa are on the ship waiting for us. Doctor Sosa wanted to stay, too, in case she was needed."

"Pilar should've gone earlier."

"She refused," Barto said. "She's already lost her best friend. She has nobody else and feels safest with us."

I nodded. I wasn't sure *this* was the moment she should finally stand her ground, but there was no other option now. "Gabriel?" I asked.

"Haven't seen him," Max said. "I assume he went already."

"When all this is over, find him if you can. Help him. He's a good kid. He'll be a good man."

Max nodded.

"What's this about? Why am I here?" Barto crossed himself. "To help with Natalia's body?"

I looked to him, my ex-comrade, a man of his word, and someone who, despite our history, I could depend on in my youth and now, when I needed him most. Then to Max, my friend, my confidante, and right-hand man.

"You and I, we've been together a long time, Max." I pinched the inside corners of my tired eyes. "I don't need to tell you how the plan plays out."

"I never truly believed it would come to this," Max said.

I nodded. "But it has."

I was silent a long time. There was only one option, but

facing it meant coming to terms with the fact that Natalia was really gone.

I turned to Barto. "Belmonte-Ruiz is here for blood. They won't stop until they get it. Until someone pays—and I will. They'll continue to hunt me. If they don't make an example of me, someone else will. I'm no longer good to anyone—I'll only bring danger wherever I go."

Barto raised his chin. "Are you asking for my help to get you out of the country?"

"No." I paused. "The Badlands is rigged so that in an emergency, it will detonate."

Silence fell over the room. Max closed his eyes briefly but straightened his back.

Barto's expression finally eased. "Smart. Better to perish than be captured."

"Even better if you can take the enemy down with you," I said.

Barto looked between us as my intent registered. "Anyone within the Badlands' walls will go with it."

I nodded. "Belmonte-Ruiz wants me—they'll have to come into the Badlands and get me. And their entire cartel, plus any other faction that has joined them, will be wiped out. The explosion will completely level the town, the mountain—everything."

My death would stop this. Belmonte-Ruiz could be obliterated, and Costa, Max, Alejandro, and the entire population of the Badlands would be safe from them.

In one fell swoop, I could end this war and make a considerable dent in human trafficking. It wouldn't be forever, but every life held value, and many would be spared during the time it would take to rebuild the operation that would crumble with Belmonte-Ruiz's fall.

Barto looked almost impressed. "You'd give all of this up?"

"To save lives, yes."

Barto shifted feet, nodding slowly. "And Costa?"

"Say he was forced into this arrangement against his will. I had his daughter. He's respected enough that once our partnership is dissolved, he'll be left alone."

"It will be the end of BR and their operation," Barto said. "But it won't finish anything. One leader steps down, and another takes his place. There are others who'd like to see you dead."

"And they will. My life in exchange for many others. It's a sacrifice I've always been willing to make. Only my death will stop this."

Barto glanced at the ceiling, then nodded with pursed lips. "How does it work?"

Max widened his stance and crossed his arms, in full strategy mode. "There are two ways to detonate. From the control center in the basement, or remotely, within half a kilometer."

"If you can push the button from the water, why would you stay?" Barto asked.

I took a breath. Not because I was hesitating—I had no reason to doubt my decision. But because once I said it, the life I'd known would truly be over. "Without Natalia, nothing's keeping me here," I said. "She's gone. I'll die today. You were good to her—" I cleared my throat to keep my voice even. "Even after all we've been through, I consider you a friend."

I offered my hand. Barto looked at it a moment. Perhaps now he finally realized how deep my love for Natalia ran, but whether he did or didn't was no longer important. We shook.

"If you're willing to do this to avenge her," he said, "and to save the rest of us—then the feeling is mutual."

"This is why I asked you here. I appeal to your logic,

not your emotion, and Costa would've tried to talk me out of it. I . . ." The next part didn't come easily. I wanted Natalia here with me for the end. It wouldn't make a difference in the afterlife—if there was one, I'd find her. Selfishly, I wanted to hold her until my final breath, but I'd been greedy enough when it came to her. The right thing to do was to give her a peaceful final resting place, not incinerate her with the rest of us.

"Take Natalia with you," I said. "Costa shouldn't go back until things have settled, but I'm counting on you to leave here and take her home. To bury her where she belongs—with her mother."

A hint of despair softened his features. "You have my word."

That was it, then. There was nothing left to stay, and time was up. The longer the final ship remained in port, the more everyone on it would be at risk. They were counting on me to be strong.

A deep ache pounded in my stomach, but I ignored it and turned to walk back up the aisle to Natalia. I had to pause at the top of the steps to force breath in and out of my lungs.

There was no other way, though.

Only my wife would be so beautiful in death. I could almost convince myself that her pallor had lifted. That her cheeks had pinked. As I slid my arms underneath her body and lifted her, I felt warmth, not death—self-preservation allowing me to look upon her for the last time as I had always known her.

Beautiful, vivacious, as stubborn in death as she'd been in life.

Butterfly in the sky, monarch in my arms as we'd danced the night of the costume party. She'd buzzed against my body with fear, trepidation, and excitement as our wits had sparred and our feet had tangoed.

Mermaid in the water, showing me how the curves of a woman could soften my hard, sharpened edges.

Owner of my cold, black heart.

I pressed a final kiss against her lips.

"*Mi vida. Mi amor.*"

My life. My love.

My need for her was so willful, so gripping, that I felt her soft breath caress my lips. I drank in her sweet sigh. My descent into madness had begun, and its timing was perfect. I forced my mouth away from hers and my feet down the stairs.

It was the hardest thing I'd ever do. Even lighting dynamite under my own feet would be easier, I knew.

I handed Natalia's body over to Barto.

Reaching into the holster at my side, I removed the White Monarch I'd brought for her, opened her hand, and curled her fingers around the grip. My tired eyes hallucinated her thumb twitch against the pearl. "Bury her with it. For protection."

Barto nodded once, a promise to see my command through, and took her away.

"*Suerte.* Be prosperous, be good," I told Max. "Don't return to México ever again."

"I hope you'll change your mind," he said as we shook hands. "If you do, I'll be waiting for you."

I wouldn't. I wasn't leaving any chance Belmonte-Ruiz would get to walk away from what they'd done, and what they'd stolen from me.

I took comfort in the fact that eradicating them would save even one life. Every life held value.

But Natalia's life had been worth everything. And in the end, it was worth my own.

29

CRISTIANO

In the moments before dawn broke, I blew out the candles in the chapel, not that it mattered if it burned down. Belmonte-Ruiz would be here any moment, and once they were inside the gates, I'd lay waste to all of this.

The Badlands had been home, but without its people, it was a shell. I made my way toward the house through the empty streets. The quiet brought a sense of peace I could only recognize knowing my pain would end soon, and with purpose. I wound up the mountain path for the final time, across the driveway, and started up the steps to the front door.

At a sound from inside the house, I froze mid-stride.

Hurried footsteps beat against the entryway tile.

Everyone was supposed to be gone.

It could only be one of my men, but I took out my gun anyway and leveled it at the front door as it flew open.

Gabriel Valverde threw both of his hands up. "*Ay*. It's just me."

I holstered the gun. "What the fuck are you still doing

here?" I asked, wiping my dusty hands on my pants. "I ordered everyone out of the Badlands. The last boat is leaving, if it's not already gone."

"I couldn't leave. Not until I knew everything I could find out about this," he said, opening his hand to show me . . .

"A syringe?" I asked with a frown.

"*Escalera al Cielo.*"

"*Stairway to Heaven*? That's a Zeppelin song. You've gone mad," I said, nearly laughing. "Both of us. You're going to die here if—"

"Max picked it up in the warehouse by Natalia's body," he rushed out. "He said you didn't know how she died, so I've been researching all night." As if that fact had only just occurred to him, he blinked hard, removed his glasses with his free hand, and rubbed his red eyes with the back of his fist. "*This* is why Belmonte-Ruiz wanted your help." He replaced his glasses and pinched the barrel between his fingers. "To take this drug to the international market—"

"It doesn't matter anymore, Gabriel."

"It does—just listen. The drug only kills with the wrong dosage, Cristiano. Otherwise, it just puts the user into a trance. This is how Diego faked his death—well, clinically, he *was* dead, but—"

"You've been a better soldier than I gave you credit for." I walked up the front steps and grabbed him by the shoulders. "Run. You may still be able to catch the boat out of here. Get your share of the money and go. Start a new life."

I walked by him into the house.

"You're *staying*?" Gabe asked, panic threading his voice as he followed me through the foyer.

"Another few seconds, and you may have to swim to the boat if you want to catch it."

"Where's Natalia's body?"

"Gone!" I snapped over my shoulder, my nerves fraying at the mention of her name. "Get out of here before I—"

"And if she wakes up and you're not there? What then?"

I froze in my tracks, my scalp tingling. I turned around slowly. "What?" My eyes darted between his. "If who wakes up?"

"What I've been trying to tell you," Gabe said, tripping over his words. "I think Diego injected her with this—a tetrodotoxin that could've put her into a cataleptic trance."

I balled my fists. "Speak English."

"Diego used Stairway to Heaven to fake his death. Too much of this could kill her, but the right amount would only put her into a state that *mimics* death. It could take twelve hours, maybe more, until the drug wears off."

My throat dried like my eyes. Couldn't swallow. Blink. Function. Think. It was taking me longer than it should to calculate how much time had passed, but we were definitely somewhere close to that. "You're saying she could still . . ."

He was insane. I'd listened to her chest for a heartbeat. Waited for her breath. I'd felt neither.

"You've really gone mad," I said. "What game are you playing with me? I don't care if you get on the boat, but if you don't get out of my sight—"

"It's no game." I'd seen Gabriel scared shitless before, and he wasn't now. He took a breath. "She could still be alive, Cristiano."

I turned and stalked away. "You're wrong."

"I could be," he admitted. "But what if I'm not?"

It hit me then. She'd stirred in my arms.

It hadn't been an illusion.

My mind hadn't been playing tricks on me.

The ache in my gut hadn't been despair but an instinct I'd ignored. The warmth I'd felt in her lips . . . the final wisps of her breath—they hadn't been final at all. They hadn't been conjured by my mind out of desperation to will her back to life.

"She's . . . she *is* alive," I whispered.

Relief exploded in me, sending pure, unadulterated joy coursing through my veins. I knew the truth without a doubt. "She's alive," I told Gabe.

Gabriel's mouth broke into a grin. "You said yourself the boat might still be here. Go. *Apúrese. ¡Corra!*"

Hurry. Run. I could catch her. I would dive into the sea and swim as long and as hard as necessary to do it.

Heaven or Hell, land, air, or sea, I will find you, mi amor, *and I will . . .*

What?

What would I do? Bring her back here? Go with her?

Dread filled me, planting my feet where they were.

She'd been given a second chance.

As had I.

I'd promised I'd protect her. Since then, there'd been two serious attempts on her life. She'd almost been taken from me more times than that. I hadn't kept her safe. I'd only put her in more danger. I'd risked her life too many times, and this was my opportunity to make it right. Natalia would wake up on the sea, and she would hear it from the people who cared for her most. I was dead. That I had died avenging her and completing the mission I'd set out to do—saving lives. It would be hard, but eventually, she would pick up and move on with her life.

I wasn't going to run into the ocean and call them back when Natalia had already set sail on a better future.

She'd be safe with Barto, Max, Pilar, Alejandro—and her father. It was a new life with them or death with me, and she would choose me if I let her. She'd stay here by my side until the end.

I had a purpose here. I needed to see it through. As soon as I'd decided to stay behind, I'd known it was the right choice, and it still was.

Heaven, Hell, or anything in between—I would find her again.

Until we met, wherever it would be, she'd be safe.

"What are you doing?" Gabriel asked. "Let's go."

"*Sal de aquí*," I said, sending him away. "You couldn't find me in time to tell me she was alive, understand? Tell her I died with dignity, and with love for her in my heart."

"Cristiano—"

I charged him, took him by the shirt, and I did for him what I'd once tried to do for Natalia. I scared the shit out of him for his own good. "Get the fuck out of here. *Now*. You can't stay here." My voice threatened to break as I shoved him away. "You still owe Natalia your life. Stay with her. Take care of her. I'm trusting you to do that for me. It's my . . ." I gritted my teeth together. "It's my dying wish."

Gabriel looked as if he'd seen a ghost. He backed away from me and glanced at the floor as he said, "Yes, sir. I promised I'd be a good soldier to you and to her. I will, in life or death. Thank you for—"

"There's no time. Go."

He nodded once, then sprinted away.

I couldn't move, barely able to breathe as it registered. Natalia was *alive*. I couldn't fucking believe it. It changed nothing, and it changed everything.

It was occasion to celebrate.

I made myself a drink, a few fingers of my finest, most expensive mezcal—then filled the tumbler to the top. Might as well finish off the bottle. I took my time cutting and lighting a Honduran Gurkha Black Dragon cigar I'd been saving for a special occasion. The birth of my son or daughter. The wedding I'd tried to convince Natalia we should repeat with as much extravagance as we could. In this case, I'd be celebrating her life, and the fall of Belmonte-Ruiz.

My love, my wife, was alive. I walked through the vacant house, by the patio where Natalia and I had eaten snails, past the dining table where I'd loved her most intimate spot with my mouth the first time, and I made my slow way up the same stairs where she'd called me back to her in her darkest hours after learning the depth of Diego's deception. Where any love she might've had left for him had finally become *mine*.

To our bedroom, where she'd killed a man.

Where I'd held her in my arms after she'd arrived here, where she'd quivered against me.

Where I'd first made love to her.

In the shower, where we'd confessed our love to each other the first time.

The closet, where I'd threatened her with a good time with *El Gallo*.

With my drink and cigar in one hand, I continued on to the closet and removed Natalia's wedding dress from its fancy, padded hanger. She had walked into the church that day tall, with curious, anxious eyes, and jet-black tendrils framing her delicate features and smooth, bronzed skin. The most beautiful thing I'd ever fucking seen, and she'd been mine. I fisted the fine fabric the way I had that day in the church. It had torn so easily and had been mended as close to perfection as it could get.

But it would always be scarred by my hand.

I was doing the right thing.

I folded the dress, set it on the closet island, and went

to the balcony for one final glimpse as they sailed away—but there was nothing on the horizon except first light.

I sat in one of the over-sized cushioned patio chairs Natalia had bought for the balcony and tried not to think of her, somewhere out there, alone.

But it was an impossible feat.

She wasn't alone. She had her father. Barto. Alejo, Max, Gabe, Pilar—everyone. Everyone but me.

Natalia was stronger for the past year. She would thrive. *I* had given her that. And she was even more beautiful.

I pinched the expensive Honduran cigar I'd only begun to enjoy between my fingers until I'd nearly halved it.

What would life for her look like without me? It didn't matter; she'd be alive. And wherever I ended up, I'd be watching out for her . . .

I wouldn't risk her life today and allow her to die for me, though there was never any question I'd die for her. She had promised me she'd go on. Live life to the fullest. Pursue happiness.

What more could I ask for? I had a front row seat to one of God's greatest phenomenon—the rise of the sun over the vast ocean. And the knowledge that I'd made the right decision, no matter how fucking badly it hurt. That my Natalia was safe.

I sipped my mezcal and heard bare feet slapping the hallway tile only a second before Natalia came crashing through the bedroom door.

30

CRISTIANO

Breathless but breathing, cheeks pink with life, fire ablaze in violet eyes I thought would never reopen —my dead wife stood in front of me with disheveled hair. Furious. "Fuck you, Cristiano de la Rosa."

I dropped my cigar to the ground as I stood. She had to be an apparition. "God in the sky, tell me I'm seeing things," I said, my voice rising as I stepped out from behind the chair. "Tell me I've gone completely fucking mad, and that I'm seeing things, Natalia—" I balled my fists. "*Tell me* you did not come back here!"

She rushed forward and shoved me in the chest. "You think you can send me away while you stay here to die?"

Alejandro appeared in the doorway and didn't look nearly as fearful as he should. He had no idea what I'd do to him for risking her life.

She glanced back at Alejandro. "What, you *pendejos* thought you could make decisions about *my* future? Fuck *all* of you assholes."

I turned my glare on Alejo. "You couldn't handle her? She was *dead* a half hour ago."

"We taught her too well. She fought back when she learned the truth." He wiped his bloody lip. "She has more will to stay than I have to make her leave."

"Then her death will be on *your* shoulders, Alejandro," I snapped, unfair as it was.

"To get back to you, she would've shot me." He nodded at her hand. "I'm certain of it."

She held the White Monarch. I frowned. "Did you shoot someone, Natalia?"

She cleared some hair that'd fallen into her face. "Not yet."

I sighed. "The boat's supposed to be far gone by now."

"We're still docked," Alejo said. "I tried calling."

I took my phone from my pocket. "*No tengo señal.*"

Nothing.

Nothing at all, in fact. I had no service. No signal. No Wi-Fi.

"Belmonte-Ruiz must've turned the area into a dead zone," Alejandro said.

They'd likely blocked the cell towers in an attempt to down our systems and hinder our attempts at escape.

I would've done the same.

And if I hadn't chosen to stay behind, it would've worked. I could no longer detonate anything remotely. I had two options left. Leave with them now and let Belmonte-Ruiz live . . . or implode the Badlands from within the walls.

It was no choice at all.

It would all come down—which meant Natalia couldn't be here. I had to get her back on that ship.

"If they're jamming the signal, that means they're here," Alejo said. "They could be at the gates any moment."

I glanced at him. "*Vete*," I ordered him out, and he shut the door behind himself.

I put my palms together in front of me. As a man who hardly begged for anything, except only things my wife could give me, I pleaded with Natalia to see the gravity of the situation. "On this, you have to trust me, *mi amor*," I said.

"Don't give me that 'trust me, *mi amor*' bullshit," she shot back through gritted teeth. "Be a man and come out from behind your excuses. Face me."

She struck a match against my anger, and it flared. Did she have any idea how difficult she'd just made this for me? I wanted her here by my side—God, I fucking wanted that more than anything. I had no desire to say good-bye. Not at all. But what kind of man would I be if I put her on my back and took her down with me?

I took her by the biceps. "I ask *one* thing of you." I enunciated every word. "Do as you're told."

"No." She shrugged out of my grip and stepped back to cross her arms. "Alejandro and Max didn't have time to explain. They only said you were planning to take Belmonte-Ruiz down and die in the process."

I pinched the inside corners of my eyes. "It's true. This was always a possibility. I hoped it was a lever I'd never have to pull, but I do." I raised my eyes. "And you can't be here for it."

"I can and I will. I'll stay and fight with you."

"I'm not fighting, Natalia," I said. "None of us are. Everyone's gone but us. We're outnumbered. You're leaving with Costa right now."

Her mouth pressed into a line as it did when she was so angry, she could cry—but wouldn't let herself. Her small hands formed two formidable fists. "And what about you?"

"I have to stay and see this through."

"And then what?"

Now that we were face to face, I couldn't bring myself to lie to her. But I couldn't tell her the truth, either. It would put her in serious danger, whereas ignorance could save her. She wouldn't go, and I had to get her out, whatever the cost. "It's not your job to worry about me. I have things under control—"

"Did you not hear me earlier? I'll repeat myself—fuck *you*, Cristiano." She charged forward and pushed my chest until I was backed up against a wall. Tears filled her eyes. "How could you do this to me? I woke up alone—no husband, no b-baby." Her voice cracked, nearly shredding my resolve. "*Alone*. My own father thought I'd risen from the dead and nearly fainted when he saw me."

"You're not alone," I said quietly. "You have people down there who love you. Who don't want to lose you."

"Without you, I'm alone," she said quietly. "I'd rather be with you. Here."

The tears in her eyes and quiver of her chin told a clear story of her pain. I never wanted to hurt her, but I would to save her. My chest threatened to cave under the weight of the truth—I loved her *too much* to let her stay.

She would be alone, yes—but she would be alive.

"You can't be here for this," I said.

"You would leave me in this world all by myself? You forced me here, you made me fall in love with you, you made me need you as I need air and water"—her voice broke—"and now I'm supposed to walk away?"

She went to shove me again, but I caught her wrists. She was crying too hard to fight me.

"Natalia . . ."

"I already lost my baby," she whispered, looking down as her body shook with more sobs, silent this time. "Wasn't that enough? Why do you continue to push me to be strong if I have nothing to live and fight for?"

I'd thought she'd broken my heart already, but now it shattered. "*Hush,*" I said, gathering her in my arms, holding her as tightly as I could. She wailed in a tortured way I'd never heard from her as she crumbled against my chest, and I had to inhale up at the ceiling to stop from shedding my own tears. To stop from breaking down and giving in to her.

"I shouldn't have fought back." Her tears soaked my shirt. "I should've waited for you to come."

"What do you mean?"

"If I-I'd played his game . . . if I'd only kept pretending, at least until you were able to come—"

"You had to fight, Natalia. You *had* to."

"I wished the baby away," she said. "I tried to convince Diego I didn't want it so he wouldn't see it as my weakness —and I lost the baby. The miscarriage was my fault."

No. No, my love. She blamed herself for it? No wonder she was inconsolable. I took her arms and shook her gently to rouse her from her grief. She looked up at me, red-rimmed eyes glistening with overflowing tears. "Listen to me," I said. "You did *exactly* what I told you to." I took a breath. "And now you have to do what I say only one more time."

"No," she said. "Please. No."

"Natalia," I said, keeping my tone as even as I could manage. "Everyone is waiting for you."

"So send them away."

Adrenaline coursed through my veins. Fear. Desperation. To keep her here with me. To pick her up and physically carry her downstairs. She was making this impossible, and I was about to lose my temper. I had to be cruel. "You'd be willing to die now, this moment? You're ready to burn alive? Because that's the fate you're asking me to give you." I stared at her. "You're not that goddamn short-sighted—you have a life to live, and it doesn't end today."

I expected her to continue railing at me, but instead, calmness settled over her. "I'm not going anywhere without you, and I don't *want* to. I would rather burn by your side now than spend an eternity in Heaven alone, so good luck trying to convince me otherwise. Now, tell me how this works."

I was wrong—it wasn't calmness. It was resolution. It was the demise of my arguments against her. My demise. Hers. "I'm going to die today—that's how it works," I said.

"Then I will, too," she responded without hesitation. "I asked you not to spare my life at the expense of others, but you did when Diego asked you to make the deal. You were willing to ruin all those lives to keep me safe." Her voice softened. "It's my turn to make a hard decision. Don't take my choice from me. Don't fail me now and treat me as Diego and my father did. I chose you because you're not them."

That wasn't fucking fair. After all the ways I'd pushed her to be her own woman, she knew her autonomy was a plea I couldn't deny.

To lead a life without Natalia would be true hell, but to take her life with mine? That was what I'd be doing.

I thumbed the corners of her mouth as she looked up at me eagerly. I searched her eyes, gripped her face, and gave it my best shot. "You know my love for you spans the world. It trumps time, space, human life. I chose you knowing hundreds would suffer. I could never make a decision that didn't put you above all. Please, Natalia. I beg you. Go."

"Over my dead body. Do you hear me? Alejandro will have to drag my corpse out of here."

I stared my very beautiful, very angry—very much *alive* —wife in the face. If I forced her to go, I'd be making decisions for her as others had.

Her determination would be her downfall. But she'd made it clear—that was her choice.

I told her the truth, start to finish.

31

NATALIA

A breeze from the sea cooled my clammy skin as Cristiano, Alejandro, and I hurried from the house down to the ship. Still docked, our loved ones were at risk—but I had one thing still to do.

I left Cristiano on the deck with Max as Alejandro escorted me onto the modern-day pirate ship. It was only missing flags with skulls and crossbones—but the Calavera presence was everywhere.

We found my father standing at the bow, looking out over a turquoise, horizonless ocean. His tall, imposing frame was no less intimidating against the lifting dawn.

Alejandro turned to face me. "For what it's worth, I think you're doing the right thing. You've always been brave. And don't worry about Pilar, all right?"

With gratitude, and my complete trust in him, I took his hands and squeezed them. "Thank you."

"No need." He kissed the backs of my knuckles. "Until we meet again in Heaven, Natalia."

When he'd left us alone, I walked forward. "Papá," I said.

He turned. "*Mija. Gracias a Dios.* You returned. Gabriel said the death was fake? What the hell happened?"

What had happened was that I'd awoken from a deep sleep of wild dreams so fantastic and realistic, I wasn't entirely sure I *hadn't* visited Heaven. I'd come down floating on a cotton cloud. Things had been fuzzy, and buzzy, my fingers and toes tingling.

As the euphoric hum in my ears had faded, irritation had ripped through me when I suddenly had eyes that tore open and a mouth that gulped air as if it would be my last breath. And I'd woken to a high-pitch whistle, the tip and sway of the sea underneath me, surrounded by men's shouts. With an empty stomach. Blood on my dress. A broken heart. And the White Monarch in my hand.

Had I woken up moments later, I would've lost Cristiano forever.

I swallowed back the horrific, gut-wrenching thought and took my father's hands. "It doesn't matter. Diego lost in the end."

"You can tell me everything on the voyage. I have no clue where we're headed, but Barto is working on it with Max." He heaved a sigh. "*¿Y Cristiano?* Has he come to his senses?"

I looked at our hands. "Yes."

"Good." Papá moved his hands to my waist, and I raised my eyes to meet his sorrowful gaze, lines deepening around his mouth. "I'm sorry to have lost my grandchild. I can't help think I'm partly to blame."

A lump formed in my throat. It wasn't his fault. It wasn't Cristiano's. And it wasn't mine. I'd had a few joyous moments as a mother, and I was grateful for that.

I tried my best to keep my sadness from showing. And I glimpsed—barely—the pain Cristiano must've endured trying to send me away for my own good just now. The doubt that surely plagued him. The deep-seated need to protect me by making the decision for me.

As I'd do for my father now. "None of us knew the depth of Diego's deception."

"Cristiano did. I should've known he wouldn't hurt Bianca, but Diego's complete confidence, and your conviction as a child, convinced me of it."

"Mija." She fought to keep her eyes open, but they went glassy as her gaze shifted over my head. "Please, Cristiano," she begged, her voice strangled. "Please don't . . ." She shuddered with the effort. "My daughter . . ."

"I was wrong. I now know her dying words had been pleas to Cristiano to protect me—not her begging him to spare my life," I said. I'd clung to the memory so many times growing up, and now I saw it for what it was . . .

"I should've trusted my gut and brought Cristiano home at once," he said.

"All is well, Papá. We have made things right."

"There will be other grandchildren," he said. "You won't make me wait long to hold them, will you, *mi corazón?*"

How could I lie to my own father, and about something like this? His heart would break with the truth.

I ground my teeth together, almost unable to hold back my tears. But I did—and I committed the same crime against him that he had against me for many years. The one for which I'd persecuted him.

I lied to protect him. "Yes, Papá. You will hold your grandchildren before long."

With a satisfied smile, he looked past me. "Where's Cristiano? We should already be gone."

"I'll go see." I went to kiss his cheek but threw my arms around his neck instead. "I love you."

"Te amo, mija."

My resolve nearly broke remembering all the nights Papá had prayed for my mother's soul and cried himself to sleep. The thought of putting him through that again was almost too much to handle.

Pray for me. I will pray for you.

All I had to do now was walk away. To say good-bye for good to the man who'd raised me.

"I understand why you ran back for him just now," Papá whispered. "Your mother would've done the same."

Emotion wracked me, threatening to take me down. I pulled back. The pride in his eyes was clear. It meant everything to me. I kissed his cheek and forced myself away before he became suspicious of my tears.

I wanted to say good-bye to Pilar. To see Alejandro's smile light up a room once more. To kiss Barto's cheek and thank him for his service to my family. To assure Gabriel he had the world at his fingertips. But it would be selfish. There was no more time. They needed to leave.

I left my father at the front of the ship and made my way back toward where Cristiano waited on the loading dock. He wore no expression as his dark eyes followed me, but I could read his torment. Maybe he doubted himself, but as painful as this would be—it was the right decision.

He'd made me a queen when others would've had me stay a princess forever. To have the choice to go and live or stay and die meant more to me than he knew. I would remain by my king's side. Now. Always.

Cristiano helped me off the ship. As it prepared to leave, worry crept in, tensing my shoulders.

With a strong arm around me, Cristiano pulled me closer and kissed the top of my head. "They're prepared," he whispered. "They'll be safe, Natalia."

"And everyone else?" I sniffled, slipping my arms

around his middle to hug him back. "Teresa and Felix? Jaz, Paula, the Zamora family—"

"They're on to new lives. They'll be okay." The contentment in Cristiano's voice comforted me until he loosened his embrace and looked down. "I have to say this one last time, Natalia. It's not too late. I can call them back. You can still go with them."

I shook my head hard. I was determined, but that didn't mean I wasn't scared.

He smoothed a hand over my hair and down my back. "This is it. Everyone you love and care about is on that ship."

My dear, thick-skulled husband with anguished eyes. I reached up to run my palm along the stubble of his cheek. It was obvious he hadn't shaved since the parade. His scratchiness was comforting in a way. It was real. "There is no possible scenario in which I leave your side. My place is here. With you."

With my husband was where I stayed. Silence fell over us as we stood on our beach for the last time and watched our friends and family go. As we said our final farewell to everyone we cared about, and to this world.

32

CRISTIANO

In a black lace dress, Natalia turned in a circle in our closet—the same gown I'd put her in at the church on our wedding day. She lifted the skirt and showed me her sneakers with Kevlar laces.

"In case you need to run in the afterlife?" I asked at the mirror where I fixed the cuff of my dress shirt.

I was perhaps overdressed for death as well—but we weren't going to go down in anything less than the best.

"In case I need to *fight*," she said, holding up *la Monarca Blanca* before placing it in our bag of emergency items.

"That's my girl." I winked and bent my head. "*Un beso.*"

She obliged me with a quick kiss.

A hum sounded above our heads, and Natalia looked up. "Helicopters?"

As I nodded, a *bang* echoed through the valley of the Badlands, rumbling like thunder.

"What's that sound?" she asked.

I turned back to the mirror, tightening the knot of my black tie. "Tanks ramming the front gates," I said.

"You know people call them *las puertas del infierno?*" she said.

Of course I did. *The gates of hell.* "For Belmonte-Ruiz, it will be true."

She left the closet and headed for the balcony.

"It's not safe out there in the open," I called.

"I just want one last look."

My mistake. If I wanted her to stay indoors, I should've told her to do the opposite.

I stepped out with her and checked the sky to make sure we were alone. When I determined it was safe enough for now, I joined her at the short wall overlooking the water.

In my bespoke suit, Natalia in her black lace evening gown, our hands locked between us, we took in the endless ocean. For those moments, it was calm, but it wouldn't last.

"We'd better get downstairs," she finally said. "Our time is up."

The calm in her voice mildly surprised me. I hoped that was due to her faith in me and the choices we'd made.

I turned, scooped her into my arms, and tipped her back to kiss her with everything I had. We had time for that, at least. There would always be time for that.

I took my wife down into the bowels of the mountain, through the tunnel that connected the house to the control center humming with the data, communication, and files we'd been collecting for years to protect others. Intelligence Belmonte-Ruiz would love to get their hands on for the opposite purpose. The precise reasons we hadn't made it explosion-proof.

We crossed that room, making our way through a maze

of hallways, passed two ironclad security systems where only one fingerprint—mine—would work. Because under any other circumstance, I would've burned, mutilated, or carved off my own flesh to prevent the wrong person from entering this space.

Once inside, I closed the door and sat at the computer system, where I followed the same steps I had a million times—all but the final step, a phase I'd never entered until now.

I put in my credentials, clicked all the systems into place, pressed my thumb to the final fingerprint scan, and waited for the facial recognition software to identify and approve me.

We got the green light.

"Now what?" Natalia asked.

"Now, we wait."

I pulled up security drone feed to monitor the progress of Belmonte-Ruiz and any other faction dumb enough to join them. I wanted as many of these motherfuckers as I could get inside the walls before I hit the button.

Natalia stood behind me, her hand on my shoulder, as the footage filled the screen.

They'd broken through the gates. They flooded the town, teeming into the alleys, filling up the arteries of the Badlands like blood.

"They move like a swarm of lame bees," Natalia muttered.

They drove tanks through abandoned homes, stores and marketplaces, and set fire to structures and farms.

Watching proved difficult. No matter my gratitude for the fact that every human life in my care except Natalia's had made it out, a piece of history would die today.

I chose the present over the past, instead, and stood from the chair to find my true home in Natalia's eyes. I pulled her into my arms. Her heart slammed against her chest. She was scared. I couldn't blame her. I was more terrified than I'd ever been. If I'd miscalculated anything, if the button didn't work, if these fuckers survived—then all of this could be for nothing. It could go fatally, irrevocably wrong.

I tilted Natalia's chin up and pressed my lips to hers. "We were lucky to have you. You have been everything I could've ever hoped for—and so much more."

She slid her arms around my neck, whispering. "I was only getting started. I'm sorry that . . ."

I put my forehead to hers. "What?"

"I'm so sorry you have to watch it all burn, and that your family has been displaced." A frown tugged the corners of Natalia's mouth. She thought of them during her own imminent end. It *was* sad to know there'd be no rebuilding this tight-knit community exactly as it had been —or, most likely, at all. Most of them would never see one another again. "What you did for these people will never be forgotten," she said, "no matter that only ashes will remain."

"None of it means anything without them. Without you." I thumbed the corner of her mouth. "I promised I'd follow you anywhere, and I would've, *mariposa*. I thought you were gone. Forever. And I was right behind you."

She tightened her hold around my neck, rising onto the tips of her toes. "Now we'll go together."

As the horde closed in and more and more of the enemy flooded our home, I took a breath. "What was it like to die?"

She tilted her head as if remembering, then shook her head. "I didn't like it."

"You don't say." I smiled at her. "But I heard the drug was supposed to be pure bliss."

"It's far better to be with you," she said thickly.

Both of our hearts were slamming now, but at least it was against the other's chest. I cupped her cheek. "You will be. This is not an ending, but the start of an eternity together. No one else. Just you and me."

"Just you and me," she said, but with less hope in her tone than mine. "I should've told you about the baby the moment I suspected—but I wanted to be sure." She reached into her neckline and pulled out the sonogram. "To show you this and watch your eyes light up."

I took it as my jaw tingled with emotion. "How?"

"Max picked it up with the syringe. He gave it to me on the boat." Her voice faltered. "I'm sorry you didn't get to experience the bliss of fatherhood, even for a little while."

"I'm sorry it was taken from both of us." I tucked the image in my jacket pocket and smoothed back her hair, falling more in love with her for how deeply she felt my pain. "You redeemed your child. Diego murdered our baby, and he paid the price."

"We will carry the loss with us when we go."

"And it is time to go," I said. "Are you ready?"

She bit her bottom lip. "I'm scared."

"I've got you. We fall together."

"We fall together." She nodded, running her hand along my jaw, her thumb over the hollow of my cheek-bone, smoothing my eyebrows as if we had all the time in the world. "I'm ready."

I focused on the beautiful violet eyes in front of me. I'd fallen for them at the gala when she'd looked back at me from behind her mask. I'd fought against it. I'd lost.

There was no question I'd won.

Nothing else mattered now. I already knew I wouldn't stay here without her. She didn't want that for herself, either. We'd leave this life together, and I couldn't ask for more than that.

I kissed my Natalia once more. "I love you, my wife. My *mariposita*."

"I love you, *mi esposo*. Cristiano, my husband."

All that remained now was to push the button and detonate. So that's what I did.

A rumble started in the depths of the Badlands, the angry beat of the ground shaking beneath our feet.

The underworld called us home.

33

COSTA CRUZ

"It was the explosion heard round the world—or México, at least. One year ago tomorrow, a mysterious, cartel-run town known as 'the Badlands' imploded, taking out its own residents, plus some of México's most pervasive crime syndicates. But none more famous, or dangerous, than two which have become household names since the explosion.

"Belmonte-Ruiz, known for their extensive trafficking ring and the development of a drug rumored to take its users as 'close to Heaven as humanly possible.' The explosion incinerated nine-tenths of their cartel, a large portion of two other factions, and two of the three kingpins the United States government had on the FBI Most Wanted list.

"There are no good guys here, but since its destruction, the Calavera cartel's legend has grown amongst the people. Once feared as an international cartel with an anonymous leader renowned for his merciless ways, *narcocorridos* tell a different story. It's one our station can't confirm, but these ballads canonize the leaders of Calavera cartel for their fight to curb human trafficking in a way the government never could.

"During this *Día de los Muertos*, we remember the innocent lives lost that day—if there were any. But what makes this a tragic tale, and one that has fascinated the public, is the love story between Natalia Cruz, the stunning daughter of Bianca King and businessman Costa Cruz—"

I shut off the television and tossed the remote on my desk. I'd heard enough the past year. It never got any easier. The way they glorified Natalia and Cristiano—didn't the media know they had a grieving father? I respected Cristiano's passion, and if he saw to it to kill himself over principle, fine. But to take my daughter with him.

I hadn't yet forgiven it.

"Legend says the explosion shook the earth to its core, changing México's geography forever," I heard behind me.

I turned to Barto as he stood in the doorway. "Legend exaggerates."

But it hadn't exaggerated my daughter's beauty. Nor my son-in-law's determination to do things his way. Determination that would get them both killed.

Narcocorridos—Mexican ballads—idolized drug lords, traffickers, and cartels, romanticizing our wins and losses. They told the story right. Natalia and Cristiano had possessed a great love, like mine with Bianca. At one time, it was all I'd wished for my daughter.

I set my elbows on my desk and put my head in my hands. "Senseless."

"But noble," Barto said, entering the room. "They certainly made a difference in the world, which you know is what they wanted. They're at peace, now, Costa."

I grumbled my agreement. The rest of the year, I could be understanding of the sacrifice they'd made for a better world. But on the anniversary of not just their deaths, but Bianca's, too, I only wanted to grieve.

I was about to tell Barto to leave when the maid knocked at the door of my study.

"Mail, *señor*," she said, hanging off a stack of envelopes and catalogues to Barto before she disappeared again.

Barto walked to the desk, sifting through everything until he stopped on the final item—a bulky, padded manila envelope. "What's this?" he asked.

I lifted my head and craned my neck to see better.

Handwriting that looked vaguely familiar. No return address, though.

The only handwriting I knew as well as my own belonged to those who were no longer with me. Bianca and Natalia. Both gone.

"Give it to me," I said.

"It could be dangerous," Barto said, turning over the envelope. "Let me—"

I stood, came around the desk, and took it from him. Danger meant something different these days. It meant nothing. I had little left of importance to lose. I tore open the envelope and a rosary fell out.

Not just any rosary, though. One centered by a polished gilt Sacred Heart and matching crucifix. Red rubies, milky pearls on a gold chain. I'd had it commissioned myself.

I'd know it anywhere.

It had been Bianca's.

"What the . . . *fuck*?" I muttered.

Barto was at my side immediately. "What is it?"

Well-loved, with some scratches in the gold and wear on the gemstones, this wasn't a replica.

I pushed the beads through my fingers as my throat

thickened with emotion. "Where did it come from?" I looked up at Barto. "Who sent it—and why now?"

Barto's eyes widened as something passed over his face.

Alarm made me straighten. Any reaction was rare with him—especially one of surprise. "I . . ."

"What is it?" I demanded.

Barto met my eyes and slowly shook his head. "I don't know, *don* Costa. I'm sorry." His gaze returned to the precious piece of jewelry clutched in my hand. Barto's tone softened. "Perhaps just a simple sign from God that your wife is at peace, and that . . ." Barto crossed himself. "That both her and your daughter are in good hands."

EPILOGUE

NATALIA

*W*e were warned, and so were you. In the end, death took what it wanted—Cristiano and Natalia de la Rosa. But in their place, Joaquin and Jenny Delgado were born.

My attacker had no idea who he was dealing with.

I nailed him in the chest with the flat of my foot, and my sneaker landed squarely between his pecs. He grabbed my ankle and twisted until I was forced to rotate around and face the opposite direction. Teetering on one leg, anyone else would've been dangerously close to falling flat on her face.

Not me. I lifted my head and met a sea of wide-eyed women, their mouths agape. "A leg grab like this while fighting back is both common and dangerous," I said. My shoulder-length hair fell forward, curtaining my face. "So in this scenario—"

Fuck.

A dark glare pinned me from the back of the room. Cristiano's arms crossed over his wide chest, displaying the massive biceps that had lovingly hugged me just this morning.

With the way his firmed jaw ticked like a time bomb about to blow, he looked more likely to kill me.

He took one step forward into the room.

"Let go, Dimitris," I hissed to the man holding my ankle in a firm grip.

"Huh?"

Poor guy didn't realize his life was on the line. Cristiano took another step.

"Release my leg," I said under my breath so I wouldn't scare the women sitting on the mat in front of us. I was sure they were already horrified enough to see me up here, even though *my* fake last name was on the banner in the registration room. "*Hurry.*"

He let go, and I lowered my foot to the ground gracefully to show Cristiano that my body was perfectly within my control. I straightened as I slipped my sandal back on and stepped back, gesturing for Dimitris to continue. "Sorry I interrupted your lesson," I said, retreating. "Go ahead. Continue."

With a funny look, Dimitris turned back to the class.

I gave Cristiano my best puppy-dog eyes since they'd served me well with him in the past. I held a finger to my lips to indicate we shouldn't interrupt. The alternative was that these women, who we'd invited here to learn to defend themselves, would watch me get reamed out.

When I met Cristiano at the door, he placed a hand on my upper back and guided me out of the small, mirrored room and into the office, where he shut the door behind himself.

"Natalia," he started.

"*Lourdes*, my love," I corrected him. Had I not been able to see his anger with my own eyes, my name, loaded with warning, would've been enough to tell me. "Or Jenny, of course—"

"We're alone." His brows lowered. "Don't change the subject."

I tried to look contrite. "I'm sorry," I said. "I was just observing the class before our date, and I get so excited to demonstrate for the girls myself. And I *feel* great—"

"And what if that *pendejo* out there had yanked on your foot and you'd lost your balance?"

I walked to Cristiano, took his hands, and placed them on my thirty-three-weeks-pregnant belly. "Everything's going to be okay, *papi*. We're safe here. Nothing is happening to this baby." I smiled up at him. "I've never been so sure of anything."

His shoulders loosened, if only a little. "I worry, *mi amor*."

I laughed. "That's like saying the Pope prays. It's very obvious."

"I'm not being unreasonable," he cried. "Everyone in that room thought you were crazy. That an eight-month pregnant woman would teach self-defense . . ." He shook his head and uttered a profanity.

His concern didn't bother me; it made him who he was. But it was unnecessary. I squeezed his hands beneath mine. "Can't you feel how strong our *bebita* is?"

As if on cue, she kicked, but her timing wasn't that strange. The baby was always moving around, always telling her mama she was ready to come out and throw some punches. I wanted that, too, considering my uterus had become a punching bag.

Cristiano grunted, smoothing his hands under my blouse and over the warm, tight skin of my stomach. "I can't wait any longer to meet her." His demeanor lightened considerably, as it often did when he spoke of the future. "Do you think she'll come early?"

I nodded. "She's very eager and persistent. Like her father."

He bent forward to place a sweet kiss on my lips. "Don't think you're off the hook. Since day one of this pregnancy, you've been strictly forbidden from teaching self-defense."

"And I have definitely abided by that rule," I said, trying not to squirm from the obvious lie.

As if Cristiano didn't know. His full lips pressed into a line, displaying his skepticism. "I'm not trying to limit you —you know that." He stepped closer and slipped his hands around the back of my neck to gather my long bob into a loose ponytail. "I've just come too close, too many times, to losing you."

I fought the urge to shut my eyes as his fingers tickled beneath my hairline. "But this last year has been quiet," I reminded him. "Nobody knows we're here but Max. And nobody's losing anybody."

One year ago, Cristiano and I had died.

Incinerated along with the Badlands.

All of México knew it. For months, we'd holed up in tiny apartments throughout Europe, never staying in one place too long, keeping our faces from the public.

The resulting baby was no surprise considering, without much else to do, we'd had sex for days on end.

Officially, we were Joaquin and Jennifer Delgado now. Cristiano hated calling me by a fake name, so sometimes he used Lourdes in public. But always, in private, I was his Natalia.

Fortunately, though we'd been major news in our home country, the story had never really made it outside of México.

And I loved our new life, basking in each other every day, getting to know the very cores of ourselves and of one another. But living a life indoors, under the radar, would never last for us—even if it meant we kept a little danger alive.

Opening a business had been risky. We owned and funded a traveling girls' school that taught self-defense to any and all women—or people—who wanted to attend. Once the course was complete, we'd pick up and change locations so we were never in one place too long.

The little bit of risk suited us. We'd already survived the most dangerous situations possible.

One year ago, we'd descended into the belly of the beast, the mountainside rumbling with its impending explosion. There'd always been a good chance we wouldn't make it out in time, so when I'd told Cristiano I was ready to die by his side, I'd meant it.

But fortunately, it hadn't happened that way.

Cristiano had had every intention of dying the day he'd thought he'd lost me to Heaven's stairway. But my revival had changed his plan back to the one he and Max had originally put into place many years ago in case of an emergency like this—faking his death. Knowing he might not make it out, he'd tried to send me away so he could come for me one day, when the time was right, and he had all of Mexico's underground off his back.

But that hadn't been good enough for me.

I'd die by his side literally, or I'd do it symbolically.

After Cristiano had pushed the button and we'd heard the underground roar, we'd passed through the tunnel system that led out of the Badlands, burrowing down into the mountain and under the ocean. We'd had to run. *Fast.* I'd never moved that quickly in my life, my hand locked in Cristiano's as we'd pulled each other along.

But we'd made it to the end of the tunnel before the explosion could catch us, where a submarine had waited complete with the documents to support our new life and coordinates already programmed into the GPS. Only Max knew the truth. To everyone else, we were nothing more than ashes, gone in the wind.

I thanked Our Lady of Guadalupe every day that my love and I had survived, and that now, we'd finally form a family. And I thanked Cristiano, too, for the devil made his own destiny and crowned his own queen.

Date night, my favorite time of week.

Holding hands, Cristiano and I walked through the cobblestone streets of the small town in Greece where we'd chosen to settle for the next little while. Soon, either here or in our next spot, we'd have to stay put to have the baby.

The sun made its way toward the horizon, casting late-afternoon light on the white plaster walls that broke up buildings the colors of blush, pistachio, and melon. We made our lazy way through the labyrinth toward upbeat music in the town center. Every Saturday night, residents gathered for a street fair.

Cristiano bought a bottle of locally distilled single malt and some *baklava*, feeding me a bite before his animalistic appetite possessed him to take a chunk out of it.

We stopped by a wall to finish our pastries. One man had covered himself head to toe in gold spray-paint and stood still as a statue in front of a bowl for tips. Another played a hauntingly beautiful melody on the violin. A teen girl skulked around the booths in a skull-and-crossbones hoodie.

A cool breeze passed through the square for a perfect November evening.

Cristiano's eyes roamed the area around us, and I knew he was thinking of his people in the Badlands, dispersed around the world now. I had complete faith they'd all made a home somewhere and were thriving, as did he.

I hoped that was true for my friends, Pilar and Alejandro, wherever they were.

For my father, I wished peace, though I knew he struggled with such an empty house. I shouldn't have sent the rosary. Cristiano hadn't wanted me to, but he hadn't stopped me, either. I wasn't sure if Papá would understand, but Cristiano had said Barto definitely would.

I slipped my hand in Cristiano's, and he turned to smile down at me. "More fine, handmade clothing here than we've seen in a while. What do you need?" he asked. "Aren't your pants getting too small?"

"Never ask a woman who can shatter your kneecap with a swift kick whether she can fit into her pants."

"*Ay, pero* you're pregnant, *mi corazón*," he said, as if I needed reminding.

"And do you know what pregnant women like?" I asked.

"Ice cream," he answered.

He knew me so well. Either that, or I'd been milking the cravings too hard. Either way, I got my gelato. Cristiano bought me a cup with a tiny spoon, and we made our way around the square, stopping to purchase little things we didn't really need, mostly to support the residents, and accepting the occasional gift for our future daughter.

As we stood at one booth admiring wooden jewelry boxes, the hair on the back of my neck rose. The steady tap of nails on glass, over and over, made a simple beat that somehow became chilling.

"Cristiano," I whispered.

He squeezed my hand. "*¿Qué pasa?*"

Slowly, I turned my head over my shoulder and met the dark, cunning eyes of an elderly woman sitting across the way. She drummed her nails on a glass ball centered atop the purple crushed velvet fabric covering her table.

My mouth dried. Shimmering gold headdress. A mélange of rings in silver and gold topped with pearls and gemstones. Veiny, feminine hands.

It had been over a year-and-a-half, but I hadn't forgotten the woman with the slender, wrinkled fingers, haunting eyes, and floral perfume from my father's annual costume gala. And rarely a few days went by that I didn't remember the fortune teller's words from that night.

"You will die for him, your love."

I *had* died. I'd been pronounced dead, my body so devoid of life that it had terminated my first child.

No good could come from this.

I stepped back and hit Cristiano's wall of a body. He squeezed my shoulders. "What is it, Lourdes?" he asked. "Do you need—"

He stopped speaking. I turned around to see why. His gaze was also trained on the old woman staring back at us.

"Who wants to know their future?" she called out in that same craggy voice. Her cackle turned into a hacking cough.

"She gives me a bad feeling," I said.

"And me," he agreed.

"Do you know her?"

He nodded. "I believe we met once."

And had she told Cristiano his future?

This soothsayer had said I'd die for the love of my life, and I had. Not just once, but twice. I'd come clawing back to life once for Cristiano, and we were strong and healthy now. I couldn't take any more despair.

I grabbed Cristiano's hand and started to pull him away.

This woman could bring *nothing* but bad news.

Cristiano

"Lovely young couple," the old woman said, slowing us in our tracks as we made for a getaway. "And with a *chiquita* on the way."

Clever woman. She knew the sex of my child. Any other time, I'd have called it a lucky guess. Now? I wasn't sure. I still didn't believe in this kind of hocus pocus. But my fortune *had* been eerily spot on.

Was it premonition that my drink had been drugged at the political event? Or something more?

I soothed my wife with a hand up and down her biceps, bringing her closer to my body. "What did she tell you?" I whispered over Natalia's head.

Her back went rigid. "That I would die," she said and wriggled away from me to march toward the woman's table.

I followed, staying at Natalia's back as she accused, "What do you want, *vieja*? Am I supposed to die a third time? My husband and I are happy. Enough harm has been done."

The woman pressed a hand to the base of her neck. "I

simply deliver messages. I'm not so different from your beloved monarch."

All right, that was a bit too far. The monarch was private between Natalia and me. I gripped Natalia's elbow to pull her back. "Let's go."

But she couldn't be moved. "That was just a silly costume," she said.

"And yet you're considering naming your baby after . . ." Her eyes traveled up to mine. "Well, I won't spoil it. I'll let you tell your husband the name you've chosen."

Natalia's face drained of blood. I had no idea what the woman meant, though. Had Natalia picked a name and not told me?

"Stay away from us," Natalia said.

The woman sighed. "I don't create anyone's fates. I warned you, didn't I? You should listen next time."

Next time.

She *had* warned us—Natalia that she would die, apparently—and me, to get back up when I fell. Moments after I'd seen her, I'd literally fallen to my knees.

And now she was here again.

To give us a warning.

"What is it?" I narrowed my eyes on *la bruja*. "What did you come here to tell us?"

Her sparkling eyes fell to Natalia's stomach. I put my arms around my wife, spreading my hands over her belly, shielding it.

"It's hard to see the future of a dead man. And you are, aren't you?" Her gaze bounced to Natalia as she smiled and squinted. "However . . ."

This didn't mean a damn thing. And yet, I found myself leaning in, my heart thumping against Natalia's back.

"I see nothing."

I released a breath. After a lifetime of non-stop violence and death in the name of revenge, love, and sex, I muttered, "Nothing would be *fucking* great. For a while."

"For a while," the sorceress agreed, nodding. "But not forever. I see light and love, too. Well into old age." She lifted up and resettled in her seat, a smile tugging at one corner of her mouth. "And a daughter," she added.

"That we know," Natalia said.

"I'm speaking of the one *after* this."

Huh. Two daughters. I was glad for it. I deserved it, and so did Natalia. No girls would be loved more in the world.

The woman sat back with a sigh. "Then again, I've been wrong before." She glanced at her crystal ball. "I can look a little harder if you like? I may see something after all . . ."

"No," Natalia and I answered at the same time.

"Well. I'll be here next weekend, too." She took a pack of cigarettes from somewhere under her table. "Do you have a light?"

"I quit," I said.

"Right."

I put my arm around Natalia and guided her away as she cast a final glance over her shoulder at the woman. "Feel better?" I asked.

"*Me?*" Natalia's brows lifted. "I could've knocked you over with a feather, you were so interested in what she'd say."

I chuckled. "*Nah.* I don't believe in any of that."

"Sure." She rolled her eyes. "So you don't think we'll have a second girl?"

The thought put a smile on my face all the way back to the third-floor apartment we'd rented for now.

As Natalia changed, I opened all the windows overlooking a small courtyard. Fresh, cool air breezed in. I turned on the record player, sat on the edge of our bed to remove my shoes, and leaned back on the mattress with an arm behind my head. Something I hadn't gotten to do very much in my old life—sit and listen to music.

I thought of the Badlands often—I couldn't help it. It had been my life for twelve years. But between my childhood with my parents, my service at Costa's compound, and the Calavera cartel, I'd lived several lifetimes. This one, with Natalia, would be just another adventure, and there was nobody I wanted by my side more.

Speak of the she-devil, she strolled out of the bathroom in a black silk slip with lacy red edges that stopped just below the tops of her thighs. She smoothed her palms over her belly, curving her hands underneath and turning to the side so I could see how far along she was. I liked to watch her grow. To look at her as much as possible and commit these days to memory. Once the baby came, things would be a little more chaotic. Traveling around wouldn't be as easy. I'd have to keep looking over my shoulder everywhere we went, with even more on the line.

But it was a good problem to have. After the life we'd led, I was confident there wasn't anything my wife and I couldn't take on.

She poured me a whisky neat from the bottle we'd picked up during our trip to the square and brought the glass and a lit candle to my bedside. "It's Day of the Dead, and we didn't do anything," she said, sitting on the edge of the bed.

"I think we should be thankful for an uneventful holiday for once." I winked. "But yes, we honor those we've lost. Your mother. Our baby. My men, your father's, too, and our friends."

She nodded and glanced at her purse, where she kept the sonogram she'd received this time last year, and then to her suitcase, which held her mother's wedding dress, one of the only things she'd brought with her.

I took her hand, brought it to my mouth and pressed a kiss to the back of it.

With a smile, she passed me my drink. "How is it?"

I took a sip. "Not like the Zamora's blue agave," I said. "But very nice."

She took the glass from me, set it down on the night-stand, and climbed onto the bed on her hands and knees. The woman acted as if she wasn't pregnant at all. Agile as ever—always down for anything, constantly on the move, participating in hand-to-hand combat despite my explicit prohibition. She was only twenty-two, though. At thirty-six, I probably had more aches and pains *without* carrying a human the size of a cantaloupe.

"You asked earlier if there's anything I need," she said.

"Tell me," I responded. "You know I don't rely on anyone to deliver my wishes to the gods. I make them happen myself. I will grant you anything."

She climbed on top of me. "Just you."

Straddling my waist, she opened my fly. Put me inside her. Rocked on me.

It wasn't the throne I'd once envisioned for my under-ground queen, but I couldn't complain.

Bienvenido al infierno. Welcome to Hell, my friends.

It happens to look and feel quite a lot like heaven.

"The fortune teller said you picked a name. Was she right?" I asked.

Natalia leaned forward, still gyrating on me as her dark hair brushed her shoulders, eyes bright as they met mine. "Mel," she said. "Short for Oyamel."

"The forest where the monarchs make their winter

homes," I said. "The one you *died* in. I cursed those butterflies, *mi amor*."

She smiled, her hands curling against my chest. "But I *didn't* die," she said. "They protected me."

I cupped her jaw, touching my thumb to the corner of her mouth. "Every day I think to myself, I've never seen you more beautiful. How is it possible?" I took her hips. "Mel is very nice. Oyamel Cruz de la Rosa."

"But to the rest of the world, she'll be Mel Cristina Delgado."

"Cristina?"

"For her Papá."

"Do I get a say?" I asked. "We should put Bianca somewhere in there, too. Perhaps we pretend it's your *apellido*."

"And curse her with a long, traditional name?" She smiled. "Yes—let's. Oyamel Bianca Cristina Delgado."

". . . De la Rosa," I added. "There won't be any names left for the next girl."

"Angelina," she said at once.

My heart threatened to rupture, overflowing with love. Natalia understood what the name meant to me. Angelina it would be.

Natalia's smile gave way to a moan as she used my chest as leverage to push back on me, her hips sliding back and forth faster.

After she'd been at it a while, I put my hands around the back of her neck and held her in place. I took over with a languid, easy rhythm. "Slow down with me. Relax."

Apparently, this was what one did in the afterlife. He ate a good meal, drank fine whisky, and fucked his eight months pregnant wife. Nobody had to die. Nobody depended on us for anything. Nobody cared what we did. Because nobody knew we were still alive.

And nobody ever could.

It was a good life. One I was more grateful for considering I'd almost lost it. I had all I needed in my wife and our child—or children, as the old lady would have it.

So now you know the truth. It's a lot of responsibility. Don't tell anyone.

ACKNOWLEDGMENTS

Endless thanks to my own personal Badlands, the proverbial village that helped me pull together this series. A thrilling, tasking journey not without its potholes—and payoff.

To my editor (never-let-me-down Maksim), Elizabeth London Editing: you put me through the wringer on this one, but I believe this time, the result were our best yet. Thank you for helping me bring Natalia and Cristiano to the world.

To the people on the ground, my beta Katie at Underline This Editing, proofreader Paige Maroney Smith, sensitivity readers, Chayo Ramón and Maria Dominguez—the foundation of the story was laid, but you helped make it a book.

To my release PA, Serena McDonald for rallying the troops and keeping things moving when I can't.

And special thanks to the ones who've made my bookshelf look like a piece of art. The pages needed a home, and you gave them the most beautiful one possible: Najla Qamber

Designs for the cover design, Michelle and Cameron for gracing the books, and Perrywinkle Photography for the shooting them (with her camera . . . death's day has come and gone).

ALSO BY JESSICA HAWKINS

LEARN MORE AT WWW.JESSICAHAWKINS.NET

White Monarch Trilogy

"Exciting and suspenseful and sexy and breathtaking." (USA Today Bestselling Author Lauren Rowe)

Violent Delights

Violent Ends

Violent Triumphs

Right Where I Want You

"An intelligently written, sexy, feel-good romance that packs an emotional punch…" (*USA Today*)

A witty workplace romance filled with heart, sexual tension, and smart enemies-to-lovers banter.

Something in the Way Series

"A tale of forbidden love in epic proportion… Brilliant" (New York Times bestselling author Corinne Michaels)

Lake Kaplan falls for a handsome older man — but then her sister sets her sights on him too.

Something in the Way

Somebody Else's Sky

Move the Stars

Lake + Manning

Slip of the Tongue Series

"Addictive. Painful. Captivating…an authentic, raw, and emotionally gripping must-read." (Angie's Dreamy Reads)

Her husband doesn't want her anymore. The man next door would give up everything to have her.

Slip of the Tongue

The First Taste

Yours to Bare

Explicitly Yours Series

"*Pretty Woman* meets *Indecent Proposal*…a seductive series." (*USA Today* Bestselling Author Louise Bay)

What if one night with her isn't enough? A red-hot collection.

Possession

Domination

Provocation

Obsession

The Cityscape Series

Olivia has the perfect life—but something is missing. Handsome playboy David Dylan awakens a passion that she thought she'd lost a long time ago. Can she keep their combustible lust from spilling over into love?

Come Undone

Come Alive

Come Together

ABOUT THE AUTHOR

Jessica Hawkins is a *USA Today* bestselling author known for her "emotionally gripping" and "off-the-charts hot" romance. Dubbed "queen of angst" by both peers and readers for her smart and provocative work, she's garnered a cult-like following of fans who love to be torn apart...and put back together.

She writes romance both at home in New York and around the world, a coffee shop traveler who bounces from café to café with just a laptop, headphones, and a coffee cup. She loves to keep in close touch with her readers, mostly via Facebook, Instagram, and her mailing list.

Stay updated:
www.jessicahawkins.net/mailing-list
www.amazon.com/author/jessicahawkins

www.jessicahawkins.net
jessicahawkinsauthor@gmail.com

Made in the USA
Coppell, TX
12 November 2019

11277184R00222